Mrs. Poe

He was the literary genius of nineteeth-century
New York, magnetic and mysterious.
She was a gifted young poet, vulnerable and filled with
desire. Only one person could stand in the way
of their all-consuming passion. . . .

Mrs. Poe

Lynn Cullen's acclaimed historical novel illuminates
the shattering love affair between Edgar Allan Poe
and his mistress, Frances Osgood

"Evocative, compassionate, intelligent, sexy, and utterly addictive.
The passion between Frances Osgood and Edgar Allen Poe burns
up the pages, while her relationship with Mrs. Poe makes your heart
ache. Truly a book to savor!"

—M. J. Rose, international bestselling author of *Seduction*

"Masterful. . . . Rich with period detail and compelling characters,
Mrs. Poe weaves a thread of creeping menace into the true story
of an obsessive liaison for a thoroughly unforgettable and chilling
read. Enthralling."

—Deanna Raybourn, bestselling author of
A Spear of Summer Grass

"Bewitching. . . . Danger, sensuality, mystery and passion fill the pages."
—Stephanie Cowell, author of *Claude and Camille*

"Brilliant . . . a wonderful and fascinating novel. . . . Poe absolutely comes to life in Cullen's novel. . . . *Mrs. Poe* is truly one of the best historical fiction novels of 2013 and possibly ever."

—Examiner.com

"*Mrs. Poe* is an entertaining tale with interesting characters, a vibrant locale, a good dose of romance, and even some intrigue, which is what an historical novel should be."

—*The Copperfield Review*

"A fascinating fictional rendering. . . . I fell under the spell of Cullen's exquisite imagination and appreciated every single facet of this gemstone, from the accurate and evocative description of pre–Civil War New York and its literary salons to the magnetic and stark characterization of Poe. Cullen's luminous and eloquent prose is remarkable, absorbing, and convincing. A riveting read."

—*Mina's Bookshelf*

"*Mrs. Poe* is a captivating novel. Cullen's attention to historical detail, lush prose and enlightening evocation of an interesting moment in American literary history make this story a fascinating read."

—*Arts ATL*

"Cullen weaves a dark, sensuous love triangle . . . and in the midst of many real historical details, she creates something truly and wonderfully surprising. . . . Don't miss it."

—*BookPage*

Mrs. Poe

Lynn Cullen

GALLERY BOOKS

New York   London   Toronto   Sydney   New Delhi

G

Gallery Books
A Division of Simon & Schuster, Inc.
1230 Avenue of the Americas
New York, NY 10020

First Gallery Books trade paperback edition May 2014

GALLERY BOOKS and colophon are registered
trademarks of Simon & Schuster, Inc.

For information about special discounts for bulk purchases,
please contact Simon & Schuster Special Sales at 1-866-506-1949
or business@simonandschuster.com.

The Simon & Schuster Speakers Bureau can bring authors
to your live event. For more information or to book an event
contact the Simon & Schuster Speakers Bureau at 1-866-248-3049
or visit our website at www.simonspeakers.com.

Interior design by Esther Paradelo and endpapers by Christopher Sergio
Jacket photographs: Photo of Frame by Luther Holman Hale/Library of
Congress, Prints & Photographs Division, LC-USZC4-12731;
Woman's Face © Chris Tobin/Getty Images
Endpapers Art: © Geoffrey Clements/Corbis

Manufactured in the United States of America

10 9 8 7 6

Library of Congress Cataloging-in-Publication Data is available for the
hardcover edition.

ISBN 978-1-4767-0292-6
ISBN 978-1-4767-0293-3 (ebook)

For Lauren, Megan, and Ali

The Raven

Edgar Allan Poe

Once upon a midnight dreary, while I pondered, weak and weary,
Over many a quaint and curious volume of forgotten lore,
While I nodded, nearly napping, suddenly there came a tapping,
As of some one gently rapping, rapping at my chamber door.
" 'Tis some visiter," I muttered, "tapping at my chamber door —
         Only this, and nothing more."

Ah, distinctly I remember it was in the bleak December,
And each separate dying ember wrought its ghost upon the floor.
Eagerly I wished the morrow; — vainly I had tried to borrow
From my books surcease of sorrow — sorrow for the lost Lenore —
For the rare and radiant maiden whom the angels name Lenore —
         Nameless here for evermore.

And the silken sad uncertain rustling of each purple curtain
Thrilled me — filled me with fantastic terrors never felt before;
So that now, to still the beating of my heart, I stood repeating
" 'Tis some visiter entreating entrance at my chamber door —
Some late visiter entreating entrance at my chamber door; —
         This it is, and nothing more."

Presently my soul grew stronger; hesitating then no longer,
"Sir," said I, "or Madam, truly your forgiveness I implore;
But the fact is I was napping, and so gently you came rapping,
And so faintly you came tapping, tapping at my chamber door,
That I scarce was sure I heard you" — here I opened wide the door; —
         Darkness there, and nothing more.

Deep into that darkness peering, long I stood there wondering, fearing,
Doubting, dreaming dreams no mortal ever dared to dream before;
But the silence was unbroken, and the darkness gave no token,
And the only word there spoken was the whispered word, "Lenore!"
This *I* whispered, and an echo murmured back the word, "Lenore!"
                                        Merely this, and nothing more.

Then into the chamber turning, all my soul within me burning,
Soon I heard again a tapping somewhat louder than before.
"Surely," said I, "surely that is something at my window lattice;
Let me see, then, what thereat is, and this mystery explore —
Let my heart be still a moment and this mystery explore;—
                                        'Tis the wind, and nothing more!"

Open here I flung the shutter, when, with many a flirt and flutter,
In there stepped a stately raven of the saintly days of yore;
Not the least obeisance made he; not an instant stopped or stayed he;
But, with mien of lord or lady, perched above my chamber door —
Perched upon a bust of Pallas just above my chamber door —
                                        Perched, and sat, and nothing more.

Then this ebony bird beguiling my sad fancy into smiling,
By the grave and stern decorum of the countenance it wore,
"Though thy crest be shorn and shaven, thou," I said, "art sure no craven,
Ghastly grim and ancient raven wandering from the Nightly shore —
Tell me what thy lordly name is on the Night's Plutonian shore!"
                                        Quoth the raven, "Nevermore."

Much I marvelled this ungainly fowl to hear discourse so plainly,
Though its answer little meaning — little relevancy bore;
For we cannot help agreeing that no sublunary being
Ever yet was blessed with seeing bird above his chamber door —
Bird or beast upon the sculptured bust above his chamber door,
                                        With such name as "Nevermore."

But the raven, sitting lonely on the placid bust, spoke only
That one word, as if his soul in that one word he did outpour.
Nothing farther then he uttered — not a feather then he fluttered —
Till I scarcely more than muttered, "Other friends have flown before —
On the morrow *he* will leave me, as my hopes have flown before."
                    Quoth the raven, "Nevermore."

Wondering at the stillness broken by reply so aptly spoken,
"Doubtless," said I, "what it utters is its only stock and store,
Caught from some unhappy master whom unmerciful Disaster
Followed fast and followed faster — so, when Hope he would adjure,
Stern Despair returned, instead of the sweet Hope he dared adjure —
                    That sad answer, "Nevermore!"

But the raven still beguiling all my sad soul into smiling,
Straight I wheeled a cushioned seat in front of bird, and bust, and door;
Then upon the velvet sinking, I betook myself to linking
Fancy unto fancy, thinking what this ominous bird of yore —
What this grim, ungainly, ghastly, gaunt, and ominous bird of yore
                    Meant in croaking "Nevermore."

This I sat engaged in guessing, but no syllable expressing
To the fowl whose fiery eyes now burned into my bosom's core;
This and more I sat divining, with my head at ease reclining
On the cushion's velvet lining that the lamp-light gloated o'er,
But whose velvet violet lining with the lamp-light gloating o'er,
                    She shall press, ah, nevermore!

Then, methought, the air grew denser, perfumed from an unseen censer
Swung by angels whose faint foot-falls tinkled on the tufted floor.
"Wretch," I cried, "thy God hath lent thee — by these angels he hath sent thee
Respite — respite and Nepenthe from thy memories of Lenore!
Let me quaff this kind Nepenthe and forget this lost Lenore!"
                    Quoth the raven, "Nevermore."

"Prophet!" said I, "thing of evil! — prophet still, if bird or devil! —
Whether Tempter sent, or whether tempest tossed thee here ashore,
Desolate, yet all undaunted, on this desert land enchanted —
On this home by Horror haunted — tell me truly, I implore —
Is there — *is* there balm in Gilead? — tell me — tell me, I implore!"
                                                    Quoth the raven, "Nevermore."

"Prophet!" said I, "thing of evil! — prophet still, if bird or devil!
By that Heaven that bends above us — by that God we both adore —
Tell this soul with sorrow laden if, within the distant Aidenn,
It shall clasp a sainted maiden whom the angels name Lenore —
Clasp a rare and radiant maiden whom the angels name Lenore."
                                                    Quoth the raven, "Nevermore."

"Be that word our sign of parting, bird or fiend!" I shrieked, upstarting —
"Get thee back into the tempest and the Night's Plutonian shore!
Leave no black plume as a token of that lie thy soul hath spoken!
Leave my loneliness unbroken! — quit the bust above my door!
Take thy beak from out my heart, and take thy form from off my door!"
                                                    Quoth the raven, "Nevermore."

And the raven, never flitting, still is sitting, still is sitting
On the pallid bust of Pallas just above my chamber door;
And his eyes have all the seeming of a demon that is dreaming,
And the lamp-light o'er him streaming throws his shadow on the floor;
And my soul from out that shadow that lies floating on the floor
                                                    Shall be lifted — nevermore!

My first meeting with the poet was at the Astor House. . . .
With his proud and beautiful head erect, his dark eyes
flashing with the elective light of feeling and of thought, a
peculiar, an inimitable blending of sweetness and hauteur in
his expression and manner, he greeted me, calmly, gravely,
almost coldly; yet with so marked an earnestness that I
could not help being deeply impressed by it. From that
moment until his death we were friends. . . . I maintained
a correspondence with Mr. Poe, in accordance with the
earnest entreaties of his wife, who imagined that my
influence over him had a restraining and beneficial effect.

—FRANCES SARGENT OSGOOD, letter to R. W. Griswold, 1850

In person [Mrs. Osgood] is about the medium height,
slender even to fragility, graceful whether in action or
repose; complexion usually pale; hair very black and glossy;
eyes of a clear, luminous gray, large, and with a singular
capacity of expression. In no respect can she be termed
beautiful, (as the world understands the epithet,) but the
question, "Is it really possible that she is not so?" is very
frequently asked, and most frequently by those who most
intimately know her.

—EDGAR ALLAN POE, "The Literati of New York City. No. V,"
Godey's Lady's Book, September 1846

Mrs. Poe

Winter 1845

One

When given bad news, most women of my station can afford to slump onto their divans, their china cups slipping from their fingers to the carpet, their hair falling prettily from its pins, their fourteen starched petticoats compacting with a plush crunch. I am not one of them. As a lady whose husband is so busy painting portraits of wealthy patrons—most of whom happen to be women—that he forgets that he has a family, I have more in common with the girls who troll the muddy streets of Corlear's Hook, looking to part sailors from their dollars, than I do with the ladies of my class, in spite of my appearance.

This thought bolted into my mind like a horse stung by a wasp that afternoon at the office of *The Evening Mirror*. I was in the midst of listening to a joke about two backward Hoosiers being told by the editor Mr. George Pope Morris. I knew that the news Mr. Morris was obviously putting off giving me must not be good. Still, I laughed delightedly at his infantile joke, even while choking on the miasma created by his excess of perfumed hair pomade, the open glue pot sitting upon his desk, and the parrot cage to my left, which was in dire need of changing. I hoped to soften him, just as a "Hooker" softens potential customers by lifting a corner of her skirt.

I struck when Mr. Morris was still chuckling from his own joke. Showing teeth brushed with particular care before I had set off to confront him after a silence of twenty-two days, I said, "About the poem I sent you in January. . . ." I trailed off, widening my eyes with hopefulness, my equivalent of petticoat lifting. If I was to become independent, I needed the income.

No sailor considering a pair of ankles looked more wary than Mr.

George Pope Morris did at that moment, although few sailors managed to achieve the success he had at toilet, particularly with his hair. Never before had such a lofty loaf of curls arisen from a human head without the aid of padding. It was as if he had used his top hat for a mold. Whether by design or accident, one large curl had escaped the mass and now dangled upon his forehead like a gelatinous fishhook.

"Might you have misplaced it?" I asked lightly. Maybe he would appreciate putting the blame on his partner. "Or perhaps Mr. Willis has it."

His gaze slid down to my bosom, registered the disappointment of seeing only cloak, then snapped back to my face. "I'm sorry, Mrs. Osgood. To be quite frank, it is not what we are looking for."

"I'm certain that your female readership would enjoy my allusions to love in my descriptions of flowers. Mr. Rufus Griswold has been so kind to include some of my poems in his recent collection. Perhaps you've heard of it?"

"I know Griswold's collection. Everyone does—he's made sure of it. How that little bully got to be such an authority on poetry, I'll never know."

"Threats of death?"

Mr. Morris laughed, then waggled his finger at me. "Mrs. Osgood!"

Quickly before I lost him: "My own book, published by Mr. Harper, *The Poetry of Flowers and the Flowers of Poetry*, sold quite well."

"When was that?" he asked distractedly.

"Two years ago." Actually it was four.

"As I thought. Flowers are not what is selling of late. What everyone is interested in these days are shivery tales. Stories of the macabre."

"Like Mr. Poe's bird poem?"

He nodded, causing the great greased curl to bounce. "As a matter of fact, yes. Our sales soared when we brought out the 'The Raven' at the end of January. Same thing happened when we reprinted it last week. I suspect we could reprint it ten times and it wouldn't be enough. Readers have gone Raven-mad."

"I see." I didn't see. Yes, I had read the poem. Everyone in New York had since it had first been published the previous month. Even the German man who sold newspapers in the Village knew of it. Just this morning, when I asked him if he had the current issue of the *Mirror*, he'd said with an accent and a grin, "Nefermore."

My dearest friend, Mrs. John Russell Bartlett, part of the inner circle of the New York literati, thanks to her husband, a bookseller and publisher of a small press, would not be quiet about him. She had been angling to meet him ever since "The Raven" had come out. In truth, I had thought I might get a glimpse of the wondrous Mr. Poe in the office that morning. He was an editor at the *Mirror* as well as a contributor.

Mr. Morris seemed to read my mind. "Evidently, our dear Mr. Poe is feeling his success. He is threatening to leave the magazine. Wherever he goes, I wish them luck in dealing with his moods."

"Is he so very moody?" I still hoped to cajole Mr. Morris into friendship and, therefore, into indebtedness.

Mr. Morris gestured as if tipping a glass to his mouth.

"Oh." I made a conspiratorial grimace.

"He's really quite unbalanced, you know. I suspect he's more than half mad, and it's not just the drink."

"A shame."

He smiled. "Look, Mrs. Osgood, you are an intelligent woman. You've had some luck with your story collections for children. My own little ones loved 'Puss in Boots.' Why don't you go back to that?"

I could not tell him the real reason: money. Writing children's stories did not pay.

"I feel that it's important for me to expand my writing," I said. "I have things I would like to say." Which was also true. Why must a woman be confined to writing children's tales?

He chuckled. "Like which color brings out the roses in one's complexion, or how to decorate at Christmas?"

I laughed, good Hooker that I am. Still smiling, I said, "I think you might be surprised at what I am capable of."

His parrot squawked. He fed it a cracker from his pocket, then wiped his hands on his pantaloons, his sights making their habitual rounds from my eyes to my bust and back again. I forced myself to keep a cheerful gaze, although I wished to slap the curl off his forehead.

He frowned. "A beautiful woman like you shouldn't have to trouble your head with this sort of thing, but what if you came up with something as fresh and exciting as 'The Raven,' only from a lady's point of view?"

"Do you mean something dark?"

"Yes," he said, warming to the idea. "Yes. Exactly so—dark. Very dark. I think there might be a market for that. Shivery tales for ladies."

"You'd like me to be a sort of Mrs. Poe?"

"Ha! Yes. That's the ticket."

"Will I be paid the same as Mr. Poe?" I asked brazenly. Desperate times call for uncouth measures.

He marked the inappropriateness of my question with a pause before answering. "I paid Poe nothing, since he was on staff. I should think you'd want to do better than that."

Although already envious of Mr. Poe for his recent success, I felt a twinge of sympathy for the man. Perhaps he was independently wealthy, as was Mr. Longfellow or Mr. Bryant, and did not need the money or my compassion. In any case, he was not wed to a philandering portrait painter.

Mr. Morris led me to the door. "The *Mirror* is a popular magazine, Mrs. Osgood. We're not interested in literature for scholars. Bring me something fresh and entertaining. Something dark that will make the lady readers afraid to snuff their candles at night. You do that, and I'll see what I can do for you. Just don't turn your back on us when you've reached the top, as did our Mr. Poe."

"I wouldn't. I promise."

"Poe's his own worst enemy—he no sooner makes a friend than he turns him into a foe."

"I wonder what has made him such a difficult character."

He shrugged. "Why do wolves bite? They just do." He held open the door, letting in a cool draft. "Give my regards to Mr. Osgood."

"Thank you," I said. "I will." If he ever tired of his current heiress and came home.

I soon found myself on the sidewalk of Nassau Street and, it being a mild day for February, ankle-deep in slush. Gentlemen passed, encased in buttoned overcoats and plugged with top hats. They flicked curious gazes in my direction, not sure whether I was a lady to whom they should tip their hat or a Hooker who had wandered into their inner sanctum. Few females of any sort ventured into the hallowed business precincts of New York—the engine room of what was becoming the greatest money factory in the world.

I bent into the biting wind, ever present in winter in this island city, and rounded the corner onto Ann Street. A landau clattered by, its wheels flinging melted snow. Across the way, a hog rooted in refuse, one of the thousands of pigs who plied the streets, be it rich district or poor. The wet had brought out the smell of the smoke rising from the forest of rooftop chimneys as well as the stink of horse manure, rotting garbage, and urine. It is said that sailors can smell New York City six miles out at sea. I had no doubt of it.

Two short blocks later, across Ann Street from Barnum's American Museum, with its banners advertising such humbuggery in residence as President Washington's childhood nurse and the Feejee Mermaid, I arrived upon the shoveled promenade of Broadway. Vehicles poured down the thoroughfare before me as if a vein in the city had been opened and it was bleeding conveyances down the bumpy cobblestones. The din they made was deafening. The massive hooves of shaggy draft horses clashed against the street as they pulled rumbling wagons bulging with barrels. Stately carriages creaked by behind clopping bays. Hackneys for hire rattled alongside omnibuses with windows filled with staring faces. Whips cracked; drivers shouted; dogs barked. In the midst of it all, on a balcony on the Barnum's building, a brass band tootled. It was enough to test one's sanity.

Clutching my skirts, I hurried through a gap in the thundering traffic. I landed breathless on the other side of the street, where the Astor House hotel, six stories of solid granite gentility, sat frowning down its noble pillars at me. It seemed aware that I had only two pennies in the expensive reticule on my arm.

Just a month previously I had been one of its pampered residents. I had been among the privileged to bathe in its hot-running-water baths. I, too, had enjoyed reading by the gaslights and dining with the rich and beautiful at the table d'hôte. Samuel had insisted that we take rooms at the Astor House when we had moved to New York from London, to make a good impression.

Had I known of the ruinous state of our ledgers, I would have never agreed to it. But Samuel thought that as the daughter of a wealthy Boston merchant, I expected no less of him. He could never get over the inequality of our backgrounds, no matter how much I assured him that it didn't matter to me. I, on the other hand, had gotten over it the moment he first kissed me. I had no care if we took up housekeeping in a soddy, as long as I spent the night in Samuel Osgood's arms. Samuel, though, could never quite believe this. There is no more prideful creature than a man born poor.

Now, hunched against the icy wind and feeling the pinch of my thin pointed boots and the stabbing of my corset stays, I marched up the assault on the senses that is called Broadway. The loud swirl of striving people and their beasts dazzled the eyes, as did the brightly painted establishments bristling with signs that bragged LIFE-LIKE DAGUERREOTYPES! WORLD'S FRESHEST OYSTERS! MOUTH-WATERING ICE CREAM! FINEST QUALITY LADIES' FANS! The stench of rotting sea creatures commingled with the sweet scent of perfumes, as did the spicy odor of unwashed human flesh and the aroma of baking pies.

Soon the flapping awnings of tobacconists, haberdashers, and dry-goods emporiums gave way to mansions with ornate iron fences that fringed their foundations like chin whiskers. Although the richest man of them all, Mr. Astor, refused to budge from his stone pile at Broadway and Prince, the fashion was to show off one's newly minted money by constructing a castle in the neighborhoods north of Houston Street. It was in this vaunted district that I turned westward on Bleecker. In boots made to stroll across a manicured square, not march up a mile and a half of flagstones, I minced painfully past ranks of stately brick houses at LeRoy Place, in many of which I'd had tea. Near the writer James Fenimore Cooper's ostentatiously large former home on Carroll Place, about which his wife liked to complain often and loudly that it was "too magnificent for our simple French tastes," I veered right onto Laurens Street.

With an end in sight, I picked up my pace as much as my cursed corset and destroyed feet would allow. I hobbled elegantly by a tumbledown row of stables, smithies, and small wooden dwellings meant for those who served the denizens of the palaces around them, until at last, a block short of Washington Square, I came to Amity Place, yet another enclave of new four-story Greek Revival town houses caged in by black ironwork fences. From a third-story window, through an oval that had been cleared in the frost by the sun, peered two young girls.

My heart warmed. I opened the wrought iron gate, climbed the steep flight of six stone steps, and pushed open the door.

Five-and-half-year-old Vinnie was running down the narrow staircase as I entered the hall. "Mamma, did he buy your poem?"

"Hold on to the railing!" I exclaimed. Behind her, my elder daughter, Ellen, three years older than her sister and worlds more cautious, took the stairs at a more judicious rate.

Vinnie threw herself against me. A loud crash descended from an upstairs room, followed by a wail and the exasperated voice of my friend Eliza.

Ellen made a safe landing and held out her arms to take my mantle and hat. "Henry is being bad."

I glanced above her. "Yes, I can hear him."

"Mamma," Vinnie demanded, "did the man buy your poem?"

"He didn't buy that one. But he did ask to see more." I opened my gloved palm, upon which lay two peppermint drops. I had taken them from a dish on Mr. Morris's desk when I had waited for him to arrive.

Vinnie's grin revealed a newly naked arch in her upper gums. She popped in the candy.

Ellen shifted my things in her arms, then took her piece. Not yet nine and she was as somber as a Temperance lady on Christmas. "You should write more stories for children," she said as I peeled off my gloves. "They always buy your children's stories."

"I'm trying to spread my wings. What do I say about birds who don't spread their wings?"

The candy rattled against Vinnie's remaining teeth as she moved it to her cheek to speak. "They never learn to fly."

"You don't need to fly, Mother," Ellen said. "You need to make money."

How did she know these things? At her age, I was dressing paper dolls. Blast you, Samuel Osgood, for stunting her with worry and spoiling her childhood. I could spin all manner of tales about his care and concern for us and she always saw right through them.

"What I need to do now is to help Mrs. Bartlett," I said cheerfully. "Vinnie, how is your ear?"

She gingerly touched the ear with the tuft of cotton sprouting from it. "Hurts."

Just then, a young boy in a rumpled tunic trampled down the stairs, followed closely by a plain but kindly looking gentlewoman of my age, who was in turn followed by a pretty red-cheeked Irish maid carrying a toddler.

"Fanny!" cried Eliza. "Thank goodness you're back. I have news!"

Although I had lived with Eliza Bartlett and her family for several months, my heart still swelled with gratitude at the sight of her. She and her husband had taken me in when the Astor House had turned me out. It seemed that prior to decamping for lusher pastures in November, Samuel had not paid the bill for the previous three months. After I showed up on Eliza's doorstep with my shameful story, she made no verbal judgment, just said, "You're staying with us." Nor did she speak up when our other friends inquired about Samuel, but silently sat back and let me lie about his imminent return. She thus saved me from the pity that our circle would have rained upon me for being the abandoned wife of a ne'er-do-well. I would have gained their sympathy but lost my place and my pride.

She took little Johnny from her maid. "Mary, please take Mrs. Osgood's things downstairs to dry and Henry along with you. Henry: *be good*." To me she exclaimed, "Goodness, you look frozen. Why didn't you take a hackney home?"

"What is this news?"

She removed little Johnny's hand from inside her blouse. "Mr. Poe is coming!"

"Here?"

She laughed. "No. Not unless he wishes to change a diaper. He's going to appear at the home of a young woman named Anne Lynch— this Saturday! And we, my dear, are invited."

I found my excitement to meet the renowned writer was tempered by the fact that I had just been encouraged to be his competitor. "Wonderful! Do we know this Miss Lynch?"

Eliza gave little Johnny to Vinnie, who'd been silently begging for him with open arms. "She's new to this city from Providence—she's a friend of Russell's family. She stopped in his shop and told him she was attempting to start a salon—not just for the usual bon ton but for artists of all kinds, rich or poor. I daresay she might have a chance at success after having snagged Poe."

"I wonder how she lured him in."

"She might come to regret it. He's sure to be horribly ruthless. Poe doesn't like *anything*."

It was true. I had seen his reviews in *The Evening Mirror*. Prior to "The Raven," he was best known in literary circles for his poisoned pen. For good reason he was called the Tomahawker, happy as he was to chop up his fellow writers. He regularly tore in to gentle, gentlemanly Mr. Longfellow with a savagery that made no sense. In truth, I had wondered about his sanity even before Mr. Morris's accusation, or at least his motives for such abuse.

"The gathering is to be at seven. Say that you'll come with me. I told her about you—" She saw my wince. "That you are a poet."

Bless you, Eliza. "I'll go, if the girls are well by then."

Vinnie jogged little Johnny on her hip. "I will be!"

"There you have it," I said with a nonchalance that I did not feel. If I became his competition, I, too, might soon be on the wrong side of the dangerous Mr. Poe.

Two

I woke up the next morning shivering from the cold. Leaving the girls curled up together under the quilts in our bed, I went to the window and cleared a spot in the frost. Snow was coming down, muffling sidewalks and streets, blanketing rooftops, capping the ornate iron railings of the stoops across the way. The milkman passed in a sleigh, the mane of his horse thick with icy crystals, as was his own hat and shoulders.

Wrapping my robe more closely around me, I went to the fireplace, uncovered the banked embers, and gave them a poke. One of Eliza's Irish maids, the "second girl," Martha, the cook's and parlor maid's helper, slipped into the room with a bucket of coal and a can of water, then whispered her apology when she saw me crouching there. As she took over tending to the fire, I wondered once more how I would have survived without the generosity of her employers and where I would go once my welcome wore out. There was no question of returning to my mother. She had never gotten over the disappointment of my marriage to Samuel. Father's death the following year had further turned her against me; she blamed the blow of losing me for weakening his health. The doors to my sisters' and brothers' homes were equally closed, nor could I find shelter in the arms of another man, at least not a decent one, if I divorced Samuel for abandonment. No one wanted a divorcée as a wife. I did not even have the luxury of conducting an affair. Should I fall for a man while still married, Samuel had legal right to take the children. Only the Bartletts stood between me and deepest poverty and isolation.

As Martha finished stoking the fire and began pouring water into my pitcher, I thought of the ragged children I had seen outside the neighborhood coal yard, scrambling to pick up nuggets that spilled from the wagons as they left to make deliveries. Even as I imagined myself among them, scurrying to beat a waif out of a lump in my destitution, I saw the image of my husband before a cheerfully crackling fire, helping himself to marmalade for his toasted bread, his current mistress, young, blond, and very rich, smiling as he ate his egg. Was there a man ever born who was more supremely selfish than Samuel Stillman Osgood?

I was twenty-three when I met him, ten years ago. He was twenty-six, tall, and handsome in a rough, raw-boned way. He had hair and eyes the brown of fresh-turned earth, the high cheekbones of a Mohawk, and a strong, straight nose. I had come upon him in the paintings gallery of the Athenæum in my native Boston, where I had gone to write some poetry, hoping the art would inspire me. Little did I know that this confident young man with the fistful of paintbrushes would forever disrupt my comfortable life.

He was working at an easel set up before the famous Gilbert Stuart portrait of George Washington. I walked by quietly as to not disturb him, noting the nearly finished copy of the portrait upon his easel. I had just passed him when my pencil slipped from my notebook and clattered on the marble floor.

He looked up.

"Sorry," I whispered.

He retrieved my pencil and held it out to me with a gallant flourish. "Madame."

I could feel the heat rising up my neck. He was much too handsome. "Thank you. Sorry to disturb you." I turned to go.

"Don't leave."

I stopped.

He smiled. "Please. I could use your opinion."

"Mine?"

"Does Mr. Washington seem to be holding a secret?"

I peered at the portrait that I had seen so often as to ignore it. The eyes did seem wary. Only the slightest trace of a smile animated the president's sealed lips. It was the face of a man under strictest self-control. With a start, I wondered how well we knew this most famous of men. "Is he?"

"Yes. Do you know what it is?" He leaned forward. When I stepped closer, he whispered, "His teeth are bad."

I stifled a laugh. "No!" I whispered back.

"Shhh." He pretended to scan the room for eavesdroppers. "They say that even in his youth, he was so conscious of his teeth that he rarely smiled, even though he was quite the ladies' man, believe it or not."

"Old Martha's husband?"

He put hands on hips in mock protest. "I'll have you know that 'Old Martha's husband' kept a lady love across the Potomac from Mount Vernon when they were young. His best friend's wife."

"Maybe it's Martha who didn't feel like smiling."

He chuckled, making me feel witty. "You'd think so, but as it happens, Old Martha was wild about him. All the women were. They fought to be his partner at dances and elbowed their way to shake hands with him in reception lines."

"Even though he didn't smile?"

"Maybe because of it. Women do love a mysterious, brooding man."

"I don't."

He laughed. "Good for you. Then maybe you won't be disappointed to know that the reason Dashing George was sullen at the time of this picture was because he hadn't a tooth left in his head."

"Poor George."

"Poor George, indeed. His new dentures were a fright. It seems his dentist never could get the springs on the hinges to fit."

"Ouch." I put out my hand. "You are quite the authority on Mr. Washington and his dentistry, Mister—?"

He gave my gloved fingers a genial tug. "Osgood. Samuel. And you are—?"

"Frances Locke."

"Nice to meet you, Miss Locke. In all seriousness, I'm not really an expert on either Mr. Washington or his teeth or even his lady friends. I just did a little research because I had to know why his jaw looked so misshapen in Stuart's portrait." He gave the original portrait a loving glance. "Stuart wouldn't have painted such an awkward smile on Washington's face unless it truly was awkward. In case you can't tell, Gilbert Stuart is my hero."

I studied his reproduction of the Stuart. "Your copy of his painting is perfect."

"You are probably wondering if I can paint originals as well as copy from masters."

"No," I protested with a laugh, although that was precisely what I was thinking.

"May I borrow your notebook and pencil, please?"

I gave them to him. He studied my face as if I were a statue or a painting, not a living woman, then, as I winced under his scrutiny, he held up my pencil, took a measure of my features, and made a few markings before setting to drawing rapidly. In the time it takes to brush out and braid one's hair for bed, he finished his sketch and turned my notebook toward me. It was a perfect quick likeness in pencil, down to the skeptical look in my eye.

"Do I really look this doubtful?"

He only smiled.

"I must show this to my family. They accuse me of being outrageously impetuous but it's *not* impetuous to bring home a stray dog or to feed the cats roaming in the alley or to give one's allowance to orphans, it's reasonable and practical. Actually, I do have doubts, all the time. Any thinking person does. There are so many sides to every question."

"You must have trouble in church."

I met his grin. "And then there are times, Mr. Osgood, when one must just let go."

His gaze softened. "I believe," he said after a moment, "that those are the happiest of times."

We smiled at each other.

He bowed. "Would you allow me to paint you, Miss Locke? It would be a great honor." I must have looked leery of his intentions because he added, "I would do it right here. The librarians could serve as chaperones."

"I trust you."

"The great doubter? I'm flattered."

We both laughed. We made arrangements to meet there the next day. Before my portrait was completed, he had proposed to me. We were married within a month, in spite of my parents' strenuous objections. I thought they would come around to see his true worth in spite of his negative ledger, but they never did. Love was not everything to them, as it was to me. My father cut me out of his will. My mother refused to see me. I was so drunk with love that I didn't care. Before our honeymoon ended, I was with child.

It had been in the eighth month of this first pregnancy, while we were in England so that Samuel could paint the cream of British society, that I had learned the reason why he was so popular with his female sitters: he bedded them with the same enthusiasm that he painted them. I found that I was just one of many, although, as far as I know, and for my daughters' sakes I hope, I was the only one that he married. He claimed that I was so beautiful that he had to possess me—a dubious honor.

Now the girls were awake. After a quick washing at the basin, they were dressed, swathed in shawls, and settled at Eliza's basement family room table with their books after breakfast—no school for them that day, as Vinnie's ear was still draining and Ellen's cold had not improved.

Eliza had gone out to pay a call upon an ill friend; the younger Bartlett children were upstairs being tended by the maid. Mr. Bartlett was at the little bookshop he ran in the Astor House to satiate his own mania for the written word. My girls and I had the cozy, low-ceilinged room to ourselves, with the homey sound of banging pans murmuring through the wall shared with the kitchen. With a glance out cellar windows so frosted over that they revealed only a shadowy glimpse of the trouser legs and skirts of the passersby on the sidewalk, I took out a copy of *The American Review* and spread it open to my own lesson for the day: "The Raven." Tapping my finger in time with the rhythm, I silently recited the verses.

Barely into the poem, I muttered, "What trickery. It's just a word game." Out loud I read:

> *But the raven, sitting lonely on the placid bust, spoke only*
> *That one word, as if his soul in that one word he did outpour.*
> *Nothing farther then he uttered—not a feather then he fluttered—*
> *Till I scarcely more than muttered, "Other friends have flown before—*

On the morrow he will leave me, as my hopes have flown before."
                              Quoth the raven, "Nevermore."

Wondering at the stillness broken by reply so aptly spoken,
"Doubtless," said I, "what it utters is its only stock and store,
Caught from some unhappy master whom unmerciful Disaster
Followed fast and followed faster—so, when Hope he would adjure,
Stern Despair returned, instead of the sweet Hope he dared adjure—
                              That sad answer, "Nevermore!"

I stopped when I saw that the girls were listening.

"Are you writing a new poem?" asked Vinnie.

"No. This is one by a Mr. Edgar Poe."

"Read us all of it!"

"Shouldn't you be working on one of your own?" said Ellen.

"Yes," I said. "I should. Go back to work. If you're able to go to school tomorrow, you won't want to be behind."

I started again at the beginning, with the hope of understanding how this silly piece captured the imagination of the reading public. I came to the next verse.

But the raven still beguiling all my sad soul into smiling,
Straight I wheeled a cushioned seat in front of bird, and bust, and door;
Then upon the velvet sinking, I betook myself to linking
Fancy unto fancy, thinking what this ominous bird of yore—
What this grim, ungainly, ghastly, gaunt, and ominous bird of yore
Meant in croaking "Nevermore."

"That's it!" I dropped the magazine.

"What, Mamma?" asked Vinnie.

"This silly alliteration—it's clinking, clattering claptrap."

Ellen's face was as straight as a judge's on court day. "You mean it's terrible, trifling trash?"

I nodded. "Jumbling, jarring junk."

Vinnie jumped up, trailing shawls like a mummy trails bandages. "No! It's piggily wiggily poop!"

"Don't be rude, Vinnie," I said.

The girls glanced at each other.

I frowned. "It's exasperating, excruciating excrement."

"Mamma!" breathed Ellen.

"What's that mean?" Vinnie cried.

Ellen told her. And thus a torrent of alliterative abuse was unleashed on Mr. Poe's poem. The girls were still trading outrageous insults as I got out paper and pen and opened an inkpot. Banter does not fill a pocketbook.

Something fresh, Mr. Morris had asked for. *Something entertaining. Something dark that will make the lady readers afraid to snuff their candles at night.*

But try as I might, with two little girls giggling at my table, no frightening subject would come to me, although the precariousness of our well-being was truly terrifying in itself. From Samuel's abandonment I knew the fear of want. I knew firsthand anguish and despair and how they soon blackened into fury. But I had not yet come face-to-face with sheer malevolence, with the dark and ill side of humanity that is inured to the suffering of others. To know such is a necessity if one is to write something truly chilling. That would come for me later.

Three

Gaslight flickered in the sconces of Miss Anne Charlotte Lynch's Waverly Place double parlor, bathing the intelligent faces of the guests in pale orange. I recognized many of the usual members of the New York literary crowd, but there were others: a Bohemian poetess in her gypsy hoop earrings and loose vest; the elderly Mr. Audubon in his buckskin costume; one Mr. Walter Whitman, who belligerently wore the long-tailed frock coat and ruffles from an earlier era. In contrast to the elaborate offerings at the table that were the usual part of salons, Miss Lynch fed this mixed group simply: butter cookies and little dishes of Italian ice, washed down with cups of tea. There were no maids to serve us—everyone was on equal standing here. Nor was there planned entertainment. All that was offered was discussion and encouragement to read short clips from one's recent work or to play one's newest composition. Ideas were the centerpiece, Miss Lynch insisted. She herself dressed as if ready to teach class, which she did by day at the Brooklyn Academy for Young Ladies. Indeed, this humble scene of intellectual earnestness untainted by the crass influence of money would have been completely believable had it not been for the row of handsome carriages waiting outside in a queue that reached to Washington Square. But the illusion was nice.

Now, an hour into the event, I sipped my tea, turning whenever a newcomer entered the orange-lit room. Like everyone else there, I anticipated the imminent arrival of Mr. Poe. He had the New York literati under his thrall. While the discussions that I listened in on that night may have *started* on the inhumanely crowded tenements of Five Points, where Irish immigrants were being packed three families to a filthy windowless room, or on the growing problem of slavers who seized free black men from the streets of New York and sold them into bondage in the markets of Baltimore or Richmond, or on the continuing removal of the Plains Indians from their lands by the War Department, sooner or later, the conversation returned to Poe.

"Do you know that he married his thirteen-year-old first cousin?" said Margaret Fuller, addressing the group next to whom I cruised. "I understand that they've been married ten years now." Besides being the literary critic for Mr. Greeley's *New York Tribune*, the best-read female in New England, and one of the few women in America to support herself by her writing, Miss Fuller was an expert on the Great Lake Indians. This evening she wore a Potawatomi bib of bones over her wool serge bodice. Indeed, with her hawklike nose and piercing black eyes, her face resembled an Indian war club.

Helen Fiske, who herself was but fifteen years of age, butter-haired, and as soft as Miss Fuller was hard, said, "Perhaps all Southerners marry young."

Miss Fiske was quickly attacked all around for being ignorant of Southerners, who were just like us if not a tad more old-fashioned. The unspoken truth was that New Yorkers considered everyone in the world to be just a tad—well, more than a tad, a lot more than a tad—old-fashioned, compared with themselves.

Mr. Greeley, who was also present, lifted his teacup. The nails of his thick fingers were permanently stained with printer's ink, although as publisher of the *Tribune*, his days of setting type had long since passed. "I'll tell you a new fashion that I find ludicrous: this notion of Free Love. Claiming that 'spiritual holy love' is more important than a legal marriage—I wish them luck with that."

"Hush," said Miss Fuller. "Mr. Andrews can hear you."

The little group glanced toward the fireplace, where the founder of the Free Love movement, Mr. Stephen Pearl Andrews, was speaking earnestly to Miss Lynch.

"Besides," Miss Fuller said, "I'm not sure that Andrews is all wrong."

"Don't tell me you're one of those Free Lovers, Margaret," said Mr. Greeley with a rubbery-faced grin.

"No, but I do agree with him that marital relations without the consent of the wife amounts to rape."

Mr. Greeley seemed not to hear her. "We ought to ask Poe what he thinks of the Free Lovers. He seems to have an opinion on everything."

"I have heard that he was court-martialed from the army," said the daguerreotypist Mathew Brady. Although a young man, he wore spectacles with thick round lenses that magnified his eyes to thrice their size, giving him the appearance of someone much older. When he sipped his tea, I saw that his hands were tinged with the umber color of the iodine he used in developing his daguerreotypes, a kind of portrait done by exposing chemicals to light, a fad that my husband felt sure would soon fall out of favor.

"No surprise." Mr. Greeley swallowed his mouthful while dusting off the crumbs that had fallen upon his long gray coat. "I hear he's got a weakness for the bottle."

"Be that as it may," said Miss Fuller, "I find his poetry touching if a bit elementary, although his stories are entirely too preoccupied with the dead."

"Is it a wonder?" said Miss Fiske, her yellow ringlets nearly trembling. "I've heard that he lost his mother as a tiny child."

Miss Fuller frowned. "Poor Poe."

Behind the prisms of his glasses, Mr. Brady's eyes grew even bigger. "Why do all you ladies say that? You rush at him like you are his long-lost mothers."

A quiet fell over the room. A slim, immaculately dressed man stepped into the parlor with Miss Lynch, whose heart-shaped elfin face was tilted at him in adoration. His broad forehead, cleared of the unruly waves of his hair, emphasized the dark-lashed gray eyes from which he now stared with a cold intelligence. His mouth, beneath a silky mustache, was delicate in its cut yet hard and disdainful. Erect as a soldier, he held himself so tightly that he seemed ready to either lash out at whoever approached him or to stalk from the room. I didn't know whether to run to or from him.

"I don't think being his mother is what the ladies have in mind," Mr. Greeley said under his breath.

"Everyone," Miss Lynch exclaimed, "may I present Mr. Poe!"

No one moved. Into the wake of silence, a slight young woman with robin's-egg-blue-colored ribbons fluttering from her hair, neck, and sleeves swept through the parlor door on the arm of Mr. Nathaniel Willis, Mr. Morris's partner on the *Mirror*. She was beautiful in a fragile way, thin and pale, and with hair so black as to have undertones of blue. Her features were much like Mr. Poe's—wide forehead, shapely mouth, dark-rimmed eyes. They appeared to be brother and sister, with he the elder sibling and she the adorable baby of a notably handsome family.

Miss Lynch reached back and put her arm around the young woman's delicate shoulders, bringing her into the room. "And this, my dears, is Mrs. Poe!"

The woman-child smiled sweetly. From his little wife's side, Mr. Poe glared at our gathering as if to eat us.

The elderly Mr. Audubon stepped forward and put out his hand to Mrs. Poe, the fringe of his buckskin dangling. "My dear lovely lady, where were you when I was young?"

Mr. Poe stared at him as if deciding whether to take offense.

Shielded from fear by age and self-preoccupation, Mr. Audubon pursued Poe's wife further. "From where do you hail, dear? I know you're not from New York. You are much too sweet."

"Baltimore." Mrs. Poe's voice was as silvery as a little bell. She sounded like a young girl, although if Miss Fuller was correct, Mrs. Poe was twenty-three years of age.

"Baltimore—ah, a name I adore. You are familiar with the Baltimore oriole?"

"No, sir."

"No? Well, I shouldn't expect such an innocent young thing to know *everything*. They are birds, madame, birds." Mr. Audubon folded her hand onto his arm. "I saw my first oriole in Louisiana, in 1822. I paint birds. Did I tell you that?"

They strolled off, the aged illegitimate son of an aristocrat, dressed like a frontiersman, and the wife of the toast of New York, as pretty in her ribbons as a child's doll. At any other soiree, such a pair would be remarkable. At Miss Lynch's party, which she preferred to call a conversazione, they were just part of the colorful crowd.

Seeing an opening, Miss Fuller detained Mr. Poe. Reluctantly, conversations renewed around me. I pretended to listen to Mr. Greeley and Mr. Brady as I observed Mr. Poe and then his wife. It was uncanny how much they looked alike. I wondered if they had grown up together and, if so, when they knew that they were more to each other than blood kin.

"Fanny."

I started.

Eliza laughed. "I scared you."

"You didn't."

She edged in closer. "Does Mr. Poe?" she whispered.

I drew in a breath. "Frankly, yes."

She chuckled. "I know what you mean. But I believe he might be a gentleman once you get to know him."

"Tell that to poor Mr. Longfellow and the scores of other poets he has shredded."

Eliza peered over the crowd. "Quick—Poe looks bored. Now's our chance to meet him."

She pulled me across the room redolent with the smell of hair pomade, butter cookies, and perfumed flesh. We stopped before Mr. Poe, who was listening coldly as Miss Fiske related how her mother had died in the previous year and how her mother's passing had only deepened her poetry and enabled her to truly *feel*.

"I believe she is with me still, Mr. Poe." Miss Fiske peered up into his face with earnestness. "Whenever I see a fallen feather, I know she has sent it. I collect them. See the one she has sent me today?" She pulled a brown feather from her reticule.

He glanced at the feather and then at Miss Fiske. "Not resting comfortably in heaven, is she?"

Miss Fiske flinched as if poked.

Eliza chose this moment to interrupt. "Mr. Poe?"

He turned his baleful gaze upon her. I nearly winced at the pain and fury in his dark-lashed eyes. What had happened to this man to make him such a wounded beast?

Dismay flitted across Eliza's face. She recovered her equilibrium with the speed of an experienced socialite. "I believe you have met my husband, John Russell Bartlett."

"The publisher? He has a bookshop in the Astor House."

"That's correct," she said, delighted. "I am his wife, Eliza. I would like you to meet my dear friend."

Mr. Poe cut me a doubtful glance.

"Mr. Poe, this is Mrs. Samuel Osgood—Fanny, as her many friends and admirers call her. She's well known for her poetry."

He let his beautiful, terrible gaze fall upon me. As discomfiting as it was, I refused to look away. I would not let this second-rate poet, as popular as he was, frighten me. He put one leg in his pantaloons at a time, just like every other man.

Although his expression remained cool, his eyes registered surprise, then amusement. Did he find me that ridiculous?

Eliza glanced between us. "Fanny has written several collections for children. 'The Snow-drop,' 'The Marquis of Carabas, and Puss in Boots,' and 'The Flower Alphabet.' We are so proud of her."

I must sound as childish as my tales. "I also write poems for adults."

"She does!" cried Eliza. "She has written about flowers for them, too."

"Flowers," he said flatly.

I was saved from melting into the carpet in shame by the vigorous approach of the English actress, Mrs. Fanny Butler née Kemble, who was advancing upon us with a swish of pumpkin-colored skirts. With her chestnut curls, milk-and-roses complexion, and soulful brown eyes, she was even prettier in person than in the hoardings that were still plastered around London when I had lived there, several years after she'd left the stage for marriage.

"Mister Poe!" she said in her plummy stage voice. "I have been dying to talk with you!"

He glanced at me as if he thought to say more, then regarded her coolly. "You look fairly alive just yet."

She laughed. "Thank you, you are quite correct," she said, her voice less affected. "We must be mindful of our words. We do get lazy; at least I do."

She held out her hand to me as one would to a man. "And you are?"

I shook with her. "Frances Osgood."

"So very nice to meet you."

I caught a glimmer of sorrow behind her brave smile. Even though she had just taken up residence in the city, everyone knew of her recent estrangement from her American husband over the issue of slavery, he being one of the largest slaveholders in the nation. After living on their plantation when newly married, she had grown to despise human bondage and her husband in equal measures and had publicly denounced both. Now that she had left him, she was thought of by many to be an unnatural woman, not just for breaking with her husband over a principle, even one as important as this, but for abandoning their children, to whom she had no legal claim upon leaving her husband. Now that Mrs. Butler was so vilified, Miss Lynch had been every bit as brave to invite her as to have invited Mr. Andrews and his Free Lovers. At other, less intellectual, more "respectable" gatherings, "decent" women would have left the room had Mrs. Butler entered. It was astonishing how rapidly she had gone from being the cosseted darling of the stage to a much-despised pariah.

"I'm glad for this chance to speak to you," she said to Mr. Poe. "I have wanted to ask if you would be interested in staging 'The Raven' as a short play for charity."

"I am my only charity, Mrs. Butler."

She laughed again.

"I do not joke." He stared at her until her brightness dimmed. "I never joke."

Just then Miss Lynch called everyone's attention to Mr. Whitman, who wished to read a poem.

Everyone gathered around with their teacups—Mr. Poe, I noticed, with Mrs. Butler.

I had no other chance to talk to him that evening. But had I been like the other moths fluttering to his light, I would have soon felt his withdrawal, for shortly after Mr. Whitman's reading, Poe's little wife, who'd been standing behind Mrs. Butler, began to cough. When Mrs. Poe could not regain her composure, Mr. Poe excused them from the gathering.

They left quickly, with his little bride holding a handkerchief to her mouth, but not before she had flashed Mrs. Butler the most startling look. For a blink of the eye, her innocent young face twisted into a lacerating glare. Or had I imagined it? By the time I could mark it, it was gone, replaced by a cough, making me wonder what I'd seen. Then Miss Lynch pressed me into service to help refresh everyone's tea and the thought was snuffed like a candle in the rain.

Four

Is there a name for the phenomenon in which once one's attention is brought to a new word, subject, or acquaintance, one begins to see it everywhere? I experienced such with Mr. Poe and his bird poem during the weeks after I had met him. I heard two ladies swapping verses of "The Raven" as we waited at Broadway and Amity for the omnibus to pass. A gentleman standing outside an oyster cellar on MacDougal Street had a copy of the *Mirror* open to the latest reprint. Little girls skipping rope on the sidewalk of Sullivan Street chanted, "Quoth the raven, quoth the raven, quoth the raven, 'Nevermore!'"

That very morning, at the Jefferson Market, as I struggled with frozen fingers to pinch some pennies from my reticule for some apples, I heard the grocer, yet another German, ask the man behind me if he'd read the parody of "The Raven" called "The Owl."

"The Defil himself should be so clefer," he said. "De Temperance Owl will not drink de whiskey—"

"Let me guess," said the man. "—nevermore."

I glanced up as they laughed. The grocer was watching my hands, unaware of the enviousness he had unleashed in me. Why couldn't I have thought of writing a parody? Better humor than horror—the shivery sort of poem or story that Mr. Morris had requested was not exactly spilling from my pen. In fact, I did not like reading frightening stories let alone writing them. I did not enjoy how they openly played upon people's fear of death, dying, and the dead. What was wrong with Mr. Poe that he should be so preoccupied with these subjects? Why should he be so dark? Why should people want him to be so dark?

Yet his fame was growing among unlearned and literary folk alike.

Just the previous evening, the Bartletts and everyone else I knew had gone to hear him give an address about American poetry at the New York Society Library. Although I had several poems in the collection he was to discuss, I had made my excuses to stay home, secretly unable to bear hearing him praise other, more important authors when my own writing was foundering. I did wonder, however, whom he had tomahawked, and so was sorry to find when I came down to breakfast that there would be no report. Eliza had gone out with her maid.

Now, by the front parlor window at the desk that the Bartletts had so generously set up for me, and after eating an apple, brushing and coiling my hair into a bun, and paring three pens, I turned back to the story I was trying to write. I picked up a pen, dipped it into the inkwell, stared at the blank paper, then set the pen down. A glance at the picture on the wall—a portrait of Mr. Bartlett's stern grandfather, reminding me that I had no house of my own—caused me to pick it up again.

In an hour, I had a poem about a fallen angel. I hated it. That did not stop me from bundling up for a walk downtown.

Mr. Morris lowered my manuscript. "Angels, Mrs. Osgood? It is demons that are selling now."

"Fallen angels are a sort of demon," I said, not convincing even myself.

He tapped the top page. "Not yours. They are decidedly angelic. And your angel did not fall hard enough. People want to see *despair*. They want to see *horror*. They want the living daylights scared out of them."

"I know," I murmured.

"All this is," he said, handing the manuscript back to me, "is sad."

I put it in my reticule.

"Maybe you should stick to ladies' magazines."

"Thank you for your time, Mr. Morris."

He accompanied me to the door. When I turned around to propose another idea, his wide form was already receding down the hallway.

I began the long trudge home. Few vehicles were on Ann Street, and most of them were on runners, the weather having turned frigid after a two-day thaw, thus hardening the slush on the streets and sidewalks into ice. On the way to the office of the *Mirror*, I had slipped several times and, in trying to avoid a fall, had pulled a muscle in my back. Now, without the prospect of a sale, I felt the pain of it more keenly. I minced along on the ice, racking my brains for the premise of a clever poem—no, a *ghoulish* poem or story.

I was looking at the banners draped from Barnum's hall of hokum, trying to draw inspiration from his fantastical creatures, when I slipped and dropped like a sack of coal. In the moment that I sat there, the icy pavement chilling me through my petticoats, a gloved hand came into the view before my bonnet. My gaze trailed upward from a pair of neatly pressed trousers, up the buttoned front of a butternut-colored army greatcoat, to a pair of black-lashed gray eyes calmly regarding me from beneath the brim of a glossy hat.

"Take it." Mr. Poe motioned with his hand. "I don't bite."

I reached up. He tugged me to my feet, then looked away as I straightened my garments.

"Are you all right?" he asked.

"Yes."

He glanced back to verify if this were true. "That was a hard fall. I was just crossing the street when I saw you go down."

"I must have been a sight."

"Not so much," he said. He tamped back a smile. His eyes were almost kind when lit with amusement.

Just then he glanced across the street. His smile retreated to his typical cold expression. "If you are certain you are well . . ."

"Yes. Thank you for your help."

He tipped his hat, then strode down Ann Street.

I peered across Broadway. Margaret Fuller was waving from the sidewalk in front of the Astor House.

I made my way through a break in the stream of sleighs gliding down the street.

"How are you?" she said when I reached the other side. "I haven't seen you since Anne Lynch's little party the other week."

"I'm well, thank you. And you?" Although Miss Fuller and I

knew each other socially, we hardly ever spoke. As someone known for children's poetry, I did not carry much cachet. It was my husband who had attracted her attention on the occasions that we had seen her, with his charm and good looks and ability to dash off flattering sketches of the ladies.

"I saw you conversing with Mr. Poe just now," she said without further ado. "Did he tell you how much he liked your last book of poems?"

I could feel my smile fade. Was she mocking me?

She peered from her bonnet with those bird-of-prey eyes. "Don't tell me you haven't heard about his lecture at the library last night. Were you there? I didn't see you."

"I couldn't make it."

"No one has told you about it?"

"Not yet."

"My dear, you were the talk of the evening. Everyone wondered if you two were lovers."

"What?"

"They were joking, of course. Tell your charming husband not to worry." She laughed, then grasped my arm. "Come inside to lunch. I'll tell you all about it."

"I really can't." I could not bear for the hotel manager who had cast me out to see me.

At that moment a handsome sleigh pulled by four gleaming horses rounded the corner of Barclay Street. Its passenger was an older woman wearing a magnificent fur bonnet and cape.

"You wouldn't think she'd gloat so openly about building her fortune on the heartache of women," Miss Fuller said after the sleigh had passed. When she saw my puzzled face, she said, "Madame Restell."

"I don't know her."

"I wrote a column about her last year. She keeps advertising in the *Sun*, claiming to know the 'European secret' of ending a pregnancy. I'll tell you what the 'secret' is: abortion. Administered by someone without a shred of training."

I watched the sleigh head up Broadway, a rich plum of a vehicle among workaday carts. What a gold mine she'd struck. As long as women felt the pull of a man's embrace, she would have plenty of trade.

"So," said Miss Fuller, "what do you say to lunch? My treat. You'll want to hear what Poe had to say."

I let her tug me into the hotel.

Inside the overheated womb of the lobby, Miss Fuller raised her voice over the disconnected conversations echoing from the high ceilings. "You really should have come last night. Poe was in rare form. In his weird, polite way, he proceeded to rip through everyone's work in *The Poets and Poetry of America*. He accused Mr. Longfellow of plagiarism."

"Not again," I murmured, looking around. Plush drapery clotted the windows, snuffing out any natural light that might have supplemented the artificial orange glow cast by the gas chandeliers. In this otherworldly dim, well-dressed ladies and gentlemen moved languidly, as if suspended in some kind of fluid. I was relieved to not see Colonel Stetson, the proprietor who had presented me with our unpaid bill, among them.

Miss Fuller nodded. "Oh, yes. Again. He called Bryant 'trite.' And the poor defenseless dead Davidson sisters—dear me, he destroyed them. You should have heard what he said about Rufus Griswold. Poe crushed him for choosing such poor work for his collection. Rufus was sitting next to me. His face was something to see. These sofas aren't as red."

"A shame."

"That's why I was excited when I saw Poe just now. I wanted to get him to make a statement for my column. He was bound to say something outrageous. But then he ran off. Did he say what the matter was?"

"We didn't really speak. He was just helping me up—I had fallen on the ice."

Miss Fuller's nose was even more hawklike in the strange light. "Are you sure?"

"I don't think he remembered me from Miss Lynch's party."

She dismissed me with a snort. "Don't kid yourself. Pretty girls like you are always remembered."

We reached the table d'hôte, a room that was as excessive in its use of heavy wood as the parlor was of marble and satin. How had I ever stood living in this place? Its opulence suffocated me.

Our wraps were taken, revealing that Miss Fuller was not wearing her Potawatomi bib on this occasion, but a bracelet that looked to be made of bone. "No one was immune from Mr. Poe's vitriolic," she said after we were seated. "Except one person." She blinked with a flash of white lids. "You."

"I really don't understand."

She laughed harshly. "Your modesty is a good role for you. Men love that sort of thing. Wish I could adopt it."

She continued before I could protest. "In his entire lecture, you were the only poet he consistently spoke highly of. He said you had a 'rosy future.' Do you know what a feather in your cap that is? It made me want to scramble to get a copy of your works. Surely you have some connection with him. Poe wouldn't crow like that for the sport of it—the man hates to puff. Do tell, Frances. It can be off-the-record if you wish."

Denying a connection would be throwing away an opportunity to climb the ladder to professional recognition. But recalling his unaffected smile, even though it had been at my expense, made me feel a twinge of protectiveness toward him. "Unfortunately, we have no connection whatsoever. I met him briefly at Miss Lynch's conversazione. That is all. As I said, I don't think he recognized me just now, although he seemed almost nice."

"Poe? Nice? I knew something was up. Poe is never 'nice.'"

The waiter came. I cringed—I knew him from my stay there. To my great relief, he inquired politely about my husband and daughters as if we were guests of good standing. Still, I wondered what Miss Fuller knew about Samuel. The woman seemed to have antennae for scandal.

The waiter had just served us our soup when the maître d'hôtel came to our table and, bowing as if he, too, knew nothing of my empty coffers, presented me with a folded newspaper.

"From the gentleman, madam."

I looked over my shoulder. Just inside the entrance to the table d'hôte, Mr. Morris's diminutive partner, Mr. Willis, saluted in his hasty manner. With his slightly flattened balding head and his forward-pitched posture, he reminded me of a grasshopper.

"Tell him to come over," Miss Fuller instructed the maître d'.

I unfolded the paper. It opened to a copy of 'The Raven.' The hair raised on my arms.

Miss Fuller gave me a conspiratorial smile. "Last chance to come clean about Mr. Poe."

Mr. Willis sprang across the room. "Sorry to interrupt. I was leaving the office just now when Mr. Poe came in. He asked me to give you his poem, Mrs. Osgood, and to ask your opinion of it."

"My opinion?"

He crossed, then recrossed his arms, then put them down altogether, as if aware of the twitchy appearance he was making. "He said you might tell him in person. I believe, Mrs. Osgood, that this is our dear Mr. Poe's way of saying he would like to speak with you."

Why?

Miss Fuller lifted her brows. "If you really don't know him, Frances, you ought to take him up on it. He would be useful to have as an acquaintance. Your husband won't object, will he?"

"I don't believe so."

"Well?" asked Mr. Willis.

I wanted to tell them that I found Poe's bird poem childish and strange. If I were ever able to figure out how to write a "shivery" work for Mr. Morris, let it have depth and something to say about the human heart and not just be a game with words.

But my husband had run off, and even if I did sue him for divorce, it would do me no good—he had no money to support me. I was in no position to turn up my nose at Mr. Edgar A. Poe and the recognition his backing might give me. Surely no harm could come from that.

"Tell him, please, that I admire his poem greatly."

Five

Two weeks later, I was tucked beneath a thick buffalo robe, riding downtown in Miss Fuller's carriage. I had been too nervous to enjoy the trip or to appreciate Miss Fuller's carriage, pulled by a clopping bay. That Miss Fuller was the only woman in New York to support herself by writing, let alone to have enough leftover to buy her own buggy, mattered little to me at that moment. Why had I agreed to meet Poe? And why would he want to meet me? He had already made and broken an appointment the previous week. I had been relieved by the cancellation, only to become agitated once more when he set up a different date. As suddenly and inexplicably as he had championed my poetry at the New York Society Library, he could withdraw his support if I said something wrong. Who knew what triggered the man's tomahawk?

Miss Fuller jerked on the reins. "Here we are." She looked at me expectantly, as if I should climb out of her trim little gig without her.

"Shouldn't we wait for the doormen to take your reins?" I asked.

"Take my reins? Oh—did you think I was coming with you? No, no, dear, I'm off to investigate a slum on Hester Street. You really thought I was coming with you? I only meant that I would take you here. I thought your husband would appreciate my escorting you since he is, as you say, out of town."

"Would you rather I came with you to the slum?" I asked.

"And have you jilt Mr. Poe? I wouldn't dare." Miss Fuller steadied her horse, then waved me toward the hotel. "Go on. It will be good for your books."

Reluctantly, I climbed out from under the heavy robe. I held my breath as the carriage rattled away.

I found myself on the sidewalk before the hotel, contemplating an immediate about-face up Broadway when I felt someone's presence behind me. Before I could move, a man said, "Lord help the poor bears and beavers."

I turned to find Mr. Poe, his black-lashed eyes trained upon the building before us. Without a hello he said, "Davy Crockett's words, upon first seeing this pile."

I hesitated. "Because of Mr. Astor's fur trade?"

He continued as if I had not spoken. "But Crockett was mistaken. It wasn't the bears and the beavers that made Astor's fortune. It was the opium he bought from the Chinese."

I looked at him in surprise. "Mr. Astor deals in opium?"

He kept his gaze upon the hotel. "Whenever you see this much wealth, assume that someone dirtied his hands. Fortunes don't come to saints."

"I've never thought of that."

He gave me a sharp glance. "Really?"

I drew back, chastened.

"Mr. Astor prefers to be known for the slaughter of animals rather than for his association with opiates. I wonder why that is." He lowered his sights to me. "Shall we enter, Mrs. Osgood?"

So he did recognize me. I preceded him inside, into the hot maw of the lobby. As we walked past impressive people dressed in beautiful clothes, I felt low and insignificant, a ne'er-do-well's abandoned wife, although my gown was as fine as anyone's. What a sham I was.

I stopped to face him. "Congratulations on the success of 'The Raven.'"

He frowned as if insulted.

"People love it. I hear talk of it everywhere I go."

"'People' have no taste. Don't tell me that you think it's a work of genius."

Was this a trick? I scanned his dark-rimmed eyes for clues.

When I did not answer he said, "Thank you, Mrs. Osgood. You're the first honest woman I have met in New York." He shook his head. "It is my luck that I will become famous for that piece."

Still not sure that I shouldn't be gushing, I switched to safer ground. "May I ask what you are working on now?"

"A book on the material and spiritual universe."

I laughed.

He watched me coolly.

"I'm sorry. I thought you were joking."

"I never joke."

"Of course not. Excuse me."

"Although I wish I were. It will never sell."

"Your work always sells," I said lightly.

"Not any of my works with a true idea in them. People want to be titillated or frightened. They don't want to think."

I smiled hesitantly. What did he want with me?

"This is why I singled out your poems in my lecture," he said. "They have real feeling in them, if one reads between the lines."

I could not help but be disarmed. "Thank you. I find that the thoughts spoken between the lines are the most important parts of a poem or story."

"As in life."

I reluctantly met his intense gaze. "Yes."

"I am particularly taken with your poem, 'Lenore':

So when Love poured through thy pure heart his lightning,
On thy pale cheek the soft rose-hues awoke—
So when wild Passion, that timid heart frightening,
Poisoned the treasure, it trembled and broke!

I swallowed my surprise. "You memorized it."

An elegant couple drifted by, he in succulent wool and she in layers of costly lace. Mr. Poe frowned. "It spoke to me somehow, and not just because I had written a poem with the same title and had used the name in 'The Raven.'"

"A coincidence."

He stared at me.

I looked away. Why had Mr. Poe called this meeting? Surely he had better things to do than to raise the hopes of an unknown writer.

"You are probably wondering why I wished to meet you."

I drew in a breath.

"Actually, it is on behalf of my wife."

"Mrs. Poe?"

He frowned slightly at my unnecessary question. "She is a great reader. I have taught her all of the classics. I like to encourage her when she shows interest in good work, and your poems, Mrs. Osgood, delight her."

I pictured the pretty woman-child I had seen at Miss Lynch's conversazione. I wondered if it was my poems for adults or for children that she admired.

"Thank you for your kind words, Mr. Poe. I wish she were here so that I could thank her, too."

His expression hardened. "She has had bronchitis. Her recovery has been long and difficult. There was no question of her going out today."

"I am sorry to hear that."

"The few times she has ventured beyond our home have only served to set her back."

"I am truly very sorry."

He glanced away, then glared as if I'd offended him. "You will not hear her complain. She's a brave, good girl. If I could only take her to Jamaica or Bermuda or some such hot clime, I'm certain she would become well."

Why did they not go, then? With his success, surely he had the money.

"I hope she gets well soon."

His expression settled back into cool civility. "It is bold of me to ask—we are perfect strangers, and you have obligations to your husband and family—but might you come visit her someday? I know from looking into your eyes that you are a good person, and kind, and that your gentle association might help her."

That was why he wished to meet with me? Ashamed of my disappointment, I exclaimed, "I should like very much to meet her! Might I have the pleasure of visiting her at your home?"

"Mrs. Osgood, you are too kind. Yes. Yes, we'd like that very much."

"When would you like me to come?"

"At your convenience."

"Would next week suit you?"

"Name your day. Any day. I will arrange my schedule around you."

"Monday? In the afternoon?" I saved my morning hours for writing . . . writing, that is, what I hoped would be my imitation of his work.

He bowed, as stiffly formal as if in a royal court. "We would be so grateful."

He gave me directions to his home on 154 Greenwich Street, then bowing again, left me in Astor's parlor with all the frippery that bears and beavers and opium could buy.

Six

That Saturday, at Eliza's insistence, I attended another of Miss Lynch's conversaziones. The talk was provocative, as usual. In the orange gaslight amplified by the many mirrors upon the walls, Miss Fuller, wearing the beaded headband of an Iroquois maiden, regaled the assemblage with some the colorful expressions she had learned while visiting the poor families in the Bowery—"slang," they called it. Men were "b'hoys"; women were "g'hals." A friend was a "chum" or a "pal," and to die was "to kick the bucket." "Good-bye" was the perplexing "so long."

Assuring us "chums" that he had no intention of "kicking the bucket," Mr. Greeley next spoke about the state admitted to the Union the previous week. Florida, a malaria-ridden swamp to which the Seminoles clung, was a land, all agreed, that would never amount to much. Georgia plantation owners just wanted it for expansion for when their cotton fields went barren. The conversation then turned to slavery, which few in the gathering supported, but when Mrs. Butler began to relate the horrors she had seen on her husband's plantation, the implied subject of her divorce raised its unsuitable head, provoking some chilly stares around the overheated room.

To keep the conversation civil, Miss Lynch had us break for cookies and tea. I offered my services to man the samovar, the subject of estrangement too close to me for comfort. I remained in my position behind the urn as the crowd reassembled in small knots with their refreshments. I was surprised when Miss Fuller motioned for me to join her and Mr. Greeley. Warily, I stepped over.

"I wonder if he'll bring his wife," Mr. Greeley was saying.

"I hope so," said Miss Fuller. "They make such an interestingly odd pair. Frances, here, is going to their house next week."

"You are!" exclaimed Mr. Greeley.

"You remember Mrs. Osgood?" she said.

"With the talented painter husband?" Mr. Greeley scanned the crowd. "Where is he? I don't recall seeing him of late. He used to dash off sketches of the ladies as easily as buttoning his shoes."

"He's had a commission out of town."

He looked at me more closely. "You're going to Poe's?"

I nodded, wondering if it had been a bad idea to tell Miss Fuller of the invitation.

"What's your connection to him?"

"I don't really have one." I could not tell them that he'd memorized my poem. For reasons I did not fully understand, that recollection was too precious to share.

"That's what Frances keeps claiming," Miss Fuller said to Mr. Greeley.

"But I don't."

Mr. Greeley's pliable features bent into a rubbery-lipped grin. "'The lady doth protest too much, methinks.'"

"I have been trying to interview Mrs. Poe for weeks," said Miss Fuller. "And Frances here sashays out of the Astor House with an invitation to their home."

Mr. Greeley smiled. "Well, with a beautiful woman like Mrs. Osgood—"

Miss Fuller cut him off. "Do you realize on how many levels you offend?"

"Forgive me." Mr. Greeley bowed to us both. "I only meant to compliment. Are you working for the *Herald*?" he asked me. "Because if you are, give me your feature and I'll pay you double whatever they're paying."

"It's to be purely a social visit," I said, "to Mrs. Poe."

Mr. Greeley grabbed my hand and rubbed my knuckles. "Let me rub off some of your magic. Poe won't let anyone near his child-bride."

"As you recall, he also praised Frances's poems at his lecture at the Society Library," Miss Fuller said, "the evening that he crucified Longfellow."

Mr. Greeley winked. "And you don't know the man at all."

"I don't," I said.

He called over Mr. Brady, who was passing by with an empty cup of tea. "Did you know that this little lady is a friend of Poe?"

Mr. Brady put down his cup, took my hand in his own chemically stained ones, and gazed at me through his prismatic lenses. "I've been trying to get Poe to sit for a portrait since January. Tell me how to influence him."

I laughed. "I have no idea."

"Poe's asked Mrs. Osgood to visit his wife," said Mr. Greeley.

"You're kidding. You'll have to tell us what she's like at home."

Miss Fuller pushed up her headband as she peered toward the entrance. "Maybe Mr. Poe will delight us with her tonight."

"I don't think so," I said. "She's not well."

My fellow conversationalists grew silent, waiting for me to continue. I found that their interest felt good.

"She's had bronchitis," I said.

"She did have a terrible cough when she was here last," said Miss Fuller.

"Mr. Poe said that going out had set back her recovery," I said.

"I could see that he was worried," said Mr. Brady. "One cough and he whisked her right out of here."

"I had wondered if it wasn't because he was ashamed of her," said Miss Fuller. When the others frowned, she said, "Well, she is just a child. Don't tell me I am the only one who finds that it's strange that he married his adolescent cousin."

"She may have been thirteen when they married," said Mr. Greeley, "but you told me yourself that they've been together ten years now. Show me a man who wouldn't want a pretty twenty-three-year-old wife."

"Mrs. Poe is well educated," I found myself saying. "She's familiar with all the classics."

"Oh?" said Miss Fuller.

Again all gazes were on me. I felt a heady surge of power. "Mr. Poe told me that he taught her himself."

"Really," said Mr. Greeley.

We were joined by a young dandy wearing jeweled rings over

his gloves. From the marble dome of his forehead, laid bare by the retreat of his hair, to the almost pretty curve of his lips and flare of his nose, his pinkly shaven face was the picture of elegance, as graceful as Michelangelo's *David*. Only the severe cleft between his brows marred his manicured surface, giving him a quarreler's scowl.

"Poe?" he said. "Did I hear you say Poe? Never believe a word that madman says."

"Mrs. Osgood," said Miss Fuller, "surely you have met the Reverend Rufus Griswold? He is visiting from Philadelphia. Rufus, you know Mrs. Osgood."

"We've corresponded by mail." He pressed shapely lips to my hand. "You are much more beautiful than I pictured. I find women poets as a whole to be prettier on the page than in person."

Mr. Greeley reached over to the table for a cookie. "Always winning hearts," he said drily.

I held back a smile. Getting on the wrong side of Rufus Griswold was suicide for a poet. Somehow this prickly young man had become the arbiter of taste for American poetry while still in his mid-twenties. Inclusion in his annual editions of *The Poets and Poetry of America* could make or break a writer, as could his reviews or lack of them. No one's reviews were followed as closely by the reading public—except for, recently, Mr. Poe's.

"How nice to meet you in person at last, Reverend Griswold," I said. "I hope this edition is selling well for you."

"It was," he said bitterly, "until Poe ripped it to shreds a couple of weeks ago."

"Oh, pooh, Rufus," said Miss Fuller. "I should think that your audience has increased. Poe devoted a whole evening to your book."

"To slashing it!"

Miss Fuller shrugged. "Free promotion."

"He publicly humiliated me!"

"Margaret's right, Griswold," said Mr. Greeley. "The literary papers were filled with it for weeks. Controversy sells. He's making you a pretty penny."

"Whose side are you on?" cried Reverend Griswold. He saw the frowns of the others. "Just don't imagine that he's not promoting himself. He thinks he's so clever, being the Tomahawker. I wonder how he'd feel on the other end of the hatchet."

Mr. Greeley brushed at his chin whiskers. "No doubt about it, Poe is a clever one when it comes to self-promotion. I wouldn't put it past him to have written the owl parody of his raven poem himself."

Miss Fuller took my arm, causing me to start. "Frances has been invited to the Poes' house, Rufus."

"Going into the lion's den, are you?" Reverend Griswold studied my face with a shrewdness that made me squirm. "You'd better be careful. He'll eat up a pretty little thing like you."

"I suspect that this 'pretty little thing' might wend her way into Poe's confidence faster than you could bludgeon your way in," said Miss Fuller.

Mr. Greeley stretched his lips in a grin. "Bring us back a report."

"While you're at it," said Mr. Brady, "convince him to come sit for me."

Miss Fuller rubbed my arm companionably. "Rufus, get her some tea. You will tell us all about it, won't you, Frances?"

I accepted the cup that Reverend Griswold frowningly poured. I would have liked milk in my tea, but it was so unusual to be served by a man instead of serving one that I kept my peace.

"So you'll give us a report?" said Miss Fuller.

I looked into the brown liquid in my cup and then up at the group silently waiting for my answer. At Eliza's house, two little girls depended on me to make a life for them. It was not as if I would learn anything that would harm Mr. Poe by its revelation.

"Yes," I said. "Of course."

"Good," said Miss Fuller. Then pushing back her headband, she speculated whether the new president's wife might indeed be with child, when it had long since been thought that an operation for kidney stones had left Mr. Polk as sterile as a jug of boiled water.

Seven

I walked down lower Greenwich Street, giving wide berth to the hog feasting on a rotting pumpkin shell. Across the way, a well-dressed Temperance lady handed out tracts to the men emerging from one of the saloons that dotted the neighborhood like the dark kernels on an ear of Indian corn. A peddler trudged by, leaving a trail in the refuse-strewn pavement with the wheel of his barrow. The block, now fallen upon hard times, had once housed merchants and bankers in plain sturdy homes built of brick. But when yellow fever had swept through the city twenty-some years ago, many of those wealthy enough to flee had departed for the village of Greenwich or the countryside surrounding it, and have continued to settle north-ward ever since, making it passé to live downtown. In the dwellings they left behind, now four families crammed instead of one—families from foreign shores, most often Germany and Ireland.

Now I passed a German man carrying a pile of white cloth followed by his kerchiefed wife, who would be turning the heap into collars or cuffs at their kitchen table. Worn clothing flapped from lines strung above an alley down which a pack of Irish children kicked an empty patent-medicine bottle; a baby in rags toddled after them. At the end of the street several blocks away, the masts of sailing ships could be seen cruising behind the naked treetops of Battery Park, where the island gave way to the sea.

I came to the address that Poe had given me, Number 154. I had to be mistaken.

It had been a long while since a merchant had taken pride in this home. A fist-size hole in the glass of the window nearest the door had been stuffed with rags. Nearly slatless shutters sagged at the upper story windows and the door was shaggy with peeling paint. Even the doorknob, hanging by its stem, was in an advanced stage of neglect. Surely the poet who had captured the imagination of the city lived in a more comfortable situation than this.

Reluctantly, I climbed up the steps and tapped on the battered door, cringing at the thought of the lout who I might be disturbing in error. When no one answered, I turned away in relief. At that moment, a handsome private carriage pulled up to the building several doors down. I watched as a heavily veiled figure left the vehicle. Before she could enter the building, the driver whipped the horses and the carriage rumbled off, not waiting for its passenger.

The door of Number 154 opened behind me, sending the knob rolling to my feet. With a gasp, I picked it up and turned around. Mr. Poe, dressed in a spotless black frock coat and holding a large tortoise-shell cat, stared at me as if I should speak.

"Hello," I said stupidly.

He held out his palm. I placed the knob upon it.

He stood aside so that I could enter the dismal dwelling.

My fear flamed into anger as I did so. Why should he be so cool? I would not have come if he'd not invited me.

Just inside, quivering next to the stove that served for both cooking and heat, was a woman who looked to be what Mr. Poe might become in a few years had he been a woman and in a constant state of worry. She had Mr. Poe's high forehead and dark lashes but her square-jawed lined face and rounded eyes bristled with an anxiety completely foreign to him.

"Mrs. Osgood," said Poe, stroking his cat, "this is my aunt, Mrs. Clemm."

She bustled forward to shake hands, the long lappets of her white widow's bonnet flapping. Was it her daughter who had married Poe? She glanced between us, obviously bursting to speak.

"You might tell Virginia that she has a visitor," Mr. Poe said mildly.

Her bolster-like breast lifted in a sigh before she trundled into a back room.

I kept my gaze trained forward, pretending that I did not see the contents of the grim chamber: a threadbare sofa; a table set with a linen cloth browned at the edges from too much ironing; three lyre-backed chairs; the stove. Books lined the walls without the benefit of shelves. Besides a service of bone china on the table, the only fine piece in the room was a small, polished desk. It looked lost in its position beneath the rag-stuffed window.

"I hope you had no trouble in finding your way here," said Mr. Poe.

I could hear whispers and scuffling sounds coming from the back room. "None at all."

He put down the cat, who waddled over to the sofa, then jumped up and took a spot on it. "May I take your coat?"

Framing and discarding excuses to flee, I let him help me remove my wraps. His closeness discomfited me. I was trying to shake off my awkwardness when Mrs. Poe appeared in a schoolgirl's gray wool dress, her face as bright as a child's in a candy store.

"Mrs. Osgood! Thank you so much for coming! I have been dying to meet you ever since I read 'Puss in Boots!'" She glanced at her husband. "I love your poems on flowers as well."

Before I could thank her, she cried, "Please excuse our temporary lodging! Eddie had to find something close to his work, and this was all that was available at short notice. At least we don't have to share it with filthy strangers."

Mrs. Clemm grimaced. Mrs. Poe seemed not to notice. "You have heard that Eddie's the owner of *The Broadway Journal*?"

"Congratulations," I said to Mr. Poe. "So you have left the *Mirror*?"

"That monster Morris cheated him out of payment for his poems!" exclaimed Mrs. Poe. "Did he really think he could get away with that?" Her angelic voice dripped with vindictiveness. "Just wait—you'll see. Eddie will get his revenge."

Taken aback, I said, "Your husband's talents will be much more appreciated at the *Journal*, I should think, with its more literary leanings."

Mr. Poe's expression remained rigid. "I fear my position at the *Journal* is not as lofty as it might seem. As one of three owners, I put in sixteen-hour days. I seem to be the partner elected to supply the elbow grease."

"I should not take up your time then." I started to rise.

"Oh, please stay!" said Mrs. Poe, all sweetness again. "You only just got here."

Mrs. Clemm, hovering in the background, cried, "Would you like some coffee?"

Mr. Poe's face remained neutral.

"Mother just made it," Mrs. Poe added as further enticement. "We can't possibly drink it all by ourselves. Please!"

I lowered myself, cringing. There seemed to be no polite way out. "Maybe just a cup."

I soon found myself on the sofa with Mrs. Poe and the tortoise-shell cat perched on either side of me, the table moved to our knees. Mrs. Clemm poured the coffee into the china cups and then after passing them out, sat on one of the spindly chairs, her hand poised on the coffeepot, ready to replace my smallest sip. Mr. Poe, erect as a soldier, stood next to the sofa, quietly paging through a book.

Mrs. Poe smiled at me over the rim of her cup, her eyes a remarkable clear violet within the familial frame of dark lashes. Her skin, I noticed, was nearly as translucent and white as the cup itself. One could just make out the tracery of blue veins beneath it, giving one the odd sense that another creature altogether lurked just inside her flesh.

She put down her cup as carefully as a child playing at tea. In an overly serious voice, she asked, "Tell me how you came to write 'Puss in Boots.' "

"It was a few years ago," I said. "I was reading the stories of Charles Perrault to my children—"

"Oh, you have children! How old? Boys or girls? How many?"

"Girls. Ellen is going on nine and May Vincent, whom we call Vinnie, is nearly six."

"Oh, how lovely! Eddie and I are dying to have children! I want to fill a house with them."

"First we must get the house," said Mr. Poe, turning the pages.

"I do like the countryside!" said Mrs. Poe. "We just moved from the prettiest farm overlooking the North River. It had orchards and cows and chickens, but we had to be closer to Eddie's office. I do miss the lovely fresh air. Do you find the city air agreeable for your daughters?"

I raced to keep up with her train of thought. "More agreeable than in London."

"You've lived in London!"

"My girls were born there."

"I want to live in London! I want to live in Paris!" She pushed out her lower lip. "But Eddie won't let us." She changed the subject before I had to. "Where are you from?"

"Boston."

Mr. Poe looked up.

Mrs. Poe glanced between us. "Eddie? Did you know that? That's where Eddie's from. No wonder he likes you."

Mr. Poe "liked" me?

"I was merely born there," he said coolly. "I have no memory of the place."

"More coffee?" asked Mrs. Clemm. When she flew forward with the pot, I saw that her bonnet bore the same singe marks from ironing as the tablecloth.

"It's so wonderful that you write stories for children," said Mrs. Poe. "I want Eddie to write them when our children come. I won't let him read them his scary stories. They would frighten our poor babies to death. You must think Eddie is terrifying, but he's not. Are you, Eddie?"

He did not respond.

"Do you read much French, Mrs. Osgood?" asked Mrs. Poe.

I scrambled to connect the loose ends of the conversation—oh, the Perrault. "At times. 'Puss in Boots' is my translation—with my own twists, of course."

"Eddie does likewise." A hint of boastfulness crept into Mrs. Poe's voice. "He takes German and French stories and makes them into his own."

"Actually," said Mr. Poe, "they are more like inspirations."

"His stories are better than anyone's." She gave me a challenging look.

"Yes," I said. "I'm sure that's true."

Mr. Poe scowled.

"A little more coffee?" cried Mrs. Clemm.

"Eddie has taught me French," Mrs. Poe announced. "He says I speak it like a Parisian. Might you have any books you can recommend to me in that tongue?"

She was smiling expectantly at me when she started to cough. I sat back, sipping coffee politely as she coughed first into her fist, then into the handkerchief Mr. Poe produced from inside his coat. The cat fled from the sofa. Mrs. Clemm urged her daughter to drink the hot coffee, and when Mrs. Poe could not down that, she jumped up, retrieved a bottle of medicine from the back room, and poured Mrs. Poe a spoonful. Mrs. Poe could not stop coughing long enough to take it. On she barked as Mr. Poe rubbed her narrow back, each paroxysm wringing her lungs tighter until the flesh around her nose and lips were blue.

"Shouldn't you get her out into the air?" I asked helplessly.

"Virginia!" Mrs. Clemm bleated, spilling the medicine on her spoon. "Breathe! Breathe!"

Mrs. Poe convulsed in silent spasms, until at last, mercifully, she stopped. Mr. Poe held her, his face tight with fear.

Mrs. Poe smiled weakly as she leaned against her husband. "Sorry," she whispered to me.

My gaze went to the handkerchief, which had fallen from her hand. In its center was a coin of liquid crimson.

My skin tingled with fear. "I should go now and let you rest," I said.

"No," she whispered. She pulled away from Mr. Poe as her mother draped her own black shawl over her. "Please. Stay."

I laid my hand on her arm. "I will come back at another time."

"Promise?"

"Yes. Of course."

Reluctantly, Mrs. Clemm moved the table to release me from the sofa. After a tearful good-bye, Mrs. Poe sank against the sofa and watched as Mr. Poe helped me with my cloak.

He followed me outside and shut the door behind him.

"Thank you for coming," he said quietly.

"It was my pleasure," I said.

"You cannot know what this means to my wife."

I felt a rush of sympathy for the man. His fragile young wife seemed so helpless and ill. Again I wondered why a person of his means did not take her to a more suitable clime to heal her sickened lungs, when he so obviously doted on her. I was beginning to understand that Mr. Poe might not be so wealthy after all.

"I was glad to do so. I hope your wife gets better soon."

His silence told more of his worry than could words.

The wind tossed his hair, shining black in the weak March sun. I became conscious of how handsome he was and how noble in his restraint. He was as buttoned-up as his frock coat, as if he felt that all who depended on him would fall apart should he relax for one moment.

"Thank you again for the coffee."

"May I see you safely to a cab?" he said.

"You are hardly dressed warmly enough for the cold. At any rate, I walked. It's not so far." I would not mention that I did not want to waste money on a hackney.

"I would like a little air. Do you mind if I accompany you for a ways?"

"Doesn't Mrs. Poe need you?"

He kept any emotion from his face. "She is probably asleep by now. Her mother will watch her."

We walked silently along the pavement, the soggy flotsam left by the melted snow oozing under our feet. I wondered how long Mrs. Poe had been suffering with bronchitis, or if she was consumptive and that was why she had not borne the children she so fervently wished for.

A woman swathed in veils rounded the corner and commenced in our direction. I tried to see her face when she passed us but she was so heavily covered that it was impossible to get a measure of her. I turned to see her hurry past Mr. Poe's home and toward the building beyond, where I had seen the other shrouded figure enter earlier.

"Is there a nunnery on your street?"

"Nunnery?" He turned to see what I was watching. "No. Not a nunnery."

He offered no further explanation as we strolled on. "What are you working on now?" he asked.

"Not much." *Except on projects meant to siphon from your glory.* I could feel my face radiating with shame. "How is your book coming along on—what was it—the spiritual universe?"

He glanced at me. "You remembered."

"Of course."

He returned his gaze forward. "Unfortunately, I've had to put it aside for something that might actually sell."

I gave him a look of sympathy. "Something frightening?"

"There is nothing more frightening than cold reality. But readers don't want that, do they?" He allowed me a rueful smile. "What do you think I should write about?"

"I needn't tell you. You are the most popular writer in New York."

"Do you think so?" He scanned my face as if to detect any insincerity.

"'The Raven' is on everyone's lips. My friend Eliza heard 'nevermore' worked into a scene in a play at the Castle Garden Theatre. The little girls jumping rope in my neighborhood were chanting it. I have listened to ladies gush about meeting The Raven, as if you and your poem were the same. How does it feel to suddenly be adored by thousands of readers?"

He grimaced. "To be truthful, Mrs. Osgood, I have striven my whole life to be famous. Oddly enough, now that I have had some measure of success, I don't feel any more at ease. In fact, if anything, I feel less so. It is as if I am standing on the brink of a precipice, looking into the abyss."

When I saw that he was serious, I said, "Maybe you should take some time to enjoy your fame. You said you are working sixteen-hour days. You must be exhausted."

"Journals don't put themselves together nor do books write themselves."

"Maybe you could hire someone to take over some of your editorial work."

"If I'm ever to run a journal of my own, I must know the business from the inside out."

"Is that what you are working toward, having your own journal?"

"Yes. That is one of my goals." He smiled slightly. "You have caught me out."

I thought of my own goal of establishing my literary reputation, yet it was important to me to be a good mother as well. "There are so many ways in which our hours can be claimed each day. What a shame that we only have one life."

"Do we, Mrs. Osgood?"

I saw that he was serious. "Do you think we have another chance?"

"At this never-ending and mournful remembrance? No. Our maker would not be so cruel."

"Then what do you suggest that we have to look forward to?"

"You and I are poets, Mrs. Osgood. Our job is to raise questions, not to answer them."

I sent him a silent thanks for thinking of me as an equal.

Just then he grasped my arm. From the open door of a saloon reeled a man with his greasy hair falling in his face, shouts and laughter trailing after him. As we waited for him to lurch from our path, I looked down at Mr. Poe's hand. He met my eyes.

Time strangely and sharply suspended. We were gazing at each other guardedly, as if something within us was making a connection that we ourselves feared, when Mrs. Clemm came bustling down the sidewalk, her bonnet askew and her shawl riding slipshod over her shoulders. "Eddie! Eddie! Come quick. It's Virginia."

His hand trailed from my arm.

I watched them go, he upright and polished, even at a run, she shambling and flyaway. Long after they'd gone, I could feel his touch upon me. I hoped that his fragile young wife would be well even as a silky voice whispered, *I wish he were mine.*

I went up to the Historical Society Library in Washington Square on the way home. My association with Mr. Poe had the exhilarating effect of making me want to write. Maybe I could support myself and my family, if I only applied myself harder. With this in mind, I strolled through the gallery, peering at the portraits for inspiration as gentlemen conversed quietly around me. A poem about Time drifted into my mind, but like so many poems and stories that shine like gems in one's imagination, once I found paper and pencil and sat down to write, it had turned to dust.

Frustrated, I scratched out the inane lines that I'd produced, then bent my imagination toward creating a dark tale to sell to Mr.

Morris. Strangely, Mrs. Poe sidled into my mind. As I stared at the writing table, I saw her as an angel of darkness who'd come to earth in the form of a fair young woman. She charmed her admirers with her sweetness and innocence, lulling them into complacency, only to swoop in and—

And what? Snap their necks? I laid down my pen. Not even Mr. Morris would wish to print such rubbish. Where had I gotten such an idea? Shuddering at my perversity, I packed up my reticule and left immediately.

Eliza was sewing in the downstairs family room when I returned. She greeted me with an inquiring smile. One would never guess that a desperate sadness lurked just below her cheerful blue eyes, that she was still grieving for her two-year-old son, lost to scarlet fever not yet three years ago, and for a seven-year-old daughter who had fallen to diphtheria. She clung to her surviving children, a nine-year-old girl, Anna, and the two boys, with a quiet fierceness made more heartbreaking by her attempts to hide it.

"Mary took the children to the park." She tugged on her thread. "I hope you don't mind."

I removed my hat. "Thank you. Truly, I don't know what I would do without you."

"Never mind that. How was Mr. Poe?"

"In truth, very pleasant."

She laughed. "Poe?"

"Surprisingly, yes."

"We are talking about the man who regularly bludgeons Long-fellow?"

"The same. But he didn't cudgel anyone today. He was actually almost courtly." I thought a moment. "Especially once we left his home."

She raised her eyebrows.

I laid my hat on a table and sat. "It's not like that. He's very devoted to his wife. I think she causes him a great deal of worry. She's really very sick."

"He wouldn't be the first man to turn away from his obligations."

I gave a rueful laugh. "No, Samuel has already charted that territory."

She stopped sewing. "I'm sorry, Fanny. I didn't mean to imply that."

"No harm done. We both know what Samuel is."

She sighed. From behind the closed door to the kitchen came the clink of crockery as the cook, Bridget, prepared for dinner.

"What was Mrs. Poe like?" asked Eliza. "Beyond her illness."

I took up my own basket of mending. "I can't say exactly."

She dipped her needle into the cloth. "What do you mean? What does she seem like? Sweet? Sharp?"

"Both, oddly enough. But more of the former, I would say. I think she means well."

She plucked the needle out the other side. "That's a strange thing to say."

I absentmindedly picked at one of Vinnie's stockings. "She was very hard to fathom even though she talked a great deal. To tell you the truth, she rather disconcerted me."

"So you don't like her—"

"That's not it."

"—but you do like the husband and he evidently likes you."

"I did not say that!"

"He invited you to his house."

"At his wife's request."

"And you talked to him alone."

I put my finger through a hole in the heel. "Only for a moment. He walked me partway home."

I could feel Eliza's affectionate look of concern before she returned to her sewing.

As if taking a precious jewel from its hiding place, I replayed my conversation with Mr. Poe in my mind. I was gleaning his words for all possible warmth—and finding, to my great wonder, much—when Eliza spoke up.

"Fanny, be careful. You are vulnerable now, what with the wound from Samuel's leaving so fresh."

I laughed. "Mr. Poe is in love with his wife. You are making something from nothing."

"Perhaps I am." She sewed silently. After a moment, she said, "Did I tell you who left his calling card today? The Reverend Mr. Griswold."

"I am glad that I was out."

She laughed. "Fanny!"

"I'm sorry. That sounded rude. He just— Do you find that there's something a little off-putting about him?"

"I don't know him. But maybe you ought to. He could be very important to your writing—Russell says that he has everyone's ear in publishing." She tugged at her needle. "It is possible that he came here for Russell."

"*Please* let that be the case."

She chuckled, then bit her thread, the repair having been made. And so the subject of Mr. Poe was equally sewn shut, at least for the afternoon.

Eight

Saturday came, and with it another literary soiree at Miss Lynch's house. For reasons I refused to acknowledge, I dressed with utmost care. It struck me as Eliza's maid Mary buttoned up the back of my frock that Miss Fiske and the other rich young ladies would be taking pains to look less rich in order to fit in with the modest tone Miss Lynch set, while those less wealthy would be mustering all their forces to give the appearance of having money. How Samuel would have scoffed at Miss Lynch's insistence on moderation, especially had he learned that she and her mother, with whom she lived, were actually quite well-off. It infuriated him when those who had money would not flaunt it. He thought them dishonest. Only the rich, he said not a little bitterly, can afford to act like income does not matter. I wondered if he would ever return to New York. He was missing the opportunity to fish in this new pool of wealthy beauties while mocking their intellectual pretensions. Whoever had hooked him now must have pots of gold to be keeping him away for so long. Or maybe he just cared that little about his children and me.

Vinnie stroked the shiny satin of my skirt as Mary arranged my low-cut neckline around my shoulders. "You look pretty, Mamma. You're going to be the prettiest lady there."

She did not know of Mrs. Butler, whose beauty was renowned on both sides of the Atlantic, nor of Miss Lynch, with her kittenish pink-and-white sweetness.

"I hardly think so, dear, but thank you. Thank you, Mary," I said when she'd finished.

"You do look nice, ma'am."

I smiled at Mary, whose plain dress could not hide her own bright beauty. With large dark blue eyes accentuated by a beauty mark below the left one, and the red cheeks and mouth and dark hair of the Black Irish, she was as breathtaking as the green countryside from which she'd come. Some man would claim her soon and Eliza would be out a competent children's nurse.

Ellen, sitting on my bed, said, "I wish Papa could see you. Then he'd never go away."

I stepped over and gathered her to me, furious at Samuel for hurting his daughters and, worse, for being so self-involved that he had no idea he was hurting them.

"I don't think there is anything that you or I could have done to make him stay here, love. He'll come back, as soon as he can. It has nothing to do with us."

Ellen's face crumpled with doubt. "Has he written yet?"

"No."

"Maybe you should have been nicer to him."

I opened my arm for Vinnie, suddenly tearful, and brought her close, too. "Your papa loves you both very, very much. How can he help it?" I kissed the tops of their heads in punctuation: "You are the most lovable, most clever, most adorably silly girls in the world."

I stood back with a smile, although my heart was breaking for them. "Well," I said brightly, "what kind of necklace do you think Miss Fuller will have on tonight—made of shells, bones, or animal's teeth?"

Vinnie wiped her eye. "Bones." Both she and her sister had met Miss Fuller on afternoon promenades down Broadway last fall, when the weather had been fair. As one would guess, Miss Fuller's distinctive dress had left an indelible impression on them.

"Teeth." Ellen retreated again into her solemn facade. "People teeth."

"That is possible," I said. "Maybe she'll stop off at the dentist's on the way to the party and get herself a few."

Ellen frowned. "Maybe she steals them from people."

"Ellen!" My overly shocked tone brought out her smile.

As they exchanged gory and inappropriate ideas for how Miss Fuller might bolster her supply of teeth, I examined a sudden thought for a shivery story. What if a beautiful woman who had lost her teeth due to illness forced her maid to give up her own teeth and had them implanted in her gums, only to find that she was starting to think and speak like the maid . . . ?

I shook my head to clear it of ugliness. How could I ever write the kind of poetry that was selling well when dwelling on the dark side unnerved me? How did Mr. Poe bear it? You would think that his mind was ill. Yet the Mr. Poe I was beginning to know did not seem ill at all, but steady and even thoughtful, when I spoke to him alone. To be honest, more honest than I could be with Eliza, I found that I liked him a great deal.

As I fastened on my ear bobs, a pair Samuel had given me when he had been courting me—a set of pearls that had falsely given the impression that he had money—I felt dread at having to speak of Mr. Poe's private circumstances to Miss Fuller and Mr. Greeley. Mr. Poe had trusted me enough to let me meet his ailing wife. It seemed wrong to betray him.

And so I was relieved at the party that night to find that Miss Fuller and Mr. Greeley weren't there. I operated the samovar with cheerful vigor, happy to help Miss Lynch serve as I listened at the edges of conversations. It was freeing to be able to observe the various personalities without the distraction of having to interact with their owners: Miss Lynch's genuine modesty and earnest friendliness, which relaxed even pompous elitists like Senator Daniel Webster, glowering by the chimneypiece in his flamboyant purple coat; Mrs. Butler, with her actress's great energy and her natural good spirits, even while being rebuffed by some of the more traditional members of the assembly; and the Reverend Mr. Griswold with his Midas's touch of negativity, capable of puncturing anyone's mood with a single sour word. Soon after the cookies had been dispensed, we pulled around chairs and sofas to see the young spiritualist, Andrew Jackson Davis, give an impromptu performance in the art of mesmerization.

He looked around the crowd, his long, attractive face lifted in a grin. "Any volunteers?" he asked. He would have been very handsome had not his glossy mound of beard been trimmed so precisely to his jawline, making him look like he was wearing a fur ruff.

"What does it feel like to be mesmerized?" Eliza asked cheerfully. At her elbow, her husband, Russell, never one for nonsense, shook his head.

"The subject goes into a trance and feels nothing," said Mr. Davis. "While they are in the state of nervous sleep, I shall ask them to perform a few simple tasks. They will remember nothing when I awaken them."

Mrs. Butler stepped before him. "Use me. I should like to try it."

Mr. Davis seated her before the crowd, then pulled a leather case from his vest. At that moment, Mr. Poe walked into the salon, his top hat in his hand.

Miss Lynch flitted over to him. "Come in, Mr. Poe! We were just getting ready to see Mr. Davis put Mrs. Butler into a nervous trance."

Mr. Poe caught my eye as she led him over to the chair she had been occupying. I smiled, ridiculously shy. He blinked in acknowledgment just before the gaslights were turned down low.

I could not fully focus on the mesmerization. Yes, I watched Mr. Davis take a curette from his case and wave its shining blade just high enough above Miss Kemble's eyes so that she had to look up without lifting her face. Yes, I heard him command her to follow it with her eyes from side to side, and heard him tell her that she was getting sleepy. I witnessed her lids growing heavy, and Mr. Davis's stepping forward and closing them by simply putting his thumb in front of them. But although my face was trained toward the performance, my outer gaze was upon Mr. Poe, who was watching the proceedings closely. I could not help but wonder if Mrs. Poe's health was improving. Had he found a new house? And, absurdly, had he thought of me?

A stirring behind us revealed Mr. Greeley tiptoeing into the room with Miss Fuller and a man who I recognized to be another editor at the *Tribune*.

"Shhh!" one of the ladies hissed. "A mesmerization!"

"That humbug?" Miss Fuller said under her breath. She took a place on a chair that Miss Lynch had quickly found her.

Soon Mrs. Butler was meowing like a cat at Mr. Davis's command. He commanded her back to sleep, then asked her what she saw.

"My sister," she said in a strange voice.

"Where is your sister?" asked Mr. Davis.

"There!" Mrs. Butler flung out her arm. In doing so, she knocked over a Chinese urn on a pedestal. It broke apart on the floor like an egg tapped against the edge of a skillet.

Mrs. Butler opened an eye. "So sorry, Anne," she whispered to Miss Lynch.

All laughed, except Mr. Davis and, I noticed, Mr. Poe. As people broke into animated groups, he took aside Mr. Davis. They were talking quietly when Miss Fuller tapped my arm.

"How was your meeting with Poe?" she said in a low voice.

I gazed at her necklace—stone, tonight—as I grasped for a non-committal answer.

Mr. Greeley ambled over with a cookie. "What did I miss?"

Miss Fuller strained to see if Mr. Poe were still occupied. "I just asked her about Poe," she whispered. "So tell us, what was his house like?"

I lowered my face. "I can't say. He was living in temporary lodging."

"Did you talk to his wife?" asked Mr. Greeley.

I looked up. "She was very sweet."

"Sweet?" cried Miss Fuller. "I can't write a column on 'sweet'!"

I glanced at Mr. Poe, still engaged by Mr. Andrews. "I really don't know the Poes. At any rate, maybe there's not enough about Mr. Poe's personal life on which to write a column."

Miss Fuller gave me an incredulous stare. "Edgar Poe married his thirteen-year-old first cousin when he was in his twenties. He regularly scalps America's best poets. His stories are filled with dead people who haunt their killers. And you mean to tell me there's nothing about his private life to write about?"

I saw Mr. Poe coming our way. My frown made Miss Fuller turn.

"Mr. Poe!" she cried. "Good evening."

"It is good-bye, I fear. I have been at the office all day and must return home. Mrs. Osgood—" He bowed. "I had hoped that I would catch you here. My wife asked if you could possibly call on her next week. Perhaps Tuesday?"

I felt Miss Fuller's smile upon me. "Certainly," I said.

"At ten o'clock?"

"Ten is fine."

With nods to all, he backed away, then left.

"Well," said Mr. Greeley, "that was fast."

Miss Fuller chuckled. "And you don't know the Poes."

I kept my expression pleasant. Mr. Poe had walked a mile and a half from his office to Washington Square and the walk home was equally far. It seemed like a lot of time and trouble just to deliver an invitation.

Reverend Griswold arrived at our circle. "Where's Poe going?"

"Home," said Mr. Greeley.

"Well that he should run!" said Reverend Griswold. "If he thinks I will forgive him for insulting my book, he's got a big surprise coming."

"I doubt if you'll take him by surprise, Rufus," said Miss Fuller. "Unless you actually did forgive him."

Reverend Griswold raised his smoothly pink face in a superior smile. "Why should I forgive Edgar Poe, when ruining him would be ever so much more fun?" His rings crunched my fingers as he plucked up my hand with his own dove-gray-gloved one. He smelled strongly of crushed roses when he leaned in to kiss it. "Wouldn't you agree, Mrs. Osgood?"

Nine

Frozen pellets of sleet rattled on my bonnet and served as tiny ball bearings under my feet as I gingerly shuffled along the lower stretches of Greenwich Street that Tuesday. The children had gone away. The Temperance lady had abandoned her position at the groggery. The pothouse itself was shuttered up tight, only to issue forth a roar when a patron stumbled out into the whistling curtain of ice. Why I was making a trip to the Poes' home in these conditions, I did not know. Or perhaps I did know and would not admit it to myself.

Ice crunched under my boots as I climbed the steps to their house. Through the rag-plugged window, I saw a candle burning. *Let Mr. Poe be here*. I knocked resolutely on the door.

Mrs. Clemm answered. Her worried expression melted into a grin. "Come in!"

Mrs. Poe was seated on the sofa when I entered, the tortoiseshell cat in her lap. "Mrs. Osgood! You came! I didn't think you would."

Mrs. Clemm took my hat, cloak, and gloves. "Coffee?" she cried.

Mrs. Poe nodded enthusiastically for me to take some.

"That would be nice. Thank you."

Mrs. Poe patted the seat next to her and the cat. No sooner had I taken it than Mrs. Clemm rolled the table in front of me, effectively blocking me in. I shivered although the stove was nearly glowing with heat.

"Eddie's not here," Mrs. Poe said. "In case you were expecting him."

I covered my disappointment. "I came to see you. Thank you for inviting me. How are you feeling?"

Mrs. Clemm brought over the coffeepot from the stove. "We are quite well! Two more newspapers have printed Eddie's bird poem."

She poured a stream from the rustic pot into one of the delicate bone china cups. "That makes twelve magazines or papers in all, not including the ones that printed it twice."

"It's a wonderful poem," I said.

Mrs. Poe held on to the cat, which kept trying to jump from her lap. "Do you think so?"

I took the cup Mrs. Clemm offered me. "Oh, yes. Once you hear it, you can't get it out of your mind."

"Like a curse," said Mrs. Poe.

"Dear me, Virginia," said Mrs. Clemm, "there you go, talking about curses. You're as frightening as Eddie."

Mrs. Poe smiled with satisfaction. "That's because he and I are just alike."

"Two more independent children, you have never seen." Mrs. Clemm shook her head, the long lappets of her widow's cap swaying. "They would run from me when I called them, though Eddie was older and should have known better. Virginia was always the instigator of the two. When just a wee mite of a girl, she led poor Eddie down the primrose path."

Mrs. Poe laughed as if her mother had just paid her the highest compliment.

I smiled, wondering if Mrs. Clemm, too close to the pair to have a proper perspective, might be a poor judge of their abilities. It seemed particularly telling that she thought of Mr. Poe, elegant, successful, and in his thirties, as a child. Virginia, on the other hand, seemed less mature than my Ellen.

Wishing to change to a more comfortable subject, I said, "Did Mr. Poe write as a boy?"

"Dear me, yes," said Mrs. Clemm. "It was all he had, what with losing his mother as a toddling child and then being cast aside by his foster father. I think sometimes his pen was his only friend in the world."

Her worried expression brightened. "He got quite good with it, though, even while young. As a matter of fact, he wrote me the cleverest poem apologizing for breaking the teapot to this set."

Mrs. Poe held down the cat as she sipped at her coffee. "I broke the pot."

Mrs. Clemm looked at her, startled. "You did?"

Mrs. Poe continued sipping, holding her cup with her pinky finger raised.

After a strained silence, I said, "Mr. Poe must have done very well in school."

Mrs. Clemm returned her attention to me. "Oh, very well, indeed! I always knew he would be someone special."

"You must be so proud now."

Mrs. Poe daintily put her cup upon her saucer. "Tell us about your husband."

I met her inquiring gaze. "There's not much to tell."

"Is he rich?"

"Virginia!" Mrs. Clemm exclaimed.

I laughed with feigned ease. "I don't know about that, but he does paint rich people."

"He's a painter?" asked Mrs. Poe.

"A portraitist," I said. "After the school of Gilbert Stuart."

"Gilbert Stuart is very good?"

"He was the best in his day. Have you ever seen a portrait of George Washington?"

She nodded. "In magazines."

"Most likely the portraits were from engravings done from paintings by Mr. Stuart. Many of the portraits that hang in the President's House in Washington were painted by him."

"So Mr. Stuart's famous?"

"Very much so."

"Is your husband?"

I drew in a breath. "He's trying to be."

"Will you have him come paint my portrait?"

"Virginia!" cried Mrs. Clemm. "You must not ask. Perhaps he is busy."

I considered Mrs. Poe with her beautiful child's face, shining with excitement. "I'm certain that Samuel would love to paint your portrait. Unfortunately, he's not in town at the moment." Heaven help Mr. Poe if he were in town. Mrs. Poe was just the sort of adulating, soft-centered subject Samuel favored. He would sweep her off her feet before she knew to draw breath.

"I could strike a dramatic pose for him." She stuck out her narrow chest and called in a booming stage voice, "MIS-TER POE!" The cat took the opportunity to leap from her lap as Mrs. Poe thrust her face near mine. "'Would you mind staging a play for charity?'"

Her imitation astonished me. "You must be an admirer of Mrs. Butler."

She shrugged. "No."

"You sounded very much like her," I said, trying to keep the mood light.

"Virginia's a quick study." Mrs. Clemm poured herself another cup. "Every bit as smart as Eddie."

"I'm sure you are," I murmured.

Mrs. Poe began to cough. She handed her cup to her mother, who could be seen to visibly stiffen. But although the paroxysms seemed to come from deep within her, on this occasion the attack was short in duration. By the time Mrs. Clemm had rushed into the back room and returned with the bottle, Mrs. Poe's spell was over.

Mrs. Poe continued speaking as if there had been no break in the conversation. "If you are interested, I have written some poems."

I sighed inwardly. So that is why she wanted to meet me. Like so many others, she thought that because I had work published, I held the key to the secret of success. Little did she know how hard I scrambled to get my own work in print. I could hardly help myself, let alone help someone else. But why would she come to me if she were eager to publish her poems? Surely her husband had better connections.

"I would love to see them," I said.

With that, Mrs. Poe dove from sight. She resurfaced with a sheaf of papers, retrieved from under the sofa. She was handing them to me when the door opened.

Mr. Poe entered, his top hat and the shoulders of his tan military greatcoat spangled with ice.

"Eddie!" Mrs. Clemm exclaimed.

"Dearest!" cried Mrs. Poe.

Mr. Poe removed his greatcoat, hat, and gloves. As he was doing so, Mrs. Poe snatched the papers from me and shoved them back into their hiding spot.

He came over and kissed both aunt and wife, then nodded gravely at me. "Mrs. Osgood."

"You don't have to work?" asked Mrs. Poe.

The cat trotted out. Mr. Poe picked it up and began to pet it. I could hear its loud purrs from where I sat on the sofa.

"We had all the manuscripts for the issue on time for once. It's in the typesetter's hands now. I thought I would come home."

"Mrs. Osgood is here."

"Yes." His demeanor became more reserved. "I see."

"Did you know that her husband was a famous painter?" asked Mrs. Poe.

"You are most kind," I murmured.

"A painter?" Mr. Poe stroked the cat. "That sounds like an interesting line of work."

"He does portraits," said Mrs. Poe. "I asked her if he would paint me."

Mr. Poe put down the cat and took the coffee offered by his aunt.

"How soon might he do one?" Mrs. Poe asked me.

"I'm not sure," I said. "I don't know when he will return to town."

"Might I be next when he comes home?"

"I can ask him."

She clapped her hands. "I have never had a portrait done. Eddie has had his done lots." She gave her mother a nod, which prompted Mrs. Clemm to jump up and trot out of the room. She returned with a hatbox full of magazines and newspaper clippings, then rifled through them until she found what she was looking for. She folded open a magazine and held it out to me. "This is from last month's *Graham's*. What do you think?"

The engraving of Mr. Poe made him look like a jolly office clerk in possession of a curiously sloping forehead. Save for his generous sideburns, his face was as smooth and hairless as an egg.

"Very nice."

"I look to be made of wax," said Mr. Poe, "and have been placed too long next to the fire. Muddy," he said to his aunt, "put it away. I am ugly but not that ugly."

Mrs. Clemm examined the picture closely. "I think you look very sweet. You look better without a mustache."

Mrs. Poe rubbed her lips. "He *feels* better without a mustache, too."

Mr. Poe pointedly turned to me. "Has your husband painted you often?"

My mind went back to the gallery of the Boston Athenæum. I saw myself sitting for Samuel; he was dabbing at my portrait on his canvas. Even as two old women examined the pictures around us, I was fixated upon Samuel's hands, so active and strong. I yearned for them to be upon me. Hours passed—or was it minutes?—before finally the ladies strolled into the next gallery. The moment they were gone, he threw down his brushes, stalked over, and swept me off my feet. He pressed his mouth and body hard against mine. The pleasure had been excruciating.

"He did, once."

Mr. Poe stared at me as if he could read my mind.

I glanced away, flushed, as Mrs. Poe cried to her husband, "Is it so very much for me to ask to have one portrait done before I die?"

Desperation passed through Mr. Poe's eyes, then vanished as quickly as it had come. "We have decades in which to have dozens made of you, Virginia, if that's what you wish." He looked at me. "What does your husband think of daguerreotypes? Does he fear for his business?"

The conversation shifted to the safe subject of daguerreotypes versus portraits done in oils: Mr. Poe arguing for the daguerreotype's accuracy in depicting a subject, and I defending my husband, astonishingly enough, by arguing for the artist's ability to capture the essence of a person in a way chemicals processed in a tray never could.

Mr. Poe had taken a seat next to his wife, and with the cat upon his knees, had to speak over the upright animal to address me. "You would argue that the way a person is perceived by an artist might differ from what a daguerreotype mechanically records?"

"As strange as it seems," I said, "yes. Gilbert Stuart, my husband's mentor, was said to have 'nailed his subject's soul to the canvas.' That was the highest compliment a critic could pay him. And it's true—Stuart's subjects seem lit with an inner light. You don't get that from daguerreotypes."

He stroked his purring cat. "To say that he 'nailed a subject's soul to the canvas,'" he said quietly, "makes the assumption that we persons, as well as artists, can see one another's souls."

"Maybe we do," I said. "Maybe we all have the ability to perceive another's soul, and do so every day, only we take it for granted and don't even know it when we're doing it. We call it knowing someone's 'character' or 'personality.'"

Mr. Poe stared at me as if I had said something profound.

I could feel Mrs. Poe looking between us as I sipped my coffee. She gave me a small odd smile. "Then I must have my portrait painted. I should like to have my soul pinned to a canvas." She turned to her husband. "Then you could have my essence forever, Eddie. Even when I'm gone."

Mr. Poe seemed to cringe, although he had not outwardly moved a muscle.

"This is very fine talk!" cried Mrs. Clemm. "Pinning things to canvases. I can think of nothing so very ghoulish!" She hopped up from one of the cheaply made chairs. "We should celebrate Mrs. Osgood's visit and your coming home at this hour with an early dinner. Eddie, you must be half-starved, hurrying out of here this morning without breakfast. Do you have a half dime? I will run down the street and get us a meat pie."

The cat jumped down when Mr. Poe reached in his pocket to pull out a few small coins.

I started to rise. "I should be going."

"No!" cried Mrs. Poe. "It won't be a treat without you."

"Yes, do stay," said Mrs. Clemm. "It's so nice to have you here."

"Please," said Mr. Poe. "Stay." In spite of his rigidly polite demeanor, he suddenly looked so desolate that I sat back down.

Mrs. Clemm retreated to the back room, returned in a dusky pelisse that was fraying at the cuffs, and after taking a coin from his palm, hurried out the door.

At Mrs. Poe's insistence, we looked at the clippings that her mother had brought out, with Mrs. Poe recalling what she had been doing when he had composed the various stories and poems, and Mr. Poe staring at the words. The only time he responded strongly was when she produced a faded watercolor from the bottom of the pile and held it up to the light.

"Behold, the most important place in the entire world—at least according to my husband." She gave him a sidelong smile.

I peered closer. "The Boston Harbor?"

Without a word, Mr. Poe took it from her hands, rose, and then stalked up the stairs, the cat strolling after him.

"Caterina, you're such a traitor," Mrs. Poe called after the cat. "You can at least pretend to like me."

"I'm sorry," I said, nonplussed. "Did I offend your husband?"

"Don't worry, he won't hurt *you*."

Just then Mrs. Clemm returned with a meat pie. There would be no escape for me. The table was set, Mr. Poe was restored to us, and dinner, meager as it was, was served.

Over a pork pie oozing with grease, Mrs. Poe chattered on about the games she and "Eddie" played as children. Mr. Poe seemed to have regained his equanimity, for he quietly ate as his wife explained how they had spent much of their childhood apart, she growing up in Baltimore, he living with foster parents in Richmond and England. It wasn't until after he returned from military service at West Point, Mrs. Poe said as Mr. Poe cut his pie into tiny bites, that he renewed his acquaintance with her. Again I wondered what I had questioned when I'd first seen them at Miss Lynch's salon: How had they gone from being cousins playing blindman's bluff at Christmas to lovers who wished to marry?

The thought reminded me of Miss Fuller, waiting for my report. My pie turned in my stomach. In spite of Mr. Poe's fame, the pair made me feel out of sorts and sad. In one of the busiest cities in the world, they seemed to exist on a bleak island of their own making, their backs turned against the social tide lapping at their battered door.

After our meal, Mrs. Clemm spooned out a dose of medicine to Mrs. Poe, who soon got so sleepy that I excused myself and left.

Outside, the weather had improved. Although it was cold, the sky was that crisp, joyful blue that is only possible after a storm. Down the block from the Poes' temporary lodgings, a band of children had taken to the street. They were gathered around a boy whose shaved head indicated a recent bout of lice. He held something in his cupped hands. As I grew closer, I saw what it was: a gray kitten, perhaps a month or two old.

Another boy, dirtier and smaller than the ruffian with the kitten, ran up with a gunny sack. He held it open. The bigger boy dropped in the kitten, took the bag, and slung it over his shoulder.

He marched off, the other children following. I watched in growing horror as the ragtag band paraded past a saloon and a row of houses to a blacksmith's workshop, where they stopped before the watering trough. The boy suspended the bag over the water.

Before I could scream, Mr. Poe rushed over and snatched away the bag. I had not heard him leave his house.

"That's mine!" cried the boy.

"Not anymore," said Mr. Poe.

"You can't have it!"

Mr. Poe gave a stare that made most of the children run. Only the boy remained, fists doubled up like a Five Points brawler.

"You must not know," Mr. Poe said calmly, "that if you kill a cat, it will have its revenge."

"That's not true!"

"No?" Mr. Poe smiled. "I have seen it happen. You cannot keep them down. I saw one black cat come back to haunt its murderer even after it had been bricked inside a wall. Its mauled, dead body yowled from behind the bricks: Meow. MEOW. *MEOW*." He stamped at the boy. "*HISS!*"

The boy pelted away.

Mr. Poe delved into the sack and pulled out the kitten, which clung to the burlap with its clear pink claws.

I hesitated, then approached Mr. Poe as he extricated it. "I saw you save the kitten."

He looked up, stroking the crying animal.

I touched the fur that grew in fine furrows on the top of the kitten's head. "That was an excellent tale to scare the bully off."

"It's from my story, 'The Black Cat,' changed a bit for the occasion."

I had not read the story—in truth, of his works, I'd only read "The Raven," as I did not want his style to influence mine. Even that poem had been enough to get a view through his dark, severe lens. But he did not seem to see my look of embarrassment for he turned the kitten to his face and said, "What to do with you?"

"It seems that your wife was better today."

He glanced up sharply.

"Her cough was better."

"Do you think so?"

His expression was so bleak that I said, "Yes. Much better than when I saw her last."

He stroked the kitten's cheek. Weary from its ordeal, it had stopped mewing and had closed its eyes.

I smoothed the kitten's face in a similar manner. "Poor little fellow."

"I appreciate your coming," said Mr. Poe. "This is the best day we have had in a long time."

With all his recent success? But I saw that he was serious.

He regarded me deeply, as if trying to speak with his eyes. "I was touched," he said quietly, "by your remark about seeing one another's souls."

"Do you believe that's possible?"

"First you must believe there is a soul."

"Do you?"

"If by a soul one means the creature who lives within each of us, a creature born loving, born joyful, but who with each worldly blow shrinks more deeply into its shell until at last, the poor desiccated thing is unrecognizable even to its own self, yes. I do."

I could feel him gazing at my face, urging me to look at him.

"Our soul is as much a part of us as our hands or our voice," he said quietly, "yet we are terrified to acknowledge it. Why is that?"

Slowly, I lifted my eyes to meet his. I would not look away even though it was wrong for me to interact with a married man in this intimate manner. And what I saw within his dark-rimmed eyes—not just with my own eyes, but perceived powerfully, clearly, with an un-named sense—made my chest ache with joyous recognition. A smile of wonder bloomed simultaneously upon our faces.

I became aware of the blacksmith leading a horse toward his shop. Mr. Poe glanced away, then shielding the kitten, stepped aside. The smith and horse passed.

The connection, so vivid only a moment ago, had been broken. Now that we had experienced such intimacy, we could no longer bear to look at each other. We focused on the kitten, cradled now against Mr. Poe's chest.

"I am looking for poems for my journal," he said as we petted it. "I realize that all of your work must be spoken for, but if you should ever be looking for a venue, I would be honored if you thought of me."

"Thank you," I said quietly. "I will."

Almost shy now, he looked down upon the kitten, which had begun again to mew. "I think he's rather desperate."

"May I?" I reached for it as a hackney carriage rattled up the cobblestones. The vehicle stopped down the street from Mr. Poe's lodging. A woman got out, her bonnet hung with veils.

"Who are these shrouded women?" I asked. "I've seen them several times now. Are they in mourning?"

He glanced in the woman's direction. "So to speak, yes."

"Who have they lost?"

"That is Madame Restell's place of business." He saw that I knew who he meant. "I did not know it when we took the place for rent or I would have thought twice. Virginia has not yet discovered it. I fear it will not sit well with her." He drew a breath. "She can be very judgmental."

"Of course."

He gave me a sharp look.

"Any woman would react strongly," I said. "It is a sad business."

I felt him withdrawing into himself. After a moment he said, "I must find other lodging soon. I can do nothing to set Virginia off."

"No," I said earnestly, "you mustn't."

A terrifying fierceness flashed through his eyes. He opened his mouth as if to speak, then seeming to think better of it, nodded his good-bye and strode away.

I stood there shivering on the sidewalk with the kitten, its weight-less bones trembling along with me. I knew that I should dislike the man, should fear him, should keep my distance at all costs. I knew that I would not.

Ten

On Miss Lynch's stone porch steps the following Saturday evening, Vinnie stopped and leaned against the scrolled plaster railing to look into her coat front.

"What is it, Vinnie?" I asked.

She pulled back the corner of her lapel to reveal what was slowing her progress: A kitten popped up, its pale eyes curious.

"Poe wants to see."

As Eliza's own young ones entered Miss Lynch's house with Mary—children having been invited to a special conversazione that night—she paused next to us on her husband's arm. "Is there a problem?"

I sighed. "Vinnie brought the cat."

"Poe wanted to go to the party," Vinnie explained.

I sighed. "Well, we're here now. Please tuck in Poe until we get inside." I winced after I said it. When I had brought the kitten home and told the girls how Mr. Poe had saved it, after getting Eliza's permission to keep it, they had insisted on its taking his name, even after we had determined that it was a girl. This is what happens when you let a child name a pet.

We were greeted by Miss Lynch inside the vestibule. From within, came the melodious groan of a cello.

"Mr. and Mrs. Bartlett! Mrs. Osgood! Are these your lovely children?"

We introduced them to Miss Lynch, who shook each of their hands in turn.

"I have a special treat for you," Miss Lynch told them. "One of my friends has learned some very nice stories for children by a man who lives far, far away. She is going to tell them to you tonight."

"My mother writes children's stories," Ellen said.

"Yes, I know," said Miss Lynch. "These stories are by Mr. Hans Christian Andersen, all the way from Denmark. They are not as good as your mother's, I'm sure, but you might like them, too."

Miss Fuller marched into the hall, her large bangle earrings—a gift from an Algonquin woman, she would tell us later—in full swing.

She nodded to Eliza and her husband. "Bartlett. Mrs. Bartlett." To me she said, "Hello, Frances. Are these your little girls?"

I reintroduced her to them, though she had met them in seasons past. Miss Fuller shook their hands, and those of Eliza's children, then waited as we removed our wraps and piled them in Miss Lynch's maid's arms to take upstairs.

"What do you have there?" she asked when Vinnie took off her coat.

"A kitty."

"Darling," she said flatly. "What's its name?"

"Poe."

A sly smile slid over Miss Fuller's face. "Oh?"

"Mr. Poe saved her," Vinnie explained earnestly. "Some boys were going to hurt her."

"Good for Mr. Poe." She thumped the kitten on the head as one would a dog. "Be sure to give it some milk tonight."

"I will."

"Go on up, now," I said.

Vinnie ran up the stairs after Eliza's brood, Ellen and Eliza's maid Mary trudging after her. Miss Lynch left for the parlor with Mr. Bartlett. I threw a helpless glance at Eliza as Miss Fuller took my arm and ushered me toward the salon at a tortoise's pace.

"Should I assume that you kept your appointment with Mrs. Poe?"

"Who is playing the cello?" I pretended to be listening.

"Some Swede. Poe was there, yes?"

"He dropped home before I left. It was all very brief."

She smiled. "What are they like together?"

I looked longingly toward the entrance of the salon. "Like any other married couple."

"Which is . . . ?"

"Very kind to each other."

She laughed. "That's not the sort of behavior I have observed in your typical married couple. Our friend Greeley won't even live with his wife, although they reside in the same city. She has the house on Turtle Bay. He has rooms in the Astor House. Ditto for five other gentlemen I could name."

"They seem happily married."

"The Reverend Mr. Griswold lived cities apart from his wife while she was alive. It wasn't until after she died that he developed a yearning for her. I've heard that when he got home he had to be forcibly pried from her dead body, then after the funeral, he wouldn't leave her grave until a relative intervened. As if that weren't gruesome enough, he had her dug up forty days after her burial. He clipped locks from her hair then clung to her blackened corpse, sobbing like a baby. Guess he had a bad case of regret."

"Horrid." With her prying ways, she had to know about Samuel's abandoning me.

We came to the entrance to the salon. "Look around," she said as if she owned the room and everyone in it. "For every married person here there is a story of rejection and betrayal. Some stories are sadder than others. But everyone has their wounds."

"Not necessarily."

She studied me a moment, then walked me toward the other guests. To my relief, Miss Fiske of the heavenly feathers, and her dreamy-eyed young friend visiting from Massachusetts, Miss Louisa Alcott, came forward to greet us. Miss Fuller soon stepped away—evidently there were bigger fish to fry than these young ladies. Even as the three of us compared mutual acquaintances in Boston, I commended myself again for submitting a small cache of unpublished poems to Mr. Poe's journal under a pen name, with a note explaining to him that I preferred for my identity to remain unknown. If he accepted them and published them as mine, Miss Fuller, with her taste for scandal, would be sure to make a sensation of it.

I was just breathing easier when Miss Fuller marched up and latched on to me again. She guided me over toward the table where the tea was soon to be dispensed.

"You don't strike me as naïve, in spite of your books for children."

I felt my anger welling up. If that was a compliment, it certainly felt like an insult. Who was she to push me around Miss Lynch's party? I'd had just about enough of it.

"I'll come to the point, Frances: I am looking for an article on the lives of Mr. and Mrs. Poe."

"An article?"

"Yes. From you. I want scandal. How much is he drinking? What do they do in private? What's behind his buttoned-up appearance? You can't tell me that the man is not ready to explode."

"I can't—"

"You'll get your own byline in my column in the *Tribune*. If it's money that you need, I'm prepared to pay you ten dollars in advance and ten dollars upon submission." She paused. "Not that you need it."

That was a great deal of money. My unstable situation pressed itself upon my mind. Payment for my poems at *The Broadway Journal*—if Mr. Poe accepted them—would go only so far. Terrifying stories for Mr. Morris were not yet flowing from my mind. Two of the scant handful of women who supported themselves by their writing in America wrote columns for periodicals, Miss Fuller for the *Tribune* and Mrs. Sarah Hale for *Godey's Lady's Book* in Philadelphia. I must give Miss Fuller's offer, as repugnant as it was, my serious consideration. Perhaps my future was as a magazinist.

"If I would take on this project, it would be at the consent of the Poes."

She shrugged. "If you wish to jeopardize your chances, by all means, ask them."

Mr. Greeley arrived, all shining top hat and rubbery smile, with the happy effect of drawing Miss Fuller's attention away from me. I took my position behind the samovar, to put distance between her and me so that I could think.

Eliza stepped over beside me. "What is the bee in Margaret's bonnet?" she whispered.

In hushed tones, I said. "She wants me to write an article on the Poes."

"For the *Tribune*?"

I nodded.

She looked at me. "Do you want to?"

At that moment Reverend Griswold approached. "Ladies, may I join you?"

The pink dome of his brow shone in the gaslight when he bent to kiss my hand. I shuddered, picturing him clasping his dead wife.

"Please do," Eliza said politely.

"I wanted to speak to the most beautiful woman in the room. Everyone pales next to you, madam." He smiled at me intently. I felt bad for Eliza, but it was she who flashed me a look of sympathy before stepping away.

"Her husband's the publisher, yes?" he said, watching her go.

"Yes, Russell Bartlett."

"A good man—he puffed my book in a review for the *Mirror*. I shall be glad to return the favor for his publications. That is how the world turns, wouldn't you say?"

"I'm afraid that I must go check on my children. They're upstairs."

"Perhaps your husband could do it?" He caught my glance.

"He's not here tonight."

He waited for further explanation. When none was forthcoming, he only smiled. "You might have heard, Mrs. Osgood, that my collection has been tremendously successful. I confess this is true. It has been very humbling that so many people trust in my taste in poetry. I think they must know that I feel a great responsibility to give them America's finest. Imagine, then, my *honor* when my publisher recently offered to bring out yet *another* edition of *The Poets and Poetry of America*. Might I expect some more selections from you?"

I knew that I should leap at the opportunity. It brought little money—Reverend Griswold paid his poets a small fee up front and then took the profits from the sales for himself—but the recognition it gave me was priceless. Yet why did I feel like I was making a bargain with Rumpelstiltskin, with my firstborn in the balance?

The crowd went silent. The Swedish cellist stilled his bow. I looked toward the door. Mr. Poe stood alone, holding a posy of snowdrops bound together with a linen handkerchief. I could not help thinking how imperiled the delicate white flowers looked against the unrelenting blackness of his frock coat.

"Him again," muttered Reverend Griswold.

Miss Lynch rushed to greet him, but Miss Fuller beat her to it. Mr. Poe looked on calmly as Miss Fuller pumped his hand. With a gracious nod to Miss Lynch, he let Miss Fuller lead him off, her earrings jangling as she spoke with great animation.

I returned my glance to the Reverend Griswold, who was in the process of listing the authors to be included in his new collection.

"Great friends, all of them," he said in conclusion. "I make it my business to know my poets well. I will make it my business to become familiar with you, too. In fact, I shall relish it."

I smiled, my attention upon Mr. Poe, who was disengaging himself from Miss Fuller.

"You will be in excellent company, madam," said Reverend Griswold. "My dear friend Mr. Longfellow has already promised me his latest. I consider him to be the greatest poet of our times, no matter what Mr. Poe says."

"And what is it that I say?" Mr. Poe calmly stepped next to him.

Reverend Griswold's pink face turned crimson. "You err when you besmirch Mr. Longfellow, sir. I'll say it—I'm glad that fellow Outis is giving you a thrashing in the *Mirror* for accusing Longfellow of plagiary! You richly deserve it."

"Perhaps so." Mr. Poe turned to me, then presented the snowdrops. "For you. From my wife."

I forced myself to be calm. "You must thank her for me." Reverend Griswold's scowl deepened as I smelled their blooms. I was surprised to find that the simple white blossoms had a powerfully seductive scent.

"She picked them in the countryside," Mr. Poe said quietly. "I took her for a ride up by our old farm this morning. We were able to get in a little picnic before the weather turned."

"That must have cheered her." I peered over the crowd. "Is she here tonight?"

The cellist resumed his playing. Mr. Poe shook his head. "The day wore her out, I fear."

"Look here," said Reverend Griswold, "we were having a conversation."

"I did not realize. I thought Mrs. Osgood looked ready to leave." He held out his arm. "Mrs. Osgood?"

I nodded my leave from Reverend Griswold. Self-consciously, I put my hand on Mr. Poe's forearm. I tried to deaden myself to the feel of his sinuous flesh radiating though my glove.

When we had gone five paces, he said, "Where do you want to go?"

"As far from him as possible."

We crossed the room, nodding to persons along the way but not pausing. I could sense their inquisitive stares on my back as we left the parlor for the hall.

"Far enough?"

"Not yet."

We processed down the hall to an alcove under the stairs, a book-lined nook lit by a single lamp on a doily-covered table. He seated me on the sole chair, where I was enveloped by the old-fashioned smell of burning whale oil and decaying paper. The melancholy song of the cello moaned in the distance. From upstairs came the murmur of a woman's voice, rising and falling as she told a story to the children.

"Now far enough?"

I tamped back a smile. "I think so."

He stood by the chair, within plain view from the hall, should anyone come looking.

When he did not speak, I said, "How did you know I needed saving?"

"Everyone in the room knew, except Griswold."

"Oh, dear, am I that transparent?"

"No. He is that unbearable."

We smiled at each other briefly. I then sniffed at the snowdrops again, not knowing where to put my gaze.

He peered at the books as if to find something. Abruptly, he said. "I'm glad that we have a moment to speak. I have been thinking about our conversation the other day."

I glanced up.

"About the painter nailing a soul to a canvas."

I laughed. "I fear that sounds rather grim at the moment."

He regarded me calmly, as if waiting for me to grow serious.

"Please continue," I said. Did he know how his dark-lashed eyes unnerved me?

"I wrote a story a few years ago," he said, "'The Oval Portrait,' about an artist who is painting his new bride's wedding portrait. In it, his wife sits for him day after day, week after week, as he tries to perfect the painting. You see, he wishes to achieve what no painter has done before: to make a portrait as real as life. For weeks he works, then months, until at last, he sees to his joy and disbelief that he has *finally* made the portrait seem as alive as his beautiful bride. Her very soul has come to life in the painting! Exulting in his great good fortune, he turns to her to show her his masterpiece. But alas, his wife is dead."

A chill slid down my spine.

"You see why your statement affected me so," he said. "I had actually written a story about it."

"A coincidence."

"Is it? Most would call it that, I agree. But there are some who would say that such a 'coincidence' is not a coincidence at all, but evidence of two spirits in communication."

"I'm not sure that I understand."

"In truth, who does? At least not completely. Our world has no name for the sense that detects the realm of which our spirits are part. Yet all of us are swimming in the matter of this other dimension. It is flowing in us, through us, over us, bathing us in its light. Now and then we get a glimmer of its existence. Do we ignore it, fight it, or accept it?"

"Have we a choice?"

"Yes."

I sniffed at my snowdrops, my heart beating faster. "What if a person accepts it? What then?"

"She faces it."

By degrees, I raised my eyes to him. He was waiting for me.

Nothing in my past experience prepared me to so baldly receive another person and to not pull away, to let myself be penetrated even as I was penetrating him. I sensed the hurt and pain and sweetness within the man standing above me, while at the same moment

I absorbed the blow of having my innermost self exposed. It became too much. I looked away, elation charging through my body.

When I glanced up again, he did not hold me fully within his gaze.

"I apologize," he said.

"No need. I am honored that you share your ideas with me."

"They are not just ideas."

Our gazes met again, briefly. The jolt of it tingled to my toes.

The cello throbbed in the other room. He drew in a breath. "Virginia is very ill."

"From your trip today?"

"No."

When he said no more, I said, "She seemed to be coughing less when I last saw her. You must not worry. She is young and strong and will recover fully, you'll see."

His face was bleak. "Will she?"

Miss Fiske and Miss Alcott rustled into the hall. "Ah, there you are!" exclaimed Miss Fiske, blond curls atremble. "Mr. Poe, we were wondering if you might read 'The Raven' to the gathering. Miss Lynch said that you might if we asked you nicely."

"It is the perfect dreary night for it," said Miss Alcott, her eyes as dreamy as a calf's.

"Miss Lynch said she would turn down the lights." Miss Fiske shivered. "It will be most frightening."

Mr. Poe looked to me.

"Your audience awaits," I said lightly.

He let himself be ushered from the alcove.

I stayed, listening to the murmur of the children asking questions of the storyteller upstairs. As strange as it sounds, I could feel Mr. Poe's presence lingering with me. Why had he chosen me as a confidant? I was honored, although I knew it was wrong. But how could I fight against the unspoken current of communication between us? I craved it even as I shied from it.

"Fanny!" Eliza hurried toward me. "There you are! I've been looking for you. Poe's going to read now—are you coming?" She peered at the flowers wilting in my hand. "Are those snowdrops?"

"Mrs. Poe sent them."

Her honest face clouded with a frown. "Odd. I always heard that bringing snowdrops indoors was unlucky. To do so is said to cause a person's death." When she saw my expression, she pulled me to my feet. "Never mind—it's just a silly old wives' tale. Come on, before we miss Mr. Poe."

Spring 1845

Eleven

It was April Fool's Day, of which I felt every inch. For days after the conversazione, I had found myself waiting, ridiculously enough, for a word from Mr. Poe, for a tap on the door at any moment. *He does not know where you live*, I chided myself. When I reminded myself that he did indeed have Eliza's address, that I had included it with the poems I had submitted to his journal, I argued back that even if he accepted my poems, why would he come in person to say so when a letter would do? There was no reason for him to trouble himself to come this distance.

Yet, as I sat at the dining table in Eliza's basement family room with paper and pen, ostensibly to compose a poem, I felt Mr. Poe's presence in a way that I could not explain. It was as if I knew that he was thinking about me but he could not act upon it, as if our souls were communicating in the strange dimension about which he wrote.

Surely this was not just my imagination. I looked around the room. Could I not *feel* Eliza's concern for me as she sewed on the sofa, her son Henry playing with his tin soldiers at her feet? Could I not *feel* the maid Mary's disconnection from our group, her soul wandering off—to her homeland?—even as she sat sideways at the table and bounced Baby John on her knee? Could I not *feel* Vinnie's love for her doll as she fed it at a tea party given by bossy Anna Bartlett, or Ellen's discomfort with being in someone else's house even as she read a book, a small girl in a big upholstered chair?

A brisk tapping sounded on the steps outside our window. The doorbell jangled.

I gasped.

"What, Mamma?" asked Vinnie.

Ellen sprang up. "Father?"

Vinnie's eyes widened. "Really? Is it, Mamma?"

I cursed myself for setting them off. "I don't think so, dears. He has been very, very busy."

They ignored my words, listening as the parlor maid, Catherine, went down the hall upstairs and answered the door: a woman's voice. They visibly sagged.

Miss Fuller came downstairs wrapped in what looked to be a deerskin shawl hung with jingling cockleshells. Catherine followed after her, rubbing her hands in dismay. Manners dictated that callers stay put in the vestibule until the lady of the house agreed to have them in.

"Margaret!" said Eliza. "Please excuse our humble quarters."

"No, it is I who should beg your pardon. I insisted upon coming down." Miss Fuller scanned the room. "I hope you don't mind."

"Not at all," said Eliza.

"I came to have a word with Frances, if I may."

"Certainly." Eliza raised her brows at me. "Would you like to chat upstairs in the back parlor? Catherine, please make sure the fire there is sufficient."

"Thank you," Miss Fuller said, although all of us knew that there was little danger of Margaret Fuller not doing whatever she liked. "I won't linger. I plan to meet with a woman who arranges to send poor women who have borne children out of wedlock to respectable homes to serve as wet nurses. An ambitious program, if not tenable."

We went upstairs. She waited until we were seated on the black horsehair sofa. "I have spoken with Mr. Poe about my interest in writing an article about his life. He was not open to it."

"I shouldn't think so," I said.

"Until," said Miss Fuller, "I told him that you would be his interviewer."

Her audacity was boundless. "I had not agreed to that."

"I know, I told him that you hadn't. He looked rather disappointed."

"Perhaps," I said, "you confuse his disappointment with relief that his tale was not to be told. I get the sense that he's a rather private man."

Miss Fuller smiled. "See? This is why you are the perfect candidate. You understand Poe, odd as he may be."

"We are two poets who respect each other's work, that's all."

"Call your relationship whatever you want," she said. "He has agreed to your interviewing him for an in-depth piece."

"He has?"

"Are you taking the job then?"

"I don't know. I'm surprised he would want this."

Miss Fuller drew a coin from her reticule. "I believe this is the amount we had agreed upon. Take it—easiest money that you ever made." She drew my hand to her, then placed a ten-dollar gold piece in it. "Poe expects you at the Astor House tomorrow at two."

I frowned at the eagle shining on my palm.

"Why the glum face? The recognition you will get from writing this article will do you good. You do want to be famous for your work, yes?"

I had never voiced such. Was my ambition that apparent?

"Well, so long, chum, and good luck." She turned to go, the cockleshells rattling on her shawl, then stopped. "Oh, and if you want to write more features for the *Tribune*, I'd dig up all the dirt on him that you can. There's something deliciously wrong with him though I can't quite put my finger on it. I hope you can."

And so it was that I found myself perched on the edge of a red satin sofa in the Astor House, watching a manly promenade of the powerful young lords of commerce and the idle spoiled sons of the newly wealthy. It was easy to distinguish between the two groups, even without noting the ivory-handled canes, monocles, and gold chains favored by the latter. One just needed to look at their shoes.

No-nonsense boots, buffed to a brilliant shine, peeked from the trouser legs of the commerce kings as they strode through the room. Those who had inherited their family's wealth favored gaiters and soft kid pumps, as if their feet never trod anything more coarse than a Turkish carpet. I supposed, in fact, that they hadn't.

I was conducting my study of footwear when a whisper rippled through the crowd. I looked up to see John Jacob Astor, the builder of this hallowed hall of money, being carried king-like through the parlor on a sumptuous sedan chair. Although it was not a cold day, the old man was swaddled in furs of all sorts: fox furs, mink furs, lynx furs. Only his cross, wizened face appeared from within the pile of them. It was as if the old trader were drowning in the very commodity that had made his fortune.

"I think the bears and the beavers might be getting their revenge."

I turned around. Mr. Poe was standing behind my sofa, his hat in his hands. The man moved as quietly as a wolf.

I stood, happier to see him than I had a right to be. "I was just thinking something similar."

He smiled.

The color in his cheeks, heightened by a walk in the damp wind, brought out the soft gray of his eyes. I thought how beautiful they were within their lashes of black, and how intelligent, and searching, until I realized it was possible that he was perceiving my thoughts.

I fished in my reticule for my writing things. He came around the sofa.

"Thank you for agreeing to this interview," I said, not looking at him. "Miss Fuller was quite insistent upon my writing an article about you." I pulled out a pencil and pad of paper. "I want you to know that I objected. I did not want to pry."

"Thank you for your discretion," said Mr. Poe. "And I must thank you, too, for taking on this project. You are doing me a favor in writing about me. But would you mind so much if we walked outside? It's a fair day, and I've been cooped up in my office for too many hours."

"I would prefer the fresh air myself."

"Of course you do. We think alike."

We exchanged a smile. I staunched the happiness bubbling up within me. *It was a simple interview. Don't be ridiculous.*

Outside the hotel, we stood on the pavement with the carriages and wagons rumbling past us down Broadway. "Which way?" he asked.

At that moment, two large men carried Mr. Astor down the steps of his hotel. He blinked from within his mound of skins like a creature unused to the light. Horses were halted in both directions as he was decanted into a gilded carriage.

"To the park," I said. "Before the bears and beavers attack."

Laughing, we ran across Broadway in the hiatus caused by the preparations for Mr. Astor's departure. We landed on the sidewalk before Barnum's American Museum, on the corner of Ann across from City Hall Park. In the balcony above the museum marquee, a band blared its atrocious way through a festive march. When I put my hands to my ears, my shawl slipped from my shoulders.

Mr. Poe lifted it back in place. "They say Barnum hires the worst band he can find to drive people inside."

My shoulder tingled where he had touched it. "I do believe he has found it."

Our eyes met. I fought against the delight blooming across my face even as I saw his own similar struggle.

A man dressed in a garish checked suit and sandwiched between signs for Mr. Barnum's museum stepped close and waved an illustrated guide book at us. "Would the Mr. and Mrs. like to see the latest attractions?"

I opened my mouth to correct him but found that I did not wish to do so.

Mr. Poe suppressed a smile. "Well, Mrs., would you like to?"

The sandwich-sign man, whose thick florid lips and narrow face gave the impression of a fish wearing a top hat, poked the program at me. "How 'bout it, Mrs.?"

I nodded to Mr. Poe. "Well, Mr., if it would tickle your fancy, it would tickle mine."

"You heard the Mrs." Mr. Poe put my gloved hand upon his arm as if it were the most natural thing in the world. "Show us to the show."

We followed the man into the museum, my inner self focused upon my hand on Mr. Poe's arm, my body humming with excitement. After Mr. Poe paid our admission of twenty-five cents each, we found ourselves to be the sole patrons in a dim hall lit only by gaslight.

"Waxworks," said Mr. Poe.

I drank in his touch as we walked along, admiring the pantheon of famous persons. We stopped before the wax bust of William Shakespeare.

"A smart fellow," said Mr. Poe.

"I believe you bear a resemblance."

He frowned. "It's the forehead. And the curls. Only I hope mine cover more of my scalp."

I laughed. "I was talking about your intelligent bearing." I nodded to the bust. "Most Famous Writer of the Past, meet the Most Famous Writer of the Present."

With his free hand he pretended to shake with the bust. "What advice might have you for me, kind sir?"

"It's true," I said. "You are the most famous writer in New York now—in the entire United States, I would say. Someday your bust will be here next to Mr. Shakespeare's."

"A frightening thought."

"But it could happen."

"It hardly seems possible." He looked down at me. "I used to think that in spite of my hard work and a goodly amount of little-known publications, I was not a success unless I was famous. Only after I was famous would I really be alive."

"Don't all writers believe that? It's as if we are dolls who only come to life when touched with fame." I smiled up at him. "So is it true? Do you feel changed?"

He thought, then grimaced. "No."

I sighed. "As I feared."

He caressed me with a grateful gaze. "How well you understand me. I cannot say I have ever felt this from another person—I knew it the minute I met you. Thank you."

"For what?"

"For brightening my life."

We beamed at each other as openly as children. When at last we strolled on, the very air between us felt buoyant.

Beyond the busts was the first of several life-size tableaus. It was labeled "The Drunkard's Family" but no explanation was necessary. Ragged wax children much like those from Mr. Poe's street were depicted in various acts of mischief: breaking bowls, taunting one another, spilling flour. In the center of their frozen hubbub, their parents slumped at a table, asleep, the cause of their slumber evident by the jug marked with Xs before them. Off to the side, with a gaslight trained upon his pinched white face, a young son lay dead on his small and narrow bed.

I could feel Mr. Poe's good spirits recede. I wished to pull away from his arm but felt that I could not for fear of upsetting him.

At last Mr. Poe said, "They got it wrong."

I waited for him to continue.

"It is the mother who should be on the death bed, with her little children being led to her side to touch her. At least, that is my recollection of such a scene. My father, who I had not known before, and whom I would never see again, was the one slumped at the table with the bottle. My brother, William, and I were being made to say our good-byes. I was not yet three." I could hear him swallow. "My aunt made me touch my mother's face. It was cold. No face should be so cold. My mother had become something inhuman."

"I am so sorry."

He drew a breath. "I do remember her. When she was alive. She had a glow about her, an incomparable joyous light. I wanted only to please her—" His knotted jaw spoke of his struggle to contain himself. "I regret that she could not live to see my success. Maybe then I would truly believe it."

Only our footsteps and the rustling of my skirts broke the silence as we walked on to the next tableau. The scene was of a happy family, with aged grandparents reading the scriptures while the rest of the family gathered around the mother playing a pianoforte.

His tone was that of forced levity. "Is that us, Mrs.?"

But the spell had been broken. I saw us for what we were: two persons married to others, alone in a public place. I pulled away from him. "Tell me about the real Mrs. Poe. Your wife."

His face took on a closed look. "Am I being interviewed now?"

I shook my head. "No. I ask you as your friend."

"A friend wouldn't ask me about her."

"A friend would, and that's why I ask."

"Are we just friends, Mrs. Osgood?"

I did not know how to answer.

Agitated, I continued with him past wax figures of the famous Siamese twins, Eng and Chang, past a Chinese mandarin, a pair of giants, and a tableau of Christ's birth and death. No one disturbed our solitude. It was as if the museum were open only for us.

We stopped at a grand staircase. I turned to confront him.

"What *are* we, Mr. Poe?"

"Is it necessary to discuss this?" he said. "Can we not just be what we are to each other?"

Offended that he had brushed off the very question he had provoked, I walked down the stairs in taut silence.

At the foot of the steps, a life-size looking glass loomed before us. When we took our places in front of it, our images grew to gigantic proportions. My eyes, large as melons, stared at my fantastically sized partner.

His monstrous reflection soberly considered mine. "I wrote a story once, 'William Wilson.' In it, the narrator is hounded by a fellow who is like him in every way in appearance and manner, even in name, except for in one disturbing way: his duplicate is evil. This bad twin dogs him every step of his life, behaving disgracefully, creating havoc, destroying William Wilson's reputation as everyone mistakes the bad William Wilson for the good. Finally, the good William Wilson cannot bear it anymore. He flies into a rage and stabs his twin to death. Seized with the horror of what he was done, he stumbles away, then glances into a mirror. His doppelgänger, now pale and bloodied, smiles back at him." He looked down at me. "I have not liked mirrors since I've written it."

I would not take my gaze from our reflections. "This is not a tale. This is you and me."

His amplified image attempted a smile. "Yes, you and me, Mrs., writ large."

I was not his "Mrs." His real wife was sick and helpless. And I had a husband, whom I had once loved with all of me, and I had his daughters, the lights of my life, who depended on me to behave, even if their father was a scoundrel.

I turned away. "I can't do this."

"Do what?"

Carry on this flirtation. I searched his face. "Interview you."

"Would it make you feel better to interview my wife?"

I wanted nothing to do with her. I wanted to kiss him. I wanted him to kiss me.

"Yes."

"You shall then," he said quietly. "Tomorrow, if you like."

We left the museum soon after, the amusements having lost their power to amuse. We were standing on the sidewalk, letting our eyes adjust to the light, when the leading edge of a flock of passenger pigeons flew overhead. The birds soon darkened the sky, their million whistling wings drowning the din of the wheels on the cobblestones, muffling the pulse of the city. We parted under their disorienting shadow, going our separate ways beneath the endless whirring primordial wave.

Twelve

At last Mrs. Poe's coughing spell wound down to a wheezy halt. She sat back and blinked at me, as haughty as a child playing queen. "Could you repeat your question, please?"

I took my gaze from around the room. Several weeks after my first visit, the Poes' lodging was beginning to have a less temporary look to it. An ornately carved shelf had been hung and the books that had lined the walls now filled it. A hooked rug had been laid on the floor and the broken pane had been glazed. Even the dangling doorknob was now secured. It seemed that Mr. Poe meant to keep his family here. I thought he did not like having his wife living so near to Madame Restell's establishment. Why would he choose to stay in such a dreary place, so far away from everyone?

I looked down at my notebook. "What was Mr. Poe like as a boy?"

"If you mean when he was a *little* boy," Mrs. Poe said importantly. "Mother would be a better judge. I wasn't alive when he was very young. There are thirteen years between us."

Mrs. Clemm, perched on the edge of her rickety chair like a thief being interrogated for her crimes, deepened her permanently worried expression. "You must think that is a large gap in their ages."

"Oh, no," I said.

"It would be for most people," said Mrs. Clemm, "but Virginia has always been very mature for her age."

"Of course."

"As for Eddie, when he was a boy, he was such a sad little thing." The lappets of Mrs. Clemm's cap swished against her shoulders as she shook her head, remembering. "His papa abandoned his mama when he was two, and his mama herself died later that same year."

"Yes, he told me."

Mrs. Poe gave me a sharp look. "He did? When?"

Mrs. Clemm seemed unaware of her daughter's stare upon me. "All his Mamma left him was a miniature of herself and that picture of Boston Harbor. Such a sad, sad inheritance, poor little creature. I would have adopted him myself, pitiful as he was, but Mr. John Allan of Richmond snatched him right up from his Mamma's bedside. Mr. Allan's wife couldn't have her own children, you see. I suppose she wanted little Eddie as a plaything. No wonder—he was a beautiful child, with black ringlets and big gray eyes. Just like my Virginia. You'd think they were twins."

"The Allans must have doted upon him," I said. Must Mrs. Poe keep staring?

"Oh, yes," said Mrs. Clemm, "I never met Mrs. Allan myself, but Eddie said she treated him like a prince. But then her bad health caught up with her and she became bedbound. So Mr. Allan sent Eddie off to boarding schools, both here and in England, when he was still a little boy."

"Six." Mrs. Poe's mouth puckered in a babyish frown. "From the time he was six."

I made a notation, wishing she would look away. "So Mr. Poe received a good education?"

"Mr. Allan wouldn't let poor Eddie come visit him from school," said Mrs. Clemm, warming to her subject. "Not in England, not in Richmond, not anywhere. Then, when Eddie went to college at the University of Virginia, Mr. Allan wouldn't give him enough money to eat, let alone buy books. It was a terrible, terrible hardship on him."

Suddenly, Mrs. Poe demanded, "When did he tell you about his childhood?"

I looked up, startled by her tone. "Yesterday. He gave me an interview. For this article—he must have told you."

"He didn't. I wonder why."

I saw myself standing before the funhouse mirror with her husband. "It was very brief. Nothing worth mentioning."

The doorknob turned. Mr. Poe entered.

Mrs. Poe watched me when he came over to kiss her and his aunt.

He patted his cat who'd come strolling out, then nodded in my direction, carefully avoiding eye contact.

"I was just about to tell Mrs. Osgood how you cheated in college," said Mrs. Poe.

Only a twinge of brows marked Mr. Poe's disapproval. Mrs. Clemm exclaimed, "Virginia, that's not true! He gambled but he didn't cheat."

"I really don't need to know," I said.

"He was just a boy!" cried Mrs. Clemm. "He lost everything and more."

"'Cheaters never prosper,'" Mrs. Poe sang.

Mr. Poe stared at his wife, his face blank.

"Maybe you won't want to put that in your article," said Mrs. Clemm doubtfully.

"Why ever not, Mother?" said Mrs. Poe. "We're proud of what we've become. When Mr. Allan died, he was one of the richest men in Richmond, but he didn't leave Eddie a cent. He must be turning over in his grave to see Eddie become so famous."

Mrs. Clemm gave me a crumpled smile. "Oh, Mr. Allan had the loveliest house! I saw it when Eddie moved us to Richmond. Moldavia it was called. It had big white columns in front and two sleeping porches in the back. There was no finer house in the—"

"That's enough," Mr. Poe said sharply.

Mrs. Clemm started.

"I'm sorry," Mr. Poe said quietly. "I should not have taken that tone with you, Muddy. But I thought the article was to be about my writing."

"Is it?" said Mrs. Poe. "I thought it was about us."

Still avoiding my eyes, he said to me, "I'm sorry to have interrupted your interview. I only stopped home to retrieve a manuscript that I'd left." He gave his wife a peck on the head. "Good-bye, my dear. Good-bye, Muddy." Then, with a cold nod to me, he scooped some papers off the desk and left.

After the door shut, Mrs. Clemm said proudly, "He's very busy."

I nodded, feeling deflated by Mr. Poe's aloofness. I could see now why he protected his wife. She was even less capable than I'd thought. I would never allow myself to be the cause of pain to someone dealing with such a person. Did he not trust my judgment enough to know that I would never try to be anything but a friend to him?

"Eddie was always writing," said Mrs. Clemm, whisking at her lap. "That boy came into this world with a pen clutched in his hand. He sold his first poem when he was twenty. He wrote it when he was fourteen, I believe. He'd sold several before he came to live with us in Baltimore."

My energy was flagging. "How old was he then?"

"I'm not sure," said Mrs. Clemm. "Let me think."

Perhaps I could simply ask Mr. Poe to provide me a list of his publications and be done with it. I reached for my reticule and began to pack up my things.

"He was twenty-two," Mrs. Poe said.

I looked up. Her eyes were fierce in her childish face.

"He was twenty-two and the most handsome, most intelligent man I'd ever seen. And I knew he was going to be mine."

Mrs. Clemm laughed. "Can you tell Virginia took a shine to him?"

"And he, evidently, to you," I told Mrs. Poe.

"From the moment he came to live with us, she tagged along wherever he went," said Mrs. Clemm, "even to his lady friends' houses. When Eddie was courting Mary Starr over on Essex Street, he made Virginia his little go-between. She had to run between their two houses with their love notes. Virginia even delivered Eddie's proposal for marriage." She rubbed her nose. "That didn't work out like he thought it would."

Mrs. Poe laughed. "He didn't make things easy for himself by going over to Mary's house drunk."

"Virginia!" Mrs. Clemm glanced at me.

"It's a funny story, Mother," said Mrs. Poe. "When I gave Eddie Miss Mary's note of rejection, he got so mad that he drank down the whole bottle of rum that I found, then went charging over there. Miss Mary's mother must have seen us coming because she sent Mary upstairs. But Eddie was out of his head. He went right upstairs after her when I dared him to. If he ever had a chance with Mary Starr, he didn't after that."

Mrs. Clemm shook the lappets of her cap. "Dear me, Virginia! What kind of impression are you giving our guest?"

"Don't worry," I said. "We are off-the-record now."

"Do you have enough for your article?" Mrs. Clemm asked doubtfully.

"I want you to know," Mrs. Poe said as I began to rise, "that my husband has not touched the bottle since he met you."

I paused, taken off guard. "That is . . . wonderful. Frankly, I don't even remember when it was that we met."

She smiled, serene as a cat. "At Miss Lynch's party, in February. February fifteenth, to be exact. You had on a green dress."

The hair raised on my arms.

"Virginia has an eye for detail," Mrs. Clemm said proudly.

"Indeed you do," I said, more stoutly than I felt. "I fear we didn't even speak."

"We didn't. But I found out who you were. When you were talking to Eddie, I asked that nice Miss Fuller."

"I'm sorry that you and I didn't get to speak then. I would have liked to have met you."

"It doesn't matter. We are friends now. You and I must always be friends."

"Yes. Certainly."

"And Eddie, too?"

"Of course. Whatever you think is best." I could feel her gaze boring into me as I moved to the door. Good manners forced me to turn to say good-bye. "Thank you for your time, Mrs. Poe, Mrs. Clemm. I'm sure we will be speaking soon. I will get the article to you for approval before it is published."

I sprang from the house like a bird freed from a snare.

Blind to the drunkards and peddlers and hogs on the street, I hurried northward, disturbed by what I had just experienced. Was Mrs. Poe hostile toward me? Or was my guilt coloring my judgment, making me misinterpret what was simply her social ineptness? I could not find my footing with her. I resolved to associate with her as little as possible once the article was published.

Thirteen

The next morning, after the children had left for school and Eliza had gone to pay calls in the neighborhood, I sat at my desk in the Bartletts' front parlor, looking at my notes. How was I to write an interesting article about the Poes with the material that I had? For Mr. Poe's sake, there was precious little of my interview that I could print. No wonder he kept his wife from the public eye. Strangely naïve and physically frail, it would be difficult for her to keep up with the rigors of New York society life. I felt honored that he trusted me not to expose her.

Yet all the pride I felt for being allowed into his inner circle was dashed when I thought about his cool treatment of me in her presence. It hurt to think that he did not trust my judgment. Did he think so highly of himself that he feared I would throw myself at him in front of his wife?

An idea nudged at a corner of my consciousness.

I began to write, crossing out, correcting, as a poem formed. The stanzas slowly swelled into being, word by word, phrase by phrase, until at last the piece, fragile as a soap bubble, glistened in its entirety on the edge of my mind. I dashed off the remaining verses, reciting the final two aloud as not to lose them:

The fair, fond girl, who at your side,
Within your soul's dear light, doth live,
Could hardly have the heart to chide
The ray that Friendship well might give.

But if you deem it right and just,
Blessed as you are in your glad lot,
To greet me with that heartless tone,
So let it be! I blame you not!

I sat back, wrung out, as I always am after I have brought forth a true and honest work, regardless of its subject or length. It is as if producing a creative work tears a piece from your soul. When it is ripped completely free of you, the wound must bleed for a while. How similar it is to letting go of a dream, your hope, or your heart's desire. You must open up and let it drain.

I became aware of the bells of the Baptist church at the next corner, ringing eleven. I pulled myself together, folded the paper, put it in my reticule, shrugged on my wraps, and left. On Broadway, four short blocks away, I hired a hackney. I was at Mr. Poe's establishment before I had time to reconsider.

A lanky young man with carrot-orange hair leaped up from a heaped desk near the door.

"I've come to see Mr. Poe." Even as I said it, I saw him sitting at a desk upon which piles of paper were neatly stacked.

Mr. Poe rose. Although he kept his face composed, I saw the gladness in his eyes. "Mrs. Osgood." He came and grasped my gloved fingers a second too long before letting go.

Forcing myself not to feel, I dug for the poem in my reticule. "I would be gratified if you would consider this piece for publication."

"In addition to the ones you recently submitted?"

"Yes. It is the best of them."

"May I read it?"

"Please do," I said, coolly.

He scanned the paper, then looked up at me. A sharp glance to the office boy sent the lad out of doors.

"What am I to make of this?" he said quietly.

I gathered myself. "I believe your lady readers who have had a genuine friendship with a married gentleman might find this poem refreshing."

"Do you think there are many such readers?"

"More than you would realize."

He nodded as if considering my point. "This poem assumes that the wife approves of the friendship. That is hardly a typical reaction a wife would have, I would think."

"You give the wife little credit, Mr. Poe. Can't she be wise enough to know her own good hold on her husband? Why should she feel threatened, when she knows the other woman has no ill intent?"

"I don't know, Mrs. Osgood. Why should she?"

I was suddenly angry. "I think she doesn't. In fact, to think she does feel threatened is an insult to her. And it is vanity on the part of the husband."

"Vanity?" He allowed a small light of amusement to come to his eyes.

"Yes, vanity. It is vain of him to feel the need to slight a lady friend to prove to his wife that he is faithful."

"My lady readers will understand this?"

"They will, I assure you. They will understand, too, that not only does he offend the wife but the lady friend as well. By snubbing her, the gentleman does not give her a chance to prove that she can conduct herself properly. It's very insulting all around, Mr. Poe."

"I'm still not sure that my married lady readers will completely agree with this poem."

I held out my hand to retrieve it.

"But," he said, folding the paper, "I have never been afraid of what people say, Mrs. Osgood, as you must be aware." He tucked it inside his coat. "I will publish this. Immediately. I will pay you two dollars for it. Is that acceptable?"

"Yes," I said stiffly. "Thank you."

He went to his desk to write a check. He spoke without looking up. "My wife wishes for me to ask you to come with us to a play tonight. *Fashion* is the name of it. As a matter of fact, I was preparing to send you a message just as you came. You entered as I was writing your name." He glanced up to gauge my response.

"Coincidence," I said.

His long look told me what he thought about coincidences. "Will you come?"

"It appears that I am fated to go."

"Pay attention to fate, Mrs. Osgood. It will always have the last word."

I turned away. We were playing a dangerous game, one I was not sure I had the nerve for.

He brought me the check and then walked me to the door. Another wave of passenger pigeons was passing overhead as I stepped onto the sidewalk. Its ranks were thinner than the previous two days, with dribbles of individuals straggling behind.

The wind ruffled the edges of my mantelet as I shielded my eyes from the sun to watch. "Maybe this is the last of them."

"I admire them," said Mr. Poe. "I admire any wild thing that won't be ruled by man."

"I believe these birds have the upper hand."

"Do they?" He fixed me with his dark-lashed gaze. "Fifty years ago there were so many trees in America that a squirrel could jump from a treetop in New York and keep leaping until it reached Indiana. Now it wouldn't make it out of Manhattan."

"How quickly the world changes, yet we are so busy trying to live that we don't notice it."

"And yet," he said quietly, "it does not change quickly enough."

He bowed to me. "Good day, madam." And then he returned to the confines of his office, captive to the demands of his work.

Vinnie's soft hand was on my chin. "Turn your head, Mamma." She was on a chair in our room on the third floor of the Bartletts', my ear bobs in hand. I felt a nervous pit in my stomach as I leaned toward her so that she could affix one. Why had I agreed to go with the Poes to the play? How quickly I had broken my resolution not to associate with Mrs. Poe. Now what seemed like a simple invitation had taken on an ominous prospect as the day had wore on. While Mrs. Poe had nothing to fear from me, her odd frame of mind unnerved me. It was sure to be an awkward evening at best, no matter how well-meaning my intentions. I was glad when at last Eliza came to my door and I could get on with it.

"Mr. Poe is here," she said, her eyes full of curiosity. I had answered her earlier questions about my visit to the Poes' intentionally vaguely. Talking about them disturbed me.

I nodded cheerfully, pretending to be sure of myself.

Downstairs, Mr. Poe stood in the hallway, rain dripping from his furled umbrella.

We greeted each other with reserved civility under Eliza's interested gaze. It was determined that I needed my long mantle due to the weather, and once that was fetched from upstairs by the maid and donned, Mr. Poe escorted me to a hackney carriage standing at the curb.

Mrs. Poe was waiting inside. She allowed me to kiss her cheek as if we were old friends and then I settled next to her. Mr. Poe entered the carriage from the other side and off we went with a jolt.

"Such a rainy night!" said Mrs. Poe.

"Yes," I said.

"Eddie says *Fashion* is a very good play."

"Thank you for inviting me to join you," I said. "It's been a while since I have been to the theater." Since the previous year, in fact, before Samuel had left.

We jostled along. Mrs. Poe cheerfully named all the plays that she and Eddie had attended over the past few months as guests of the management of various theaters. She then proceeded to give her impression of each, her stream of thought only broken by the occasional spate of coughing. Her observations took us all the way down Broadway to City Hall Park, where we rounded the corner to approach the Park Theatre, within sight of Barnum's museum to the south. Although Mr. Poe was silent, I could feel his presence on the other side of his wife, as tightly wound as a coil.

The carriage stopped. I waited for Mr. Poe to help out his wife, who under her cloak, I noticed when she stood up, wore the same beribboned little-girl frock she had worn the first time I had seen her. Once she had alighted onto the sidewalk before the theater, and I was transferred by the cabman to the shelter of Mr. Poe's umbrella, we took our place in line. The rain drummed on the canvas over our heads.

Mrs. Poe knotted together her hands at her chin. "Cozy, isn't it?"

"Very," I said.

She cocked her gloved thumb toward the right. "Have you ever been there?"

I turned to look.

"To Barnum's," she said.

I saw the edifice of the museum down the street, its lurid banners lit up by gaslight. I could hear strains of a poorly rendered march coming from its direction.

I paused. "Yes."

"Recently?"

Mr. Poe kept his gaze pointed toward the theater.

"Yes."

She smiled. "Lucky. I've never been. Eddie says it's not educational." She made a pouting face within her hooded cape. "Everything I do must always be educational."

Mr. Poe took her elbow and turned her toward the theater door. "The show will be starting soon."

She sighed to me. "I am his creature, you know. Everything I am, I was taught to be by him."

"I did not know that you resented it, my dear," he said mildly.

"I don't! Why would you say that, Eddie? Who wouldn't be proud to be taught by the Shakespeare of our generation?"

I could feel the heat rush to my face. Had Mr. Poe told her about our excursion to Barnum's? I glanced at him. He gave a slight shake of his head as if to deny it. But how strange that she had echoed my own conversation with him. I shivered. A coincidence?

Mrs. Poe turned to scan the line that had formed behind us. "Do you see anyone that you know, Eddie?"

"It is not polite to gape around behind you," he said.

She gasped, then whirled to face front. She cut a gaze to her side, indicating that I should look behind us.

"See them?" she said loudly. *"Whores."*

I noticed two gaudily dressed women in the line.

"What are they doing here?" she said. "They are supposed to use a different entrance."

"I really must insist that you stop this, Virginia," said Mr. Poe.

"They're not supposed to mix with us!"

"They'll take their place in the upper tier," he said, "and then we won't see them."

"Like the ladies who visit Mrs. Restell? If people are doing wrong, they should be punished."

"It's not our place," he said.

"Then whose is it?" She smiled at me as if to enlist my support. "Don't you agree, Mrs. Osgood?"

I was saved from answering by the opening of the theater doors. I followed Mr. Poe and his wife inside. Immediately upon entering the lobby, Mr. Poe was hailed by a well-heeled gentleman who introduced himself as Mr. Stewart, owner of a large mercantile concern on Broadway. He told Mr. Poe how greatly he enjoyed 'The Raven' and then introduced his wife, who then asked to be introduced to Mrs. Poe. This pattern repeated itself until a large crowd had formed around the Poes, congratulating him on his success and admiring her for her youth and freshness. I stood at the edge of the circle, noticing with each greeting how Mrs. Poe grew more animated and gay, and Mr. Poe less so. Only when the five-minute bell before curtain rise rang were they released from their admirers. By the time we were ushered to a box in the first tier, very near to the stage, Mr. Poe was glowering.

I took my place on the other side of Mrs. Poe. She leaned in to her husband. "Eddie, Eddie, what's wrong? Why were you so rude to the people?"

"You must apologize to Mrs. Osgood."

She looked at me. "For what?"

"You forgot our guest."

"There is no need to apologize," I said.

She ducked her head and frowned. "I'm sorry, Mrs. Osgood. I meant no harm."

The bell rang, announcing the start of the play.

She squeezed my hand. "If I did anything wrong, Frances," she whispered, "I truly am sorry."

The play commenced. It was a fair enough comedy. The woman who played the silly wife lusting after status drew all the appropriate laughs, and the actor playing her cringing husband, who nearly ruined himself trying to appease her, commanded chuckles of sympathy. But as I sat there in the dark, I could feel Mrs. Poe's spirits still soaring from the admiration she had garnered and, disturbingly, what felt like her sense of triumph over me. If she had wanted me to recognize her possession of her husband, she had succeeded.

At the intermission, Mrs. Poe sprang up, prompting a little spate of coughing. "Eddie, I do believe I need a punch. Will you buy me one?"

"If you like. Perhaps it is best if you stay in your seat and rest— I'll bring it to you."

"And be cheated out of seeing your people? No!"

"I have no 'people,' as you yourself will sometime learn. Mrs. Osgood?" he said to me. "Are you coming?"

I told him no and begged to stay in my seat, claiming that I wished to jot down my thoughts about the play.

"Eddie's the one who's the critic," said Mrs. Poe. "He's already written it up."

"I'd like to be able to describe it to Mrs. Bartlett when I get home."

"But you must come out!" exclaimed Mrs. Poe.

"Please forgive me," I said, "but I must insist on staying."

They left. I was gazing at the curtain, hating Samuel for abandoning me and leaving me in this vulnerable position, and loathing myself for being ruffled by Mrs. Poe, when Mr. Poe returned, carrying a cup of punch.

"We cannot have you wasting away."

Our hands touched when I reached for the cup. He let go reluctantly.

"It was a bad idea to come," he said.

"Oh, no." I glanced out over the rail, fighting against the pressure building in my chest. "I'm very much enjoying Mrs. Smith's performance."

"Hers is nothing compared to the rats."

"The rats?"

"They are very well trained here. They understand their cues perfectly. They know precisely the time when the curtain rises and the exact degree in which the audience is spellbound by what is going on. They know just when to sally out to scour the pit for chance peanuts and orange peel, and when the curtain is about to fall and they should disappear."

I laughed. Our smiles settled into a quiet probing gaze. *You must not do this.*

He broke away first. "I apologize."

"For what?" I said lightly.

He glanced away, then looked fiercely into my eyes. "My wife."

"She will be looking for you."

I could feel him retreat into himself. "Yes."

Stiffly, he asked my pardon and left. Some ten minutes later he returned with Mrs. Poe, who was filled with tales of the important wives who had spoken to her, and a count of the invitations she had received to pay calls upon them. Only the curtain's rise hushed her, and even then I could feel her beaming victoriously my way.

Deflated, I missed much of the final acts of the play. Only the rats lifted my spirits. They were as talented as Mr. Poe claimed. They conducted their own play within a play—a more dramatic one, it turned out, than the comedy featured on the marquee. Would the rat get its bit of peel before Mrs. Smith stepped on it? Would it wrest its peanut from under the edge of the curtain before being swept away by its closing?

But I could not report even these small findings to Mr. Poe after the play. Before we could leave our box, he and his wife were mobbed by eager readers wishing for a glimpse of the celebrated Mr. and Mrs. Poe. The well-wishers shouted for an impromptu reading of "The Raven" as we descended the stairs. Their cries of "Nevermore! Nevermore!" dogged us through the lobby, where three ushers had to clear our way to the door. By the time we landed in our cab, Mrs. Poe was giddy with the adulation.

The carriage started away from the curb.

"Did I tell you that Mr. Brady invited us to have our daguerreo-types made?" Mrs. Poe exclaimed to her husband. "I have always wanted one. To see what I really look like."

"I thought we had mirrors for that," said Mr. Poe.

"Eddie." Mrs. Poe nudged her husband playfully. "Did you know that Mr. Astor's daughter-in-law commented on my dress? She said it becomes me. She's really very nice."

Her exhilaration loosed a fit of coughing. Mr. Poe patted her back, first distractedly, then as her coughing deepened, with genuine concern. On she coughed as our horse clopped down the dark streets. By the time we reached Eliza's house, Mrs. Poe was curled against her husband's chest, her coughs now wretched little spasms as he stroked her damp brow.

I insisted that Mr. Poe stay with his wife and let the cabman take me to my door. I faded back into the hallway, as with the jingle of reins, the carriage rolled into motion and away.

Eliza had not waited up for me but left an oil lamp turned down low on the hall table, along with a note:

You must tell me about everything in the morning!

Too unsettled for sleep, I took the lamp to the desk in the front parlor. With a sigh, I pulled a sheet of foolscap and pen before me.

I stared at the page as if to will a story to life. But the magic of creativity had abandoned me. Without it, I could no more will my imagination to produce than I could have willed the onset of labor for my daughters' births. Like childbirth, creativity came when it came, beyond one's control. Empty of productive thoughts, my mind wandered where it should not go: to Mr. Poe.

I laid my head down on my hands.

I was awakened by a tap on the window.

I froze. Had I imagined it?

The tap came again. Quickly, I blew out the lamp so as not to be seen. Who could it be at this hour? I inched to the window, my heart pounding.

Mr. Poe stood on the stoop, rubbing his hands as if to ward off the cold.

I pulled back. Was I dreaming? Had I conjured him up with my desire? I laughed with incredulousness.

Trembling, I went to the door, then drawing a breath, opened it.

He stood there silently as a hackney clattered down the street. He raised his hand. My reticule was slumped on his palm. "You left this."

"I forgot it."

"Did you? Or was I meant to return?"

We beheld each other in the moonlight. His face was anguished and furious and resolute. I glanced away. When I looked back, he grasped me to him. He gazed down upon me as if to devour me, then, with a groan, seized me to his lips.

Fourteen

Mr. Bartlett put down his coffee cup. "There she is. Sleeping Beauty."

I entered the family room and sat down at the breakfast table. "Sorry I'm late."

"Mary took the children to the park," said Eliza, lowering her fork. "It's such a beautiful morning. I hope you don't mind that I let your girls go along."

"No, I'm glad for them to get out—thank you. I should have gotten up earlier." The fact is, so electrified was my mind and body from the touch of Mr. Poe, I had not been able to sleep. Not until dawn had I been able to drift off, only to fall hostage to dreams as vivid and violent as if induced by opium. When I awakened, the dreams dissolved, replaced in my consciousness by an overwhelming feeling of foreboding. I was aware that my life had changed, wonderfully, painfully, permanently.

"How was the play?" Mr. Bartlett asked coolly. Golden-skinned and blond-haired, he would have been handsome had his forehead not been so high, his lips so thin, and his quick intelligence not quite so given to judgments. As it was, his large brow and golden complexion put me in mind of a duckling—an image I am certain he was not trying to cultivate.

Eliza frowned at her husband. "What he really means, Fanny, is how was Mr. Poe?"

The hair rose on my arms. Had they seen me and Mr. Poe last night?

"Both were enjoyable enough." For more reason than one, I was grateful for Martha's offer of coffee at that moment.

"Poe—enjoyable?" Mr. Bartlett shook his head. "I must be missing something. I can't understand why so many women are fascinated with him."

"You would if you were a woman," said Eliza. "He's so handsome and mysterious. The more standoffish he is, the more the ladies swoon."

She tried to catch my eye but I could not look. My mind was flooding with remembered sensations: the warmth of Mr. Poe's body when he clasped me to him; the heartrending sound of his groan; the sweet leather and soap smell of his flesh as he cupped my face to kiss me once more.

Mr. Bartlett poured cream into his coffee. "I should think women would have more sense. Any student of phrenology can see that he's a dangerous man."

"Must we talk about this now?" said Eliza. "Fanny hasn't had her breakfast yet."

I kept my gaze upon Martha, bringing over my cup, even as in my mind's eye I saw myself pulling back from Mr. Poe's lips. We had marveled at each other, joy welling up from our very cores. No words were exchanged before he left. None were necessary.

"Both you and Eliza would do well to steer clear of him at Miss Lynch's conversazione tonight," said Mr. Bartlett.

I willed myself into the present. "Pardon me?"

"It's all written upon his skull. Those swellings at the sides of his frontal bone, just above his temples—surely you've noticed them? They're quite remarkable."

Eliza sighed. "Oh, Russell."

"What meaning do you find in them?" I asked.

"Thank you for taking me seriously. My own wife won't listen to me." Mr. Bartlett drained his cup and set it on his saucer with a clink. "Those bumps, located where they are, represent a highly conflicted nature of the most volatile sort."

Eliza gave me an apologetic grimace.

"We do have to talk about this," said Mr. Bartlett. "We would not be good friends to you if we didn't. As you know, phrenology is a proven science. Poe himself subscribes to it in several of his tales. And those frontal bone protrusions of his are enough to make any student of phrenology shudder. I wonder if the man has ever taken a look in the mirror. If he knows phrenology, he won't like what he sees."

"Is it possible that you're overstating it?" said Eliza.

Mr. Bartlett put his napkin on the table. "Not really. If you combine the severe moral confusion indicated by those bumps with the superior intelligence implied by the extreme breadth and height of his forehead, you have one very dangerous individual indeed."

My gaze traveled to Mr. Bartlett's own high forehead, framed by two swoops of yellow at his temples. He responded to my gaze with a stern, "It's all in the location of the bumps."

Eliza bit back a smile.

He deepened his frown. "It follows, Mrs. Osgood, that when such a mind comes under added pressure, not only is its possessor endangered but so are those who are close to him."

"I'm sorry, Fanny," said Eliza. "This is not exactly nice breakfast conversation."

"I don't think it's wise for you two to continue to court him at Miss Lynch's soirees." Mr. Bartlett raised a hand against Eliza's protest. "I should have said something earlier. I thought it would take care of itself. But now that Mrs. Osgood has gone to the theater with that pair, I feel that it is my duty to warn her against any further personal involvement. It is critical that you give him no encouragement should he come to Miss Lynch's this evening."

"You do know," said Eliza, "that Fanny is writing an article on him for the *Tribune*."

"Yes. And I regret that. I think you should consider abandoning that project."

"Russell," said Eliza, "you are scaring us."

"Good." He sat back. "I meant to."

Had he seen us? Why should he be so alarmed about my involvement with Mr. Poe if he had not?

Martha brought me a soft-boiled egg. I began to crack it with the blade of my knife. "Thank you for your concern," I said evenly. "But I have seen nothing of this in Mr. Poe. In all the time that I have been with the Poes, interviewing them for my article, he has been patient and kind, even when Mrs. Poe is . . . not feeling well."

"You do not see behind their closed doors," Mr. Bartlett said gravely. "Things may be different than they seem. I wouldn't be surprised if his wife is terrified of him."

"This is frightening," Eliza murmured. "Like his stories."

"Where do you think Poe gets his ideas for them?" said Mr. Bartlett. "Haven't you ever noticed that men are always mourning the deaths of their beautiful young wives or lovers in his tales, that is, when they are not actually murdering them? Doesn't it make you wonder if he is plotting or at least wishing for the death of his wife?"

I lifted the severed top from my egg. The man I knew was kind to his wife, even when challenged. With Mrs. Poe's odd propensity for boasts and inappropriate comments, he'd had many occasions to correct her but had been scrupulously courteous. Not many husbands would humor such foolishness. The closest I'd seen him come to losing his temper was when Mrs. Poe and her mother were speaking of his foster father. Even then, his outburst had been brief and directed toward Mrs. Clemm, quickly followed by an apology.

"Mr. Poe has been nothing but a gentleman." I dipped my spoon into the liquid yolk. "I would trust him with my life."

"You might not want to put him in that position," said Mr. Bartlett.

"Now you're going too far, Russell," Eliza said. "The man is a writer, not a murderer."

I stared at Mr. Bartlett, the yellow yolk dripping from my spoon. "I can't just shun the Poes. I haven't finished my article, and to be frank, I need the money."

He held my gaze. "Then tread lightly, my dear. Tread lightly."

At the conversazione that evening, I was so agitated by my desire that Mr. Poe should arrive, and by Mr. Bartlett's warning that I should have nothing to do with him if he did, that I could do little more than to observe and drink my tea. Even so, it struck me, as I sipped from my cup, that Miss Lynch's utopian forum for ideas was no longer quite working as she'd hoped. Her guests had taken to sorting themselves by status. The established poets and writers and darlings of the stage held forth in the front parlor, where they were courted by politicians and society wives and deep-pocketed consumers of art. Poorer sorts, including upcoming poets and rising actors, and those with unpopular views, such as Mr. Stephen Pearl Andrews and his Free Love, congregated in the back parlor. There they proclaimed loudly and showed off, trying to catch the attention of the denizens of the front, as did young Mr. Walter Whitman in his loud ruffles and Mr. Herman Melville with a cigar that was more formidable than he was. Only an open archway separated the two parlors, but the haves and have-nots were divided as effectively as if walled off by bricks. One key unlocked the invisible gate between them: fame.

How keenly the lack of fame was felt by the back parlor residents, of which I, as a children's author, was part. Even in my distracted state, I knew too well how envy lay on the back of one's tongue, weighing down one's every word, sickening one with its taste. As I choked that evening on Mr. Melville's aggressive smoke, I couldn't help but consider which parlor I would have inhabited if Samuel were still in town: the front, if Samuel had anything to do with it.

Now I redirected my sights upon Mr. Melville, who was regaling our group of second-raters with his tales of the Pacific. I felt sorry for him, for though his was a fair enough story, if you liked ships, most of our group kept glancing toward the front parlor, where the wealthy poet and newspaper editor, William Cullen Bryant, was declaiming about the need for a park for all New Yorkers. Judging from the interested expressions on the faces of his congregation, it was obvious that he had struck a chord. But even if Mr. Bryant's "central" park had not been sinking Mr. Melville's ships, I would have had difficulty in giving Mr. Melville my full attention. My gaze kept slipping from Mr. Melville's anxious young face to the entrance hall, looking for Mr. Poe.

Reverend Griswold stepped up next to me, cradling his teacup with lilac-gloved fingers heavy with rings. I flashed him a polite smile, then returned my attention to Mr. Melville.

Reverend Griswold pinged his rings against his cup. "Have you been listening to Mr. Bryant?" he said loudly.

I pulled away from Mr. Melville's circle. "No," I whispered. Poor Mr. Melville. Must Reverend Griswold be so disrespectful?

"He proposes a park for all of New York, Knickerbockers and Irishmen alike. Imagine!"

I glanced at Mr. Melville to imply that Reverend Griswold should listen to him like the rest of us.

He continued on, uninhibited. "I am an admirer of Mr. Bryant's poems—I've puffed enough of them, haven't I? He's had me to luncheon a good half a dozen times. But I cannot say that I like his idea about parks for the public. With all that mingling, soon our own dear children will be talking in the uncouth accents of County Cork."

At that moment, Mr. Poe appeared in the entrance hall. I could feel heat surge into my face.

"We shall all be saying words like *ya* instead of *you* and cutting off the endings of our *-ing* words." Reverend Griswold smiled archly, waiting for my comment.

"I wouldn't mind." I saw that Mr. Poe was talking to Miss Lynch. She was leading him into the front parlor. His wife was not with him.

"You wouldn't mind!" exclaimed Reverend Griswold. "You would want your beautiful little girls speaking Hibernian trash?"

Eliza, in Mr. Bryant's circle with her husband, saw Mr. Poe enter with Miss Lynch. She sought my gaze.

"I see nothing wrong with the Irish, Reverend Griswold," I said. "They are good people, doing the best that they can in spite of their poverty. In fact, my girls spend much of their time with the Bartletts' Irish maid and they do not speak 'Hibernian trash.'"

I could feel Mr. Poe looking my way. I turned as does a flower to the sun. When our eyes met, I felt the heat of his intensity. Exhilaration poured through my veins like hot nectar.

Reverend Griswold blinked in alarm at my flushed face. "I did not mean to upset you! If you say the Irish are good, I must believe you. I should—I should like them, too!"

Mr. Poe excused himself from Miss Lynch. He was coming toward me. Should he seek me so openly? I glanced at Eliza and her husband. Both were watching intently. "I'm glad that you like them, Reverend Griswold."

Delighted to have seemingly scored a point, Reverend Griswold beamed. "I have noticed some Irish girls to be of singular beauty— not nearly as great as yours, Mrs. Osgood—but they are pretty young things."

I could feel Mr. Poe arrive at my side.

His expression was cool, belying the tumult I could feel within him. "Good evening."

I forced all emotion from my face. "Mr. Poe."

"Hello, Poe," Reverend Griswold said sourly.

From across the room I saw Eliza's concern and Mr. Bartlett's scowl. I remained motionless even as my spirit joyously reached for Mr. Poe.

"We were talking about the Irish," Reverend Griswold said belligerently. "Mrs. Osgood and I have much in common in our admiration for them."

Mr. Poe flicked a glance at Reverend Griswold as if surprised to still find him there, then began to steer me away.

"What about the Irish?" Reverend Griswold demanded.

"We should stay," I murmured.

Mr. Poe gave me a sidelong look, his face calm.

"Mrs. Osgood!" Reverend Griswold cried.

We kept going.

"Mrs. Osgood!"

Still we kept walking.

"Mrs. Osgood! What," Reverend Griswold exclaimed shrilly, "about Mr. Osgood?"

I stopped. The groups in both parlors fell silent.

I turned to him. "Pardon me?"

Reverend Griswold was stunned only momentarily by his success. He threw a defiant gaze at Mr. Poe and me. "What does *Mr. Osgood* have to say about the Irish?"

I made myself smile. "I really don't know."

"Well!" the reverend sputtered. "You should!"

Conscious of all eyes upon me, I felt gentle pressure at my elbow. I let Mr. Poe guide me into the front parlor and to the place of pride next to Mr. Bryant.

Those of the upper circle stared at us, none more so than Mr. Bryant, displeased with having been interrupted. Even his side-whiskers, as tangled and stringy as an unwound ball of yarn, seemed to rise up in indignation. Although I held my head high, I writhed inwardly.

Mr. Greeley spoke up. "We've been talking about the necessity of a park in the city, something centrally located and—"

"—and good for driving horses, like in the great cities of Europe," said Mr. Bryant, not yet ready to give up the reins of the conversation. "Something supremely civilized."

"What say you to that, Mr. Poe?" said Mr. Greeley.

"As you always have an opinion," added Mr. Bryant, not altogether kindly.

When Mr. Poe did not immediately reply, Eliza, seemingly aware of her husband's grim stare upon him, and my own discomfort, said in mollifying tones, "Mr. Bryant says that if space for such a park is not created now, soon there won't be a blade of grass left in New York, as fast as the city is growing."

Mr. Poe gazed at the expectant faces gathered around us. At last he said, "I like the notion of a park." His sights came to rest upon Eliza. He gave her a slight smile. "As long as there are no ravens."

The circle laughed in appreciation, save for Mr. Bartlett, on principle, and Mr. Bryant, who must have felt his hold loosening on his audience.

"Mr. Poe," said Miss Lynch, "could you be convinced to recite 'The Raven' for us now? There are some people here who've not yet heard you and it's such a treat. Mr. Bryant, have you heard Mr. Poe's recitation?"

"I read the poem," Mr. Bryant said shortly.

Mr. Poe nodded at Miss Lynch. "Thank you for your interest, but I'm publishing a far better poem next week in the *Journal*. Perhaps you'd rather hear it."

Miss Lynch's elfin face brightened with enthusiasm. "Oh, yes, Mr. Poe, please! I think we should all like that."

All in the upper echelon clapped in encouragement, except Mr. Bartlett and Mr. Bryant, and Reverend Griswold, who had marched up, his nostrils flaring in righteous anger. The back parlor crowd eased toward the separating arch to listen.

Mr. Poe reached into his coat. He drew out a paper, then handed it to me. "As it is your poem, Mrs. Osgood, you should read it."

Someone gasped. Surprised smiles followed on the faces of many. No one was more surprised than I.

I shook open the paper. It was my poem "So Let It Be," in which I had scolded Mr. Poe for not believing that his wife would trust us. I felt the blood prickling in my face as I began to read.

When I finished, I was afraid to look up. The room reverberated with silence. Then: the sound of a single pair of gloved hands clapping. This pair was joined by another and then another, until the parlor rang with applause. Slowly, I looked up. Every woman in the gathering was clapping.

Mr. Poe waited until they were done. Quietly, he said, "Mrs. Osgood assured me that my women readers would understand her poem. She said it was vanity for a male friend to feel the need to slight his lady friend just to prove to his wife that he is faithful. It appears that she was right."

"Yes!" cried Miss Lynch. "Thank you for speaking up, Mrs. Osgood. We women are so often misjudged by our men. Our every move is not a means to entrap a male, you know."

After the other guests laughed, she said, "Let's discuss this over some refreshments." Linking arms, she led me to the table, then allowed me, with an Italian ice in hand, to receive the praise and acclaim saved for the most famous of her guests.

Fifteen

Skirt flounces, bonnet brims, coattails, and shop awnings flapped in the sharp April wind. The laughter of children punctuated the crashing of hooves against the cobblestones as huge-wheeled phaetons drummed past, driven by bachelors intent on showing off to young ladies squeezed to the point of breathlessness by their corsets. Sunday-afternoon-promenade season had returned.

The poor tumbled along, their bright ready-made clothes announcing the very poverty that they wished to forget. The middling sort sailed by in plain dark clothes that showed their grasp of taste and refinement. If *they* had a salary of two thousand a year, *they* would know what to do with it. The rich floated past as if on swans' vaunted wings, their costumes showcasing their wearers' wealth and importance. Incomes could be calculated by the number of yards of glossy silk in a skirt or in the height of a gentleman's collar. Even the poor in their gaudy checks could read the signs of a healthy ledger, or at least they thought they could. But who really was to know if a man was actually bankrupting himself by putting his wife in diamonds? Who knew if he could not pay for the glossy beaver hat perched upon his head? As I joined the Nile of humanity pouring down Broadway during the customary hour between three and four, I thought to myself: *Is there anyone alive who is not hiding something?*

Now I flowed amid the human current with Eliza and her husband. Our children—Eliza's blond trio and my dark pair—bobbed just ahead of us with the pretty young Mary. Among the crowd we greeted Mr. Clement Clarke Moore, known, much to his chagrin, for his children's poem "A Visit from Saint Nicholas" which famously began " 'Twas the night before Christmas . . ." and not for his professorship in Oriental

languages at the seminary that he founded. We nodded at Mr. Philip
Hone, who as mayor had come up with the idea of covering over the
paupers' burial ground in Greenwich Village to make it into a fashionable park. The land in Washington Square is still unstable; cannons on
military parade have been known to sink into the settling graves.

"Look who's coming," said Eliza.

Beyond a large Hessian family stumping along in tight shapeless
jackets and an upright Knickerbocker couple trying in vain to pass
them, I caught sight of an arch pink face beneath a stovepipe hat.

"Oh no. Do you think he has seen us?"

Eliza caught my arm. "He's your editor, Fanny. You must be polite. Maybe he'll go away if we don't encourage him."

Reverend Griswold hastened forward when he saw me. He took
off his hat, releasing the fringe of curls above his ears, and then bowed
to the Bartletts and me. "May I have the honor of joining you?"

"Yes." I did not know how to refuse him. "Please do."

The crowd on the sidewalk necessitated that we separate into couples. Reverend Griswold marched next to me as we processed along,
giving a solemn tip of his hat to the James Fenimore Coopers as they
passed, prompting the author to glance at his wife before bowing. The
reverend called a hearty hello to the astonished current mayor, William
Havemeyer. When an earnest young gentleman approached, my escort
waved him away, crying, "Not now, Hawthorne! I'll read your draft of
The Scarlet-whatever as soon as I can." I could feel a strong emotion ex-
uding from his nearby presence—pride of ownership of me? I shivered.

A mustachioed youth sauntered past, twirling a cane and arranging his face in a superior sneer, a task made difficult by the squint
that was necessary to keep a monocle to his eye. Even Reverend
Griswold's oppressive company could not dampen my amusement.

Reverend Griswold gladdened to see my expression. "It is a fine
day, isn't it?"

"Oh dear," I said, "Does young Mr. Roosevelt realize what a ridiculous figure he cuts?"

His smile faded. "I didn't realize that men were such figures of
fun to you."

"They aren't, not usually." I suppressed a smile, recalling the
dandy's silly monocled wink.

"Well! Let us not talk about the folly of women! This new con-traption that women wear to stretch out their skirts—"

"Crinolines," I said, taken aback by his vehemence. "I imagine they are much more comfortable to wear than a score of petticoats."

The cleft between his brows deepened. "I did not mean for you to say articles of unmentionables aloud. But I just now saw young Caroline Schermerhorn *in one*, and the wind caught hold of her and nearly set her sailing like a hot-air balloon. I am pleased to say that *I* did not laugh."

"A pity," I murmured.

He glanced at me.

"A pity she should look so foolish," I said.

"Exactly!" he cried. "I do believe, Mrs. Osgood, that we are of the same mind. I have often felt so in your presence."

"You are very kind."

"I'm not kind," he said. "I am speaking the truth, though it makes me blush to do so. What must you think of me, saying such, when you are a married woman?"

"I think very little of you," I said.

He blinked.

"Other than as having the best of intentions," I said.

"Oh, yes! You do perceive me well! This is the very thing I speak of."

I smiled. If only Eliza would turn around and save me.

He waited until a phaeton with enormous yellow wheels and small grim driver rolled by. "Other men might try to take advantage of a married woman when her husband is absent, but never me. I am here to guard and protect you."

"Thank you, Reverend Griswold. I'm sure my husband would wish to thank you himself, when he returns, very soon."

"Very soon?"

"Any time now—perhaps today."

"I was under the impression—" He stopped, balling his gloved hands at his side.

"How is the new edition of your poetry collection coming along?" I asked.

An immodest smile nudged through his frown. "Coming along

well, coming along well. I must have read a thousand new books to choose for it. I do believe that I have the largest library of American books in the country. But this edition will not be complete without some new works by you—can I count on you?"

"You are most kind."

"Not kind," he said. "Truthful—remember?"

I held back a sigh as I nodded.

"The truth shall set us free, yes?" His smile soured as he peered ahead. "Oh no."

I peered ahead. My heart leaped as I caught sight of Mr. Poe, hatless among the river of black stovepipes. And then I saw his wife. They were promenading in our direction, along with Mrs. Clemm.

"Why does he not stay at home?" said Reverend Griswold. "Does he not think of the health of his wife? She is obviously consumptive—I think he wishes to hasten her to her grave!"

I felt a stab of guilt. Did her condition seem that severe? I recalled Mr. Bartlett's accusation that Mr. Poe's characters often murdered their wives. *Don't be absurd.*

I caught at my bonnet, lifted by the wind. "Surely they are just enjoying the fine weather like the rest of us."

"Are they? Is he? I find that there is nothing about Edgar Poe that is remotely like the rest of us. He is a predator, plain and simple. A wolf in wolf's clothing."

Eliza, a pace ahead, turned to seek my attention, having spotted Mr. Poe. When he and his family were even with our children, she extended a gloved hand to him. "Dear Mr. Poe! How lovely to see you today!"

As his wife and her mother nodded their hellos, Mr. Poe gazed at each of us in turn until his sights settled on me. A wildness leaped from his eyes, then receded back as if whipped into submission.

A thrill charged through me as I outwardly carried out my social duties, introducing Mrs. Poe and her mother to the Bartletts, then to our children, who had been made to stand quietly by Mary.

Ignoring the Bartletts and their offspring, Mrs. Poe looked between my daughters, curiosity sharpening her face within her bonnet. "Such delicious little girls."

I nodded for them to respond.

"Thank you," they said in unison.

"Mother," Mrs. Poe asked Mrs. Clemm, "don't you want two little girls like these?"

"Indeed I do!" cried Mrs. Clemm.

Mrs. Poe bent down and dabbed Vinnie on the nose. "I could just eat you up!"

Vinnie shrank back. Then, shyly, she said, "We have a cat named Poe."

"Really?" Mrs. Poe's face hardened as drew herself upright.

"Mr. Poe saved her," said Vinnie, "and gave her to Mamma."

"You did?" Mrs. Poe demanded of her husband. "When?"

"Recently," Mr. Poe said shortly.

The fluttering of skirts and bonnet strings filled the awkward pause. Eliza frowned at her husband, who was rudely staring at Mr. Poe's forehead. To the group she exclaimed, "Pretty day!"

"Very," said Reverend Griswold in a scolding tone. "We should be going. Mrs. Osgood?" He put out his arm for me to take.

I ignored his offer. I could feel Mr. Poe's intense gaze upon me. It had the singular effect of panicking and calming me at once.

"It is the warmest day so far this year," said Mrs. Clemm.

Mr. Bartlett stared coolly at Mr. Poe. "It's getting very warm indeed."

In spite of their sister's sternly administered pinches, Eliza's boys, having stood still beyond their limit of patience, began to fidget. "Would you care to join us?" Eliza asked Mrs. Poe. "We're going one more block south and then heading home."

Mrs. Poe peered down the sidewalk as if weighing other invitations.

Just then, a plump woman stuffed within a lavish eruption of peacock-blue silk approached, followed by her lanky red-faced husband.

"Mr. Poe?" she asked tremulously.

He waited.

"Mr. Poe, we are your most ardent fans. I—we—loved 'The Raven.' May I ask you, please, could you say 'Nevermore'? In your own voice."

"I have no other voice to use," said Mr. Poe.

"Please excuse my husband's sense of humor," said Mrs. Poe. "He's always joking."

The woman's mouth rounded in an *O*. "You are Mr. Poe's wife?"

Mrs. Poe extended her hand prettily. "I am Virginia Poe."

The woman appeared ready to burst with her great good luck. "*Mrs.* Poe! What an honor to meet you! You must be so very proud."

The attention invigorated Mrs. Poe like a potion. "Indeed, I am!"

Mr. Poe made a small smile. "Perhaps, madam, you would be interested in meeting one of New York's shining stars."

"Another star?" The woman gasped. "There is no one greater than you, Mr. Poe!"

Reverend Griswold, who'd been quietly fuming, sweetened. He turned toward the woman with proud expectation.

Mr. Poe touched my elbow. "This is Mrs. Frances Osgood."

I reeled from the audacity of his touch as I nodded civilly.

The woman drew back to look at me. "Oh. Do I know you?"

"She is known by all persons of taste," said Mr. Poe.

"I think I have heard of you," the woman said haltingly.

Her husband patted her on the shoulder. "Come along, dear, let these good people take their air."

"Eddie," said Mrs. Poe as they walked away, "I'd like to go home."

He turned to her with a slight frown. "If you wish."

"You should get home, too," Reverend Griswold said to me, "since your husband is coming."

Mr. Poe glanced at me. The girls raised their faces to me with surprised delight.

I took their hands, hating Reverend Griswold. "It's time to go. Good-bye, Mr. and Mrs. Poe," I said, "Mrs. Clemm." I parted ways with them distractedly, and shedding Reverend Griswold, turned for home.

I spent much of our return keeping my anger in check while explaining to the girls that Reverend Griswold had been confused. I had not, in fact, heard from their father, I told them, but they should not worry about it, not at all, as it could only mean that he was finding plenty of work, wherever he was. Their sad expressions devastated me. So caught up was I in smoothing over their disappointment that I thought little of the glances Eliza was throwing my way. It wasn't until we had arrived at the house at Amity Place and sent the children to the kitchen for an early supper that she said to me, "Oh, Fanny, you are in trouble."

I perched next to Eliza on the black horsehair sofa, waiting while the parlor maid, Catherine, lit a whale-oil lamp upon the mantel; Mr. Bartlett had not wanted to use the gas that night. The wick took the fire; a flame blazed up. Catherine replaced the glass chimney, setting the prisms hanging from it ajingle, casting rainbow spots upon the shadowy wall. She moved on to the companion lamp on the mantel, then to the lamp on the center table, and with the room now glittering with light reflected from the many mirrors, left us.

Mr. Bartlett, in the place of honor in the arm chair next to the fireplace, tamped tobacco into his pipe. That they should call a meeting upstairs in the back parlor instead of the family room off the kitchen signaled the seriousness of the matter at hand. The ticking of the tall clock in the corner filled the uncomfortable silence, along with muffled thumps overhead as the children were prepared for bed. There came the scratch of a match against its box, followed by the sucking sound of Mr. Bartlett drawing on his pipe as the tobacco grew orange in its cherrywood nest.

"Well, Mrs. Osgood"—Mr. Bartlett removed his pipe stem from his mouth—"I'll come out with it." He blew out smoke. "It's clear that Mr. Poe is forming an attachment to you."

I tried to laugh it off. "Mr. Poe?"

Mr. Bartlett pressed his lips in a flat line, adding to his duckish appearance. "I am serious."

What did he know? "We do respect each other's work," I said more cautiously.

"We're your friends, Fanny," said Eliza.

"I know you are. Very much so. I cannot thank you enough for providing a home for—"

"What we mean to say," Mr. Bartlett said, interrupting, "is that it appears that Poe has gotten the wrong idea from your poem. He seems to think he can carry on a flirtation with you in front of his wife as long as you and he claim you are just friends."

"That's not why I wrote it."

Eliza's plain, sweet face crumpled with concern. "We aren't here to accuse you of anything, Fanny. But if we can sense his attraction to you, what about others?"

"People talk," said Mr. Bartlett.

I pushed away the proud thrill of knowing that it might be obvious to others that Mr. Poe was attracted to me. The reality was that as persons married to others, even the appearance of our being drawn to each other could destroy our reputations. Anyone who broke the rules was severely punished, with those who wore the yoke most heavily meting out the strictest judgment. No one escaped from the institution of marriage unless by a spouse's death.

"I warned you about Poe's instability," said Mr. Bartlett. "You cannot truly believe that he will behave like a gentleman."

I braced myself. "What evidence do you have for his inappropriate conduct?"

"He can't keep his eyes off you," said Eliza.

"No one ever committed a crime just by looking," said Mr. Bartlett. He lowered his pipe to the arm of his leather chair. "But I am concerned by his involvement in your career."

"Reverend Griswold is involved in my career as well. I cannot help that publishing is in the hands of men."

Mr. Bartlett dismissed my evasion with a frown. "Poe cannot be trusted."

Mr. Bartlett must not have seen the kiss. Now was the time to give up Mr. Poe, before any real harm was done to my reputation and my good standing with the Bartletts. But how could I ever do so? Just the thought of it filled me with despair.

"We are frightened for you, Fanny," said Eliza. "There's no telling what boundaries he will overstep. He seems to have little care for convention."

"How do you know this?" I said. "Even if he does behave in a manner in which we are not accustomed, what is the harm in it?"

The doorbell jingled in the hallway.

We sat back in our respective corners as footsteps sounded up the kitchen stairs, then down the hall. I heard the murmur of voices.

The maid Catherine came into the room. "A Mr. Poe is here, ma'am. He asks to see Mrs. Osgood."

"What did I tell you?" Mr. Bartlett said. "The man is bolder than I thought."

"Tell him we are out," Eliza told the maid.

"No," I said.

They looked at me.

"What if this is about my article for the *Tribune*? I cannot afford to jeopardize my chance at making money." I almost laughed at my outrageousness. As if I wished to pursue that article. Writing it sickened me.

Eliza exchanged glances with her husband, then pursed her lips. "You may send him in, Catherine."

Mr. Poe entered. My body quickened at the sight of him, darkly handsome in his mysterious way, an untamed beast just barely under control. Mr. Bartlett rose to shake his hand, after which Eliza received him, seated. He came to me. My heart thumping, I put out my hand.

He took it briefly. "Mrs. Osgood." His manner was the perfect combination of professional friendliness and courtly reserve, the animal in him shackled and hidden. "Thank you for receiving me at this hour."

"What brings you this way?" Mr. Bartlett said, a little rudely.

"An invitation for Mrs. Osgood from my wife."

I cringed inwardly. Why wouldn't she leave me alone?

He turned his dark-lashed eyes to me. "She would like to invite you to come with us to Mathew Brady's studio on Wednesday. It seems he insists that he do our portrait."

"That's very kind of her," I said, "but I'm afraid that I would only be in the way."

"On the contrary, you'd be doing her a favor. She's looking forward to having her portrait done, and having a witness to the event would only double her pleasure. I'm afraid that my own lack of enthusiasm for the project has not been much good to her."

Mr. Bartlett puffed on his pipe. "What would Mr. Osgood say about your entering enemy territory?"

I felt a rush of anger. "Excuse me?"

Mr. Bartlett took his pipe from his teeth. "How would your husband feel about your frequenting the studio of his competition?"

"Mr. Osgood has nothing to fear," said Mr. Poe. "A tray of chemicals can never replace the artistic eye, as his wife has so rightfully advised me." He turned to me. "I would like to invite your husband, too. It might be very interesting to him."

"Thank you, but he has not returned from his travels."

Mr. Poe nodded. "Perhaps he can join us another time, then."

"I'm sure that he'd like to talk to you," Mr. Bartlett said pointedly.

Mr. Poe did not take the barb. "I understand, sir, that you have launched an ambitious undertaking." He gave Mr. Bartlett a rare smile. "Collecting words and phrases particular to America—my hat is off to you."

Mr. Bartlett raised blond brows. "You heard?"

"Mr. Willis told me. A worthy project."

"What project, Russell?" asked Eliza.

Mr. Bartlett staunched a grin. "That Willis—the man cannot keep a secret. I didn't want to tell you until I was a little further along with it, Eliza, but yes, I am working on a project, a spectacular one: a dictionary of Americanisms." He beamed unabashedly.

"Russell!" Eliza exclaimed. "How wonderful. How have you been able to keep this from me?"

Mr. Bartlett puffed cheerfully on his pipe. "It wasn't easy."

Released from his secrecy, Mr. Bartlett spent a happy hour discussing his method of collection and his criteria for classifying words with Mr. Poe, during which Eliza shot me several searching looks. At last the tall clock struck nine and Mr. Poe excused himself, saying that his wife would worry about him if he did not start for home.

"Not such a bad fellow," said Mr. Bartlett after the front door shut.

"Should you reconsult your phrenology chart, Russell?" asked Eliza. She bit back a smile at me.

Still sanguine from delving into a topic that he obviously held dear, Mr. Bartlett calmly tapped his empty pipe into an ashtray. "Perhaps."

I noticed Mr. Poe's gloves on the arm of the chair where he had sat. I rose as quickly as dignity would allow and retrieved them. "I think I might still catch him."

"It's no use," Mr. Bartlett called after me. "He'll have gone too far. His office is near the bookstore—I'll take them to him in the morning."

"Just in case—" I hurried to the door. Down the stone steps I rushed, oblivious to the evening chill. I flung open the iron gate and ran down the sidewalk. Three short blocks up, I stopped abruptly. At the corner, under a tree outside the graveyard of the Baptist church, stood Mr. Poe.

My heart beating in my throat, I approached.

I held out the gloves.

He caught my wrist. "I need you."

"This cannot be."

"Then why did you come?"

"We'll be outcasts."

"I don't give a damn." He crushed me to him. In the dim glow of a gas-lit street lamp, I could see the wildness in his eyes. His raw yearning thrilled and terrified me.

His voice was thick with furious urgency. "You are all I ever wanted. I have waited for you my whole life."

I pulled back. "Your wife. I fear she cannot stand a blow."

"You don't know her."

"I don't want to know her. I can't bear to think what this would do to her."

He let go of my waist. "Yes, you are right. It's best that you don't know her. For your sake."

I stared at him, my lips aching for his. I didn't care about his wife. I wanted his body against mine.

He took my arm. I cried out in surprise as he led me swiftly back to my door. With a curt good-bye, he strode away, leaving me with his gloves in my trembling hands.

He had treated me like a child. I hated him, and what's more, I feared him.

I lifted his gloves to my lips. They smelled like leather, cold air, and his flesh.

I would possess him, no matter if it killed me.

Sixteen

It was a sunny day, rich with the promise of spring, but little of the fine day penetrated the gloomy hackney in which I rode down Broadway. With my gloved hands folded upon my reticule like a trussed bird, I breathed in the odor of cigar smoke and sweat—a souvenir from previous passengers—and listened as Mrs. Poe recounted the details of the ball that she and Mr. Poe had attended the previous night. It seemed that neither the food nor the acclaim that she and her husband had received there had its parallel in modern history, or so one would think, hearing her glowing account as we jounced along.

"Everyone who was important was there," she was saying in her silvered voice. "The William Backhouse Astors, the Coopers, the Vanderbilts. Do you know them?"

"Yes." They were the new-money crowd whom Samuel had courted vigorously. The coal of fury smoldering in my heart reddened at the thought of him.

"Oh, the ladies were so lovely! Do you know that Mrs. Vanderbilt's dress, including her jewels, cost thirty thousand dollars? I know. I asked her." She smiled. "She seemed glad for a chance to tell."

Maybe Mrs. Vanderbilt really was happy for the opportunity to divulge the price. It was customary among the well-heeled for the value of things to be *understood* but not divulged. Perhaps it was refreshing to get exact credit.

Across from us, Mr. Poe seemed to be staring at the dust motes shimmering in the shaft of sunlight pouring through the open carriage window. He had not looked at me since they had retrieved me at Eliza's house. Did his body still hum, too, from when we had touched three long nights ago?

"The talk was of a new dance step," she said, "the polka. Have you heard of it?"

"No," I said. "I'm afraid I haven't."

"You haven't?" Mrs. Poe gasped in delight. "It's just divine! You've never heard such happy music."

"An insane Tartar jig," muttered Mr. Poe.

She made a pouting face.

I laughed to show my support of Mrs. Poe as guilt seeped from my pores. Yet face her I must. The pain of doing so while in the company of her husband seemed the proper punishment for having the feelings that I had for him. Maybe it could be my cure. If only suffering through her discomforting company could break me of my dangerous attraction to him.

Mrs. Poe gazed out the window, picking at the low neckline of her dress. With its revealing neckline and cinched waist, her gown was the most stylish that I'd seen her wear. In fact, I realized with a jolt, it was similar to the one I had worn when I'd first met Mr. Poe.

"I like your dress," I said.

"Do you?" She stroked the front of it. "I had it made from the advance money of Eddie's new book."

"A new dress does wonders for the spirit," I said.

She gazed at me for a moment. "You must know all about his book."

"I don't," I said lightly. "Which book is this?"

"Really? I thought that he might have told you at one of those *conversaziones*." She pronounced the word in mocking tones.

"I'm afraid not," I said with false good humor. "I'm just another of his readers, waiting to see what treat Mr. Poe has in store for us."

"Didn't he come to your house?"

A wave of heat swept over my face. "The Bartletts' home, you must mean, where I am staying. Yes, he did, but I fear Mr. Bartlett kept him rather occupied. What is this new book, Mr. Poe?" I said brightly.

He glanced from the window long enough to give his wife a baleful look. "Tales."

"People can't get enough of his frightening stories." Mrs. Poe studied me as our carriage shuddered along. "Which ones have you read?"

I felt my blush deepen.

Mrs. Poe crooked half of her pretty mouth in a smile. "You really should bother with reading them, you know."

"Why should she?" Mr. Poe snapped. "I've had quite enough of them."

Mrs. Poe plucked at the fabric of her dress. "You will never be done with your scary stories, Eddie. Never. Don't you know that?"

I busied myself with my reticule, feeling the friction between them. But Mr. Poe and I *had* to play the part of jolly friends if I was ever to see him at all. "So Let It Be," written so innocently, now served as a map as to how we must behave.

"When should we expect your article on Eddie to be published?" Mrs. Poe asked.

Firmer footing. I leaped at it. "It's almost finished. I've yet to put the final touches on it."

"Do you need more information? Eddie, why aren't you talking to her?"

I gathered myself. "Actually, the public wants to know about both of you. They want a glimpse of your happy married life together."

Mrs. Poe giggled. "Do they?"

"Kill the article," Mr. Poe said suddenly.

Mrs. Poe blinked as if slapped.

"My privacy has already been ruined," said Mr. Poe. "If one more person asks me to say 'nevermore,' I shall throttle them."

"Eddie!" Mrs. Poe protested. "So vicious."

"This time, Virginia, you don't get what you want."

Just past Saint Paul's Chapel, the carriage stopped. I looked out the window as an omnibus rumbled by. On the pavement before Mr. Brady's studio, a boy hoping for a half cent was trying to sell a stolen apple to a gentleman.

"Here we are." Mrs. Poe slid out her bottom lip. "But you've spoiled the occasion."

"You'll find a way to enjoy it." He got out and held the door for his wife. It struck me how in the sunshine, the blue-black of her hair was the very color of a raven. Had he been gazing at his wife when he was writing the poem that would make him famous? A shard of jealousy twisted in my heart.

I was helped from the carriage by Mr. Poe. He let his agitated gaze linger upon me, exciting and frightening me with his boldness.

Inside the studio, the three of us strolled by a gallery of portraits of the rich and famous. Many I recognized from Anne's conversaziones: Mr. Audubon, Mr. Greeley, Senator Webster, the aged Mr. Astor. We were examining them, Mrs. Poe coughing daintily from time to time into her handkerchief, when Mr. Brady trampled down the stairs, wiping his hands on a towel.

"Mr. Poe!" He shook hands, his blue eyes enlarged to comic proportions behind his spectacles. "And the beautiful Mrs. Poe." He kissed her hand, then came to me. "Mrs. Osgood? What a surprise."

"I see you have Dickens," said Mr. Poe.

Mr. Brady turned around. "Ah, yes." He gazed fondly at his work, hanging on the wall. "I had the honor of making his portrait when he visited New York several years ago. I had just bought my equipment and didn't yet have my studio. He was most kind to sit for an unknown like me. Of course *all* daguerreotypists were unknown two years ago; it's such a new art."

"He was clever to have his portrait made," said Mrs. Poe.

Mr. Brady's huge eyes nearly danced with merriment. "Indeed! If ever a person knew the value of publicity, it was Dickens. He orchestrated his every move with the press, from his dinner at Delmonico's, to his carriage ride afterward through the slums of Five Points, to his tour of the lunatic asylum on Blackwell's Island."

"See, Eddie?" said Mrs. Poe. "*He* courts attention."

Mr. Poe's expression darkened. "I'll not imitate his usage of the poor and ill to sell my books. If that's how an author wins his readers' attention, I'd rather be unknown."

Mrs. Poe shook her pretty head. "See what a difficult husband I have?"

Mr. Poe frowned at Mr. Brady. "What did you have in mind for us today?"

"I thought to make a portrait of each of you separately, if you don't mind."

"And Mrs. Osgood, too?" asked Mrs. Poe.

Mr. Brady glanced at Mr. Poe as if to see if the great man had time to wait for a portrait to be made of his wife's friend.

Mr. Poe gave a short nod.

"Yes, yes," said Mr. Brady. "Of course. If you will step this way." He motioned for us to go up the stairs.

We climbed three flights, a task made slower by Mrs. Poe's coughing. The studio was on the top floor, in a room that was bright from the sunlight pouring through the glass roof. A red velvet drapery covered one of the walls. Opposite it, Mr. Brady's assistant was atop a ladder, latching a compartment of a metal cabinet that was set high upon a shelf.

"Ladies first." Mr. Brady directed Mrs. Poe to a small stage before the curtain. "If you will allow me." He arranged her body so that her head was turned to face us, then adjusted a small table covered with a Turkey carpet and rested her arm upon it.

He pulled an iron stand behind her. "If you will pardon me, I must affix this brace to the back of your neck."

"A brace!" said Mrs. Poe.

"I apologize, but it is necessary to keep you perfectly still. Once I have exposed the plate, you must remain absolutely motionless for one minute exactly, while your image develops. It doesn't sound like a long time to keep still, but it is surprisingly difficult to do without an aid."

"What happens if I move?" she asked.

"Why, you'll disappear! Any motion will erase your image. I have many pictures of towns that look to be empty even though they were teeming with horses and people. It was the movement that wiped them out."

He put a clamp against her neck and tightened the screws, then gingerly arranged her black knot of hair over them. "Comfortable enough?"

She blinked her affirmation.

He stood back. "Now, try not to breathe. Ready?" He nodded to his assistant on the step ladder, who then opened a chamber in the little cabinet. I found that I was holding my breath, too, as Mr. Brady attended to his watch.

After what seemed much longer than a minute, Mr. Brady called, "Time!"

He released Mrs. Poe from the apparatus and helped her down

while his assistant hurried the tray containing the exposed image to an adjoining room.

I took my turn on the stage. Mr. Brady positioned me toward the camera, readjusted the table for my own lower height, and aligned my arm upon it. Once he had clamped the brace to my neck, he took his place with the watch.

"Ready?"

Motionless as a dressmaker's doll, I blinked my yes. He signaled to his colleague, now back upon the ladder.

I heard the sound of metal sliding against metal when the assistant exposed the plate. The screws dug into my flesh as I held my breath and stared into the camera. What would the image reveal of me? Would the guilt be visible in my eyes, my painful yearning for Mr. Poe?

"Oh!" cried Mrs. Poe.

I jerked my head in her direction, the screws raking my neck.

She touched her gloved fingers to her mouth, blinking her eyes like an innocent child. "Excuse me!"

Mr. Brady looked doubtfully at his watch. "The exposure *might* have been long enough."

"Oh no. Did I spoil it?" said Mrs. Poe. "I'm so very sorry!"

"We might be all right," said Mr. Brady. "Mr. Poe? Your turn."

Mr. Poe submitted himself to Mr. Brady's ministrations. Afterward, we went downstairs and were entertained by a violinist as Mr. Brady's assistant worked his chemical magic in their little laboratory. We spoke little, other than Mrs. Poe commenting to Mr. Brady on whom among the portraits of the famous that she knew personally, and those of whom she would like to know. She then lit upon the idea that Mr. Poe could have the daguerreotype engraved for usage in the *Journal* once he owned it.

"I cannot wait until your name is the only one on the masthead," she told Mr. Poe.

Mr. Brady's eyes bounced behind his thick glasses. "Is that news to the other owners?"

Just then, the assistant came down with a glass plate.

"I'm sorry to disturb you," he said to Mr. Brady.

"What is it, Eakins?"

The assistant showed the plate to Mr. Brady, who then looked up, the concern in his eyes amplified by his lenses.

Mr. Brady turned the plate to our group. On it was a perfect reproduction of my body standing before the curtain on the stage, with my dress flawless and my clenched hand lying upon the table. But where my head should have been was a blank. It was a portrait of a headless woman.

Mrs. Poe's laugh was as merry as a jingling bell. "Oh, Frances, I think you've lost your head!"

That evening after supper, Vinnie hunched on the wide rim of the tin tub, trying to draw warmth from the rapidly cooling water at her feet. The water had been hot when the maid Martha had started up the three flights of stairs to our room. As second girl to the parlor maid and cook, the one with the most difficult physical labors although the slightest of the Bartletts' four maids, Martha had hauled up many buckets that night. A midweek bath had been in order for all of the children. They had gone on an outing with Mary to see the men digging out a new street and had returned caked in dirt. They wouldn't have had to go far to find excavations. Twenty-some years earlier, to make flat, uniform blocks for investors like Mr. Astor to purchase, the city commissioners had decreed for the entire island of Manhattan to be made level, and the destruction had commenced. The rocky hills that covered the island were slowly being pulverized into plains. Bogs were being filled with debris. The substantial farmhouses were rolled away on logs; squatter's shanties were knocked flat and plowed over. The countryside, which only recently started at the bottom of Union Square, was receding to the north each day. Mr. Bryant, as self-important as he was, had been correct to call for a new park, before there was nothing green and natural left on the island.

Now I dunked a pitcher into the bucket and poured a stream of water over Vinnie. Pale rivulets ran through the dirt on her neck. "How did you get so dirty?"

"Ellen and I were playing lost girls. We made stew. We had a big stick." She put her hands together and demonstrated how she had stirred her pretend cauldron.

I soaped a flannel facecloth and lifted the wet strings of her hair. "Where was Mary while you were making your stew?" I asked, scrubbing her neck.

"Talking to a man."

"A man?"

She nodded.

I examined her scalp. Grit sparkled on the skin of her part. Her hair needed washing, even though it had been done on Saturday.

I applied the Castile soap-cake to her hair. "Who was this man?"

"Her friend."

"How do you know he was her friend?"

"She was smiling when she came back." She dabbled her fingers in the grimy water.

I lathered her hair. "Came back from where?"

"I don't know. I was playing."

I did not like the sound of this. "Did you get a look at him?"

"He was too far away. He had on a hat. He looked like Henry and Johnny's papa."

So Mary had a beau. I wondered who he could be. I tried to recall the deliverymen who came by the house. "What did Mary do when she came back?"

"Took us home."

"Lean forward."

Vinnie sputtered and blinked as I rinsed her head.

Very well, Mary could chase after a man if she liked, but I was furious that she put the children in harm's way when doing so. I had seen the work crews in action. Dozens of men chipped at the hills with pickaxes, while others blasted away the biggest rocks with gunpowder. Another army shoveled the rubble into ox-drawn wagons that shed debris as they rumbled along. Mary shouldn't have had her eyes off the children for one minute near such a place.

"Next time Mary wants to go see the workmen, ask me first, all right?"

"All right."

I heard the doorbell jingle downstairs. Someone for Mr. Bartlett, no doubt. It was past the hour for our lady friends to come calling.

Satisfied that Vinnie's head was clean, I held out first one downy arm and then the other to scrub them. I had worked my way down her back and had her stand for me to wash her legs when Eliza came to the bedroom door.

A quizzical expression darkened her plain honest face. "Fanny, Mr. Poe is here."

I stopped. Vinnie sat down in the tub.

I pulled her up. "The water's dirty."

"He came to see Russell. They're in the parlor, talking. I thought you'd like to know."

"Thank you," I said firmly. "Did you know that Mary has a beau and that is why she took the children out to the digging site? I'm sorry to complain, but it's such a dangerous place, and she wasn't watching the children."

"Yes, she was," Vinnie protested, now shivering from being wet.

"She has been a bit distant lately," said Eliza. "I wondered what was wrong with her. I'll speak with her. But would you like her to take over for you now, before Mr. Poe leaves?"

"Mamma, you said you'd read me 'Puss in Boots' when I got in bed!"

I must not run to Mr. Poe. I must sever the connection between us.

"I did," I told Vinnie, "and I will."

Eliza looked surprised. "Very well. We'll be in the back parlor."

I tried not to hurry the rest of Vinnie's bath. I put her and Ellen to bed and read them the story, straining all the while to hear the murmuring of voices downstairs. Knowing that Mr. Poe was close and that I could not be with him was a torment. But torment was what I deserved for loving another woman's husband.

At last I had tucked in Vinnie and Ellen. In the hall, I straightened my skirt and pinched my cheeks, and biting color into my lips, I descended the stairs. Deep breath: I entered the back parlor.

The gas chandelier had been lit in honor of the guest. Mr. Poe rose from a chair flanking the fireplace. Joy leaped through my body when our eyes met. I fought to erase all emotion from my face as I gave him my hand.

Mr. Bartlett rose, too. "Good heavens, Mrs. Osgood. Are you well?"

"Of course." My fingers burned where Mr. Poe touched them. I took a seat next to Eliza on the black horsehair sofa. I could feel Mr. Poe watching me in the tawny glow of the gaslights.

"You are just in time for the most interesting conversation," said Mr. Bartlett. "We have just determined that at last I have found a source for Southern expressions for my dictionary." He gave Mr. Poe an enthusiastic nod. "None other than our esteemed guest. Southernisms had been my weakest category—I had only a few rather poorly written novels to go by. Now, thanks to Mr. Poe, I have an expert in the field."

"I am glad that my childhood in Richmond is good for something," said Mr. Poe.

Mr. Bartlett laughed, not knowing, I guessed, what a miserable childhood Mr. Poe had. "I look forward to picking your brains."

"I hope you won't use too fine a point," said Mr. Poe.

Mr. Bartlett paused, then laughed. Seeing Mr. Poe was serious, he said, "It is a grisly expression, isn't it, as are so many of Americanisms."

"We do seem prone to them." Eliza pulled her thread through her ever-present sewing. "When we are frustrated with someone, we wish to 'wring his neck.' We speak of 'twisting arms' when we want a favor. When we're angry, we could 'just kill' persons."

"Eliza, my goodness," said Mr. Bartlett. "I am not compiling *The Dictionary of the Violent*." Realizing the sort of material that his visitor wrote, he smiled uncomfortably.

"The human animal has a taste for the violent," Mr. Poe said smoothly. "That is why my readers insist that I write in that vein."

"We are hardly animals," said Mr. Bartlett.

"Oh, but we are," said Mr. Poe.

"Don't tell me, Poe, that you are one of those who believe that animals have spirits."

"I do not see why that is unreasonable."

"Why don't you go as far as the Swedenborgians and claim there are spirits in rocks, too?" Mr. Bartlett grinned at Eliza and me for approval.

"I will leave those musings to Mr. Emerson and Mr. Longfellow," said Mr. Poe. "I am just saying that, like animals, we have spirits within us, and whether you realize it, they are reacting to one another this very moment."

Eliza shivered. "How chilling."

"Not really," said Mr. Poe. "They are with us all the time." He glanced at me. "As someone I respect once said, 'We just aren't used to attending to them.'"

"I believe," said Mr. Bartlett with raised yellow brows, "that attending to them might be a definition for madness."

Eliza plunged her needle into the cloth. "Mr. Poe, could you enlighten me? I'm afraid I have not given this subject much thought. My day is taken up with the commonplace: stubbed toes, teething pains, bee stings."

Selfishly, I did not want him to answer. I wanted to keep my understanding of his most treasured thoughts as my own special privilege.

Mr. Poe seemed to hear my mind. "The commonplace," he told Eliza, "deserves every bit as much attention as the sublime." He then reached into his coat and drew out a packet of letters. He held them out to me. "For you."

"Me?"

"From your admirers. You were right—my lady readers did appreciate your scolding of the arrogant gentleman in 'So Let It Be.' My congratulations."

I fanned the letters to count them.

"Nine, and your poem was only just published." He reached down to offer his hand to his namesake kitten, which had pulled itself from under his chair. "This is the most enthusiastic response a poem has received since I've been at the *Journal*."

I wondered why he did not give the letters to me before we went to Mr. Brady's studio that morning. They could not have all arrived this afternoon. Did he not want his wife to see them? "Thank you."

"Thank you for thinking of the *Journal*. I hope you'll send more poems. Especially since I've asked that you hold your article for the *Tribune*."

I saw Eliza's surprise. "I won't be writing the article about Mr. Poe and his wife," I explained.

"Oh no," said Eliza. "I was really looking forward to that."

"Mrs. Osgood's talents might be better spent on her poetry," said Mr. Poe. He picked up the kitten. "I believe I know this cat."

"You've heard what the children named her," said Mr. Bartlett. "'Poe.'"

He smiled. "She's an improvement on the original."

Eliza was frowning. "Have you told Miss Fuller, Fanny? I can't imagine that she took this lightly."

"I will write to her this week," I said.

Mr. Poe's tone became more formal. "Mrs. Osgood, I would like to offer you an advance for further poems, to offset the income you will be losing from not writing your article."

"Perhaps, Mr. Poe," said Mr. Bartlett, "you should ask her husband."

My flesh prickled with offense. "He need not ask Samuel. Samuel would not care."

Mr. Poe put down the kitten. "I was under the impression that Mrs. Osgood makes her own decisions."

Mr. Bartlett's golden brow knotted in disagreement. "I would hope that she would consult her husband on business as well as personal matters. She is a married woman, you know."

"And as such," I said, my voice becoming strained, "do my wishes no longer matter?"

"It is the law, Mrs. Osgood," said Mr. Bartlett.

"Samuel does not own me."

"Legally," said Mr. Bartlett, "he does."

"Oh, Russell," said Eliza, "must you make it sound so grim?"

He shrugged. "Facts are facts."

"So I may make no decisions when my 'owner' is not present?" I stood before he could infuriate me further. "If you will please excuse me. I find that I need a little air right now." I left without bothering with my hat. I was nearly to the Baptist church when Mr. Poe caught up to me.

"You should not have run out like that," he said coolly. "You will give the impression that you are upset."

"I am upset." I turned onto Mercer Street and strode along the iron fence of the graveyard. The piney smell of the evergreen trees in the cemetery overlaid the refuse-tainted air. A carriage rattled by, more easily heard than seen in the faint gauzy glow of the half-moon; the next streetlight was at the next corner, at Fourth Street.

"If you let your closest friends think that something foul is afoot," Mr. Poe called from behind me, "what do you think your enemies will do with that same information?"

A barking dog bounded from a stable across the street, then receded with a low word from Mr. Poe. I turned down Fourth and kept going until I reached the corner of Washington Square. With an angry swish of skirts, I turned to confront Mr. Poe.

"I don't have enemies."

"I do. And if you are with me, they will become yours as well."

"Am I with you? Or am I a pathetic love-starved married woman overreacting to some kisses and a few longing looks?"

Quietly, he said, "You know what you are to me."

A man was coming our way down the sidewalk. I turned away until he had passed. "I don't know what we are. Perhaps 'something foul' is exactly right."

"I should not have put it that way." In the lamplight, I could see the agitation in his dark-rimmed eyes. He was close enough that I could smell his masculine musk. "I didn't know you cared so much for convention."

"I have more than myself to worry about. What about my girls? What about your wife?"

Two more gentlemen approached from the university buildings just down the street. We remained silent until out of their hearing.

"If only I had not married Virginia," said Mr. Poe.

"But you did."

"I married her when she was thirteen."

"Yes, I know. But you weren't thirteen."

"No. I was twenty-six—you're right, old enough to know better. But at the time, Virginia was the more grown up of the two of us." He paused. The wind whispered through the trees at the edge of the park. His voice was low and urgent when he continued. "I was at a desperate point in my life. I was too penniless to stay in the army and had been shut out of a home by the man I knew as a father. I thought I'd be a writer, but had nothing to show for it other than a childish epic poem that had been published when I was fourteen: "Al Aaraaf." Even the name was foolish. Virginia and Aunt Muddy offered stability. They looked up to me when no one else did. I was alone and vulnerable."

"But you married her."

"My marriage was not so much a union between two consenting adults as a hasty bid for security by two frightened children. Virginia was as poor as I was—no, poorer. Muddy had been scratching together a living by sewing and taking in boarders to supplement her paralyzed mother's war-widow's pension, but it wasn't enough. They were frantic with want. It was a relief to be a hero to someone poorer and weaker than I. The problem is that while I have grown up, Virginia has not."

"She's young."

"She's almost twenty-three."

"She's sick."

He stared at me.

"Her cough," I said. "Is she improving?"

I could hear him breathing. At last he said, "I swear she doesn't want to get well. Each cough is an accusation: I haven't taken her to Barbados to take the air. I haven't found her a good doctor. I haven't bought her a house in which we didn't freeze throughout the winter."

"I think she's very proud of you."

He made a mirthless laugh. "She's like a suit of clothes that no longer fits. It pinches and inhibits and makes me look foolish."

"Her mother claims you two are just alike."

He stopped breathing. At last he exhaled. "That's how much she knows."

"We must break this off."

"Virginia doesn't own me," he said fiercely. "Does your husband own you?"

"If so, he does not think much of his possession."

"He's a fool."

We began walking along the fence surrounding the park. The new shoots on the trees added their earthy scent to the night-cooled air. What did I expect him to say—that he would leave his wife? To do so was the province of fiction. Real life was not as easy as that.

We came to an entrance to the park. Although it was dark—too dark to be proper for a man to be escorting a woman who was not wife—we passed wordlessly through the iron archway. Conscious of the unspoken decision that had been made, I continued on by his side, our presence obscured within the grove of ancient elms that had been there when the land had been part of the paupers' burial ground. Only the sounds of hooves clopping on cobblestones through the neighborhood, strains of far-off fiddle music, and an occasional disembodied shout in the distance intruded upon our dark and private Eden.

We stopped under a sleeping giant. Gently, Mr. Poe tipped up my chin. Even in the fallen light, I could sense him smiling into my eyes. He kissed me tenderly. I could feel my spirit giving in to him.

Voices arose nearby. We froze, listening. When the group of young men passed—Irish toughs, by the sound of them—he turned me around and folded me against him. I melted at the touch of his body.

"Do you see that lit window on the third floor?" he said. His breath was warm against my ear.

Through the trees I could see the moonlit outline of the Gothic towers of New York University. I could hardly think with his body against mine. I could feel the strength coiled within his arms. "Yes."

"Those are the rooms of Samuel Morse."

I sighed deeply, not wanting to talk, knowing each moment that we spent together was precious and dangerous and possibly our last.

"You may know him for his work on the telegraph, but he was an artist before that."

I savored the vibration of his voice against my back as he spoke.

"A few years ago, he was in New York, working on the commission of a lifetime—the portrait of the Revolutionary War hero, the Marquis de Lafayette. He was deep at work on his painting when a horseman arrived, carrying a one-line message from his father in New Haven: 'Your wife is unwell.'"

I looked up over my shoulder at him.

"Morse dropped his things and rode to her directly. But when he arrived, his wife was dead. She had been buried the previous day."

I sighed. "No."

He kissed my temple. "The thought of his wife's lonely death devastated him. He vowed to create a means of long-distance communication so that this would never happen to anyone again. At the university"—he nodded through the trees—"he found some men who had developed a way of sending electric impulses through wire. It was up to him to create a language for this new medium, and so the Morse code was born."

I closed my eyes, drawing in his sweet spicy musk. What were we doing?

"They are stringing lines now between here and Washington City. Messages will be sent instantaneously between the two cities. Soon wires can be strung all over the nation, and long-distance communication will be more than a dream—all because a man failed to reach his wife in time."

He looked down at me. "You and I, we need no devices or codes to communicate over distance. You feel it, don't you?"

I rested my cheek against his arm, storing up his scent and the feel of his shoulders as I gathered the strength to part from him. "Yes."

His chest rose against my back. "I can be at work on a story, or walking to my office, or just brushing my coat, and I can feel your longing for me. If you ever need me, just bend your thoughts toward me, and, Frances, I shall come."

"If only that were true."

"It is true, as long as you believe that it is." He stroked my throat. "Animals can do it. Have you not heard tales of them coming to their masters' need, even when separated by great distances? Why should it not be for us"—he kissed where he had stroked—"if we but turn our wills toward it? All we must do is to believe in the power of our bond."

I drank in one long last draught of his touch, then pulled from him, although the pain of doing so left me nearly breathless. "We cannot do this."

He drew back as if slapped. I could sense his hurt, and then felt it quickly harden into anger.

"It's too dangerous," I pleaded.

"As you say."

"It's not the way I want it."

"Evidently, it is." He led me from under the trees into the lamplight.

I looked into his proud, wounded face. "We must break with our spouses if we are to truly be together. Make this an honest relationship, although we will be reviled by all"

His voice was harsh: "We can't."

"Why?"

He stared as if wishing to speak, then, with a resolute exhalation, took my elbow and guided me home. We walked in silence. I would not apologize for wanting what was right.

We stopped at the iron gate before the house.

"Is it because your wife is so ill?" I asked. "I do honor that. I would not take a man from a wife who needed him." I sighed. "Maybe we are not meant to be."

"We *are* meant to be," he said fiercely. "I feel it in my very marrow."

"I feel it, too."

He opened the gate.

"I am sorry," I said.

"Good night, Frances," he said firmly.

I would not enter. "What can we do?"

"There is nothing more to say tonight."

I saw that he was closed to me. I would not beg.

I forged up the steps, although my heart was aching. Why did he punish me for wanting what was right?

Seventeen

The hummingbird inserted her needle beak into each plum-speckled foxglove trumpet, drank, then darted to the next. Lashing her tongue like a gossamer whip, she collected her drops of nectar, oblivious to me, poised on a wicker chair in Eliza's narrow backyard garden. Perhaps the hummingbird was too hungry to notice me, or maybe she sensed my benevolence. She was impossibly beautiful, a living jewel. At rest, her wings, emerald shields just right for a fairy warrior, cloaked the plump white lozenge of her body. Flying, they were a silvery blur between which she floated, busily acquisitive among Eliza's flowers. I wondered if I could tempt her to linger with a dish of sugar water.

The back door opened. The hummingbird zoomed up and away over the garden wall as the parlor maid, Catherine, approached with the silver tray reserved for callers. I picked up the topmost card, a fancy specimen edged with a fringe of black feathers:

MRS. EDGAR ALLAN POE

A chill went over me.
I discovered underneath a similar, feathered card:

MRS. WILLIAM CLEMM, JR.

"Thank you, Catherine. Are they here?"
"The lady said she would wait for your response."
"Please send her out."
I hastily turned over the paper on my lap desk, and then, on

second thought, buried it beneath some blank pages. I had been working on a poem. A love poem. For Mr. Poe. Oh, I had addressed it to someone else, "To S—," in a move designed to throw off the suspicion of others, but he would know it was for him, I'd make sure of it. I was to take it with me that evening in hopes of presenting it to him after his lecture at the Society Library—our first communication in more than a week. Wrong as it was, I could not let him go, not completely, no matter what I had told him. I was addicted to the thrill of his attention. And now words were all I had to keep him.

Mrs. Poe, pale within a spring bonnet trimmed inside with roses, slipped out onto the porch, her mother trailing like a lumpy shadow.

"You're home! Eddie said you wouldn't have time for me."

I got up. "Of course I do!" I said with clumsy brightness. She had managed to throw me before I'd had a chance to say hello. We kissed the air by one another's bonnets.

"He said never to bother you, that you are too busy."

"I always have time for you," I protested. "I'm glad that you came. Hello, Mrs. Clemm." I caught the smell of old hair when I leaned in to kiss Mrs. Poe's mother. "To what do I owe the pleasure of your visit, ladies?"

"You!" cried Mrs. Poe.

"How nice."

Mrs. Clemm's perpetual worried expression was undimmed within the scorched lappets of her widow's bonnet. "We're sorry if we interrupted your writing."

"We know how writers need to be left alone." Mrs. Poe coughed for a moment, then added, "Eddie chases us off all the time."

"You're not interrupting. Please have a seat." I indicated the wrought iron chairs opposite me on the flagstones.

"What were you writing?" Mrs. Poe asked.

"Nothing much. Would you like some coffee? Let me ring for Catherine." I rang the bell on the table next to me. In spite of the wind rattling the flowers, I was perspiring.

Catherine appeared so quickly that she must have been listening just inside the back door. I asked for coffee to be served.

When she'd gone, Mrs. Poe said, "Are you writing a story?"

"A poem."

She noticed my hesitation. "For children?"

I would not lie if I could help it. "I find that if I talk about things before they are finished that it spoils them."

She stared at me.

There was a rustling in the clump of foxgloves bordering the flag-stones. The kitten, Poe, appeared, stalking a beetle lumbering across the stones.

"Is that the cat you named after my husband?" asked Mrs. Poe.

I felt oddly hesitant to tell her, as if she might hurt it. "My children did, yes. Did you enjoy your walk here?"

Mrs. Poe watched the young cat with an intensity that raised the hair on the back of my neck. "We rode."

"In a hackney," said Mrs. Clemm. "A very good one. Very new. Very nice. It's waiting out front.

The wind, strangely heavy with dampness, plucked at my shawl. "Do you have time for coffee?"

"The driver will wait," said Mrs. Poe. "I paid him enough." She lifted her gaze to me, her black-rimmed eyes bright. "Have you seen Eddie today?"

"Mr. Poe?" I tried to laugh. "No. I haven't."

"He wasn't at his office," said Mrs. Poe. "I just checked."

"I wouldn't know where he would be," I said.

"He comes here," said Mrs. Poe. "I know he does."

A wave of fear swept over me. Caught. "He has come to see Mr. Bartlett on occasion. Did you check Mr. Bartlett's shop in the Astor House? Perhaps he's gone there."

Catherine brought out the coffee. Cups and saucers and napkins were distributed, affording a merciful break in the conversation. I sipped at my drink, wishing that Mrs. Poe and her mother would go.

Mrs. Poe kept her gaze on me. "Will you be going to Eddie's lecture at the Society Library tonight?"

I realized suddenly that I could not—not if she was going to be there. "No."

She waited for me to explain.

"I have a conflict."

"You must go," said Mrs. Poe. "It's in all the papers. There's sure to be a big crowd."

"You must be very proud," I said.

"I am. I always knew Eddie would be something."

"That's true," said Mrs. Clemm. "Back when Eddie was nothing, she thought he was something."

Mrs. Poe set her cup in her saucer, pinky raised. "Oh, I knew. Even when Cousin Neilson said Eddie was no good for me and wanted me to come live with his family, I knew."

The growing wind flapped the long lappets of Mrs. Clemm's bonnet. "My nephew Neilson Poe did take a keen, keen interest in Virginia—I think he would have married her, in time. He's a very rich lawyer in Baltimore, you know. He was all set to take us into his beautiful new home when Eddie found out. And that was the end of that!"

Mrs. Poe tittered. "You should have seen Eddie. He was ridiculous. He said he would kill himself if I went to Neilson."

My blood froze. Mr. Poe had confessed to me that he had been vulnerable at the time of their marriage. He had not mentioned the thought of suicide.

"Really, he didn't have to threaten me," said Mrs. Poe. "He even showed me the bottle of laudanum he was going to drink." She looked for and found my appalled expression. "It was so silly of him. I had my mind set on him all along. I knew what he was, what he'd be. I can see right into him." She leveled a challenging smile at me. "As strange as it sounds, I know exactly what he's thinking."

The banging of the front gate and the cries of children announced Eliza's arrival at home. A few moments later, she swept outside, her plain face bright with curiosity. After a flurry of greetings, Eliza scooped up the kitten and held it to her breast. "Goodness me," she said, stroking its head, "the temperature is dropping. I do believe it's going to storm."

Mrs. Clemm jumped up. "Sissy, we had better get you home. Your lungs will suffer if the weather turns bad."

Mrs. Poe kept a firm hold on her teacup. "Sit down, Mother."

As Mrs. Clemm reluctantly sat, Mrs. Poe said, "Too bad you aren't coming to Eddie's lecture tonight, Mrs. Osgood."

"You aren't?" Eliza looked confused. "I thought—"

"Perhaps," I said, "no one will be able to go if this weather gets worse."

"We won't let weather keep us away," Eliza staunchly told Mrs. Poe. "We have become good friends with your husband."

"Really?"

"He's been a great help to my husband. But he hasn't been by for at least a week—we miss him. Tell him that we have been waiting for him."

Mrs. Poe looked between Eliza and me, then laid her cup and saucer on the table. She pushed her slim form from her chair. "Thank you so much for the coffee."

"Are we leaving?" said Mrs. Clemm, bewildered.

Mrs. Poe put out her hand to me with all the drama of Mrs. Butler on the stage. "I hope to see you tonight, regardless of the weather."

"She's coming," said Eliza. "I promised your husband."

Mrs. Poe studied her a moment. "Good." She turned to me, then nodded toward the stand of foxgloves, waving in the wind. "Those are poisonous, you know. If I were you, I'd watch your little cat."

The weather worsened as the day wore on. The winds picked up strength, snapping branches from trees and sending milk cans clanging down the street. The second girl, Martha, prepared a fire in the downstairs family room around which we huddled as the house popped and groaned in the swiftly gathering cold. The view outside our basement window grew ominously dark until just after five, when the rain thudded down as if dumped from a heavenly basin.

"I suppose we should cancel our plans for tonight," I said, looking out the window. I had been watching the weather closely, hoping it would supply an excuse to cancel our plans to go see Mr. Poe. Had I been mad, thinking that I could slip him a love poem there? And it was clear that Mrs. Poe suspected something. How had I ever thought that we could carry on a relationship? I must let him go now, before we went too far.

Over in her chair by the fire, Eliza was winding a ball of yarn with the help of her daughter, Anna. "It might clear."

I kept my peace, hoping otherwise while taking the precaution of mentally devising excuses, most of which involved my health. When

Mr. Bartlett arrived from his shop soon after, with the legs of his trousers soaked to his knees, I thought I might be safe.

"A pity about the weather." He gave Eliza a kiss, then patted Anna, and swung his boys in the air. "Poe's talk is sure to suffer." He put down little Johnny, who uncharacteristically did not demand more horseplay.

"We must go and support him, Russell," said Eliza. "He's been so interested in your project. We can't let him down because of a little rain."

"You're right. I owe him." He plucked at his wet pant legs. "I'd better go upstairs and change."

When the rain had not let up after a quick supper, I thought they might change their mind, but the same loyal nature that made the Bartletts such good friends to me prevailed in the face of a storm for Mr. Poe. I could not think of a way to back out when they were standing behind him so resolutely.

An hour later, I found myself in a hackney carriage—the weather was too foul for Mr. Bartlett to drive his own open-air trap—and heading down Broadway to Leonard Street. Hail began to thump on the roof.

Eliza looked upward. "Uh-oh."

"The driver had better get the horses out of the storm," said Mr. Bartlett.

"Poor man."

We fell into a silence, picturing the bewhiskered cabman hunched in his cape above us, open to the elements on the driver's seat. But the pelting stopped as quickly as it had begun, and we continued on, the wheels crunching over the hailstones.

Only a few hearty souls were standing in the entrance to the library hall when we arrived. I recognized young orange-haired Mr. Crane, Mr. Poe's assistant at *The Broadway Journal*, and Mr. Willis of the *Mirror*, appearing more than ever like a cricket in a wet black suit. After checking our wraps with a thin German girl of about twelve, we went up the grand staircase to the lecture hall. In it, in the sea of empty chairs, sat the Reverend Mr. Griswold, looking supremely satisfied in rose-colored gloves and a lush burgundy cravat.

He jumped up and loped over when he saw us.

"Poor Poe," he said cheerfully as he neared. "Bad night for a lecture." He grasped my hand, his pink face triumphant. "Mrs. Osgood, I am so pleased to see you."

"Is Mr. Poe's little wife here?" asked Eliza.

"See for yourself." Reverend Griswold spread his arm as if he were lord of the empty hall. A scant handful of ladies and gentlemen were dispersed among the chairs.

Mr. Griswold tightened his hold. "You should have stayed where it is warm and safe, too."

I was easing from his grip when a stout feminine voice rang from the foyer. "Where is everyone?"

Moments later, Miss Fuller appeared, strung with a necklace of brown feathers and the bottom ten inches of her dress dark with rainwater. "Good evening, chums."

Eliza moved first to kiss her. "A fellow survivor."

"I saw a Huron Indian woman give birth outside in the winter. I'm not going to let a little rain stop me from hearing Mr. Poe slice up a batch of poets."

She chatted with the Bartletts and me, with Reverend Griswold hovering over my shoulder like an ominous cloud. When Eliza and her husband moved to find seats among the wooden sea, Miss Fuller pulled me aside.

"How's the article coming along?"

I drew a breath. I had written her a letter but not yet summoned the courage to post it. "I'm not writing it."

She blinked with a flash of a hawk's white lids. "What?"

"Mr. Poe asked me to withdraw it."

Reverend Griswold craned his neck around me to hear. "What's this?"

Miss Fuller ignored him. "I paid you."

"I will give the money back. Or if you like, write about someone else."

Reverend Griswold flared his nostrils with disapproval. "You were writing about Poe?"

"Why did you agree not to do it?" said Miss Fuller. "An article about him would get you noticed." She put her balled fist to her mouth then jerked it away. "Do it anyhow."

"No."

At that moment Mr. Poe entered the lecture hall, a sheaf of notes in his black-gloved hand. He paused as if stunned by the empty room, started up again, then seeing me, stopped.

Miss Fuller beckoned to him.

"Too bad, Poe," said Reverend Griswold when he neared. "Nobody showed."

"It's the weather," said Miss Fuller. "Sorry, Edgar. A rotten shame."

Mr. Willis trotted over with the man in charge of the program. "Poe—so sorry. We can reschedule if you'd like."

"You'll *probably* get more listeners that way," Reverend Griswold said, gleefully doubtful.

Mr. Poe gave me a sidelong look, his dark-rimmed eyes coolly questioning.

"Are you going to speak tonight or not?" Reverend Griswold demanded.

Mr. Poe glanced at him. "No."

Miss Fuller folded her arms, catching the base of her feather necklace. "What's this about your not wanting Mrs. Osgood to write about your family?"

"I changed my mind."

"Tell me that you'll reconsider," she said.

"There are more interesting subjects than myself."

Miss Fuller gave a dry laugh. "Not right now there aren't."

Mr. Willis announced to the smattering of seated attendees that the program had been postponed until a later date. The Bartletts rose and came up the aisle.

"May I escort you home?" Mr. Poe asked me, his face fierce.

I was too ill to heed Reverend Griswold, squinting between us. Mr. Poe had a suspicious wife at home—suspicious and sickly. As much as every fiber of my body yearned for him, it was not meant to be. It was over. "No. Thank you. I'm with the Bartletts."

Mr. Bartlett shook Mr. Poe's hand. "Sorry, old man, about the nasty weather."

His face was grim. "I cannot be angry about what I cannot control."

"Perhaps it is best this way," I said. "Surely you would rather be at home tonight with Mrs. Poe."

"Yes," said Reverend Griswold, watching him. "Surely."

Mr. Poe's anguished glance said otherwise.

"Your wife was so excited about your speech tonight when she stopped by this afternoon," said Eliza. "Did she take unwell? It's probably best that she didn't venture out tonight."

Mr. Poe started. "'Stopped by'? At your home?"

"Didn't she tell you?" said Eliza.

He seemed to fight for mastery over himself. "I have not been home much."

"I'm afraid I only caught her as she was leaving. Fanny can tell you of the particulars."

"She was out looking for you," I said pointedly, "and was concerned that she could not find you."

"I thought that I would have a chance to speak to her tonight," Eliza said. "Such a disappointment, all around. I was anxious to hear what you had to say."

He stared at me, his jaw twitching. He turned rigidly to Eliza. "Thank you, Mrs. Bartlett. You are always so kind to me."

Warmth flowed from her gentle face. "You are a welcome guest in our home at any time."

He made a little bow. "I shall never forget your goodness, madam."

"Nor I yours," she said with a confused frown.

"Sorry to break up your mutual admiration society," said Miss Fuller, "but I've got work to do in the morning. So long, chums."

Mr. Poe took his leave, his good-bye to me more curt than to the others.

Dispirited, I left with the Bartletts. The three of us sat quietly as our carriage bowled up Broadway through the storm-freshened night, with Mr. Bartlett peering out the window, Eliza casting glances his way, and me absorbed by my own overwhelming sorrow. Mr. Poe could only be acknowledging the end of our affair by taking what sounded like his permanent leave of Eliza. What a pitiful ending to our friendship—our splendid attraction had withered on the vine. I had thought that he loved me. I was sure that he did.

The carriage hit a hole in the cobbles. The vehicle lurched forward, tumbling us from our benches.

Mr. Bartlett scrambled up and stuck his head out the window. "Watch it now!" he shouted to the driver. As he helped me regain my seat, I wondered: If Mr. Poe had not been home much for the past week, where had he been?

Eighteen

The next morning, Mary led the children out the front gate and onto the sidewalk.

"Do you have the bouquet for your teacher?" I called from the doorstep. I had cut the flowers that had been beaten down by the storm the previous evening and, except for the foxgloves—their association with Mrs. Poe disturbed me—wrapped them in a damp cloth. Now Ellen held them up as she joined her sister and Anna Bartlett in a pinafore parade down the sidewalk. I withdrew into the house, smiling in spite of the sore spot lingering in my heart.

A shout came from downstairs, followed by a thud and the sound of hurried footsteps. I heard the back door being flung open and banged closed.

The second girl, Martha, struggled up the stairs with a bucket.

"Is everything all right?" I asked.

She put the bucket on the floor with little splash. "A rat, ma'am. We got it."

"That must be a relief."

"Croton bugs is the real devil, ma'am. The cupboards is crawlin' with them. We put saucers of water under the legs of the pie safe to keep 'em from crawlin' up, but it don't do much good."

"A nuisance," I murmured.

"We never seen them before there was pipes, ma'am. Persons was never meant to have water flowin' into their houses from nowhere. 'Tisn't natural."

While most New Yorkers were delighted with the convenience of having water pumped into their homes from the recently completed Croton River Aqueduct, others were uneasy about the idea of their water coming from far away. They believed that the half-inch brown insects that were suddenly infesting kitchens across the city had traveled through the pipes. If "cockroaches," as Croton bugs were known by authorities, could invade homes through water pipes, what other undesirable agents could, too?

Mr. Bartlett appeared upon the stairs, tucking some papers into his coat. Martha snatched up the bucket.

"You should be glad of Croton water," he said, having overheard her. He came down toward us. "You would have had to pump that bucket you have there, instead of just turning a tap in the kitchen."

Martha scooted past him, head down, as if afraid of him.

"Skittish," he said to me.

A knock sounded on the front door. We stepped out of view into the front parlor and waited for Catherine to come up from downstairs to answer.

"Mrs. Bartlett is not taking company," Mr. Bartlett told her. "Little Johnny is ill and she refuses to leave his side."

Catherine returned in a moment, then offered the calling card tray to me. "The visitor is for you, ma'am."

I found myself fearing the sight of black feathers wafting over its silver edge.

But it was a simple card, in black and white:

MARGARET FULLER

"This time I made her stay at the door, ma'am."

"Have fun," Mr. Bartlett told me.

I drew in a breath. "Send her in."

I heard Mr. Bartlett greet her on his way out. Miss Fuller marched into the parlor wearing a large battered black rain calash even though it was sunny outside.

"I've come to talk sense into you," she announced.

"Oh dear."

"I want you to reconsider the Poe story."

I felt the smile recede from my face. Just hearing his name was painful. "I'm not the right one for it."

"I think you are."

"Mr. Poe will not talk to me."

She scowled.

"We've had a falling out."

"Over what?"

When she saw that I wouldn't answer, she said, "Never mind. It's Poe we're talking about. Sooner or later, everyone falls out with him."

I rose. "I need to give you back your money."

She smiled. "Has your husband returned from his commission?"

She knew the answer to that. I wouldn't be living at the Bartletts' if he had.

"Let me go upstairs to fetch my purse." It was cruel even for Samuel to not have at least written to me by now. Could some calamity have befallen him? More likely he had sniffed his way across the ocean after a buxom heiress.

"Wait!"

My gown scraped the floor as I turned around.

"I have another assignment that might interest you."

I paused, knowing it couldn't be good.

She took off her hat. "Phew—that thing smells! I am writing a series of articles on the lunatic asylum on Blackwell's Island. The conditions are deplorable there—I hope to shame the authorities into providing a more wholesome facility. Unfortunately, I had a row with the doctor in charge during my last visit. I'm afraid that he will have me escorted from the premises if I show my face. Hence this hat. I bought it for a penny from a ragpicker." She shook it with a frown. "Not much of a disguise."

She turned her hawk's gaze to me. "It occurs to me that there is another way to skin this cat. How would you like to go and be my ears and eyes?"

"Go? To the lunatic asylum?"

She nodded cheerfully.

"I'd be no good at it."

"Doesn't matter. All you have to do is go in, look around, then come back and record your impressions."

"I have no experience in this kind of reporting."

"I didn't mention it last night, but I saw Mr. Poe there."

I blinked.

She cocked a brow when she saw that she had my attention. "He said he was there while researching a tale he was writing. Something about the inmates taking over the asylum. I couldn't get much out of him about it. He was less communicative than usual, if you can imagine that."

"I have a difficult time imagining anything to do with Mr. Poe."

"Do you?" The corners of her long upper lip curved up knowingly.

When I did not answer, she said, "Go for me, Frances. It'll be easy. You can stick with the story I'd concocted when I was arranging for transport there—that you are concerned for your dear unbalanced mother and wish to know about the facility. But you'll have to dress much more plainly. No one with money would dream of putting a relative in there."

"Such a sorrowful place. I really can't do it."

"Think of the service you'll be doing for your helpless sisters. It's the female patients who are the most vulnerable. Any male member of their family can just dump them there for any reason, no matter the woman's state of mind. Essentially, they are buried alive."

She noted my look of horror with satisfaction. "Never mind. I think I want to do it after all. These are just the kind of heinous conditions that I excel in exposing—I do love stirring a rotten pot. Somehow I will get past that warden. How I shall relish making him squirm for all the harm he has wreaked on those defenseless women." She plunked back on her battered hat as I started toward the stairs to get her money. "But don't say that I didn't give you a chance to make something of yourself, Frances. Too bad. Beneath that pretty society-girl surface, you strike me as the striving sort."

Nineteen

Eliza did not accompany her husband and me to Miss Lynch's conversazione the next evening, a Saturday. She insisted upon staying at home with Johnny, whose cough still lingered although he was getting better. Having lost two children to disease, she was not about to leave his side until he was completely well. But I was free to go, and with my girls in their nightgowns and under Mary's spell as she told an Irish tale, could think of no excuse not to.

Pink-faced and immaculate, Reverend Griswold was hovering in the hall when I entered Miss Lynch's home. "There you are!" he exclaimed to me. "I had hoped you would come."

"You are too kind." I gave my hat and coat to Miss Lynch's maid while looking for an escape.

"Do you know if Poe is coming?" He pretended not to watch for my response.

"I'm afraid not," I said. "I am not privy to his whereabouts."

He smiled slightly.

I heard someone playing the scales on Miss Lynch's piano. "Who is going to play tonight?"

"Shall we go see?" He clamped my hand over his arm, then smoothed it with one of his mauve-clad own. The man had more pairs of gloves than the Hydra had heads.

"An important poet is to come here tonight from Boston," he said as he led me into the parlor. "A very dear friend of mine—Ralph Waldo Emerson. Perhaps you know him, being from Boston yourself?" He grinned when he saw my frown. "Yes, I have been checking up on you. I learned that you are from Boston and that you have also spent some time in London."

"Yes," I said. "With my husband."

He squeezed my hand, trapped on his arm. "I'm sorry to hear that your husband has been absent these past several months."

"Thank you for your concern. You'll be happy to hear that he should be returning soon."

He slid me a sly look. "I hope so, although he seems quite . . . busy . . . in Cincinnati."

My stomach knotted. So that is where Samuel had fetched up. Even I did not know that. Where did Reverend Griswold get his information?

In the front parlor, guests were forming conversational clusters, the closest of which were the companionable trio of Mr. Brady, Mr. Greeley, and Miss Fuller. To my dismay, I saw that the pianist, still intent upon the scales, was none other than the voluminously coifed connoisseur of horror stories, Mr. Morris, the editor of the *Mirror*.

Reluctantly, Reverend Griswold allowed me to pull him toward Mr. Brady's threesome, where I casually turned my back toward Mr. Morris. I was embarrassed that I had not the creative power of late to come up with a frightening story for him. Mr. Poe had consumed my mind.

Mr. Brady broke off his conversation when he saw me. "Ah, Mrs. Osgood. I see that you have your head." He grinned as if waiting for me to laugh.

"I don't get it," said Miss Fuller. "What's the joke?"

Mr. Brady's enlarged eyes brimmed with good will. "Mrs. Osgood had the misfortune of moving when the photographic plate was being exposed. When are you going to come in for me to re-make it?" he asked me.

"When are you going to make my portrait, Mathew?" said Miss Fuller.

I was aware of Mr. Morris looking our way. "I shall take my un-successful sitting as a sign that I'm not meant to be photographed," I said lightly.

"Nonsense," said Mr. Brady, "although it was pretty disconcerting. Here's this beautiful woman," he said to the others, "with a perfect figure, in an exquisite dress—with no head! It would be enough to scare Ichabod Crane. She was every bit as headless as Mr. Irving's horseman."

"Too bad Mr. Irving is in Spain and can't get a glimpse of it," said Reverend Griswold. "Who knows what new story it would inspire? The man's talent is outstanding. Do you realize that he wrote 'Rip Van Winkle' in one night? He told me that a couple of years ago, at lunch."

"Every generation has its own genius," said Mr. Greeley. "Mr. Irving was our father's. I'd say ours is Mr. Poe."

"True," said Mr. Brady. "Masterpieces seem to fall from his fingertips."

Reverend Griswold sniffed. "The only thing to fall from Poe's fingertips is his glass."

"I hope not," said Mr. Greeley. "I hope he's straightened up since his Philadelphia days. I hate to see genius wasted."

Reverend Griswold stroked my hand as if it were a pet rabbit. "You mean, wasted on him."

Just inside the arch to the back parlor, Mr. Morris bent into his playing, his gummy curl bobbing on his forehead.

"That's a Liszt piece, isn't it?" said Mr. Brady.

Mr. Greeley grinned. "Beware of Lisztomania. Cover your ears, Margaret, Mrs. Osgood."

We all had heard of the phenomenon that was sweeping across Europe wherever the pianist, Franz Liszt, played. Just the sight of him was thought to put women into hysterical ecstasy; his performances turned them into wild beasts. Women clawed their way to be near him and for the chance to snatch up anything that he'd touched—handkerchief, gloves, broken piano strings—which they would fashion into jewelry and bind to their bodies as if to possess a piece of the man. His coffee dregs were confiscated and worn in little vials. One woman was even said to wear his discarded cigar butt encased in a locket studded with *F.L.* in diamonds. Most troubling, at least to the men who reported it, was that it was not maids or shopgirls who were succumbing to Liszt fever but respectable wives and daughters, well-trained women who should have known better.

"She need not fear hearing the music," Mr. Brady said over Mr.

Morris's plinking, "it's Liszt himself who is the catalyst for the mania, not his songs. Wish I had *his* charisma."

Reverend Griswold pulled back in affront, his mauve-covered hand still clamped over mine. "You would want women behaving badly in your presence?"

Mr. Brady laughed. "Well, when you put it that way—yes."

A rise in feminine voices drew our attention to the parlor doorway. Mr. Poe entered, elegant and composed, with Miss Lynch upon his arm. Miss Fiske and her friend visiting from Massachusetts, Miss Alcott, made a dash for him with swishing skirts. A hot wave of yearning turned my knees to jelly.

"I think we might have our own Mr. Liszt," said Miss Fuller.

"The man's a drunk," muttered Reverend Griswold.

"Doesn't factor in, old man," said Mr. Greeley. "Liszt could be a dope fiend. Women don't care."

"Women do care," I said.

The group regarded me.

"What is it about Mr. Poe that women find so attractive?" asked Mr. Brady. "If you don't mind my asking."

Miss Fuller toyed with her bone necklace. "He's cool and hard and smart, with a river of passion running underneath. Women just want to dig down to that wild river. Wouldn't you agree, Frances?"

Reverend Griswold rubbed my hand. "You insult Mrs. Osgood by asking her such a thing. Ask some moral reprobate instead."

Miss Fuller let an appraising look come to rest upon him. "Why is it, Rufus, that you find a woman's attraction to a man to be so dirty?"

Beads of perspiration formed on the gray mask of his shaved upper lip. "Well! I needn't tell you! Within a marriage, a woman worshipping her man is a beautiful thing. But if unchecked, and outside of marriage, you get your Lisztomania. You can make light of it all you wish, Miss Fuller, but if left unfettered, female desire can exacerbate a dangerous medical condition that affects both the sufferer and society at large."

"What about men?" said Miss Fuller. "Shouldn't they control themselves as well?"

A tall gentleman cradling a glass of water in his spindly fingers stepped over to our group. His long, withered head, with its fibrous tuft on top, reminded me of a yam.

"Excuse me," he said, "I couldn't help but overhear. I believe wholeheartedly that the *effect* of unchecked desire, by both men and women, will be the downfall of our society, but that it's not the *cause* of it."

"Pray tell," Reverend Griswold said tetchily, "what is it, then?"

"Sylvester Graham," the man said, shaking hands all around. "From Connecticut. And my answer to your question is: greed."

Mr. Greeley laughed. "Isn't that the root of everything?"

Miss Fuller smiled wisely. "Not everything."

"I'm quite serious," said Mr. Graham. "Greed and our food supply. It is greed that compels dairymen to skim every bit of goodness from milk to make other products and then to fill the swill left with chalk and sell it at profit. Greed tempts butchers to grind up the meat of sick cows with well ones and mix it into sausage along with offal and dung to extend the amount of "meat" that they can sell. Greed motivates bakers to use flour devoid of the wheat germ and the nutritious outer husk and to add alum and chlorine to make bread look whiter and to cook faster. Americans are being poisoned, all in the name of profit, producing a weak-minded race of people who are given to lust and desire."

"And so what do you propose, Mr. Graham?" said Mr. Greeley.

"That people follow a vegetarian diet rich in whole wheat grain."

"Oh, I've heard of you," said Miss Fuller. "You want people to eat your crackers—Graham crackers."

"Others call my recipe that," said Mr. Graham, blushing. "They can call them whatever they wish, as long as they eat them along with wholesome fruits and vegetables."

Mr. Poe appeared next to me, as quiet as a lynx. I stared ahead, my pulse racing.

"And if we all eat your crackers," Mr. Poe said quietly, "what then?"

Mr. Graham gave him a nod. "There would be a reduction of desire."

"Is that desirable?" said Mr. Poe.

I dared not look at him. I pulled my hand from Reverend Griswold's grip.

"I should think so!" cried Mr. Graham. "How many people have ruined their lives by giving into their desires?"

"Here, here!" exclaimed Reverend Griswold.

Mr. Poe's voice was that of calm intelligence. "You'll excuse me, but I cannot agree. Many people have improved their lives by following their desires."

"Tell that to Cleopatra and Mark Antony," Mr. Greeley said laconically.

"They killed themselves," said Mr. Brady, "didn't they?"

Mr. Poe seemed not to hear them. "Desire inspires us to be our very best. Wouldn't you say so, Mrs. Osgood?"

I could feel his expectant stare upon me.

Mr. Morris stopped playing and joined our group. "Whatever you all are talking about, you have the most interesting expressions on your faces."

"Poe says desire inspires people to be their best," Miss Fuller said drily.

"Really?" said Mr. Morris. "I thought it just got people in hot water."

Mr. Brady pushed his spectacles up the bridge of his nose. "I'd say that, too, but maybe if desire can be harnessed, it can do a man good. You know that old saying, 'Behind every great man . . .'?"

"Tell me," said Miss Fuller, "who is behind a great woman?" She looked around our circle, then stopped at me. "That's right. No one. She has to get there by herself."

The men in our group frowned between Miss Fuller and me, as if trying to find a hole in her statement.

"Speaking of great women—well, at least very rich ones," said Mr. Greeley, "did you hear that Madame Restell's house caught fire?"

Mr. Brady laughed. "No kidding? Was it licked by a flame from hell?"

"Evidently, it started in a shed behind the house," said Mr. Greeley. "The fire brigade caught it before it spread beyond the kitchen. They say it was the work of an arsonist."

Mr. Poe's jaw went rigid. "How do they know this?" he demanded.

Mr. Greeley drew back, his rubbery face registering surprise at Mr. Poe's vehemence. "The usual sort of evidence, I suppose."

"You needn't leap down his throat, Poe," said Reverend Griswold.

Was Mr. Poe concerned because the fire had occurred so close to his home?

"I would have liked to have seen who came running out of that house," said Mr. Greeley. "It must have been a who's who of mistresses."

"That's not very charitable, Horace," said Miss Fuller.

"Before I forget." Mr. Poe turned to me abruptly. "My wife has asked you to join us on a picnic tomorrow."

I blinked away my look of disbelief. What good could come of such an invitation? Why did he not discourage her?

"She's very fond of you, you know," said Mr. Poe. He turned to address the group. "I'd like to invite everyone else here as well. We're going to Turtle Bay for a swim."

"A swim? There was ice on that river six weeks ago," said Mr. Brady. "No thanks."

"Turtle Bay is too close to home," said Mr. Greeley. "I avoid the wife and Castle Doleful whenever I can. If you want to picnic in the Astor House courtyard, I'm in."

"Count me out, too, Edgar," said Miss Fuller. "After I write up my visit to Blackwell's Island, I'm interviewing some women who have formed a league whose mission is to reform housemaids. Apparently, they think the girls are too prone to run away. Seems to me they could reform the girls more quickly if their husbands didn't keep pestering them."

"Margaret," said Mr. Brady, "you are a pistol."

The men laughed, save Mr. Poe, and then others declined his invitation, although Mr. Greeley offered the use of the horse and the wagonette he kept for the country. The topic of the fire in Madame Restell's house had been effectively abandoned.

"Reverend Griswold," said Mr. Poe, "I have not heard from you. Would you like to go?"

Reverend Griswold's lips curled in a sneer. "Only to see the cold water shock that smile off your face."

Mr. Poe nodded as if taking a compliment. "Excellent. You must come and give me a report. Will you come, then, Mrs. Osgood?"

Everyone's gaze was upon me. To refuse would raise suspicion.

And as mad and painful as spending a day with both Mr. and Mrs. Poe would be, in truth, I longed to be near him. I would take even the smallest piece of him, no matter how dear the cost.

"It sounds lovely. Thanks."

"Good. Please bring your children. We shall be one big happy family."

Twenty

Vinnie watched from our open bedroom window. "They're here!"

I came away from the mirror, before which I had been tucking hairpins into my knot. Pinching color into my cheeks, I looked down upon the street where Mrs. Poe, in a black straw hat, and her mother, in her usual white widow's bonnet, sat in the wagonette Mr. Greeley had loaned us. Across from them cringed Reverend Griswold, his air one of disgust beneath the jaunty straw boater perched on his head. I could hear Mrs. Clemm lobbing animated chatter in his direction.

Mrs. Poe tilted back to look up.

I pulled away from the window. "Girls, are you ready?"

Downstairs, Mr. Poe greeted us in the hall, looking dangerously handsome with his tousled hair and open collar. My urge to swoon like a schoolgirl was suppressed by the knowledge that his wife waited on the other side of the door.

"Mamma said we couldn't take Poe," Vinnie announced.

I knelt to tie her hat. "The cat," I explained to him.

"It's a girl." She grinned at him shyly. I was not the only one to thirst for male attention in her father's absence.

Mr. Poe smiled at her with genuine affection. "Your mother is right. You shouldn't take Miss Poe. Cats don't like water."

"We do," said Vinnie.

"That's good," said Mr. Poe. "Are you going to swim today?"

"Absolutely not," I answered for them. "It's too cold and danger-ous for that." I loosened Ellen's hat—she had tied it on too tightly by herself—then put on my gloves. "We can watch Mr. Poe give it a try and be on hand to throw him a lifeline when he succumbs to the cold."

"I'll have your mother know that I was a champion swimmer when I was a boy. I swam six miles upstream in the James River against strong tides, a record that is still unbroken." He took from my hands the hamper that Bridget had packed for us.

"I want to see you swim!" Vinnie exclaimed.

"I'm afraid that Mr. Poe's record will not be of much use to him today. The only record we are going to compete for today is in sandwich eating. But it's nice to know that we have a champion among us, isn't it, Ellen?"

Ellen crossed her arms and looked away, as if responding would show disloyalty to her father.

Mr. Bartlett came upstairs from the family room with his hand extended. "Mr. Poe. Thanks for the invitation to join your picnic. Sorry we had to decline."

"Next time," said Mr. Poe.

Outside, Reverend Griswold's well-groomed rosy face lit up under his boater as I approached the wagonette. "Sit next to me!" He patted the leather seat.

I did so as Mrs. Poe and her mother exclaimed about my dress and hat, and then about my daughters' dresses and hats. Mrs. Clemm begged for the girls to sit on her lap. Only Vinnie obliged, hesitantly. With Ellen safely tucked under my arm, and the hampers and baskets under our feet, Mr. Poe swung up into the driver's seat, took the reins, and chirruped the sturdy roan. The wagonette jolted toward Broadway.

Over the clashing of hooves against cobblestones, I asked Mrs. Poe, "How are you feeling today?"

She stared at me from within her straw bonnet. "Why do you keep asking me that?"

Ellen looked up at me. I sat back, chastened.

After a few blocks we had left the settled part of the city and were soon out on the new stretch of Third Avenue that had been macadamized. The wide dirt banks that lined both sides of the graveled road drew young men from all over town who were eager to test the speed of their horses, the superiority of their equipment, and the mettle of their nerves. Plodding among the brightly painted phaetons and tilburies pulled by glossy teams, Mr. Greeley's workaday wagonette and mare stood out like a goose among swans.

Mr. Poe eased our little wagon up a hillock off the road, joining a cluster of carriages and riders overlooking the tracks.

"What is it, Eddie?" asked Mrs. Poe.

He nodded to the two young men drawing their fancy two-wheeled gigs parallel on the shoulders of the road down below, preparing for a race. By the cut of their clothes—a dandy's country suit of tweed and the Irishman's favored red shirt and black flaring trousers—it was obvious the drivers were of two different classes.

"That Hibernian ruffian hasn't a chance," said Reverend Griswold, "even if he did sink every penny he owned into his horse. A shame—some poor child is probably going hungry because her papa or brother wants to show off."

Mr. Poe turned around in his seat. "Do you care to place a bet?"

Reverend Griswold coughed with incredulousness. "On these two? Only if I can take the gentleman."

"Agreed," Mr. Poe said calmly. "What should our wager be?"

Reverend Griswold groped for my hand. "The winner gets the privilege of rowing Mrs. Osgood around the cove."

I rested my hands on Ellen's shoulders. "That's hardly a prize."

"Bet money," said Mrs. Poe, coughing.

Mr. Poe did not look at his wife. "I accept Reverend Griswold's terms." And no sooner than they'd shaken, than did the racers start off below.

Hooves pounded the dirt track. Whips cracked. Mrs. Clemm covered Vinnie's ears as shouts went up from the occupants of the neighboring carriages.

The horses plunged down the track in a dead heat. I hugged Ellen to me, bracing for an accident.

Reverend Griswold sprang up. "He's winning! He's winning!"

Suddenly, the dandy's horse jerked as if stung in the haunches. When the gig snapped into the macadam in a spray of gravel, the Irishman lunged ahead. His horse put on distance before the dandy could recover. His pals leaped for joy as he streaked past the finish mark.

Reverend Griswold plopped down on his seat. "Foul! Obviously there was some sort of foul! Mrs. Osgood, I hope you'll not let him row you based on this travesty."

Mr. Poe coolly gathered the reins. "I recall nothing about basing our terms on the fairness of the play, just which driver was the winner."

"You should have betted money," said Mrs. Poe.

"As my wife knows, I always bet on the underdog."

"Even if the underdog is ruthless and unprincipled?" Reverend Griswold demanded.

"The principled man is merely one whose ancestors were ruthlessly *un*principled, affording him the option of acting upon fine sentiments."

"You speak like a ruffian, sir."

Mr. Poe smiled. "No, just one who lacks a sufficient amount of ruthless ancestors." He turned back around and shook the reins.

I was aware of Mrs. Poe watching me as our equipage crunched down the gravel track. I made a show of gazing intently at the view. Here and there in the distance, farmhouses perched on rocky outcrops above the road, left high and dry when the road had been cut through their land. Connected to the road by long zigzagging flights of steps, they looked like so many lighthouses isolated on cliffs.

"My, the countryside looks odd out here," said Mrs. Clemm.

"Someday everything will be the same level as this road," Reverend Griswold said. "All these farmhouses will be gone. There will be new homes—bigger, better ones."

Noting Vinnie's worried expression, I said, "Not any time soon, though."

"Oh, don't count on that," said Reverend Griswold. "The world around us is changing and there's nothing we can do about it. If you don't believe me, come this way in a year from now. And it's not just the land that is changing but you and I. Two years from now, and you won't even recognize yourself, mark my words."

Vinnie's soft brow buckled.

"Oh, look at the cows!" I said. We had come to a field at an intersection of Third Avenue with the Old Eastern Post Road. Mr. Poe turned off the macadam onto the dirt road.

The girls got on their knees to look as we rambled by the pasture.

"Aren't they pretty?" I said. "So light brown and big-eyed, they look like deer."

"Guernsey," said Reverend Griswold. "They're called Guernsey cows. I understand that they give excellent milk."

"Then those are the lucky cows," said Mrs. Poe.

Vinnie looked up at her hopefully. "Like four-leaf clovers?"

Mrs. Poe choked back a cough. "No, they don't bring you luck, it's they who are the lucky ones. They are the kind of cows that won't be eaten, at least not until they no longer give milk."

A cow near the road stopped cropping to raise its doe eyes to us.

"Hello," Mrs. Poe sang out. "We won't eat you . . . yet."

"We eat cows?" said Vinnie asked her.

I beckoned for Vinnie to come sit on my lap. "We are city people," I explained to the others as I cradled her in my arms. "We haven't thought much about how things get on our plates."

Mrs. Poe plucked at the top of her glove. "You ought to. You ought to be aware that a creature gave up its life for you."

"Virginia!" exclaimed Mrs. Clemm.

Mrs. Poe smiled sweetly. "I'm sorry, but they do die for you, try to ignore it all you want. We are all murderers."

"You must stop this right now," said Reverend Griswold. "Think of the children."

Mrs. Poe peeled back her glove, revealing a large broken blister surrounded by angry flesh on the meat of her thumb—a bad burn. She saw me looking.

"Cooking accident," she said.

Her mother drew in a shuddering breath.

Suddenly, Reverend Griswold called, "Slow down!"

Steadying himself against the rail of the wagonette, he shielded his eyes as if to search for something. "I know where we are. There! There's the stream. And there—there's the bridge!"

We looked at the stream winding its way through the fields and rocks before it disappeared under the bridge just ahead.

"This is it! There's the marker for where Fiftieth Street will come through. We are at Kissing Bridge Number Two! Stop! Stop!"

Mr. Poe halted our horse upon the low stone bridge. Wincing, Mrs. Poe rolled her glove back over her wound.

"I was just reading about the famous kissing bridges of old New York," said Reverend Griswold. "There are three of them in all, very famous, very old. In days of yore, it was the custom for a gentleman to kiss the woman in his care when they came upon the bridge."

Mrs. Poe raised her childlike face toward her husband. "Then you had better kiss me, Eddie."

Mr. Poe turned in his seat. "What if a gentleman has more than one woman in his care?"

Fire crept into my face.

"You cannot kiss everyone!" sputtered Reverend Griswold.

Mr. Poe frowned slightly. "You would have me ignore my aunt?"

"Oh!" Reverend Griswold huffed. "Oh!"

Blinking rapidly as the Poe women stood up to receive their kisses, the reverend turned to me. "Madam?"

I put out my knuckles.

His lips were removed from my glove by the jerk of the cart setting off. I put my arm back around Vinnie, wondering again how I had come to be part of such a strange group.

We trundled down the road until at last, sparkling before us in the sun, churned the broad expanse of the East River. Stout steamboats plowed the dark waters, belching smoke into the bright blue sky. To the left was the southern tip of Blackwell's Island, whose thick woods hid the penitentiary and lunatic asylum lurking within. Strange that Miss Fuller had seen Mr. Poe there. I wondered if he had finished his story about it.

"Pretty," said Vinnie.

"It is a pretty view," said Mrs. Poe. "Eddie, I would like a house here."

"First I must make the money."

"Greeley's house is just down the way," said Reverend Griswold. "Very big house, very big. He had me for lunch there one day."

"You look in one piece just yet," said Mr. Poe.

Reverend Griswold squinted in confusion as Mr. Poe tied the horse to a tree, then began to help down the ladies.

"Oh, I get it," said Reverend Griswold. "Not terribly amusing."

Mrs. Poe chose a spot under a maple tree and proceeded to empty the hamper I had brought. "I'm starved."

Reverend Griswold dug into his basket and produced a bottle of wine. "Who's thirsty? Poe, I bet you are."

"Thank you," said Mr. Poe, unruffled, "but I've brought a flask of water."

The wind nipped at skirts and hat strings as we ate a picnic of bread, cheese, and pickles, the flavors enhanced by the fresh river breeze. With no other takers for his bottle of wine, Reverend Griswold consumed it all. He then played Red Rover with the girls, Mr. Poe, and me with a ferociousness that ended the game early, and fell asleep under a bush in the middle of hide-and-seek.

My girls, sensing that he was off, left him alone. They centered their energy upon Mr. Poe as they would have done upon their father, if he had been there. Long after Mrs. Clemm retired to her knitting and Mrs. Poe to making a necklace with the violets that winked in the blowing grass, they insisted that he keep playing. Even Ellen chortled with delight when he staggered around pretending that he couldn't find them.

At last he tagged Vinnie, crouching behind a rock on the bluff overlooking the river. "It."

She popped up, laughing. "You better hide good or I'll find you!"

She went to the rock we had designated as "home," squeezed her eyes shut, and began counting aloud. I tiptoed off in the opposite direction of where I'd last hid. Feeling the frisson that comes with the thrill of potential discovery, even in a silly game, I climbed a hillock, then knelt behind a stand of poplars. I kept an eye on Vinnie—she was too close to the river for my comfort.

A touch on the shoulder startled me.

"Sorry." Mr. Poe crouched next to me.

Joy surged through my veins. I quickly staunched it. "You have quite a way of appearing mysteriously."

"Ninety-nine," Vinnie counted in the distance, "one hundred! Ready or not, here I come."

I watched Vinnie heading toward the rocks behind which I'd just hid. "She's going in the wrong direction. I should stop her before she gets too far."

"Her sister is over there. She'll do it."

"It seems, Mr. Poe, that another of your talents is knowing where everyone is."

He smiled, disarming me with maddening effectiveness.

"You were kind to invite Reverend Griswold today," I said. "He seems to be the lonely sort, in spite of the many friends he claims to have."

"He makes his own luck."

"Well, he's certainly feeling no pain now." I glanced toward where the reverend was laying under the bush.

Mr. Poe laid a finger on the back of my gloved hand. My sights trailed to it.

His voice was rich with emotion. "I want you to know that you have changed me."

The force of his gaze made me look into his eyes.

"I have not had a drink since I have met you."

He did not remove his touch. All my senses converged upon that single spot. "Your wife told me that."

"She tells you much."

"Yes. She does."

"Yet there is so much you don't know." He slid his fingers around mine then, gently, pressed. The sensation seeped down to my roots.

I watched Vinnie search through the cascading limbs of a weeping willow.

He held on to my hand. "What troubles you? It goes further than our rift the other night."

I sighed as I looked into his eyes, urgent with emotion. "It's not a rift we have had," I said softly, "but a break. A final and clean break. I think your wife suspects us."

He kept his hold, gazing intently into my soul.

"This is wrong," I murmured.

"Yet you know that it's right, Frances. We *must* be together. We have to be. I know that you feel this way, too."

"How?" I sighed deeply. "I don't see how we are to manage it."

"I am considering a solution." His gaze went to Blackwell's Island. He was drawing in a breath as if to speak when a silvery voice arose.

"Eddie?"

He slipped his fingers from mine.

Mrs. Poe was trudging up the hill, holding up her skirts. "Eddie? What are you doing?"

"Hiding, obviously," said Mr. Poe. We stood up.

She looked at us, coughing into her gloved fist. "I thought you were going to take Mrs. Osgood on a boat ride."

"You really don't need to," I said. "It was a silly bet."

"He needs to. He should do what he said he was going to do. Take her out, Eddie."

"No," Mr. Poe said flatly.

Vinnie came running up. "There you are!" She hit Mr. Poe's arm. "It!"

"Indeed, I am."

"Go hide, Eddie," said Mrs. Poe.

Vinnie bent over, panting. "Mr. Poe, can we go out in the boat now?"

He did not look at his wife, who was frowning at him with those dark-rimmed eyes so like his own. "You must ask your mother."

"Please, Mamma?" Vinnie begged. "We can all go! Please. Please?"

By then, Ellen had joined us. It was her beseeching look—from she who asked so little of me—that tipped the scales.

"I suppose there can be no harm in it if we stay in the cove. Mrs. Poe, will you be coming, too?"

"Oh, I wouldn't miss it."

We walked down to the water slowly to accommodate Mrs. Poe, with the girls traipsing in front of us. Mrs. Clemm joined us along the way. Mrs. Poe then rested on a rock with her mother until the girls and Mr. Poe had righted the boat and dragged it to the water. We climbed in and took our seats: Mr. Poe in the back of the boat, Mrs. Clemm, Mrs. Poe, and I squeezed on the middle bench, and the girls in the bow.

The rhythmic splash of the oars and the sun on my back did much to soothe me in spite of the strange company. The girls dragged their hands in the water, chatting between themselves, as I admired the stately trees and ancient rambling houses that stood guard on the magnificent cliffs of the bay. With a pang, I thought how even then, men with pickaxes were digging their way toward the shore. They would not stop until the trees and mansions and cliffs were gone.

"Oh!" Mrs. Poe exclaimed. "My hat flew off."

"Oh dear!" cried Mrs. Clemm.

I saw where Ellen pointed to the rapidly flowing water. Mrs. Poe's straw hat scudded along the surface next to me, its trajectory slowing as it absorbed water.

"Get it, Mamma!" Vinnie cried.

Mr. Poe reached with an oar, and fishing carefully, hooked the hat. He brought it, dripping, toward me.

I leaned out to retrieve it. Just then the boat began to rock violently in the wake of a passing steamship. I pulled back, teetering. I had almost regained my balance when what felt like a push to my hip toppled over me. I pitched into the river.

Dirty frigid water whooshed in my ears and drove daggers up my nose. I fought against the murky cold, my dress tangling around my legs like tentacles, dragging me down. I felt the pressure of someone diving in next to me as I thrashed toward the cloudy brown light. My head broke the surface.

Through the water streaming down my face I could see Mrs. Poe holding out an oar. I strained for it with all my might.

A hard blow struck my skull. Blue light burst in my head. My ears roared as I sank down, down, down.

Hands pushed me upward. The watery bubble split over my head as I broke the membrane between water and air.

An arm gripped me around my ribs. I blinked away water to see Mr. Poe, hauling me to the boat. He grabbed the rim and tipped my chin above water. "Breathe! Breathe!"

I clawed the side of the boat and, finding purchase, looked up wildly.

Mrs. Poe gazed down serenely. "You really must be careful, Frances. You'll catch your death in that water."

"How are you feeling now?" asked Eliza.

I drew the quilt around my shoulders and wriggled my toes against the hot water bottle that she'd ordered from the kitchen the moment she saw Mr. Poe carrying me into the house. Efficient nurse that she was, she had me stripped, swaddled, and tucked in bed in a thrice, with a bowl of broth steaming on the nightstand. Still, I was shivering what must have been an hour later. My hair was yet damp.

Eliza stood over me with another quilt. "How awful to fall into the river. It stinks so of fish."

"I can still smell it."

"Well"—she snapped the blanket over me—"let's just pray that's the worst of it. If you were unlucky enough to fall into the river, at least you were lucky in that Mr. Poe is an excellent swimmer."

Downstairs, I could hear the girls playing with the Bartlett children. Thank God I had fallen in and not them. With a chill, I could still see Mr. Poe hastily rowing us to shore and then our party jamming haphazardly into the wagonnette. Mr. Poe would not speak but flashed anguished looks over his shoulder as he urged our galloping animal ever faster. As Reverend Griswold clutched me to his chest, his wine-infused breath flooding over me as the vehicle bounced over the rutted roads, it was the worried affection in Mr. Poe's eyes that had kept me calm. I had clung to it as Mrs. Poe watched us, coughing incessantly, with the curiosity of a child.

Now I voiced a thought that had been troubling me since the accident.

"I'm not sure that I fell."

Eliza laughed. "You came home very wet for not falling."

"Eliza, I'm serious."

She looked up from tucking the quilt around my feet.

"I have this terrible feeling that I was pushed."

"Pushed?" She sat down on the wooden chair by my bed. "By who?"

"Mrs. Poe."

"Mrs. Poe? Little Mrs. Poe? She couldn't hurt a flea."

I shook my head. "I had the distinct sensation of being shoved often. I'd leaned over to get her hat."

"Could it have been one of your girls, trying to see over you? Children sometimes have no sense."

"They were sitting in the front of the boat." I paused, replaying the incident in my head. "At least, I think they were still sitting up there."

"Maybe Mrs. Poe was trying to catch you *from falling*, and that is what you felt."

I sighed. "That's possible. We were rocking in the wake of a steamboat. Maybe I am imagining the push. It's possible that I fell overboard on my own. It all happened so quickly."

She nodded. "You might actually owe her a thank you. For trying to save you."

I swallowed, not wanting to remember. "That's not all."

She picked up my empty broth cup. "What?"

"When I was down in the water, I think—" I stopped, knowing how outrageous I was going to sound. "I think she hit me with an oar."

Eliza's plain good features formed the picture of disbelief. "Surely that was an accident. Was she trying to offer the oar as a lifeline? She doesn't look very strong—maybe she dropped it and hit you inadvertently."

The image of Mrs. Poe leaning over the water, her pretty face terrible with hatred, flashed through my mind. "It's just that her expression—" I broke off. Who would believe me? I could hardly believe it myself.

"Really, Fanny, in all the confusion, how can you know what you saw? Why would she try to hurt you?"

I pulled the quilt closer. "You're right."

"You really don't want to believe something like this if it's not true," said Eliza. "Could you ask the children what they saw?"

"I hate to scare them."

She stood with a rustle of skirts. "Well, the important thing is that you are all right."

"Yes," I said, far from convinced. "That's true."

The next morning, I stationed myself at my desk in the front parlor, ready to work. What a difference a night made. Except for the slight sore throat with which I'd awakened, I felt no worse for the wear from my dunking. In fact, I was exhilarated. It was as if I'd had come out victorious from a match with a formidable foe. I had not lost Mr. Poe—far from it. I didn't know how we were to be together, but he wanted me and I wanted him. We were not done. Not at all. He said he was considering a solution. That there seemed to be none did not stop my soul from rejoicing. Oh, dear, dear Edgar—I could still feel the intensity of your gaze when you had clasped my hand as we hid. I could still hear the urgency in your voice when you said that you had changed for me. I could still see the vehemence of your concern when you'd rushed me home from the river, as if you could not live if anything should ever happen to me. Never had Samuel cherished me so much, not even in the beginning. Now, surging with happiness, I felt I could do anything, even write a frightful tale for Mr. Morris. I was charged with the power of love.

The ring of the doorbell jarred me from my jubilation. I peered out the window. Mrs. Poe and her mother were standing on the stoop.

Instinctively, I ducked, then felt like child. I eased back upright. They waved at me as Catherine answered the door.

Trapped.

I waited for Catherine to bring in the silver calling card tray, then took up their cards, so lavishly feathered. The stationer must have had a good chuckle when he sold them these.

I drew a deep breath. "Please show them in."

Mrs. Poe flitted into the room. "Bonjour! Bonjour!" she wheezed between little coughs.

Mrs. Clemm tottered in behind her. "I hope we aren't intruding. How are you feeling, dear?"

So they had come on a sick visit, then. Perhaps they would leave more quickly if I played the part. "Not like myself—thank you for asking. I do believe I must go back to bed." That evening.

"But you were writing," said Mrs. Poe. "I saw you." With eyes so disturbingly like her husband's, she watched me squirm. "Eddie says that etiquette demands that you return my call before I came here again, but I couldn't wait. I'm here on a very special mission."

My insides shrank with dread. "Oh?"

"We are looking for a new home!"

My heart dropped. Mr. Poe could not be leaving. "In the city?"

"Where else? We had to get out of our part of town." She scowled. "The houses are so old."

"Yes," I said, "I suppose they're dangerous. I hear one caught fire near your home."

She stared at me, strangely defiant. "Where?"

Her mother tugged at the lappets of her widow's bonnet, for once keeping her silence.

It didn't seem possible that they would not have heard the

commotion two doors down when Madame Restell's home burned. The bellows of the fire chief directing his crew, the chug of the engine as the men pumped in ferocious teams, and the crash of breaking glass and chopping axes would have been unmistakable.

"At least it wasn't in winter," I said to fill the frigid pause. "I once saw a blaze in January where the water glazed the house with icicles, then froze in the firemen's hoses. The house burned to the ground and took the neighboring homes with it."

She did not seem to hear me. "Guess what."

We were playing children's games now? Suddenly, I was deathly weary.

"There is a house on this very street that we are considering."

I absorbed the jolt.

"We'd be neighbors!" cried Mrs. Clemm as her daughter coughed. "Can you imagine?"

"No!"

Mrs. Poe lifted her babyishly rounded chin in self-importance. "Would you recommend the neighborhood to us? We want the very best."

Almost every millionaire in town lived within a few blocks. "Washington Square seems to be pleasant enough."

"We can afford the best, you know. Eddie is growing more famous by the day. He's been working on a scary story that's his finest yet."

"About the lunatic asylum?"

Mrs. Poe stiffened. "What do you mean?"

"Perhaps I am mistaken," I said. "I thought I heard— Please excuse me. I must be confused."

The tall clock in the corner ticked unconcernedly. Mrs. Poe's sudden stillness seemed to suck the air out of the room.

"I must be thinking of someone else," I said.

"She knows a lot of writers, Virginia," said Mrs. Clemm. "Being one herself."

"Shhh! Mother!"

I could feel Mrs. Poe's stare boring into me.

"What is his new story about?" I asked gingerly.

She would not look away. "Mesmerism. About a dead man kept alive by mesmerism."

"Doesn't that sound good?" cried Mrs. Clemm.

Mrs. Poe ignored her. "There's nothing in it about a lunatic asylum. I read every word that he writes and I would know."

"I misspoke," I said. "I do apologize."

"Sissy's his first reader," said Mrs. Clemm. "Always has been. Eddie counts on her."

"You must be so pleased with how well his work is being received, then," I said. Dear God in heaven, why did she keep staring?

"Do you know where Eddie is going this afternoon?" she asked.

I braced for another blow. "No."

She smiled. "Delmonico's restaurant. With Miss Fuller. *She's* going to write the article about us."

I felt the relief one does when a carriage accident has just been narrowly avoided. Glad for a safe subject, and to no longer have a part in the article, I found myself blathering on about Delmonico's food, its decor, even its grand entranceway with the pillars that had come all the way from Pompeii.

"What's Pom Pay?" asked Mrs. Poe.

"A city in ancient Rome. It was destroyed when a volcano erupted."

"Blown to pieces?"

"Not exactly. Volcanic gases snuffed it out. Then ash came down and preserved everything exactly the way it was—the food on the table, dogs on the chain, people on the street, everything—until it was discovered in the last century. Engineers have unearthed much, including people caught in the middle of what they were doing when the tragedy struck."

"Mercy!" cried Mrs. Clemm.

Mrs. Poe stood. "I wonder what people would be caught doing if a volcano erupted in New York?"

Mrs. Clemm clucked as she arose next to her. "Virginia, what an awful thought! You and Eddie are two peas in a pod."

I accompanied Mrs. Poe to the parlor room door. She stopped just short of it.

"Do you think, Mrs. Osgood, people would behave differently if they knew that they could be captured in the act?"

She watched my face as I made myself smile. "Fortunately, there are no volcanoes anywhere near here."

"Thank goodness!" bleated Mrs. Clemm.

"Yes," said Mrs. Poe. "Thank goodness."

She left in a swish of ribbons, her mother trundling after her. I leaned against the door.

The second girl, Martha, came up the stairs with a brush and ash pan to clean out the fireplaces. She halted when she saw me. "Are you well, ma'am?"

I pushed away from the door. "Of course. Thank you."

I went back to my desk, picked up my pen, looked at the blank paper, then put it down again. Every last drop of my creativity had evaporated.

Twenty-one

Mid-May in New York: the season for foolishness. We were all of us giddy with having the fangs of winter released completely from our hides. On Saturdays, crowds gathered to view the militias drilling in Washington Square. It took surprisingly little to encourage men who wore staid business black during the week to parade in red sashes, white pants, and plumed patent-leather hats. On Sundays, families turned out into the countryside, an easy walk from my part of town. My own group liked to head up Broadway to note the fine new homes springing up around Union Square. We then made our way eastward down the recently opened Seventeenth Street, chasing disgruntled pigs and indignant geese down the dirt road before us. Passing under the shanties teetering on outcrops not yet leveled by the street workers' picks, we then came to the meadows that were once part of a Dutchman's farm, where we could spread our blankets among the other picnickers'. Who would imagine, while the crickets strummed and rabbits bolted from their hiding holes and the sweet grassy smell of crushed clover permeated the air, that neither outcrop nor meadow would exist the following spring?

On such a Sunday afternoon, a gentleman in goggles was preparing a hot-air balloon for a flight, his limp apparatus spread across our field. I was relaxing on a rug with the Bartletts and our children, watching the gas ripple through the balloon like a pulse, when Miss Fuller drove up in her little gig. This day she was up to her chin in a tight collar of white beads. I wondered which tribe wore this uncomfortable style.

She nodded to the balloonist. "Where's he going?"

"We don't know," Eliza called back cheerfully. She grinned at her boys, galloping around our rug on hobby horses, with Mary futilely trying to hush them. "We don't much care."

Miss Fuller frowned at me. "Your Poe would say it was going across the Atlantic. I can't believe people actually swallowed his balloon hoax in *The Sun* last year. As if a 'flying machine' could ever cross the ocean, let alone in three days' time."

My Poe? My hackles tingled with guilty fear. Mindful of our circumstances, I had limited my contact with Mr. Poe in the past several weeks, as excruciating as that was to do. I had not received him at the Bartletts' nor had I gone to any of his lectures or to those that he might attend. I had avoided Miss Lynch's conversaziones. I had curtailed my promenades down Broadway. Only one type of communication had I allowed between us: poems. Sent to him to be published under false names in his *Broadway Journal*.

I knew that I shouldn't be doing it. Yes, they were only words, but I am a poet. Words are my currency. I know their value. How much more passionate I could be in poems, how terribly much more bold, than I could ever be in civil conversation. All Mr. Poe had to do was to read between the lines. Oh, I knew full well what my poetry would unleash in him. He was a poet, too. I knew just what I was doing when I begged him in "Love's Reply": *Write from your heart* to me.

He did. In spades. He wrote back calling me "beloved," his "bright dear-eye," and his "one bright island" in a tumultuous sea. Although the poems were addressed to "Kate Carol" or "F—" or other such, I knew who they were meant for. Each week when a new issue of the *Journal* came out, my hands shook as I searched through the pages for his responses. I would greedily read his poems to me, then hold the magazine to my breast as if it were the man himself. Because, in a most true way, it was.

"Poe wrote that hoax last year, wasn't it?" Mr. Bartlett helped himself to a dish of the first of the season's strawberries. "Upset a lot of people."

"Edgar is a master at stepping over the line between reality and fantasy," said Miss Fuller. "What made people angry is that they believed him, and then they felt stupid afterward for having been duped. Nobody likes to be tricked."

At that moment a band marched up Seventeenth Street, preceded by a frenzied goose flapping to get out of its way. The blaringly out-of-tune tootling of the trumpets and tubas drew our instant attention to a dapple-gray horse plumed like a militiaman and the red-painted barred wagon that it pulled. In the wagon, under a banner reading, VISIT BARNUM'S MUSEUM, paced a brawny tattered creature.

"A lion!" Vinnie cried.

"Barnum," said Mr. Bartlett. "Is there anywhere he isn't? If explorers ever penetrate the heart of Africa, they might expect to find him there."

"Too late. He's already been," said Miss Fuller, "and has robbed more than a few noble beasts of their freedom. It's unconscionable how he exploits his fellow man. That poor little Stratton boy, being paraded around Europe as General Tom Thumb. In spite of his fine clothes, the child is no better off than this poor beast."

"Can we go see the lion?" Eliza's older boy begged. The other children added a chorus of pleases.

"Go with them," Eliza told her husband. "Mary will help you."

"Not unless you go." He pulled Eliza up by the hand. "The music frightens me more than the lion."

"Do you want to come?" Eliza asked Vinnie and Ellen.

They didn't need to be asked twice.

When I got up to join them, Miss Fuller patted the seat next to her in her trap. "Frances, care to join me for a moment?"

To say no would be rude. Reluctantly, I climbed up.

"I've enjoyed your poems in *The Broadway Journal*," she said as I settled in.

I glanced at her. "Thank you," I said uneasily.

"Edgar and you have quite a correspondence going. I take it you are 'Kate Carol.' It is you who is his 'bright dear eye' with 'the bright idea,' yes?"

To deny it was me would shine the light of suspicion on our relationship. "It's silly, isn't it?"

"Is it?"

"Yes," I said. "Very. I think it's the season. We've all gone silly."

She grunted.

I pretended to watch the crowd gathering around the lion. The balloonist, his device taking shape behind him, gaped as if stunned that someone had stolen his thunder.

"I talked to Mrs. Poe today."

I felt a stab of guilt. "Oh? How is she? I heard that they were moving."

"I did, too. So I hunted them up. They live in a boardinghouse on East Broadway. With seven other boarders."

She let me digest that. I tried to keep my voice level. "That's strange. They were looking at a house on Amity Street. I wonder what happened."

"Oh, she mentioned that house. She said something about it not being ready for them in time. But believe me, no one who could afford a house on Amity would spend five minutes living in that hovel, even if they were planning to move."

I kept my expression pleasant. "So what are you saying?"

"That Poe is poor."

"I don't understand your need to tell me this. You, of all people, who champions the less advantaged in your articles about the living conditions in tenements and the abuse of those in insane asylums and prisons."

"It's not Edgar's poverty that concerns me, it is what his poverty has made him." She toyed with her whip. "He is not what he seems, Frances."

The driver of the Barnum's wagon had gotten down and was goading the lion with a poker.

I turned to Miss Fuller. "Which is what?"

"Cultured. Controlled. "

I smiled coldly. "What is he then?"

The lion roared. Miss Fuller frowned at it before answering. "A poor boy much damaged from the trauma of his childhood."

I laughed. "That's hardly a strike against him. President Jackson was born poor in the wilds of North Carolina three weeks after his father died, and he turned out all right."

"Andrew Jackson killed at least thirteen men in duels, probably more. He killed hundreds and hundreds in battle. He killed any Indian unfortunate enough to walk across his path, and beat a man to death with a stick. Yes, Americans, in their questionable wisdom, elected him to be president, but I don't think that he turned out 'all right.'"

"I still don't understand why you are telling me this."

"Because I don't like to see people get hurt."

"Did Mrs. Poe say something about our poems?" I asked.

"No. Should she?"

The lion roared again, louder, causing Miss Fuller's horse to shy. She steadied her animal with the reins.

"I'm your friend, Frances."

"If you were my friend," I said, "you wouldn't further rumors about me."

"Who said there were rumors?"

"You said Mrs. Poe was complaining."

"She wasn't complaining. In fact, she said she only wished she could spend more time with you, learning from you, but her illness keeps her at home."

I drew in a breath. "I will make a point of seeing more of her."

"Don't."

I bristled at her bossy tone.

"I think you should steer clear of the Poes altogether," she said.

"A strange bit of advice, coming from someone who insisted that I must write an article about them. I heard that you were writing it yourself. What happened to it? I haven't seen it in the *Tribune*."

"I should have never insisted that you pursue that article. Once I got a firsthand look at the Poes, I dropped my article immediately."

I glanced at her. What had she seen that discouraged her?

Miss Fuller rested the reins on her lap. "I've been rooting for you from the start, Frances, with that bounder of a husband of yours. I think you've done tremendously well, raising those two girls on your own while you work on your writing. Don't ruin your reputation as a serious writer on a man. History has a way of forgetting the mistresses of great men. Even if they have talent."

The children came back to the rug with Mary, the Bartletts strolling hand in hand behind them. "Did you like the lion?" I called, shaken.

Little Johnny shook his head. "He gots no teeth."

"They'd been taken out!" Eliza exclaimed. "So disgusting."

Miss Fuller stroked the beads at her neck. "That's one way of managing a lion."

Twenty-two

The following Saturday afternoon at Washington Square brought rock doves bobbing across the warm flagstones, children chasing one another, screaming with laughter, and a German brass band merrily oompah-pah-ing from the bandstand. On the parade ground, the militia performed a drill wearing beautiful uniforms and stern faces. Should the Mexicans harassing the Republic of Texas come any closer to New York, the Seventh Regiment was ready. So enchanting was the day that my girls and Eliza's older two could not be convinced to come home when it was time for Johnny's nap. We left them with Mary, with a promise that she would take them no farther than the park—there'd be no more straying off to see her beau, at least not with the children.

Back at the Bartletts', I had gone downstairs for a drink of water. It was a relief to be by myself for a moment. Constantly putting up a cheerful front, in spite of my cares as an abandoned wife and my involvement in an impossible relationship, had exhausted me. I was carrying my glass into the family room, scratching under a stay digging into my rib cage, when I came with a start upon Mr. Bartlett, reading a magazine by the open basement window. His oiled blond hair shone in a shaft of sunlight.

"Oh! I didn't realize that you were here."

He gave me a long look, leaned over, then tossed his magazine on the family room table.

"We have a celebrity in the house."

I glanced at the publication: *The Broadway Journal*. Mr. Poe's magazine.

"Your little romance is causing a stir."

My scalp tingled in alarm. "What do you mean?"

Eliza came into the kitchen, untying her bonnet strings. There was a little *V* of sweat on the buttoned-up bodice of her dress. "What little romance?"

Mr. Bartlett crossed his arms. "Between Mrs. Osgood and Mr. Poe."

Eliza paused for a moment, then proceeded to take off her hat. "Russell, that's not nice."

"What's not nice? They've been exchanging love poems in public. Did they not expect people to comment?"

I felt a wave of nausea. "They were just poems. Poets *do* write them."

"So you did send them." Eliza's expression begged me to deny it.

"Only under pen names." Is this why no one had come calling lately? I had totted it up to the Bartlett children's illnesses, and to my own withdrawal from public. People were shunning me?

"Your disguises did not hold up," said Mr. Bartlett. "Everyone knows you are 'Violet Vane' and Poe is 'M.'"

How?

"I didn't!" Eliza exclaimed.

"You've been busy with the children," said Mr. Bartlett. He pushed the magazine toward Eliza and me. "I had three lady readers come into the bookshop this morning asking for this. I don't usually get but three ladies a week requesting *The Broadway Journal.* They want *Godey's* or some such. I asked the last one what compelled her to get this issue." He paused. "She said she heard that Mr. Poe was breaking off his flirtation with Mrs. Osgood."

Breaking off his flirtation? I restrained myself from scooping up the magazine and flipping madly to the page.

"I hope you set her straight!" Eliza exclaimed. When she saw him look away, she said, "You did tell her there was no flirtation, didn't you?"

He held up his hand to hush her. "Mrs. Osgood, as your friend and guardian while Mr. Osgood is away, I insist that you cease writing these poems. It's gone too far."

Eliza picked up the magazine. How I itched to grab it for myself.

"Page seventeen," said Mr. Bartlett.

She turned to the page. "'To' *blank*, 'by M.'" She ran down the page with her finger, then read aloud:

We both have found a life-long love
Wherein our weary souls may rest
Yet may we not, my gentle friend
Be to each other the second best?

She looked up at me.

This is how he would end our relationship? So publicly and condescendingly?

I made myself smile. "You see? I'm just second best."

"This is no jest," said Mr. Bartlett. "You shouldn't be second best to a married man. You shouldn't be third or fourth, or even fifth. You should be nothing to him."

Obviously, that was precisely what I was to Mr. Poe now.

"As man of the house, I'm putting my foot down," said Mr. Bartlett.

Eliza studied my face. "Don't worry, Fanny. It will blow over."

I nodded, my insides roiling. Apparently, some things already had.

The evening brought a walk with the Bartletts to Niblo's Garden, across Broadway from Mr. Astor's large home. On such a pleasant night, everyone would be there. Although I wished nothing more than to repair to my bed, I had to go. I had to act as if the poems in Mr. Poe's journal were meaningless to me. But how had people figured out that Mr. Poe and I were writing the poems? Had Miss Fuller pried it out of Mr. Poe? And then to have had the tale spread—what a sickening sensation to be "known" by people I had never met.

Niblo's Garden was glittering with influential patrons when we arrived. As I feared, many of the same guests who frequented Miss Lynch's salon were there. Made close by our evenings of conversation, we naturally drifted together. I soon found myself strolling with Mr. Greeley and Miss Fuller and the others through the open-air saloon under the hundreds of colored lamps shining from the trees like fairy lights. I braced myself for questions and remarks.

Surprisingly, none came. My circle's good breeding prevailed. Yet many of the women treated me with the coldly kind and civil reserve one saves for former friends or cousins of whom one disapproves. The men tried not to smirk. Not a word was breathed about my exchange with Mr. Poe. None was necessary. The too-quick smiles, the subtle turning away when I approached, spoke volumes.

I had come to rest in a conversational knot that included a newcomer to town, a Mrs. Ellet, who was now droning on about her husband's four different degrees in the sciences, when Mr. Poe stepped into the garden with Virginia on his arm.

Reverend Griswold, who had claimed a place at my elbow, sniffed. "Speak of the devil."

Mr. Poe's expression was pleasantly quizzical as the group politely greeted him and his wife. His gaze stopped on me. In the scarlet light of the lamp hanging over us, I saw the curious looks of the crowd.

I smiled at Mrs. Poe. "Lovely dress."

Everyone looked back and forth between her and me, noticing what I'd seen when she entered: her dress was almost exactly like mine in color and cut.

Mr. Greeley grinned, then shoveled in another bite of ice cream.

Mr. Brady was not so restrained. "I give up!" he said, laughing. "Poe, this has got to be another of your hoaxes."

Mrs. Poe blinked at her husband. "What hoax?"

"My wife doesn't know what you're talking about," Mr. Poe said coolly. "Perhaps you had better explain it to her."

My face was on fire. Before Mr. Brady could upset her, I said, "You must forgive me, Mrs. Poe. I had conceived of a little game to pique the readership of your husband's journal, for which I myself received payment. I wrote some silly flirtatious poems and Mr. Poe responded in kind, until this week's issue, in which he begged to reconcile with his wife." I nodded to Mr. Poe. "It appears the scheme has worked. My friend, Mr. Bartlett, reports sales of the magazine have increased at his store."

Mrs. Poe wrinkled her nose. "You would do that to your reputation?"

"Thank you!" cried Reverend Griswold. "My sentiments exactly! I have been bursting to say something all evening long. Shame on you, sir," he said to Mr. Poe, "for injuring our dear Mrs. Osgood in this way." He swelled with righteous indignation, shrinking only a little under Mr. Poe's withering stare before he turned to Mrs. Poe. "I'm sorry, madam, but what your husband did was inexcusable."

"Blame me," I said quickly. "It was a foolish and unseemly ploy on my part to get recognition. Your husband was correct to put an end to it this week with his poem," I said to Mrs. Poe.

"What did you say, Eddie?"

The lamp above us rocked in the wind, flashing scarlet light over Mr. Poe's grim face.

"He said," Reverend Griswold announced, brave now that he had been released from Mr. Poe's glare, "that she was second best to you."

I could feel the fascinated looks of Mr. Greeley and Mr. Brady upon me, and Miss Fuller's I-told-you-so scowl and Mrs. Poe's pout. But it was Mr. Poe's torment that stopped my breath. Anger, sorrow, and dismay contorted his face until he harnessed them into murderous fury. I feared for Reverend Griswold's safety.

Just then, as if heaven-sent, a peal of chords on a harp blossomed in the air. Everyone turned to see the gentleman tuning the instrument set up under a rose-covered trellis. A buxom woman in black stood next to him, wringing a handkerchief.

The proprietor of the garden, a stout gentleman crossed with watch chains, beckoned us to gather around. "Dear friends, joining us during their tour of America, I give you Mr. and Mrs. Nicolas-Charles Bochsa!"

Mr. Poe's expression had frozen into cold disdain as we all politely moved to encircle the harpist and his wife, who proceeded to perform from an opera of the gentleman's own composition. By the time they had finished, my heart had resumed its normal beating. I applauded with extra enthusiasm, grateful for the relief they had provided.

Noting my zeal, Reverend Griswold exclaimed, "Her voice sounds just like a flute!"

"You realize," Miss Fuller said to me under our continued clapping, "that we have the privilege of hearing the 'Bochsas' in New York only because they were drummed out of London. 'Mrs. Bochsa' isn't Mrs. Bochsa at all, but Mrs. Bishop, wife of the composer Henry Bishop. They left London under the threat of death. Adultery is no more acceptable there as it is here."

I kept on applauding.

A gentleman stepped up to the couple with his violin. The two men gave a concert, the intensity of which grew as it turned into a bout of one-upmanship. Each thought to top the other in musicality and dexterity until at last the violinist contrived to play a merry polka. As the crowd clapped with delight, I slipped from my group and out the gate.

I was hurrying along the white picket fence surrounding the garden when I heard footsteps behind me. Minetta Street and its criminal element were only a few blocks away. I increased my pace. So did the walker behind me. I could tell that it was a man from the sound of his steps but the brim of my bonnet kept him from my view.

I had nearly broken into a run when Mr. Poe grabbed my arm. "Frances, what are you doing? It's not safe for you to be out here alone."

"I'm fine!"

Without warning, he swept me to him. My hat tumbled to the sidewalk as he kissed me.

I pulled from him, my lips wet from his. "You cannot do this!" I glanced around wildly.

"I thought that I could be away from you, that poems would be enough. They aren't."

"Why not? It should be easy for you to be apart. I am second best."

"I had to write that." His voice was terse. "Virginia saw your poems to me."

I held my breath as a carriage shuddered past, its lantern illuminating the dark. I turned away until it was gone. "My poems were anonymous."

"She saw your letter that accompanied one. I made the mistake of leaving it in my coat pocket."

I tried to remember what I might have said.

"She knows that you care for me." He drew a breath. "I feared for you."

"Everyone thinks we are lovers now."

"Do you think I give a damn what anyone thinks?" He took my face in his hands and kissed me.

We heard a pattering behind us. We drew apart.

Mrs. Poe minced up as Mr. Poe was picking up my hat. She looked between us, her mouth turned down like an unhappy child's.

"I'm afraid that I had to leave," I said stupidly. "I'm sorry that we hardly got to speak tonight."

She gave me a dismissive frown, then turned to her husband. "I'm tired, Eddie. What are you doing out here? I want to go home."

Wordlessly, Mr. Poe led her, coughing, away, but not before she threw a look of sheer hatred over the shoulder of the dress, a dress so similar to mine in every way.

Summer 1845

Twenty-three

The heat was stifling in the Bartletts' back parlor and yet I wanted to giggle. The very sight of Reverend Griswold, sitting next to me on the black horsehair sofa, water glass clutched in his white-gloved hand was enough to undo me. Maybe it was his outrageous bragging about his luncheons with this important poet or that, about his invitations to their lovely houses, about their glowing reviews of his collection of poems. Maybe it was the irreverent picture that kept flashing through my head of him making love to his dead wife. More likely, it was just me. Is there a creature more unstable than a woman made mad by desire?

Hardly a week after our encounter at Niblo's Garden, Mr. Poe had stopped by the Bartletts' on a Sunday to announce to us that he had moved his family into the neighborhood, just a few houses away down Amity Street. I could not believe that he would be so bold as to move so close. Bolder still, he began to drop by the house most nights after work, with a new book for Mr. Bartlett to consider for his bookshop, or a seedling to plant in Eliza's garden, or novel Southern expressions for Mr. Bartlett to consider for his dictionary. Never did he touch me or even claim me as the reason for his visit. But even with his back turned to me when presenting a new breed of rose to Eliza, or when standing at the table at which Mr. Bartlett wrote, or when loping down the hall, hunched like a monster, after the happily shrieking children, I could feel his soul reaching out for mine. The effect was devastating. Is there an aphrodisiac more powerful than forbidden fruit hanging just out of reach?

Now I grasped at any sensory distraction that would anchor me into Reverend Griswold's excruciating conversation: the murmur of the servants downstairs; the fly crawling up Reverend Griswold's lapel; the faint pop of the linen stretched across Eliza's embroidery ring when she punctured it with her needle. It was no use. I became lost in picturing Mr. Poe's calmly probing smile, the veined columns of his wrists as he held on to the chair behind me, the clean tapered fingers of his hands.

"Don't you agree, Mrs. Osgood?"

I found Reverend Griswold's pink face turned expectantly to me.

"I'm sorry, I didn't hear you."

The furrow deepened between his eyes. "That Miss Fuller's latest article in the *Tribune* has gone too far." He saw that I still didn't comprehend him. "About that madman preaching Free Love in Vermont, John Humphrey Noyes."

"I didn't read it."

"You must keep up on these things, my dear. As an important woman poet, it is your duty to speak out against false prophets."

"Thank you for the compliment. But I didn't realize that was my job."

"Your job and every other responsible person's," said Reverend Griswold, indignant. "The man is a fraud. He claims that Christ has already had his Second Coming—in seventy AD, to be exact."

"I wonder how he came by that date?" Mr. Bartlett said absently, leafing through a book.

"My point exactly!" said Reverend Griswold. "It's rubbish. He says that mankind is now living in a new age in which one only has to surrender one's will to God and let God work through him. Once God is in control, whatever one does is 'perfect,' because it's 'God's will.'"

"Sounds like a nice arrangement." Eliza tugged her silk thread through the hoop. "Do what you please and claim God made you do it."

Mr. Bartlett frowned as if annoyed by being pulled into the conversation. "Margaret agreed with this man?"

"Well, she did seem interested in his theory that conventional marriage was a sinful institution. He has the strange notion that marriage is unholy when the couple does not love each other purely, that a man does not have the right to a woman's body just because he is legally married to her."

"There are men who are unkind to their wives." Eliza looked at Mr. Bartlett, busy again with his book. "The law and society does little to protect these women. Maybe that's what Miss Fuller objects to."

"This might be true of the savages in Five Points," said Reverend Griswold, "but not in polite society. We cherish our women. I would cherish the woman who agreed to be my wife. " He set down his glass. "Mrs. Osgood, I must be frank now. I would never treat a woman in the manner in which your husband has treated you."

There was a shocked silence. Simultaneously, Eliza and I started to object.

He raised his hand. "Please. Let's stop pretending. We all know what Mr. Osgood is: a philandering, unconscionable, disgusting scoundrel. An editor friend in Cincinnati has kept me apprised of him—a most appalling case. Did you know that your husband is openly living with a rich divorcée?"

Eliza covered her mouth.

Reverend Griswold smiled grimly. "Mrs. Osgood, it's time you ripped off the bandage to let your wound heal. I'm here to help you. Won't you let me, please?"

I listened for sounds of my children. Please don't let them hear this.

He dropped to one knee, then startled me further by taking my hand. "I am considering marriage to a fine and prestigious older woman I have met from Charleston. Should I decide to wed her, I will make her the happiest of her sex. But one word from you, Mrs. Osgood, just one word, and I shall withdraw my proposal to her immediately."

"Congratulations."

He sat back, evidently expecting a different word. The tall clock ticked ominously from its corner.

"What is her name?" asked Eliza.

Petulantly, he said, "Charlotte Myers."

The jingle of the doorbell stilled us.

Catherine announced the arrival of Mr. Poe. Reverend Griswold jumped to his feet.

"Send him in." Mr. Bartlett closed his book, oblivious to Reverend Griswold's grimace and my own suppressed groan of relief.

Mr. Poe entered with kind words for all. He came to me last, and bowed with a little smile. "I've got good news."

My heart leaped.

"I've been invited to speak before the Boston Lyceum in October."

What other news did you expect? I scolded myself, as Mr. Bartlett offered his hand. "Excellent," he said as they shook. "Give them a taste of your magic, Poe."

"That's a very sophisticated crowd," said Eliza. "Congratulations."

Boyish delight leaked from beneath Mr. Poe's reserved exterior. His lower face, dark with a day's growth of beard, was wreathed in a rare open smile. "I've always wanted to address this crowd. If you can please Bostonians, you can please anyone."

"The truth," said Mr. Bartlett.

"I might try something new, see if I can kick up the dirt a little. I don't want to just be another voice in the chorus of frogs perched around the pond in the Boston Commons."

"Here, here!" cried Mr. Bartlett.

"I suppose you think Mr. Noyes is a prophet," Reverend Griswold said shrilly.

Mr. Poe turned to him. "Pardon?"

"Mr. Noyes and his Free Love, I suppose you support it."

Eliza pierced her cloth with her needle. "We've been talking about how marriage is unholy if both partners do not love each other." She cleared her throat. "Among other things."

Still in a jolly mood, Mr. Poe took the chair by the covered grate. "I do support that."

"You would," Reverend Griswold muttered.

"Do you find love so objectionable?" asked Mr. Poe.

"Of course not. But there are other important considerations to a marriage." Reverend Griswold flung Mr. Poe a superior smile. "Such as how well a man can provide for his wife. Can a man buy instead of rent a house, can he afford a carriage, *can he afford the best doctors should his wife become ill*—all these things greatly matter to a woman."

The joy drained from Mr. Poe's face.

Wicked toad! "So you support the idea of a loveless marriage, Reverend Griswold?" I demanded.

The vehemence in my tone made Eliza blink.

Reverend Griswold flared his delicate nostrils. "You make me sound like an ogre! Yes, love in a marriage is important—it's the icing on the cake—but it is respect and obligation that are essential. I'm sorry, but do you not see how society would unravel if couples split once they fell out of love?"

"I'm afraid that I agree with Reverend Griswold," said Mr. Bartlett. "Half the couples would divorce, given the chance."

Eliza stopped sewing. "Would you divorce me, Russell?"

He frowned at his book. "Don't be silly."

Her troubled expression made me look twice. I had always thought of them as such a happy pair.

"It is my belief," said Mr. Poe, "that marriage is made holy by two souls in communion, not by the order of the law."

"So you would have everyone running about having affairs?" cried Reverend Griswold.

"Is it so inconceivable," Mr. Poe said quietly, "that individuals should commit themselves to each other solely out of love and mutual understanding, not obligation?" When he sought my gaze, I boldly returned it.

Reverend Griswold glanced between us, then snatched up his glass and drank loudly. When he put it down, his smile was politely cruel. "Perhaps there is one benefit of illicit love. I've heard it said that the Spanish used to believe that children of affairs—children conceived in *amor*—were more beautiful than those produced in a marriage. But I think that can be neatly explained away by the fact that the Spanish nobility always married family. Inbreeding of first cousins makes for a very strange-looking child." He shoved his lower jaw forward and lisped, "That hideous Habsburg jaw."

Pleased at thinking he had wounded Mr. Poe, he turned to me. "You must not think that I am not a great lover of women, Mrs. Osgood."

"I assure you that I do not."

"Oh, but I am!" cried Reverend Griswold. "I think of women as superior to men. We need them to help us control our base desires."

"What if women don't want to control men's desires?" I asked.

He looked at me incredulously for a moment, then laughed.

"What if women have their own?"

He cowered away from me.

"Why must women always deny their desires? Why must men always deny theirs? It is completely unnatural to do so."

My words hung in the ensuing silence.

At last Eliza said gently, "Because to not do so will destroy our civilization. For all of us to get along, we must have rules."

Mr. Bartlett cleared his throat. "On that note, I must speak to you, Mr. Poe, about the rules for Southern speech. I'm working on a paragraph about it for my glossary."

The conversation then split into two groups: Mr. Poe and Mr. Bartlett in one; myself, Eliza, and Reverend Griswold, sulking, in another. I could feel Mr. Poe's gaze upon me as Reverend Griswold held forth loudly to Eliza about the new clock being installed in the rebuilt Trinity Church.

"It is the world's largest." As if to punish me, he kept his back turned pointedly to me, although we were both still on the sofa. "Quite a feather in Trinity's hat—it's already the tallest building in New York. I had the vicar to Delmonico's for lunch last week. He said that they have had a devil of a time hanging the minute hands. It seems that they are incredibly big—tall as a man."

"Hmm," Eliza murmured, sewing.

"It is interesting, isn't it? I would love to take you to see them, my dear. The vicar is a very good friend—I'm sure I could get him to give us a tour."

Eliza gave him a wincing smile. "Thank you for the offer."

"Nothing would make me happier, good lady." He turned his back more squarely against me. "Perhaps we could work in a luncheon at Delmonico's. Lorenzo Delmonico is a very dear friend of mine—I think I might get him to whip us up a very nice Charlotte Russe."

I could not bear my inability to speak to Mr. Poe, just across the room, when I desired him so much. I jumped up. "You will all excuse me?"

Reverend Griswold crossed his arms in satisfaction. "Oh. *You* would like to go to Delmonico's, too?"

I nodded at him and the Bartletts. "Good-bye."

When Eliza saw that I was heading toward the hall, she said, "It's awfully hot outside, Fanny."

"Just a quick errand." With a flick of a glance at Mr. Poe, I fled.

As briskly as the sultry summer evening air would allow, I walked to the Baptist church, willing Mr. Poe to come to me. *Please hurry, Edgar. How I need you. I must have your lips kissing mine.*

I let myself through the iron gate of the churchyard. The sun was bronzing the heavens and everything it touched as it sank, pouring a molten golden glow upon the tombstones, the trees, and the heat-withered grass crunching under my feet. I was reading the names carved on the glowing stones when I heard a snap behind a nearby screen of cedars.

I paused, listening. Beyond the spiked rails of the churchyard fence, horses clopped down Mercer Street. Blackbirds whistled unseen. The leaves of the graveyard trees hissed in the scorched evening breeze.

There: Another snap.

I knew I should leave. It felt wrong there, strangely threatening. The animal in me smelled danger.

Perversely, I had to see.

I eased around the cedars.

A girl in white was sitting on a headstone.

She turned around.

"Mrs. Poe?" I gasped.

She coughed and waved the broken stick she'd been holding as in a greeting. When she caught her breath, she said, "I knew that you'd come."

"Well." I patted my throat. "What a surprise. I don't often find my friends in a graveyard."

She raised one corner of her pretty mouth. "I'm glad that you think of me as a friend."

She would have had to pass the Bartletts' to get here. Did she know that her husband was in their house? It was odd that I had not seen her since she had moved so close. Mr. Poe would not speak of her, nor did I press him beyond polite inquiries about her health. I was afraid to know the extent of her illness.

My mind raced for pleasant conversation. "Such a hot evening."

She tossed away the stick. "I'm dying, Mrs. Osgood."

I felt the blow she meant to deliver.

"That's why he's turning from me." Like a child in a nursery chair, she kicked her feet against the tombstone upon which she sat. "Eddie's afraid to be alone."

"You're young and strong. You have decades left."

My words glanced off her, unheeded. "I'm his other half. I'm the William Wilson that he cannot shake. What will he do without me to be bad, so that he can be so very good?"

She had come unhinged. I must remain calm. "'William Wilson' was just a story."

"Is that what he told you?"

I swallowed.

"Don't worry. I'm not going just yet. Not without a fight."

"I don't want you to go anywhere."

She coughed against the back of her hand. "I've got consumption. My lungs are shutting down."

"It's just bronchitis—your husband said."

She laughed. "If it helps you to believe that, go ahead."

I backed away slowly, as one does from a dog that is ready to bite. "Truly, Mrs. Poe, I wish only the best for you."

"Liar."

She hopped down from the headstone, setting off a fit of coughing.

I heard the crackling of dry grass behind me. Someone was coming. We stared at each other, deadlocked.

Mr. Poe came around the hedge. When he saw his wife, he shuddered with revulsion.

"Virginia! How did you get here?"

"I walked. Mother helped me. We were going to Washington Square but this was as far as I could go. She went back to get her knitting."

If she had meant to go to the park, she could have gotten there faster by walking the other direction down our street.

"You should be in bed."

"I like it here." She spread out her arms as if to embrace the tombstones. "I feel so much closer to these people than to the living."

"Don't be a fool." He frowned at her. "You're shivering."

He saw my scowl, demanding that he care for her. He put his arm around her.

"I shall let you two be alone." I turned, my hem catching on the sere and crispéd grass.

"Mrs. Osgood," called Mrs. Poe, coughing.

I stopped.

"It's not over."

I drew a breath, then launched homeward as the remaining molten sunlight dissolved into ash.

Twenty-four

I was dreaming of Samuel. We were in the Athenæum in Boston. He was painting my portrait. My dreaming self thrilled when he threw down his brushes, climbed upon my couch, and lifted my skirts to take me. When two well-dressed matrons strolled into the gallery, he scrambled off me, then nodded to them pleasantly as they passed. They smiled until they saw my portrait. With a shriek, they flew from the chamber, their slippers tapping against the marble floor. I pushed up from the couch and turned around the painting.

It was me, naked, with legs splayed open to reveal my dark secret self.

I was writhing with shame and horror when I was startled awake. Before I could make sense of what had aroused me, a distant boom rattled the windows and bed.

I sat up. It was not yet daylight. Next to me, Ellen rubbed her eyes. "What, Mamma?"

"Shhh. Go back to sleep." Had I dreamed the explosions? Still disturbed by my nightmare, I stroked her child's silken hair. Next to her, Vinnie breathed softly in slumber. How could Samuel stay away from these beautiful children? It was July nineteenth and still I'd not heard a word from him. Whether he was with a divorcée in Cincinnati or not, I hated the man.

Another distant blast shook the room. My body rang with fear. Could we be at war? But we had no real enemies—did we?

"Stay here," I whispered to Ellen, then threw on a wrapper and went downstairs. I found the front door open and Catherine and Bridget standing on the sidewalk in the weakening darkness, the latter clutching a skillet like a weapon. Neighbors, still in night dress, and their servants stood in the street, looking south, where in the pearly gray pall of predawn, a black plume of smoke billowed into sky. Fire alarm bells began to clang from the watchtower at the Jefferson Market.

Wrapping my robe more tightly, I joined the servants. "What is it?"

"I don't know, ma'am," said Bridget.

"Where's Mr. Bartlett?"

She glanced at me, then away. "At work, I think, ma'am."

It was much too early for his shop to be open but he had been keeping strange hours since Eliza had left. She had taken the children to Providence to escape the heat that Monday, leaving the house staff and Mr. Bartlett behind. Mary was to have gone with them but had developed a sore throat that had caused her to stay home—the second girl, Martha, had gone in her stead. When Mary had recovered soon after Eliza had left, my girls had rejoiced to have her to themselves.

"Where is Mary?" I asked.

Another boom rocked the pavement under our feet.

"The British!" wailed the elderly Mrs. White, clutching her gate next door. "The British are coming!"

"They're our friends now, Mother," said her grown son Archibald. He trotted back from where he'd been watching on the street. "More likely it's the Mexicans."

I peered down Amity Street in the direction of the Poes' lodging but saw none of them through the thickening crowd. I went inside. My girls were clutching each other in the hall.

"What is it, Mamma?"

"I don't know. I'm sure it will be all right." I went back to the door and called in Bridget and Martha.

"Where *is* Mary?" I said when they reluctantly came in. "Find her, and have her take care of the girls. I'm going out."

The sound of distant fire bells infiltrated the house. "But"—Bridget's freckled pudding of a face quivered—"Mr. Bartlett!"

"He'll know what to do. Stay with my girls."

I dressed hurriedly and ran back into the street, where I pushed my way through the crowd toward Mr. Poe's house.

He flung open the door before I'd finished knocking. He was

dressed in coat and hat as if ready to leave. I could hear sobbing in a back room.

"I had to see you," I said. "Thank God you're safe."

He clasped me to him. "My darling."

He let me go when Mrs. Poe ran into the room. I stiffened with guilt but she did not seem to mark my presence.

She threw herself onto Mr. Poe. "I'm scared! It's like Pompeii!"

Mr. Poe pushed down her arms. "Don't be silly, Virginia," he said sternly. "It's a simple fire."

"Eddie! Don't go!"

"Take her," he said to me. "The fire's downtown. I must save what manuscripts I can."

"Has it spread to your building?" I said in alarm.

"I've been to the fire tower at Jefferson Market. The watchman says a warehouse caught fire on Broad Street. It set off something explosive. The whole neighborhood is ablaze."

"Close to your office."

"Don't go!" Mrs. Poe begged.

Her mother tottered after her, hands clutched. "Eddie, Eddie, you're scaring us."

"Watch them," Mr. Poe told me.

"You don't want me anymore," Mrs. Poe wailed. "You won't even touch me."

He placed her grimly into my arms. "Don't let her go outside." He stormed out the door, leaving her sobbing in my arms.

The airiness of her frame shocked me, as if her bones were hollow. She had no more substance than a sparrow.

I put an awkward hand to her forehead. It was hot, as if she had a fever. Her condition had worsened in the two weeks since I had seen her last.

"Don't worry. He'll be fine."

"He doesn't love me," she cried into my shoulder. "He loves you, not me."

"That's not true."

"It is; I know it is. All he ever talks about is you. 'Mrs. Osgood this, Mrs. Osgood that. Why can't you behave like Mrs. Osgood?'"

"Shhh. This is wild talk." I had won. Yet I was devastated.

She buried her head in my shoulder and broke into a cough. Over my own thudding heart, I could feel the rattle inside her chest as she barked. I didn't know which illness would consume her first, the one in her body or the one in her mind.

"Hush now," I said. "It's you who he loves. Didn't he say he couldn't go on living if you didn't marry him?"

"Words, words, words, words. Eddie's not a real man—he's just a shell made of words. Don't fall in love with a poet, Mrs. Osgood. All they love is their words." She sank against me in a fit of coughing.

"Mrs. Clemm," I called, shaken, "have you any tea for her?"

Mrs. Clemm, watching mutely, got up. She disappeared into the back room, then came back with a brown bottle from which Mrs. Poe drank directly. Mrs. Poe, exhausted by her fit, slid down upon the sofa. I stretched her out upon it, removed her shoes, and folded her weightless hands upon her chest. I hastily put them down again at her sides—she looked so very dead. She slept, frightening me with the depth of her slumber. Several times I felt her throat to make sure that she was breathing. Only the worry about my own children convinced me to finally leave her.

Outside, the air had become hazy with smoke. In the artificial twilight, horses screamed from their stables. Infants wailed, inconsolable. The crowd on the street had thinned, whether gone to gape at the area that was burning or to flee town, I did not know. I ran down the sidewalk, dodging weeping women and servants carrying trunks. I needed to get to my daughters. I ached from the very marrow of my bones to hold them.

I found them in the downstairs family room, playing Old Maid with Bridget and Catherine, their faces pinched with fright.

They jumped up and threw themselves against me.

"Don't worry," I said with a confidence I did not feel. "We shall be safe. The fire warden is not calling for our evacuation." Yet. Just ten years ago, nearly half of the city had burned in just such a fire.

I glanced around the room. "Where's Mary?"

Bridget and Catherine exchanged looks.

"Will you be needin' some breakfast, ma'am?" Bridget asked, her voice shaking.

If we had not been ordered to leave, then to stave off panic, we must go about our life as usual.

"Yes. Please. A poached egg—and for the girls, too, please."

I had taken my place at the table with the girls, and was confronting my egg, wondering how I could possibly choke it down, when the front door banged open. Catherine jumped up to see. I locked gazes with Bridget as dragging footsteps neared the stairs.

Mr. Bartlett came down, a hank of damp blond hair flopping on his wet brow. In his arms was Mary, her limbs hanging lifelessly.

"Get her some water," he told Bridget as he eased Mary onto the sofa. "She took in too much smoke." He marched upstairs, not waiting for praise for his heroics.

"What were you doing out there?" I demanded of Mary.

She lifted her face, smudged with smoke, then burst into tears.

She would say nothing more, but slept, with anguished outbursts of tears.

It seems incredible, but Miss Lynch insisted upon keeping her conversazione that evening, sending word by her servant Sarah that we should come. More incredibly, we did. Even as the men of the volunteer fire companies were chopping flaming timbers and training their hoses upon blocks of burning warehouses, fighting to contain the flames to the streets south of Broad, we were eating cookies and draining our tea, as if our mundane acts would hold our world together. The Astor House and Mr. Bartlett's shop within it, Mr. Brady's studio, the publishing firms on Nassau, including the *Tribune* and Mr. Poe's *Journal*—all had been narrowly missed. Now we gathered to compare losses, swap stories, and marvel at how and why we'd been spared, the separation between front and back parlor dissolved for the evening. We were kind, almost tender, to one another. Fear had equalized us.

Well into the evening, Mr. Poe, his face stern, appeared at the parlor door. I closed my eyes in a prayer of thanks. He was safe.

"Come here, come here," crooned Miss Lynch. She ran over and buried herself against him, leaving her cheek pressed to his chest a few seconds too long. Her large almond eyes glittered with tears of relief when she led him into the group. Until that moment, I had not realized that she was in love with him.

"The fire is only to the west now," he announced. "All of the manuscripts at my office are safe." He scanned the crowd. "Those of you who have sent me poems can still expect rejection."

Miss Lynch rested her head against his arm as the crowd laughed with the heartiness of those who'd just escaped peril.

Mrs. Ellet, the newcomer to our circle, wrinkled her nose flirtatiously. "You jest, Mr. Poe."

Dark-haired and heavy-featured, with an especially pendulous lower lip, she seemed to be one of those women whose doting parents had given her the idea that she was beautiful when she was a child, and she had never learned otherwise.

He ignored her, looking for me. Our eyes met. I glanced away, my heart floating, only to find Reverend Griswold's gaze upon me.

He gave me a punishing look, then turned to Mr. Poe. "How *is* your charming wife? A day like today cannot have been good for someone in her condition."

"Thank you for asking," said Mr. Poe.

Reverend Griswold waited, blinking, for the answer. His mouth snapped shut when he saw none was coming. "Well! Our gathering is always enhanced when Mrs. Poe comes. You must bring her next time, lest we forget that you are a married man."

"There's no chance of that," said Miss Lynch. She smiled bravely. "Dear Mr. Poe, may I ask a special favor? Might we lean on you tonight and ask for a reading of 'The Raven'? We so need a diversion, and your riveting poem—and particularly the way you read it—is the perfect prescription."

"Of course he reads well." Reverend Griswold took a sip of tea. "His mother was an actress—in *her* hands, with any luck, a 'noble' profession. Had she not died so young, surely, *surely* she would have become better known—at least in charming little Richmond."

The mask of civility fell from Mr. Poe's face, revealing a stare of pure, murderous hatred. I feared he would act with the violence Mr. Bartlett had once predicted, goaded by the pressure of worrying about his wife. For after seeing her today, I knew in my heart beyond any doubt: Mrs. Poe was dying.

Oblivious, Mrs. Ellet placed herself next to Mr. Poe. "I've never heard you read, sir. I understand it's quite an experience. Our mutual friend, Thomas Holley Chivers, has told me so, many times. I only wish I could do readings well. It is so *unfair* that writers are expected to do so, when by nature we are solitary creatures, spinning our delicious webs in a quiet room."

"Where is Mr. Ellet?" Reverend Griswold demanded shrilly. He seemed to have surprised himself at the strength of the effect he'd had upon Mr. Poe.

"Columbia, South Carolina." She scowled at him as if he were one of the pesky no-see-ums from that region. "He is a professor of chemistry at the university." She resumed her beaming upon Mr. Poe. "You and I are fellow Southerners, you see."

"I am thinking of wedding a woman from Charleston!" Reverend Griswold cried self-importantly.

Mr. Poe glared at Mrs. Ellet, then looked for me. Miss Lynch cried out, "Everyone, please help me move the furniture to make it cozy for our show!"

Soon the chairs were rearranged. I took one in the back. Mr. Poe caught my glance, then beckoned for me to come forward.

"There's no room," I mouthed.

He spread his palm toward the floor beneath him, indicating that I should sit there.

"Please," he said aloud.

Heads turned to look at me. I saw Miss Ellet's inquisitive gaze.

"Go on, Frances," said Miss Lynch. "Every poet needs a muse. Don't we all wish we could be Mr. Poe's!"

Conscious of gazes upon me, I came forward as the maid was dimming the lights. To balk at sitting near him would call further attention to me. I settled near his feet and turned up my face in attention, although inwardly I roiled. What would this crowd think if Edgar and I took up after his wife died? Would they accept us? Would anyone, anywhere, accept us? I shuddered. Who had I become, planning for our life together after her demise?

He began to recite the poem, his voice low and cool, almost throbbing with barely contained emotion. Around the darkened room, faces grew slack as the rhythm of his words forcefully mollified their minds. Numbed into submission, the listeners let the raven's persistence fill them with dread. There was no escape, no release for the lover in the poem. He was destined to go on loving a woman who was dead to him, to be captive to her memory, to never find release from his everlasting sorrow.

Mr. Poe looked over the crowd, every breath heaving in unison. His final word, low and insistent, resounded from a fathomless inner well.

"Nevermore."

The rhythm of our breathing filled the silence. And then, as if waking from a dream-filled slumber, first one person, and then another, clapped, until the prisms of the chandelier over our heads jingled with our applause.

When the lights were turned back up, Mrs. Ellet raced forward to cling to his side. I left the room and went outside to Miss Lynch's rear garden, to catch my breath, alone.

I was pacing by a full stand of daisies, faintly luminescent in the white light of the moon, when Miss Fuller came outside.

"Are you all right?"

"It's been a difficult day."

"It's not just the fire, is it?"

I saw that she knew everything. I shook my head.

"What are you going to do?" she asked.

"There is nothing to do."

She watched me silently, then nodded. "Let me know when you need me." She patted my hand. "There aren't many of us who would go against him."

I looked up. Did she think that I must leave him?

At that moment, the rear door opened. Mr. Poe trod down the steps.

Miss Fuller puffed herself to her fullest height as if to protect me. "Nice reading, Edgar."

"Thank you." He turned to me, his dark gaze disconcertingly fierce in the moonlight.

"Frances, would you like to go in with me?" said Miss Fuller.

"No," said Mr. Poe, his gaze still upon me. "She wants to stay with me."

I *did* want to stay with him. But it was wrong, wrong. How did I find the strength to break with him before it destroyed us both? "Go on, Margaret. Thank you."

I faced him as she went inside.

"How is your wife? She's gravely ill—more than I knew."

His voice broke with anguish. "Why must you torment me with her?"

"Because my guilt torments me!"

He drew a breath as if to control himself. He touched my arm. "I am sorry that this is so difficult."

I looked down at his hand, at his beautiful tapered fingers, so sensitive and strong. Sighing, I said, "Are we ignoring at our damnation the signs that we are not meant to be? You said there are no coincidences." I swallowed against the pain building in my chest. "If we were meant for each other, why should it be this hard?"

He waited until I looked up at him. "You can leave me if you must."

"Leave you? Edgar, I've never had you."

His voice was rich with emotion. "Oh, my love. Frances. That is where you are wrong."

His hand tightened around my arm as I searched his dark-lashed eyes. The pain in them tore my heart. I broke from him and, picking up my skirts, left him standing there, for his sake as well as mine.

The parlor was empty when I went in, with teacups and napkins abandoned haphazardly upon tables and chairs, as if their users had made a hasty departure. The gas chandeliers had been left burning, their orange flames flickering from mirrors on every wall. My distraught mind throbbed with the irrational thought that I was the last person left on earth.

I was marveling at how calmly I accepted my sentence of isolation when, through the front door, left ajar, came peals of laughter. I strode to it, and flinging it open to the lingering smell of smoke, found the other guests at the base of Miss Lynch's stoop. There they encircled a young man, who was commanding a pig to count.

That spinner of delicious webs, Mrs. Ellet, worked her way over to me as the pig pawed the cobblestones, tail wiggling. "Mr. Brady saw them walking by and insisted we all out go and see," she whispered.

"*I* resisted. After a reading by our brilliant Mr. Poe, I can hardly bear such common entertainment as Dan Rice and his sow."

I considered the possibility of continuing toward home. Climbing into bed with my girls suddenly sounded painfully sweet. I could retrieve my hat later.

"It has been a day of extremes," I said, then moved to go.

She held out her hand, large and white. "I'm Elizabeth Ellet."

The others laughed at another porcine feat.

"Where is Mr. Poe?" Mrs. Ellet asked me as we shook hands.

How my bed called. "I don't know."

"I rather got the impression that you would."

I froze as does a deer that has scented its hunter.

"I enjoyed your little exchange of poems." Her swollen lower lip smoothed into a knowing smile. "Please don't tell me that old tale about your exchange of poems in the *Journal* being a romantic hoax."

"I'm very sorry, but I was just leaving." I turned away.

"You know, I've got a mind to set my cap for him."

I stopped. "He's married."

She laughed. "I've heard that doesn't much matter."

"You've heard wrong," I said stiffly.

"I went to his office last week to offer my poems. No man happy in his marriage would look at me the way he did." She sighed happily.

The green-eyed monster raised her scaly head. "I thought you said you were married."

She heaved with a dry laugh. "I *know* that doesn't much matter." She tucked a dark lock behind her ear and peered toward the house. "Where'd you say Poe was?"

"I didn't."

Miss Lynch pattered over and linked her arms to ours. "Ladies, we are all going to sing now. Mr. Brady has talked Mr. Rice into coming inside and playing the piano. He has his own minstrel show and is supposed to be quite good." Miss Lynch led us in as Mr. Rice tethered his pig to a hitching post.

But Mr. Rice's merry minstrel tunes soon solidified into sober church hymns as the trauma of the day regained its emotional grip.

During a particularly grim rendition of "Amazing Grace," I broke free when Mrs. Ellet was wiping her eyes.

Mr. Poe was sitting on a stone bench in the garden, surrounded by a firmament of daisies and swollen hydrangea heads. The ripening blooms seemed to nearly throb with awakening life, but all that could be smelled was the reek of charred wood, coming from the burning districts of the city.

He rose when he saw me and pocketed the scrap of paper and pen with which he'd been writing. He broke into a relieved smile. "I wasn't sure if you'd come back."

I pushed away my own gladness. "Your story about the asylum?" I asked.

His smile fell.

"You had gone there for a story this spring," I said. "I haven't heard what's come of it."

He looked away, then seemed to force himself to brighten. He reached for me. "I'm working on my address for the Boston crowd."

I dodged his touch. "People will see."

Exasperation hardened his face. "Damn it, I don't care. I have acted the gentleman for far too long and what good has it done us? I'm tired of it. I'm tired of these charades. I need you, Frances. I love you. It's dishonest for us to be apart."

I laughed bitterly even as I pressed his words to my heart. "I doubt if people will give us credit for our honesty."

"Don't make light of this, Frances."

He loved me. He said he loved me. "I want what's right for my girls. I want what's right for your wife."

"What about us, Frances? Don't we deserve happiness?"

"Not at the expense of others." It took every scrap of will to keep my hands from his beautiful, anguished face.

He raked his hand through his hair, leaving it wild. "I'll make it right. I'm trying to make it good for everybody. I need you to trust me that I can." He grasped my wrist. His urgency melted into pleading. "Please."

Voices carried from the front of the house. The conversazione was concluding.

He released me. "Let me walk you home," he said quietly.

We left the gathering separately. He met me just down the street at Washington Square. We fell into step, neither touching nor speaking, as if to deny to any onlookers the feelings flying between us.

We stopped at the Bartletts' gate. I fumbled with the latch.

He laid a finger across my gloved knuckles. I drew a breath, then rattled the latch.

He flipped it up and pushed at the gate, then stopped me when I moved to enter. "I've opened my heart to you as I have never done with another living person. Why do you reject me?"

I trembled as I turned to face him. "I don't reject you, Edgar. I love you. I love you beyond reason and sanity and safety." My voice broke. "I love you so much that it terrifies me."

Pain spread across his face. "You say the words I have wanted to hear and yet—you wound me."

Shaking with mounting desire, I started up the stairs. I did not stop him when I heard him follow. I would not stop him if he followed me through the house to the Bartletts' garden, to a secluded spot I knew of behind the greenhouse, where a bower of lilies grew.

Then, upon entering the front door, I smelled it: that sharp, oily scent. An alarm jangled in my mind.

"What is it?" asked Mr. Poe.

A giggle came from the back parlor: Vinnie.

Anxiety rose from the pit of my stomach. With each step down the creaking floorboards of the hall, it inched upward like mercury in a thermometer, driving my clenched fists tighter, speeding up my heart. By the time I strode into the parlor, my temples were throbbing.

There, sitting at his easel, with our girls posing cheek to cheek before a host of gathered lamps, was Samuel.

Twenty-five

Samuel turned around, grimacing like a guilty boy. He lowered his strong-boned face in a charmingly sheepish smile. "Surprise."

I felt Mr. Poe's hand move to the small of my back.

"Mamma! Mamma! Look!" cried Vinnie.

"I see."

Samuel wiped his hand with a rag as he got up from his easel, then reached out. "You must be Poe. The girls were telling me about you."

Mr. Poe reluctantly shook Samuel's hand, then glanced at me as if to see if I were all right.

I took off my hat, steeling myself. "Why are you here?" I said evenly. The girls were listening.

"Is that how a wife greets her husband after—what has it been?"

"Eight months."

Vinnie hopped up from the chair in which she sat with Ellen. She ran over, draped Samuel's arm over her, then peered at the canvas, all transgressions evidently forgiven. "That doesn't look like me."

Samuel bent down and kissed the top of her head. "No, it doesn't, Vinneth, does it? Not yet. I work in layers, dark to light. The real you doesn't come alive until I work in the lights. You'll have to wait a few more days."

I glanced at the picture. For him to have completed as much as he did, he must have arrived just after I'd left for the conversazione.

"What do you want, Samuel?"

"To see my family. I heard about the fire."

"For you to have gotten here so quickly, you must have been close. Yet you did not come before now."

"Would you like me to see him out?" asked Mr. Poe.

Samuel's pleasant smile faded. "Remind me again who you are to this family?"

Below him, the next generation of Osgoods squinted defiantly up at Mr. Poe. How quickly Vinnie had changed allegiance, desperate to please her father. Ellen, slower to accept change, watched warily from her chair.

"Perhaps I need a few minutes with my husband," I told Mr. Poe. "Since he won't be staying long."

Mr. Poe squeezed my clenched hand, then left.

Samuel shook his head as the door closed in the hall. "By God, it's worse than I heard."

"Girls," I said, the pitch of my voice raising with anger, "could you please go upstairs and get ready for bed? It's late."

Their crestfallen faces broke my heart.

"You can come back down to say good night," I said.

"As your mother says," Samuel said when Ellen didn't move. "Scoot, then hurry back."

She took Vinnie's hand and led her skipping sister away.

I folded my arms. "How long will it take you to finish?"

He picked up a paintbrush and started wiping it with his rag. "You mean this picture?"

"Because you aren't finishing it here."

"I didn't think I would. I saw Bartlett this morning and he informed me that his wife was coming home next week. I have a feeling she won't be rolling out the welcome mat for me. He wasn't exactly the soul of cordiality himself."

"And you thought I would be happy?"

"I know. I know. I have been too ashamed to even write you. I realized that if I even had a prayer for you to forgive me, I had to come back and take my medicine."

I gave a dry laugh. "I love how I have become medicine."

"That's not what I meant."

"What am I to do, Samuel?"

"We *are* married." He plunked his brush in a jar of linseed oil, then shrugged. "Take me back?"

How did he manage to make his raw-boned weathered face so boyishly charming? "What—did your paramour in Cincinnati kick you out?"

"You heard about her?" He began cleaning another brush. "As a matter of fact, Fanny, I missed you. I missed our girls."

"You've humiliated me, Samuel. You have shamed me to my core."

"That was never my intention."

"Worse than that, you left us destitute. Did you not even worry about us?"

He had the good sense to look ashamed. "I'm sorry, Fanny. I didn't mean to hurt you. Yes, I did worry about you. A lot. But I had to disappear. Debt collectors were hard on my heels."

"They tried to collect from me."

"I'm sorry about that, but I knew they couldn't make it stick on you. Me, they could toss in Blackwell prison. I didn't want to go there. I couldn't do that to the girls, to shame them like that."

"Do you think it was easier on them to have abandoned them?"

He looked genuinely remorseful. "I've got to make it up to them. Do you think they'll forgive me?"

I thought of Vinnie's happy possessiveness of him just then. Ellen had been hurt more deeply, but her longing for him was sure to overcome her anger. "You don't deserve it."

He placed the brush in the solution and looked around the Bartletts' comfortable parlor. "You've done a good job of protecting them from my failures, and I'm thankful for that. But then you have always been resourceful. And now you've linking yourself to the most popular man in New York—bravo."

I stared at him in furious disbelief. "How dare you! You, of all people, making such an accusation."

"No accusations," he said, scraping his palette. "I'm just stating the obvious."

"There have been no improprieties. We are friends, that's all."

"That's the way you have it? 'Friends'?" He put up a hand when I started to object. "Don't worry—I've lost my right to be jealous, although I would love to punch that arrogant faker in the nose."

"How adult of you."

He frowned. "So what are we going to do?"

"Do? Nothing! You can't just walk in after eight months of silence and expect me to take you back as if you'd just gone out for a newspaper."

"I guess not. Look, I am sorry for what I've done, Fanny. Truly. And now that I have a little money, I will make it up to you."

"That hardly seems possible."

"At least think about it, for the girls' sakes. I'm their father. You can't change that. As much as you might like to."

A few minutes later, Vinnie ran back downstairs in her nightgown, Ellen following.

"I'm back, Poppy!" Vinnie sang.

He pointed to his cheek. "Good-night kiss."

After receiving their affection, he shooed them toward the stairs. "Up to bed now. I've got to go."

Vinnie's crushed expression pierced my heart. "But—our picture. When are you going to finish it?"

"It all depends on your mother."

I glared at him in disbelief. He had successfully managed to put the blame for our broken family on me. How perfectly Samuel Osgood.

"We'll see," I said. "Now go to bed. I'll be right up."

He had the good sense to not say another word.

"You can't leave your paint things here."

He put on his hat. "You're right. I'll move them."

Did the man have a response for everything? Knowing Samuel, I knew the answer to that. After the day's events, I was too drained to deal with him.

"Good night," I said, then turned away. When I looked back, he tipped his hat and gave me the hangdog smile that had broken hearts halfway around the world.

How perfectly Samuel Osgood.

At Eliza's insistence, I stayed on at their home when she returned from Providence, and Samuel, to his surprise, was allowed to visit. Oh, she knew what a bounder he'd been, what a cheat, what a reprobate, but she also knew that my girls yearned for their father. She provided a civil ground upon which Samuel and I might meet, giving me a chance to figure out if I could ever trust him again. Mr. Bartlett, on the other hand, wanted me to banish Samuel altogether, to never forgive him of his unconscionable behavior. A husband must never abandon his family. What would happen if all men just up and left their responsibilities whenever they felt like it? He made a show of quitting the room whenever Samuel came, as if to chasten him—a wasted effort, since only Samuel Osgood could decide who could make Samuel Osgood unhappy.

As it was, Samuel cheerfully gave himself up for punishment, whether it came from me or Mr. Bartlett. He accepted my cold shoulder humbly. He nodded in regretful agreement when Mr. Bartlett recounted his crimes against me. When the girls asked when we could live together again as a family, he deferred to me, making the possibility of reconciliation seem more desirable to me than if he insisted upon it himself. Fighting with him was impossible. He was as uncontainable as a handful of water: if you squeezed, it trickled away.

Yet, it was not so simple to take him back. Even if I could trust him again, there was my relationship with Mr. Poe to consider. In this regard, too, Samuel was maddeningly agreeable. Far from playing the jealous husband, he accepted Mr. Poe's presence in my life, which was still outwardly as proper and inwardly as torturous as ever. Samuel never protested when Mr. Poe came to the Bartletts' if he had been there first. Instead of removing himself during Mr. Poe's visits, he joined in our discussions, a vexingly cheerful third wheel. By the second joint visit, it was Mr. Poe who had assumed the role of the wronged spouse, his tolerance of Samuel visibly fraying by the moment. After more than a month of Samuel's cheerfully remorseful presence, everyone's nerves had unraveled to the breaking point— save for Samuel's. But even he showed surprise that stultifying dog day afternoon in early September, at who came to the house to call.

I was in the front parlor, fanning myself while ostensibly reading, as Samuel sketched our daughters for yet another painting. The girls had begged him to paint them once more, as if having him paint them was their only way to keep him anchored at home. He seemed anxious to please them, too, and relieved to have hit upon a way of staying close. Canvases of the girls portrayed singly or together, wearing mischievous smiles or wistful gazes, leaned against the parlor walls, adding the oily stink of drying paint to the stiflingly hot air. I said a silent thanks to Eliza, now working on her needlepoint by the empty grate. I could not burden her much longer with my family, our problems, or our paintings. Was I wrong to not take up with Samuel again, as disastrous as that would be? But just the idea of completely giving up Mr. Poe made my chest ache as if scraped hollow.

The doorbell jarred me out of my thoughts. Moments later, the maid Catherine presented the silver calling card tray to Eliza, who put down her knitting to receive it.

Eliza held up the card to me. Black feathers fluttered from its borders.

A chill went over me as I laid down my book. "Mrs. Poe?"

Samuel looked up.

"With Mr. Poe and Mrs. Clemm, ma'am," said Catherine.

"What do you say?" Eliza asked me.

Conscious of Samuel's gaze, I smiled. "How nice that Mrs. Poe is well enough to be out again. Please do have her in."

Samuel turned sideways on his stool as if to ready himself for a show. The girls had jumped up to see themselves on his paper when Mrs. Clemm tottered in, Mr. Poe following slowly with his wife leaning on his arm.

I fought to keep the dismay from my face. Mrs. Poe's white lawn dress hung from her shrunken shoulders; its yellow sash cinched a waist no broader than a man's hand. Within her black straw bonnet, her cheeks glowed scarlet from fever or excitement or both. What could raise such an ill person from her bed?

Eliza rushed to her. "Mrs. Poe, you're looking well.

Mrs. Poe's eyes glittered from disease as she received Eliza's kiss and then mine. In a breathy voice, she said. "I have heard the famous painter is here."

I glanced at Mr. Poe. The rigidity of his face gave more hint of his agitation than would have the blackest scowl.

Samuel stepped forward. "The famous painter—I like the sound of that." He gently took Mrs. Poe's hand. "And you would be the famous Mrs. Poe?"

She gave a wheezy laugh. "My husband is the famous one."

"Oh, no, I assure you that you are the legend around this house." He gave no hint of his irony as he kissed her hand. "It's my pleasure to meet you."

She barked into her handkerchief, then winced as if it pained her. "Will you paint my picture?" she said when she regained her speech. "My husband did not want me to trouble you, but when I told him it would be my last—" She broke off, coughing.

"It will only be your last if you have a daguerreotypist do your future portraits," Samuel said gallantly. "Which I do not recommend."

"Will you paint her?" Mr. Poe asked coldly.

Samuel frowned but would not look at Mr. Poe. "Madam," he said to Mrs. Poe, "if you would like me to paint your picture, I would be honored to do so." I grimaced at Eliza in apology for having turned her home into a studio.

She responded with a little shake of her head. "Ellen and Vinnie, would you like to go with me to the park? I'm to meet Mary and the children. Fanny, you are welcome, too."

The girls, who'd been pinned down by a doting Mrs. Clemm, happily decamped. I rose to join them until I saw Mr. Poe's desperate glance. I eased back down into my chair.

I watched, begrudgingly acknowledging the skills that had made Samuel popular with the opposite sex upon two continents. His glibness faded away as he earnestly listened to Mrs. Poe's thoughts on how she would like to appear, nodding with tender seriousness at her various suggestions. He then gently arranged her on a chair and bid her to take her ease, assuring her that she needn't worry about her position just yet.

"First," he said, standing back with a soothing smile, "I must try to find the light."

"What do you mean?" Mr. Poe said harshly.

Samuel scowled at me as if I should remove Edgar from the room. "My main care as an artist," he said, "is to notice and re-create the way light falls upon a subject. What you call color and form are simply patterns of light." He paused. "Oddly enough, while looking for light on the outside, I often find a light from within. I cannot explain how that works. Instinct, I suppose."

Mrs. Poe coughed into her handkerchief. "You should sit for a portrait, Eddie. Or are you afraid of what Mr. Osgood might see?"

Mr. Poe stared at her.

"Sure, Poe," said Samuel. "Next time you need a portrait for a magazine, come on over." He flashed me a sidelong look. "If anyone can capture the real Edgar Poe, I do believe it would be me."

Mr. Poe got up abruptly and left the room. Footsteps in the hall preceded the opening and closing of the front door.

"Please excuse him," Mrs. Poe told Samuel. "He cannot bear to see me happy."

"Virginia!" Mrs. Clemm frantically stirred her bonnet rim with her fan. "You should not talk like that."

"Go find him," Mrs. Poe said to me. "Bring him back. He'll come for you." She sank back in her chair.

Samuel exhaled a noisy breath. Already intent upon this project, he couldn't be bothered with further distractions. Sweat beading at his hairline, he fell into sketching, soon forgetting the drama around him. Mrs. Poe languished against the cushions as if the last bit of her strength had drained away the moment Edgar had left.

I perched on the edge of the scratchy red-upholstered chair, the scrape of Samuel's pencil, the click of Mrs. Clemm twitching her nails, and Mrs. Poe's strangulated breathing unsettling me more deeply by the minute. A stew of regret, remorse, anger, and terror simmered within me until my nerves boiled over, sending me fleeing.

Mr. Poe was waiting outside on the stoop.

"I should not have brought her," he said.

Storm clouds were darkening the sky. I wondered if Eliza would return soon with the children. "You were right to bring her. She seems to enjoy it."

"She enjoys torturing me."

"We have given her reason to."

He grasped my shoulders. "You are not to blame, Frances."

I turned my head in disagreement.

He waited until I looked at him. "This is between her and me. Don't you see that she wants you to blame yourself? When you do, she wins."

"I *am* to blame. She has a right to hate me. She's dying and I'm waiting like a vulture for her to go."

His voice cracked with vehemence. "Would you have me die, too?"

His extreme agitation stunned me. "You won't die. Why would you say so?"

He let me go. "Mark me, she will take me with her. She will not rest until she does."

What had his troubles done to his mind? I touched his proud and wounded face. "Edgar, what is happening to us?"

He stared at me as if willing me to understand. "Madness," he said quietly, "is as a drop of ink in water. It sends sly tendrils from the afflicted person into everyone around until all are shaded in black. Soon one does not know who is mad and who is not."

The door swung open.

"There you are!" cried Mrs. Clemm. "Are you coming in to see Sissy's picture?"

"Yes," he said. "Go."

Her worried blue eyes widened. She withdrew into the house with a bang. When she'd gone, he looked both disturbed and closed. He reopened the door for me. "If he's any good, your husband won't like what he finds in my wife."

Samuel was shading the sketch when we came back in. "Shhh." He nodded toward Mrs. Poe. Her face, slick with a feverish sweat, was twisted away from her body and turned into the maroon cushion as if she were in the thrall of death. Her chest rose raggedly in sleep. I inched toward the canvas to see, holding my breath so as not to wake her as I passed.

Her eyes flew open. I gasped.

Slowly, her sights trailed to Mr. Poe.

The parlor maid, Catherine, came in, bearing a small lamp. "Beg your pardon, but when it starts to get dark and we have company, the missus likes me to light the gas."

"The lighting will ruin the picture." Samuel put down his pencil. "Oh, well, doesn't matter. There's not enough good light left. Go ahead. I'm done for now."

Catherine caught the ring at the bottom of the chandelier, drew down the apparatus, and released the gas cock at the end of each arm. A steady hiss, like the whispering of demons, issued forth.

"May I see?" I asked Samuel.

He spread his palm toward his easel.

I pulled back in revulsion. The people in his portraits usually were faced in a flattering one-quarter turn. On occasion, someone would ask for a profile. But Mrs. Poe's face was turned three-quarters into the cushions as if her neck was broken, oddly exposing her throat and jaw. Only a single, mostly averted eye could be seen. Yet, even from this strange angle, the dark pupil seemed to watch the viewer, following one's every movement.

I glanced at Mrs. Poe. She had pushed herself upright and was keenly observing Catherine take a stick of kindling from her pocket, dip it into her lamp, and then touch it to a gas jet. It burst into light.

As Catherine went around the arms of the chandelier, setting each jet ablaze, Samuel said, "I can hear you thinking, Fanny. Yes, you're right, this is a new sort of position for me. I don't even know why I did it other than I felt called to do it this way. It was as if I had no choice."

To Mrs. Poe, he said, "Perhaps, madame, you'd like to come back another time, when I'm in a more wholesome frame of mind. I'm sorry, I don't know what's wrong with me."

Mrs. Poe seemed not to hear him. "What happens if you don't light them quick?"

Catherine looked up, seeing that she was being addressed. "Then the room explodes, ma'am, don't it?"

Fall 1845

Twenty-six

Three weeks later, Samuel and I, the Bartletts, the children, and Mr. Poe were ambling toward Broadway. To the outsiders pouring in our direction, we must have looked like a well-dressed, respectable, and congenial group: the reunited couple, the old marrieds, their children, and a family friend whose wife's health prevented her from joining them. I suppose most people only saw the friend. Mr. Poe's popularity had soared to new heights in the months since the publication of his book of tales. We could hardly take four steps without another admirer accosting him, wanting to talk about his stories.

At Amity and Broadway, Mr. Clement Moore saluted our party, his grown daughter on his arm.

"Congratulations, sir." He raised his voice over the shuffling of footsteps around us. "It seems that your Raven has firmly beaten my Saint Nick. I must thank you. Perhaps now my silly little tale shall be laid to rest."

Two short blocks farther up, Mr. Samuel Morse stopped Mr. Poe in front of the New York Hotel, causing an obstruction in the river of humanity. I recognized him instantly from the articles I had read about his invention. I smiled privately. The telegraph line between New York and Washington had been nearly completed since Edgar had spoken of him. Another was under way to Boston. Some said soon all of the county would be connected by a web of cable, giving mankind dominion over time and space—an unimaginable thought that sunny fall day as horses clopped by and carriages quaked down the street, past the flow of chatting pedestrians.

"Mr. Poe," said Mr. Morse, "pardon me, but I must ask—is it true about mesmerism, that a person might be caught at the moment of their death as was Mr. Vankirk in 'Mesmeric Revelation'?"

"It is a work of fiction," said Mr. Poe.

Blond, wiry, and possessing an expressive handsome face, Mr. Morse's air of acute observation was only exceeded by Edgar's. "Yet you have planted sufficient evidence that this could be so."

"Then I have succeeded with my story." Mr. Poe bowed. "Thank you."

"I'm intrigued with your ideas, sir. I think the potential of mesmerism is yet untapped."

Mr. Poe nodded politely. "Then you might be glad to hear that I'm at work on another tale about it."

Mr. Morse grinned. "A further look into the other realm?"

"More so about mesmerism as a means of cheating death, this time. I explore what might happen if a person is mesmerized at the point of his demise."

"Truly? Excellent!" Mr. Morse looked wistful, perhaps thinking of the wife he'd lost. "If only this could be true."

They continued their discussion, the Bartletts remaining to listen as the children gamboled ahead with Mary.

Samuel drew me aside. "So tell me, Fanny, what stories have you written lately?"

We began to follow the children, my skirts swishing in time to our footsteps. He waited, smiling.

"'Ida Grey,'" I said at last.

"You wrote that last year when I was with you. Nice to see that it finally found a home in *Graham's*."

I thanked him, although I was sure I wasn't being complimented.

"I find it amusing that readers are scrambling to read meaning into it, to connect it to you and good old Poe. Your literary romance is quite a hit these days."

"As you said," I remarked coldly, "I wrote the poem more than a year ago."

"Yes, I remember when it got rejected. Interesting that *Graham's* wants it now."

"What are you trying to say, Samuel?"

He looked down his rugged nose at me. "I've been reading your little poems in Poe's rag, too."

I gave him an irritated glance.

He was not smiling. "What I want to know, Fanny, is what have you written lately that you actually care about?"

When I did not immediately answer, he said, "Surely you've written more than this piece." He took a page from his coat pocket. When he unfolded it, I saw that it was from Edgar's *Journal*. He skimmed down a moment, and read.

I know a noble heart that beats
For one it loves how "wildly well"
I only know for whom it beats:
But I must never tell!
Hush! Hark! How Echo soft repeats,—
Ah! never tell!

He refolded it and then put it back. "There was a time when you would have made fun of a poem like this."

I grimaced. It was true.

"All I wonder is why is it that your writing is shrinking into cute little rhymes, while your Poe grows his audience like corn in manure?"

"A disgusting analogy."

"High yield," he said. "You get the point."

I did. And it stung. "I've had a lot of disturbances in my life lately," I said pointedly.

He nodded soberly, as if accepting some of the blame. "It must not be easy to watch Mrs. Poe slowly dying of consumption."

"She's not dying!" I exclaimed. "She ruptured a blood vessel while singing two years ago and cannot seem to heal it."

"Because she is dying, Fanny."

"How coarse of you to say so."

"Why? Because it's true?" He reached out and spanned my temples with his hand, then shook my head gently. "Who is in there? What is that man doing to your mind? I can hardly bear watching the change in you. The Fanny I know calls a spade a spade and is skeptical of those who don't. Doubting Fanny, where are you? I think Impetuous Fanny has eaten you up."

"Coming from a man who traipses after any pretty woman who attracts his attention!" I knocked away his hand. "Tomcats have more restraint. If you only knew what I've given up, how I've tried to make things right for everyone involved, you would say I'm the very opposite of impetuous. I'm responsible, and I pay for it."

Mr. Poe trotted up, his satisfied look dimming when he saw us. "Are you all right?" he said to me, but staring at Samuel.

"Of course."

We recommenced our walk, the three of us unhappily abreast. Eliza and Mr. Bartlett trailed behind, carrying Johnny.

I tugged at my gloves, as if to pluck away the words Samuel had lodged in my mind. "What did Mr. Morse have to say?" I asked Mr. Poe.

He swished his jaw distractedly, as if his thoughts were already elsewhere and he wished to be with them. "Morse has whet my enthusiasm for my new story about mesmerism. If only I felt as sure about my reading for the Lyceum in Boston."

Samuel leaned to ask Mr. Poe, "Is Fanny invited?"

He frowned. "She can go if she chooses."

I glared at Samuel. He knew that neither my conscience nor my reputation could bear such a trip.

Samuel raised his brows. "How nice for you to go on Poe's victory tour. Your own writing can wait. What are a few more weeks of putting it aside for your 'friend'?"

Mr. Poe saw my face. "Why don't you go back to your whore, Osgood? Don't you see you aren't wanted here?"

"By who?" asked Samuel. "You or Fanny?"

"You know the answer."

"Fanny, do you want me to go? Just say the word and I will."

I sighed with frustration. "Just go."

Gawkers strolled past as Samuel stared at me. Then, his brown eyes quiet with genuine sadness, he touched his hat and loped ahead to walk with the children.

Mr. Poe rubbed his brows. "I can't think when that man is around. All my life I have been made to eat the dust of the Boston

Frogpondians—now I have a chance to make them lick my heels. But how, Frances, with what? The most important address of my career, and I cannot think of a single worthy line."

"You will." I watched Samuel kiss each of our girls in turn and then stride away.

Mr. Poe saw at who I was looking. "Just get rid of him, will you?"

A thorn lodged in my heart. "I think I just did."

Twenty-seven

The next afternoon, I was out pacing upon the flagstones in the Bartletts' back garden, trying to compose a poem. Samuel's words about my writing had stung. He was right. I had not produced a work that had excited me or that I was especially proud of since becoming involved with Mr. Poe. Filled with my yearning for him, and made complaisant by the Bartletts' kindness and the usage of their home, my creativity had become a flimsy thing, easily snagged in a spider's web of preoccupation. The more it tried to break free, the more its weak struggles entangled it. I could not write a decent sentence.

Vinnie came skipping outside. "That lady is here, Mamma. Mrs. Clam."

Mrs. Clemm? "What does she want?" I wondered aloud.

Vinnie shrugged, her braids riding her narrow shoulders. "You."

Mrs. Clemm was in the back parlor with Eliza, sitting on the edge of the sofa, when I came in.

"There you are!" said Eliza, overly heartily. "Did you get any work done?"

Mrs. Clemm turned her head so that I could see within her white bonnet. Her eyes, round and blue as a child's marbles, held their usual worried expression.

There came a thump from upstairs, then the shrill shouts of the youngest Bartletts. Eliza got up. "Will you two excuse me for a minute? I think I need to settle a small war."

Mrs. Clemm folded, then refolded her gloved hands as Eliza walked away. "I'm sorry to interrupt. Mrs. Bartlett said you were writing."

I faced my fear head-on. "How is Mrs. Poe?"

"I came on her behalf."

"How can I help?"

She met my eyes, her foolish blue marbles filled with distress. "She's so unhappy! Eddie hardly spends any time with her."

"He works so much," I murmured guiltily.

"I thought he might be here." She peered toward the hallway as if I might be hiding him.

"He does visit with the family here, as you know. We all enjoy his company. We'd so like it if you and Mrs. Poe would come more often with him."

"We don't know where he is," she blurted.

Had he not gone home after he'd left the Bartletts' last night? "He must have gone to his office to work on his poem for the Boston Lyceum. That seems to weigh so heavily on his mind."

"He wasn't there." Mrs. Clemm heaved a sigh. "I can't be worrying about both of my children. I can only worry about them one at a time, and now it's Virginia who concerns me most."

Fear concentrated my mind. "Does she need a doctor?"

"She needs her husband."

The very last place on earth I would wish to be was with Mrs. Poe, but guilt made me say it: "May I come to see her?"

She looked startled. "Well! I never thought— That is terribly kind of you, but you really needn't."

"I insist."

"You really shouldn't." She guiltily met my eyes.

"I would like to help, Mrs. Clemm. It's important to me. Please, let me come."

She drew a shuddering sigh. "If you have to. . . ."

"I'll get my hat and coat." I went upstairs, relieved to be away from her, albeit for a moment.

How fitting, I thought as I tied on my bonnet, that I had to nearly beg her to do something I dreaded to my very marrow.

Mrs. Poe was sleeping on the sofa when we arrived. The pallor of her face shocked me. She'd become so thin that the blue network of veins stood out from her skin. You could almost see her skull.

"Hello, Mrs. Poe," I said, just inside the doorway.

"Go closer," said Mrs. Clemm. "She can't hear you."

Was she dead? I threw Mrs. Clemm a panicked glance.

"Go on."

I took two steps closer. In the shadow of her black wing of hair, I saw the blood vessel in her temple gently pulsating.

"Mrs. Poe?" I whispered.

Fingers snapped behind me.

Her eyes flashed open. I jerked back, nearly stepping into Mrs. Clemm, who in turn stepped on the tortoiseshell cat. It screeched and ran away.

"You're up!" exclaimed Mrs. Clemm, as if Mrs. Poe's waking was extraordinary.

Mrs. Poe yawned as if awaking from a refreshing nap and then smiled at me. "I was dreaming about you."

"Me?"

She coughed into her handkerchief. "It was a happy dream. I was you and you were me."

I scanned the room as if to latch upon something normal, something stable, to speak about. The furnishings had grown plusher since Greenwich Street. Matching red satin chairs had been arranged around a rosewood table. An oil lamp dripped with pretty prisms. A bookcase groaned with volumes. Over the stairs, on the wall above the banister, hung a framed daguerreotype. I peered closer: it was my headless portrait.

Mrs. Clemm looked sheepish when she caught my shocked expression. "Eddie put it there."

"Don't lie, Mother," said Mrs. Poe. "I put it there."

I smiled stiffly. Regardless of who'd hung it, why had Mr. Poe allowed that macabre portrait to remain?

Mrs. Poe reached for the bottle on the stand by the sofa and poured herself a spoonful with shaking hands. She swallowed with effort. "Eddie doesn't like that picture. But he's not here long enough to have a say in it, is he?"

I swallowed back the dismay rising in my throat. I shouldn't have come.

Mrs. Clemm showed me to a seat by her daughter. "You two have a nice chat. I'll be right outside sweeping." She bustled out the door, released from her sickbed duty.

Mrs. Poe eased back down until she was lying on her side. She watched me with too-bright eyes.

What did I say to this creature? "Have you been able to write?"

Her sigh rattled the fluid in her lungs. "Oh, thank you, Mrs. Osgood. Nobody takes my writing seriously. May I share my poem with you?"

"Of course."

She pointed to a wooden box in the bookcase. "In there."

I went to it. The box had once done service holding gloves, according to the advertisement for "finest handwear" from Brooks Brothers clothing store glued to the lid. I removed the top and extracted the first page. "May I read it aloud?"

She sighed, bringing on a cough. "Please."

I smiled, sickening myself with falseness, and began:

> *Ever with thee I wish to roam—*
> *Dearest my life is thine.*
> *Give me a cottage for my home*
> *And a rich old cypress vine,*
> *Removed from the world with its sin and care*
> *And the tattling of many tongues.*
> *Love alone shall guide us when we are there—*
> *Love shall heal my weakened lungs;*
> *And Oh, the tranquil hours we'll spend,*
> *Never wishing that others may see!*
> *Perfect ease we'll enjoy, without thinking to lend*
> *Ourselves to the world and its glee—*
> *Ever peaceful and blissful we'll be.*

I looked up when I finished.

She coughed, her eyes, overlarge in h⁄

"If you take the first letter in each line

"Oh, I see now. Very nice."

"It's every bit as good as the poe⁊

We stared at each other. A violent ru⹀

me, leaving every pore of my body bristling with fear. She knew about Mr. Poe and me. She blamed me for his neglect of her, for taking him away when she needed him most. She knew and she was going to make me suffer. As long as she clung to life, she would make me pay.

I clasped my hands to stop their tremor. "I fear my poems are just foolish pieces of fluff next to this." My voice sounded thin in my ears.

"Well," she said with a smile, "I have an idea for you."

As much as I yearned to, I could not look away from her.

"Write about what's on your mind. My husband has made his fortune upon it. His work might seem to be about black cats or birds or mansions tumbling down, but in the end, it's all about him. You just need to know what to look for to see it." She barked into her handkerchief. When she finished, her smile sharpened. "Do you know what to look for, Mrs. Osgood? Do you know my husband as well as you think you do?"

I stood up. "Thank you for sharing your poem with me." I walked toward the door.

"Why don't you write about a woman whose husband is so busy writing love poems to his lover," she called after me, "that he doesn't see that his wife is dying?"

I stopped, my hand on the doorknob.

She finished my thought as neatly as if it had come from her own head. "You're quite right. That is incorrect. He *does* see that she is dying. And so does his lover." She lifted bony shoulders in a shrug. "But somehow that would make the story less nice, don't you think?"

I could pretend no more. "Good-bye, Mrs. Poe." I fled out the door, nearly colliding with Mrs. Clemm, sweeping the porch step.

She stepped aside, her silly blue marbles puzzled within her bonnet. "Come back soon!"

I paused at the curb before their house, to cross the street behind an ice wagon. I saw something shining in the gutter. I leaned down. A smooth silver locket. I picked it up and turned it over. On it were initials: VP.

At that moment the horse pulling the ice wagon jerked forward. The rear door sprang open. A block of ice the size of a stove slid out and crashed against my shoulder. It dropped to the gutter with a sickening thud.

Mrs. Clemm dropped her rake and hustled to my side. I rubbed my throbbing shoulder—was it dislocated?—and stared at the mammoth block, chopped from the North River last winter. A fish that had been frozen in it gaped at me with cloudy eyes.

The mustachioed driver came running from the neighbor's house.

"Look what you've done!" cried Mrs. Clemm. "You could have killed her!"

"But de door, I latch!" he cried in a thick accent. "Before I go in, I latch." He whipped off his flat-topped cap, leaving his few sparse strands of hair in disarray, then knelt beside me. "Madam, did I hurt?"

"No." I touched my tender shoulder. I could move it. "I'm fine."

I looked up at the porch. Mrs. Poe was leaning against the doorjamb, watching. How long had she been there?

"Here." I held out the locket to Mrs. Clemm. "Is this yours?"

The knobs of her cheeks reddened. "Goodness me, thank you! How did Virginia's locket get out here?"

One troubling word sprang to mind: *coincidence.*

Twenty-eight

Three days passed. To my girls' dismay, Samuel remained gone, as I knew he would. Mr. Poe did not come to the Bartletts, either, time enough for Mrs. Poe's troubling words to take hold. Time enough for me to seize upon his works and pore through them for clues about the man with whom I was inextricably linked. A chilling theme emerged. In tale after tale, "The Black Cat," "The Fall of the House of Usher," "The Tell-Tale Heart," "The Imp of the Perverse," an innocent person was murdered, the body was hidden, and the culprit went free. The murderer then lived the life of his dreams until slowly, driven mad by his own relentless guilt, he crumbled. He ended up revealing his own crime, bringing on his own complete and utter ruin.

I recalled Mr. Bartlett's phrenological reading, when he pronounced Mr. Poe to be unstable and capable of violence. He said that Mr. Poe's very head shape indicated a man on the brink of explosion. Deny it as I might, there was already evidence of such. Mr. Poe's brutally scathing assessments of other writers were unprecedented in our field. The narrators of his stories so often committed heinous crimes. And although I did not wish to admit it, I could now see his terrible struggle for self-mastery when goaded by his wife. Was part of the real Mr. Poe contained in his wrenching stories?

Yet, to me, Mr. Poe was nothing but ardently adoring. I had never been so cherished, so valued, so worshipped by a man. Although clearly frustrated by convention, he struggled to restrain himself within the rules of civility. I did not know which he was: The guilt-ridden man-beast, capable of murder? Or the respectful, loving mate of my soul?

I could not bear another moment of sitting at home that afternoon, reading his stories. It being a crisp day in October, I took a stage down to Battery Park with the thought of clearing my head. I wanted to walk among boring fashionable people, persons with no other worries than if they got mud upon their shoes or if they'd dressed sufficiently for the chill.

I was at the waterfront by Castle Garden, standing among the crowd that had gathered to see an exotic Chinese junk come into port, when I felt a touch upon my elbow.

"A delivery for Mr. Astor?"

I turned around. Mr. Poe stood behind me, his black hair whipping in the wind. The gladness in his eyes nearly melted me.

"I shudder to think," he said, "how many bears and beavers paid for that ship."

I must not return his smile. Where had he been these past days? Yet, I had no real claim on him. I had no right to ask.

I kept my voice level. "Your wife has been looking for you."

The joy drained from his face. "I'm sorry. I should have told her. I should have reported in with you, too. I was thrilled to have seen you here."

"Coincidence," I said coolly, even as I marveled at the chances, in a city of thousands, of coming upon one another like this.

"The truth is, I have been wandering the streets for days, thinking to drive an idea for the Boston presentation into this skull of mine." He sighed deeply. "So far, I have nothing."

Concern for him overrode my other emotions. His address at the Boston Lyceum was in three days, the address at which his success was so important to him. For whatever reason, impressing the Bostonians was the dream of his lifetime. He had nothing for it?

"Is it necessary that you write something new?" I asked. "Surely there's a poem lying in a trunk at home that you can dust off and make brilliant."

"The Bostonians will recognize if I've merely reworked something. They are diabolically smart, damn them."

"Bostonians are like everyone else. They ride only one horse at a time, just like the rest of us."

"They aren't like everyone else"—he blew out a sigh—"and they know it."

I did pity him. "You're from Boston," I said softly. "You can beat them at their game."

The wind tugged his neck cloth from the collar of his coat, adding to his wild appearance. "Being born there isn't enough. I'm an imposter and they sense it."

"As someone who grew up with Bostonians," I said, "I can tell you, for a fact, that you are far superior to any of them whom I have met."

His dark-rimmed eyes warmed with gratitude. "Thank you. I needed that. Whether it's true or not."

His humility disarmed me. How did I resist this man? I turned to watch the skiffs swarming to the junk to unload it.

"I'd like you to come with me to Boston, Frances."

I turned back to him. "You know I can't."

"Please, Frances. I need you. Do you not need me, too?"

I glanced at a couple at the railing nearby. The gentleman's touch was resting on his wife's—or lover's—lower back as they sedately watched the boats. "Yes."

"Then come with me to Boston. We can be as we should be there—as man and wife—if only for a night."

I allowed myself the torture of cherished memories: The warm solidity of his body; the strength of his arms around me; his clean, sweetly leathery smell. I had not kissed him for so very long. To have him completely . . . I closed my eyes with a shudder.

"We are meant to be together," he said, watching me. "I know you feel it, too."

"I can't, Edgar. It's impossible."

"I know I can succeed in Boston if you are with me, I know I can. I'm a different man with you by my side, a better one—a man I could be proud of, for once in my life. Please, Frances, don't make me beg."

His hopefulness crushed me. "What would I tell Eliza? What would I tell the children?"

"It would be easy. Your mother is still living there. You are going to visit her."

"Eliza knows that Mother will not see me."

"She doesn't know that your mother hasn't changed her mind. You can even try to see your mother while you are there, if it will ease your conscience. Please. Just come. I promise"—he lifted my shawl upon my shoulder—"I shall make you glad."

My body hummed with the thrill of his nearness. I raised my eyes to him.

"I'll be at the Tremont House."

"Edgar, I would be there, if I could."

"Then you will come." He bowed, then walked away, his footsteps crunching on the oyster shell path.

I spent a miserable night, trying to be still in my bed as not to wake the girls. I kept picturing Mr. Poe on a steamboat to Boston. I saw the paddle plunging and dripping behind him as he walked the deck, pulling out his paper and pencil, revising a line and then stuffing it back in his coat, the words eluding him for the most important address in his life. He needed me. What's more, I needed him. My life was colorless and numbing without him. To be separated like this felt wrong and cruel.

The next day, tired and out of sorts, I scolded Vinnie for not wearing her coat and then hated myself for it. I could not listen as Eliza complained about Mary's increasing waywardness: Apparently the girl's growing homesickness was undoing her—that, or her male admirer. I found it hard to care at the moment if Mary stayed or if she went back to Ireland. As for writing—I could not pick up my pen. The guilt I felt over not joining Mr. Poe and the guilt I felt for seriously considering it immobilized me. By late afternoon I had decided to return a book to Miss Lynch, just to escape the house and my own tortured thoughts.

A fine drizzle glossed the yellow fronds of the ailanthus trees lining Washington Square. Shying within my hat, I turned the corner onto Waverly Place. There, marching beneath a large black umbrella was Mrs. Ellet.

I glanced around for an escape.

"Mrs. Poe!" she cried.

I looked over my shoulder with a gasp. She was up from her sickbed?

Mrs. Ellet's reticule swung as she put a gloved hand to her horsey cheek. "Oh dear. I meant *Mrs. Osgood.* Why'd I say that?"

Only years of having been polished at the wheel of social nicety allowed for me to smile. "Dear Mrs. Ellet, good to see you."

"I suppose I'm associating you with Mr. Poe."

"A compliment. Thank you." I smiled. I would take a page from Samuel Osgood's book of the slippery.

She frowned, unhappy to have missed her mark. "We missed you Saturday at Anne's conversazione."

"Was it a good crowd?"

"The usuals. Mrs. Butler was there, in spite of her husband's having served her with a petition for divorce. Few would talk to her—only Miss Fuller, who has no morals, and Mr. Greeley, ditto, and Miss Lynch, who, let's face it, has no sense, although she is darling. For Mrs. Butler to provoke her husband to divorce—well, it's unconscionable. Surely they could have just lived apart like everyone else. I was outraged to have to be in her company. Reverend Griswold claimed he was going to leave but didn't. I think he thought you might be coming, because he kept asking everyone about you."

"I thought he'd gotten married."

"Evidently, it didn't take. They were wed so briefly, I'd be surprised if he had time to take off his gloves. Is it me, or does the man have an odd penchant for hand wear?" Her eyes twinkled with what must have been her idea of charm.

I would not gossip with this woman, even about Reverend Griswold. "It was kind of him to think of me."

She wrinkled her nose. "He doesn't strike me as particularly kind. I've heard that he grew up poor—his father was a shoemaker and farmer. It's the kind of mean background that one just doesn't shake, no matter how many gloves one owns or poets one curries. But you would know him." Her pendulous lower lip stretched in a greedy grin. "And how is Mr. Poe?"

When I did not respond quickly enough, she added, "Reverend Griswold says that Poe frequents the house at which you are staying."

You damned, irritating woman. "He has. He has been helping Mr. Bartlett with a dictionary for months."

One brow cocked upward in unconvinced acquiescence.

We nodded at a well-dressed pair of women passing by. The cold damp wind—so particular to New York—leached into my bones.

Mrs. Ellet allowed the ladies to pass before asking me, "And how is *Mrs.* Poe?"

"I really don't know."

She gave me a prissy smile. "You should."

I glanced at my book, then beyond her head, sending the unsubtle message that I wished to go.

She gazed at me, serene as one of the cows in the doomed meadows beyond Union Square. "To tell you the truth, Mrs. Osgood, your name came up a lot at the party. You were being grouped with Mrs. Butler, as unfair as that might seem. You've done nothing to deserve it." Her smirk, wickedly conspiratorial, said differently.

I reined in my fury. "Whatever is being said, I am certain that it would grieve Mrs. Poe, who is in precarious health. People enjoying what might seem like idle gossip are doing real damage to an innocent person."

"What's that expression?" Mrs. Ellet tapped her cheek as if thinking. "'The pot calls the kettle black'?"

I blinked at her, astounded by her outrageous gall. "Where did you come from?"

She smiled. "Columbia, South Carolina. Or hell. They are pretty much the same."

The rain began to pick up, pattering on my bonnet. "I must be going."

"Of course." She stepped aside for me to pass. "Oh, did I tell you, Frances? I met your husband. In the lobby of the Astor House." She laughed. "I didn't realize at first that he was anyone's husband, the way he was carrying on with the Brevoort girl. I suppose it was nothing. One does have to take physical liberties when one is an artist, doesn't one, getting the subject to sit just so."

"Good day, Mrs. Ellet." I strode toward Miss Lynch's house. And I feared offending this sort of person by being with Mr. Poe? She was the offensive one. I was leaving Mr. Poe to the wolves in Boston to keep the good opinion of the likes of her. I was wrong to not have gone with him. I had let down the only man who had ever truly valued me. He nurtured my heart and my soul, yet I had not supported him in his time of need. If he failed in Boston, I would hate myself.

I left the book with Miss Lynch's maid, then heavy with sorrow, headed for home.

My head bowed in the downpour, I did not see the figure sheltering on the Bartletts' porch until I was at the gate. Rain dripped from his hat brim as he lifted his face. His cheeks were ruddy, emphasizing the grayness of his eyes. He had been in the cold for a very long time.

I ran up the steps.

Fat drops spattered on the rim of the porch as I ducked behind a pillar next to Mr. Poe. "I thought you had already left."

"I came to realize that Boston would not be a triumph if you were not there to share it with me. So for all I care, the Bostonians can go to hell. I'm not going."

I wished to throw off his hat and press his wet face in my hands. I loved this man. I would risk anything, everything, *my life*, to be with him. What good was it without him?

I brushed a raindrop from his cheek. "When do we leave?"

Twenty-nine

I lied to Eliza, saying I'd gotten word that my mother was ill and I had to go to her immediately. When she said, "Boston? Isn't Mr. Poe there?" I had the nerve to tell her that I would not have the time to see him. I lied to my girls, telling them that their grandmamma was too unwell for them to visit her with me. I lied to the man at the steamboat office, when draped in a heavy veil, I gave him my name for the passenger list. "Mrs. Ulalume." Where did I come up with such a name? Mr. Poe, in line behind me, had coughed when I said it. Later, on the steamship, I had burned with duplicity knowing that when the plunging and groaning of the paddlewheel stopped in Boston, I would join Mr. Poe on the wharf, and he would walk behind me to the Tremont House. There, still thickly shrouded, I had stood with Mr. Poe at the hotel desk and let the clerk write "Mrs. Poe." By the time we reached our room, my lies hung from me more densely than my gauzy headdress. I could not raise my head from the weight of them as I stood by the window, waiting for the clerk to bring in our valises.

The boy laid our bags on our bed. Mr. Poe reached in his pocket for a tip.

"Oh, no, Mr. Poe." The boy wore his blue livery proudly, as if it were the finest clothing he owned. It likely was. "I can't."

"You know who I am?"

"Who doesn't?" He flapped his arms. "Nevermore! Nevermore!"

Mr. Poe held out a coin. "Take it."

Reluctantly, the boy took it, then backed, grinning, from the room. "Thank you, Mr. Poe. Thank you. No murders tonight, hear?" He flapped his way to the door.

Mr. Poe waited grimly until he was gone. "I'm sorry."

"You see?" I said softly. "You are already famous in Boston."

A lamp had been lit. It threw shadows on the wall as we faced each other from across the room. A foghorn groaned in the distance; footsteps padded down the hall. I stared at him, trembling, through my filmy curtain.

Abruptly, he strode over and stood before me. We gazed at each other, my heart pounding so loudly I knew that he must hear it. When he spoke, his voice was thick with desire. "Woman."

Slowly, he lifted my veil, then, taking my face tenderly in his hands, brought his lips to mine. I melted into his kiss.

I gasped from the pain of his withdrawal when, in time, he broke from my mouth. He swept me up and carried me to the bed, and carefully, as if I were something precious, he lowered me to the velvet counterpane. He opened my bodice, first gently, and caressed my swollen flesh, until driven by need, roughly, tremulously, he pushed back my skirts. I seeped with desperate fullness as he gazed upon me, freeing himself from his clothing. I guided him to me, and crying out as I was raked with excruciating pleasure, I received him, fully, at last.

When I awoke in the morning, Edgar was standing at the window with pencil and paper. He had opened the shade; the weak morning light threw his noble profile in hazy relief. My whole being swelled with happiness as I remembered the things we had done the night before.

He turned around. "Sleep well, Mrs. Ulalume?"

I sighed deeply, the movement making me aware of the exquisite soreness in tender areas. "Yes. Very. When you'd let me."

He laughed. "Where *did* you get that name? Ulalume. It sounds absurdly Polynesian."

I grinned. "I don't know."

He came over and sat on the bed. "I've got something for you." He handed me the page upon which he'd been working.

It was a poem, written on stationery from the hotel. "Is this for tonight?"

"No. For you."

"Edgar, you should be working."

"Read it. Aloud, if you please," he added playfully.
I blew out a sigh, then began, smiling.
"'For Her Whose Name Is Written Within.'"

For her these lines are penned, whose luminous eyes,
Bright and expressive as the stars of Leda,
Shall find her own sweet name that, nestling, lies
Upon this page, enwrapped from every reader.
Search narrowly these words, which hold a treasure
Divine—a talisman, an amulet
That must be worn at heart. Search well the measure—
The words—the letters themselves. Do not forget
The smallest point, or you may lose your labor.
And yet there is in this no Gordian knot
Which one might not undo without a sabre.
If one could merely understand the plot
Upon the open page on which are peering
Such sweet eyes now, there lies, I say, perdu,
A musical name oft uttered in the hearing
Of poets, by poets—for the name is a poet's too.
In common sequence set, the letters lying,
Compose a sound delighting all to hear—
Ah, this you'd have no trouble in descrying
Were you not something, of a dunce, my dear—
And now I leave these riddles to their Seer.

I stopped. I fought back the tears of happiness that had sprung to my eyes. "Did you just call me a dunce?"

He kissed me hard. "Yes." He put his face next to mine to look at the paper. "Do you see the trick in it?"

"Edgar, you shouldn't be working on tricks. What about tonight?"

He pointed to the first letter of the first line. "What's that?"

"An *F*," I said with a frown.

"Now second line, what is the second letter?"

"*R*."

"And in the third, the third letter?"

"*A*."

"Continue on in this fashion. What does it spell?"

I scanned down the lines. "My name." I laughed. "Oh, Edgar. But what about your work?"

He took my hands. "I would rather play."

"I would, too, but—"

"Shh!" He kissed my palms. "We are living a dream, and this is a dream within a dream." He leaned in and gently bit my earlobe. "Now no one awaken me. I am about to make love to an angel."

I sank back laughing. "I feel guilty about taking you from your address."

"I have waited my whole life for this kind of happiness. Do you think I care about the Frogpondians?"

"We'll have other chances. You may not have another at the Lyceum."

He pulled down the thick white sheet, uncovering my nakedness. "Do I want this? Or to please the Froggies? What do you think my choice is going to be?"

We playfully sought each other, our fondness soon turning into sweet desperation. We didn't leave the room for many hours that day.

I did not know then the price we would pay for a glimpse of heaven.

The waiter at the table d'hôte in the Tremont House, a long-lipped, somber Swiss, laid a plate with a hushed thud upon the plush linen tablecloth. Across the crowded room dense with cigar smoke and potted palms, a violinist was making his instrument sob.

Edgar scowled at my entrée. "Pigeon?"

"Quail," I said.

"It looks like passenger pigeon. Only slaves and poor people in the South eat it. I've had my share."

"It's quail." He'd not been paying attention when I ordered. His own order had been "the most expensive thing," and he'd handed back the bill of fare without consulting it. He had been caught up in his own thoughts since I had met him after his presentation at the Boston Lyceum. It was to have been his victory dinner.

Now he ignored the slab of fat-marbled meat that the Swiss had placed before him with the reverence of one making an offering to a god. "You could see their contempt on their faces," Edgar said quietly. "Every face, set against me. They came prepared to hate me, a poor boy from the South."

I sensed that I should not talk. I pressed a fork tine against the naked bird on my plate. It wept golden juice onto the floral pattern of the china.

He shook his head. "I should have read the poem I had written. It was brilliant. One of my best. But when I saw them staring at me, just wishing for me to fail, the words spilled from my mouth." He glanced down at his steak, then, as if spying an enemy, attacked it with knife and fork.

I kept my voice calm. "Which poem did you recite?"

"I gave them what they wanted." He paused with a speared chunk. "I recited 'Al Aaraaf.'"

I lowered my utensils.

"Yes, the same poem I wrote when I was a boy. Only I called it 'The Star Messenger,' to make them think it was something mystical. They so love their transcendental tripe."

"Why?" I could not keep the dismayed astonishment from my voice.

"To see if they could tell the difference between a child's verse and a masterpiece. They deserved it. Inviting me up there to give a poem and then making me wait for almost three hours for Cushing to give his address. As if anyone gives a damn about his trip to China. I thought I had top billing. I would have never gone if I had known I would be treated like that."

"How did they respond?"

"They sat there, vacant as rocks. I suppose Cushing was partly to blame. I nearly fell asleep offstage myself, waiting for him to finish."

I had sat through many a long speech as a student at the Lyceum. We always clapped at the end of them, as much out of relief as appreciation. Even for the most boring speakers, there had been applause, if it were just lukewarm finger tapping. I could not imagine how stunned—or offended—they must have been to not applaud.

"Maybe they were in awe."

He did not acknowledge me. "Then they made me read 'The Raven.' Will I ever escape that cursed bird?"

"They must have been delighted."

"I wouldn't know. I didn't stick around to see. I walked off."

I looked down at my oozing quail. They would ostracize him for rudeness alone.

"It doesn't matter," he said. "I don't need them. All I need is you."

I tried to smile.

"Why do I punish myself? Pleasing the Frogpondians was my mother's dream, not mine. I published 'Al Aaraaf' all those years ago under the pen name A Bostonian as if it would please her. I'm not fooling anyone—I'll never be part of them."

"You don't have to please anyone."

He laughed harshly. "And I haven't, have I?

Why had he sabotaged himself in this way? My heart breaking for him, I slid my hand across the starched white linen and clasped his fingers. "You have pleased me."

A gentleman approached our table—new money, I guessed, by the heaviness of the gold watch fob dangling ostentatiously from his pocket. We withdrew back into ourselves.

"Good evening, Mr. Poe." He stuck out a hand. "Charles Wildwood." A large gold seal ring plated the knuckle of his smallest finger.

Edgar wiped his hands, then shook.

"Love your tales, old man. You working on something else?"

"Always."

He nodded to me. "Hello, Mrs. Poe."

I felt my face redden.

"You ever get scared?" he asked me.

I laughed uncomfortably.

"'Cause if I was his pretty young wife, I'd be terrified. You ever notice how he kills off all the young beauties in his stories? You see one show up, you know she's in trouble."

"It's fiction," said Edgar.

Mr. Wildwood chuckled. "There's nothing sadder than a pretty girl meeting her Maker before her time."

Edgar stared.

"I shouldn't be interrupting your dinner. You must get sick of people yammering at you night and day."

"Thank you for stopping by."

"Any time, any time." Mr. Wildwood started to leave, then pointed a finger at me. "You—keep your head now, hear?"

Edgar did not bother to smile. After the man had left, he said, "Bartlett would have enjoyed him. He was a gold mine of Americanisms."

He ate, but I had lost the little appetite that I had. I cared what people thought. I cared that I was not Mrs. Poe, but Mr. Poe's lover. I cared that my poetry was valued only in its relation to Mr. Poe. He cared, too, what people thought of him, if he were honest with himself. Only someone without even a simple understanding of this world, or without a place in society, would not care if they acted outside the boundaries of decent behavior.

A chill slid down my spine. I had just described his wife.

Thirty

The reviews came in from the Boston Lyceum. They were scathing.

Mr. Bartlett read them at dinner the evening I returned home, after the children had eaten and been sent up to bed.

"Poor Mr. Poe," said Eliza, after Mr. Bartlett had just finished a particularly brutal one. "What do you think he'll do?"

"Keep writing," said Mr. Bartlett. "He's a big boy."

"Oh, but to be called a fraud—that has to hurt."

Mr. Bartlett salted his roast beef. "He dished it out to Griswold and Longfellow. Now he's got to take his medicine from their people." He looked at me. "What was he thinking, reading a poem that he wrote when he was a boy?"

"I really wouldn't know." I smiled as if my heart were not breaking for the man I loved.

Eliza let her gaze meet mine as she cut her meat. "Did you hear about his performance while you were in Boston?" she asked evenly.

"Yes."

They both looked at me, waiting for further explanation. I gazed back, sick with anxiety. *Please do not question me. I cannot bear lying to you.*

Eliza looked away first. She stabbed a piece of meat, then asked, "Russell, have you got Mary's papers in order for her passage?"

He frowned, then nodded, mouth full.

"We've decided to let her go home," Eliza told me briskly. "She's been despondent ever since this summer—wouldn't you say, Fanny? Surely you've noticed."

I nodded, grateful for the change of subject.

She flashed Mr. Bartlett a sidelong glance before smiling at me. "I do hope it's not over a silly man. I can't get her to talk about it, although she jumped at the suggestion that we send her home."

"She'll be better off there." He cut another bite.

"Such odd timing," said Eliza. "Mary must be the only Irish person angling to go *to* Ireland these days. Their poor are coming here in droves since their potato crop failed this summer. A good many of them are starving."

"The crop will recover," said Mr. Bartlett. "It always does."

When Eliza said nothing, I asked, "Will Mary be coming back?"

Mr. Bartlett reached for some bread. "No."

Eliza stared at him. "Yes, she will. I told her that she has employment here as soon as she returns. The children love her."

"She'll not be back," said Mr. Bartlett. He resumed eating his meal.

Eliza blinked at him, then down at her plate before chewing slowly.

I pushed my bit of roast around in its puddle of gravy. The muffled clop of hooves floated through the basement window. From behind the door to the kitchen came the banging of pans being washed and put away. Treasured private images of Edgar and me together tumbled through my mind, as they did so often since Boston.

Mr. Bartlett spoke up. "Did Poe tell you that his partners made him an offer to buy the *Journal* from them?"

"No!" He had so wanted his own journal. He must be pleased. At a time like this, he needed good news.

"The scuttlebutt is that they want out."

I swallowed back a gasp.

"Does this have anything to do with the Boston disaster?" asked Eliza.

"Yes and no," said Mr. Bartlett. "I guess they've been talking about it for a while."

"Why would they want to sell out?" asked Eliza. "Mr. Poe has increased the *Journal*'s circulation. You've heard him talk, Russell—it's finally turning a profit. You would think they would want to be part of something so successful."

Mr. Bartlett grimaced. "You and I may have reached a sort of peace with him, but others are not so sanguine. Let's face it: our Poe is a hard man to understand."

"I wish people could see the Mr. Poe that we see here!" Eliza exclaimed.

"Maybe that we do see him here so much is part of the problem." Mr. Bartlett glanced at me, then took another bite.

I felt my cheeks reddening.

"We cannot let gossip ruin *our* friendship with him!" she cried. "We can't let it ruin it with Fanny."

Her acknowledgment of my involvement with Mr. Poe reverberated in the awkward pause.

Mr. Bartlett could not meet my eyes when he spoke. "I agree. But people will talk—*are* talking. Poe's partners are starting to think of him as a liability."

But we had been so discreet. I closed my eyes in grinding shame. Had we really? The poetry alone had damned us. Our proximity at the conversaziones, his frequent visits to the Bartletts'—what had I been thinking? Of course everyone knew. I had let my desire for him cloud my good sense. I knotted the napkin in my lap as my stomach roiled. How long would it be before our time together in Boston was exposed and I'd be driven from even the outer edges of polite company?

"Have you heard from Samuel lately?" Eliza asked me gently. "If you and he were to come to some sort of agreement, it might stop wagging tongues."

Until that moment, I had not adequately considered how greatly my own soiled reputation could impact her and Mr. Bartlett's position in society. How could I have been so blind?

"I should look for other lodgings."

"I didn't mean that," said Eliza.

"We aren't turning any woman out into the cold," Mr. Bartlett said brusquely.

Eating became impossible after that. I noticed, too, that Eliza had put down her fork. But according to etiquette, women could not leave the table until the man of the house had finished, and so we sat with our hands folded upon our skirts, glancing at each other as Mr.

Bartlett moved onto the subject of the likelihood of the Republic of Texas becoming a state.

The parlor maid, Catherine, came in when Martha was removing the dessert plates. "Pardon me, sir."

Frowning at her intrusion into the dining room, Mr. Bartlett lowered his napkin. "What is it?"

I noticed she was blushing. "Would you like me to light the gas in the parlor tonight?"

Eliza spoke up quickly. "Just the oil lamps, please."

Catherine nodded, then bowed out, shamefaced.

Eliza hesitated. With a glance to her husband, she said, "We had an incident with Catherine when you were gone."

"I should have let her go because of it," said Mr. Bartlett. "I still might."

"Russell," Eliza protested.

"She endangered the children. She endangered you, not to mention our home."

"What did she do?" I asked.

They exchanged looks. Eliza drew in a breath. "I didn't know how to tell you this, but Mrs. Poe and her mother came here Thursday afternoon."

"Thursday?"

"The day of her husband's presentation in Boston. When you were gone." She frowned nervously. "They were looking for you."

Panic constricted my chest. "What did you tell her?"

"She arrived at five," said Eliza, "a rather odd time, I thought then. But you know Mrs. Poe."

"What did you tell her?" I asked again.

"I had the children come down and join us in the parlor—I'll admit, to serve as a distraction. I'm sorry now that I did so."

"Eliza, where did you say I was?"

"I didn't tell her anything. But then Vinnie volunteered that you'd gone to see your mother." She sighed. "In Boston."

Every shaft of my hair prickled with fear.

She glanced at Russell, who was scowling as he chewed, before she continued. "We were having one of those awkward conversations so typical of Mrs. Poe and that frantic mother of hers when Catherine came in to light the lamps, as it was growing dark. Catherine had drawn down the chandelier and opened the gas cocks when Mrs. Poe started coughing."

She shook her head with a bounce of ringlets. "'Coughing' does not begin to describe it. You have never heard such an alarming sound! It was as if she were being strangled. She clutched at her throat and clawed for air. I rushed to her side and shouted for Catherine to bring some brandy. Catherine, who'd been standing there in shock, sprang from the room. No sooner than Catherine was gone, than did Mrs. Poe straighten. Her mother, in near hysterics, claimed that they must go home that instant—*that instant!*—it would be Mrs. Poe's only cure.

"Over my protests that she must not leave until a doctor could be fetched, they departed. Mrs. Clemm was nearly wailing and could hardly get out the door. When Catherine returned with the bottle and a glass, I told her never mind, Mrs. Poe had left. We were staring at the door, dumbfounded, when Russell arrived. He said, 'You look like you've seen a ghost—'"

"That's exactly what I said," Mr. Bartlett interjected.

Eliza glanced at him, too wrapped up in her story to acknowledge him. "Then he went to his chair, laid down his paper, and got out his pipe. He was readying to strike a safety match to light it, when your Ellen shouted, 'The gas!'"

I covered my mouth.

"We all rushed outside—"

"I threw open the windows," said Mr. Bartlett.

"—and we didn't go back in for hours."

"You were all right?" I asked.

Eliza nodded. "But it was horribly upsetting. We'd come that close to an explosion. I wish you'd give up smoking, Russell."

"That's not the problem," he said.

Eliza drew a breath. "I know this sounds absurd, but it's almost as if Mrs. Poe meant to harm us. You should have seen her face when Vinnie said you were in Boston. I have never seen such venom. It was frightening."

"We must not allow her in!" I cried.

"Now, now," said Mr. Bartlett, "you two are getting hysterical. She doesn't scare me. She's a little odd, yes, but to blame her for Catherine's absentmindedness is wrongheaded."

I thought of Edgar's words about madness coloring all those around them. Had Mrs. Poe unbalanced me? Surely she was not capable of wishing harm to my family and friends just to get at me. Surely.

Thirty-one

At first it seemed like the debacle at the Boston Lyceum had done nothing to dim Mr. Poe's popularity. It appeared, in fact, to have the opposite effect. At an afternoon tour of the Five Points slums that Miss Lynch had arranged in lieu of a conversazione that following week, everyone crowded around him when he arrived, alone, and rigid-faced, at our meeting place at City Hall Park. They wanted to know what had possessed him to try such a prank.

"Thumbing your nose at the Walden Pond group." Mr. Greeley had to speak up to be heard over the rumbling din of Broadway traffic and the gush of the great Croton Fountain, where we were waiting for the Municipal Police officer who was to protect us as we navigated the slums. "That took guts, as seriously as they take themselves."

"That's exactly why it needed to be done." Mr. Bartlett came forward to get closer to Mr. Poe, as if staking his claim on his special friendship with him. You would never guess that, at my request, Mr. Bartlett had turned Mr. Poe away from his door several days ago. "They think they have the edge over us here in New York. But we aren't afraid of them, are we, Poe?"

"H'm? No."

Mr. Poe stepped toward where I stood apart from the group. I turned away, into the spray that the wind blew from the fountain. I welcomed the sensation of the frigid mist needling my face. Better to dwell on it than on the heartbreaking feeling that he was reaching out for me with his mind. I could not look at him. To look at him would undo me. For the safety of my children and friends, I knew that I had to end it with Edgar after his wife had endangered them, but that did not mean that I didn't love him. He was all I ever wanted. I would never get over adoring him, never get over yearning for him, never get over the wounding to my soul when he called to me so pitifully outside the Bartletts' house after I had refused to see him. He had stood hatless in a drenching storm, shouting out my name, the very picture of misery as rain poured down his wretched face. I winced now at the memory.

"Well, Edgar's little ploy certainly was effective advertising," said Miss Fuller. "If you weren't already on everyone's lips, Edgar, you surely are now."

"I don't know," said Reverend Griswold, "that if being on people's lips in this way will not leave a bad taste." He had been newly restored to our circle since his brief foray into holy wedlock and now was pinkly handsome in a new beaver top hat. "I don't know if I'd want to become known for cheating an audience out of respectable material. They paid good money to hear what amounted to a joke. Don't be surprised, Poe, if people never pay to see you again."

"One thing I've seen in my line of work," said Miss Fuller, "is that there is no predicting what people will do. But your little system of mutual log-rolling has certainly worked for you, Rufus."

Reverend Griswold flared his fluted nostrils. "I'm not ashamed to puff and be puffed, if that's what you mean. Those who think that they are above it are destined to perish."

"Perish?" said Mr. Greeley. "They might lose sales, but perish?"

"Same thing in our world," said Reverend Griswold. "And those who say it's not aren't being honest." He looked at me pointedly as he twisted one of his rings around a gloved finger. "But I cannot help everyone. Not if they won't let me."

"I think all of you are missing the point." Miss Ellet expanded with importance when everyone looked at her. "If you really want to understand what Mr. Poe was up to," she said, "read his work."

I plucked at my mantle, wishing I could pluck Mrs. Ellet from my sight. Who *was* this irritating woman, claiming to know my Edgar?

But Edgar only said, "How is that, madam?"

Beneath her small net veil, her smile was smug and flirtatious at once. "Obviously, you are dramatizing the same motivation that drove the narrator in 'The Imp of the Perverse.' The narrator had escaped detection of the murder he had committed. The case had been closed and he was completely safe. The only way he could get caught was to confess the murder—an impossibility. Who would damn himself? Yet, he did. The imp within him—the imp who is within everyone—did."

"*I* have no such imp," Reverend Griswold protested.

Mrs. Ellet ignored him. "You did the very thing that would damn you, Mr. Poe, in your case, call down the wrath of the Boston elite upon you."

"And why would I want to do that?" he said coldly.

She came over and offered up her face to Mr. Poe as if it were beautiful. The netting of her veil trembled as she spoke. "Because it terrifies you."

He stared at her.

"Why would anyone want to terrify themselves?" Reverend Griswold scoffed.

"Read his story," snapped Miss Fuller. "It's brilliant, Edgar. Who doesn't at one time or another find themselves on the brink of disaster, and instead of pulling away, leaps headlong into it?"

"I did," said Mr. Greeley, "when I married my wife."

Only Reverend Griswold, and Mr. Poe and I, did not laugh.

"What else do you know about me from my stories, madam?" Edgar asked Mrs. Ellet.

"Everything." She lifted her chin to him in challenge. "That death is constantly on your mind. That you think people are gullible. That you think people are, at heart, evil."

He stared at her. "You err. I think people are, at heart, good."

The group laughed as if he were joking. I knew better.

"She got you, Poe," said Mr. Greeley, trying to make light of it.

The police officer arrived with apologies for his lateness. As he accompanied the group toward Chambers Street and beyond, to the festering boil on the city that was the slums of Five Points, I broke away from the group.

I was hailing a hackney cab on Broadway when Mr. Poe caught up with me.

"Why did you leave?"

"I cannot stand these hellish tours. I know that Miss Fuller means to educate by leading this one, but how many people go 'slumming' just to be titillated? What does it say about the fashionable of New York that it is sporting to observe the most wretched?"

"Then why did you come?"

I watched as two riders galloped by. Why had I come? I looked at Mr. Poe.

"Why won't you see me, Frances?"

"I have to go home, Edgar. I am tired tonight."

"Do not lie to me. I cannot bear your lying to me."

"Then because your wife frightens me."

He stared at me. A hackney approached, its mustachioed driver slumping at the reins. I flagged it down. When it stopped, I got in. Edgar climbed in behind me and flung himself on the opposite bench. There was no use to protest.

After the carriage jolted away from the curb, Edgar said, "What do you mean that Virginia frightens you?"

The carriage lamp cast just enough light through the window to reveal the anxiety on his face. I sighed. "To end it now would be the kindest for us all."

"What did she do?" he demanded.

"If we no longer see one another, she'll leave me alone. She is your wife. She needs you. It's only right that you care for her."

"What did she do?"

I longed to reach across the darkness and touch his anguished face. "Edgar, we had a beautiful night together. Most people never have such a night in their entire lives. Let's be glad for what we had."

"Frances, tell me."

My heart thumped to the clop of the hooves. I drew a breath. "She nearly caused a gas explosion at the Bartletts'. When we were in Boston."

He blinked as if slapped. "How?"

"She just did."

"I'll get rid of her."

"Don't say that! That makes it worse!"

He dug his hand through his hair. "I won't then!"

I wanted to tell him that I knew, now, that I had not imagined she had tried to drown me. Unless fear and paranoia had eroded my mind, I knew I was not dreaming that she had engineered my headless portrait to intimidate me. She'd had a hand in the burning of Madame Restell's quarters, I suspected, simply because she disapproved of her. It seemed that she had even somehow set up my nearly being crushed by the block of ice outside her door, although how she had achieved that, I could not imagine. Who knew what other sly acts of violence she was capable of? But I could not say these things to Mr. Poe. I could not further enrage him against her. I did not know what he might do.

"I'll do whatever you say, Frances, but I cannot bear for you to leave me." He sprang across the space between us and pressed me to him. "Promise you will not leave me, Frances."

I breathed in his sweet leathery smell. How I loved his valiant soul, fighting for his place in the world in the face of crushing hardship, fighting for me. But how could I risk my family's safety to keep him?

"Edgar, we can't."

He pulled away. "We'll be more careful, that's all, at least for a while. We'll be as invisible as ghosts. Frances, say that you will see me. I shan't let her hurt you. I promise." He squeezed my fingers. "Do you think that I would endanger my soul's true mate?"

The carriage came to a halt. I removed my hand from his. Even that disconnection was painful in its intensity.

"Oh, Edgar. All right. We can try. But we must be scrupulously careful."

He kissed my forehead, letting his lips linger, then pulled back. His smile was meant to be brave but I could see the worry in his eyes. "I will not let her hurt you, my love. You know that you can trust me."

Thirty-two

"I don't know how he does it!" cried Mrs. Mary Jones, the hostess of the Christmas ball that I was attending that evening with the Bartletts. Her effusive bulk, amplified by vast wealth, seemed to invade the air around her. That her flesh was now shoehorned into a purple velvet gown only emphasized the effect. She was fond of expensive feather headdresses and wore a scarlet one now upon her gray curls, giving her the appearance of the plumed dapple mare that had drawn Mr. Barnum's lion wagon. Now the plume bobbed jauntily as she nodded toward Mr. Poe, enthralling a group of ladies over by the pianoforte, a group I had been certain to avoid. "How does he come up with such imaginative stories?"

"I'm sure Mrs. Osgood would not know." Reverend Griswold slid up and stood as close to me as would a husband. "She has dropped him like everyone else has." He offered me a slice of cake, his well-groomed face smug with possessiveness.

I forced myself not to move away as I took the plate. It was best that Reverend Griswold felt some ownership of me. If he thought I was not involved with Edgar, maybe no one did. Edgar and I had taken great pains to appear to have been disconnected over the past two months. Oh, we had to see each other—to not do so was as sure to kill us as withdrawing water and sunshine—but our stolen moments together were at the wharves along the Hudson, or in the muddy lanes near the slaughterhouses, or in the chapel for sailors downtown, places where our set did not venture. Even there we settled for merely exchanging a few longing words or a touch upon the arm. It had to be enough. As a further precaution, Edgar had not attended the conversaziones for fear of being linked with me, and I had not attended his lectures. If I had known that he was going to be at Mrs. Jones's ball, I would have refused to come. At least Mrs. Poe was not there, or I would have immediately fled.

"I'm tempted to believe," Mrs. Jones announced, the quality of her voice remarkably like that of a bugle, "that there is some truth to Mr. Poe's musings in 'The Facts in the Case of M. Valdemar.' Is it so unreasonable to think that a person mesmerized at the point of his death could be kept alive, as long as he was being held in a hypnotic trance?"

"It's a story," said Reverend Griswold. "And not a very good one at that. I did not review it well, I'm afraid."

"Well!" She tossed her plume. "I can tell you of more than a few persons who have hired mesmerists to attend the deathbed of their loved ones."

"And did it work?" demanded Reverend Griswold.

"I did hear of one case—"

Before she could finish, a disturbance arose in the dining room. Several ladies were exclaiming around a large wicker basket that had been brought in by Mrs. Jones's manservant.

"Excuse me! Excuse me!" she trumpeted, barging through the crowd. I followed in her wide wake, conscious of Reverend Griswold at my heels.

"Daniel!" she bellowed. "What is the meaning of this?"

The servant held up the basket. I was behind Mrs. Jones's shoulder among the gathering crowd when she turned back the soft cotton blanket inside it. A beautiful infant, maybe a week old, in a clean worked linen gown and lace cap, and with a woman's gold locket around its neck, blinked in the gaslight.

Into the shocked silence, a man said laconically, "Look what the stork brought."

"Why me?" cried Mrs. Jones. "Why here?"

On the other side of the circle of shocked onlookers, Mr. Poe spoke up quietly. "Because his mother could not keep him."

"Well, I can't keep him!" Mrs. Jones exclaimed.

"Open the locket," suggested a gentleman with a lady on his arm. "Perhaps that will give you a clue to who the mother is."

The guests drew closer, as if discovering the baby's parentage were an exciting parlor game. Mrs. Jones put her gloved hand to her mouth, then, gingerly, picked up the locket. It opened with a spring. A blond wisp was curled inside.

"Hair!" exclaimed Mrs. Fish. "Mamma's or Papa's?"

Eliza drew near with the ladies with whom she'd been speaking.

Mr. Bartlett stepped forward and took her arm. I saw him whisper in her ear.

Meanwhile, as the crowd watched in a stunned hush, Edgar moved next to Mrs. Jones, then carefully lifted the child from the basket and cradled it in his arms.

"I never took you for a little mother, Poe," said Reverend Griswold.

"Shhh," Mr. Poe whispered to the child. "All will be well. Don't be frightened." He looked up and caught my gaze. There were tears in his eyes, tears for the abandoned child, and tears, I knew, for the orphan that he himself once was. How hard he had tried his whole life to hide his pain behind his cool and cultured surface. It crushed me to see his vulnerability exposed to a crowd of curious onlookers.

Without thinking, I stepped to his side and put a hand on his arm. "This child must be very well loved. His mother brought him here because she wanted him to find a home among the best in the city."

He glanced up. We exchanged a look rich with understanding.

I felt a hand upon my back.

"Fanny," said Eliza, "we have to go now. Russell is ill."

I turned to leave with a rustle of skirts. It was then that I saw Reverend Griswold watching me, his handsome pink face slack with the dawning knowledge of what he'd just seen.

Eliza spread the cooked date filling over the dough that I had rolled out on Bridget's breadboard. "Fanny, you really don't have to leave."

It was the day before Christmas. She had given the Irish girls (except for Mary, who had departed for home months earlier), the day off in which to make any Christmas purchases they needed to make. The new tradition of celebrating Christmas Day by exchanging gifts and giving presents to the children, allegedly brought by that right jolly old elf, Saint Nick, was already well entrenched in New York, where people embraced Mr. Moore's poem with an enthusiasm he still regretted.

I listened to the children, playing jacks in the family room. "You've already been entirely too generous," I told her. "I have been here for more than a year."

Surely she'd had enough of me being constantly underfoot. I had recently sold several of my old poems to *Graham's* and *Godey's Lady's Book*, most likely on the strength of the rumors of my having been Mr. Poe's lover. I could keep digging into my stock of rejects and eke out some kind of life based on my notoriety until my ability to write returned. Maybe being on my own would force it out. Need is the mother of creation.

"I have enjoyed every minute of your company," she said briskly. "I treasure our conversations. It's a relief not to have every word that comes out of my mouth categorized: Is it American? English? or both?"

I laughed. "I envy your stable life."

She paused with her spoon. "Do you? Do you really? Wedded bliss is a tale made up to keep the species going."

"Eliza!" I laughed. "What are you saying? You and Mr. Bartlett are the happiest pair I know."

She glanced at me, her plain, dear face turning red. "I'm just glad that you are here, Fanny. I don't know what I would have done without you to keep my mind off my troubles."

I looked at her. What troubles?

She went back to smoothing out the filling. "Listen to me, proof that my condition makes a woman act bizarrely."

"Your condition?"

She put a hand to her belly, then smiled uncertainly.

"Oh, Eliza! Really? You're having a baby?"

She nodded.

I rocked her in an embrace. "Congratulations!"

A jingling commenced at the panel of service bells above the square stone sink. We looked at it as if a spirit were trying to contact us from another realm. Simultaneously, we realized that none of the servants were available to answer the summons. It jangled again.

"Front door," said Eliza.

"I'll get it." I went upstairs, dusting the flour off my hands and cheek. It was probably a delivery boy with the goose for tomorrow's meal.

I swung open the door, letting in a blast of cold air. Samuel stood on the porch, holding a cedar tree that was nearly as tall as he was.

I did not know whether to feel angry or glad. Angry, I decided. Very angry. I had not heard from him since September. No matter if I'd sent him away, he could have kept contact with the children. It broke my heart how they watched for him daily from the windows. "Well, if it isn't Old Saint Nick."

"Old Nick," said Samuel. "No Saint."

"I thought you were the delivery boy with the goose."

"I am a delivery boy of a sort." He thumped the tree on the porch. "I brought this for the girls. I thought you might let me in. Don't prisoners get amnesty on Christmas?"

Some prisoner. Mrs. Ellet had not been the only one unable to resist telling me of his various conquests. He had been making good use of our separation. "Where did you get the tree?"

"I tramped up past Seventeenth Street and chopped one down. I figure I helped old man Astor and his counting house boys to clear the land." He shook the tree. "According to European tradition, you put candles on fir trees for Christmas. Thought you might want to try it." He gave me a hangdog grin. "What do you say about letting an old tree thief come inside?"

A damply cold wind rippled my skirt as I stepped aside for him to enter, if only for the sake of the children.

Vinnie bounded up the stairs as Samuel dragged the tree into the hall. "Papa! Where have you been? What is that tree?"

"A Christmas tree. You put candles on it on Christmas Eve."

"That's tonight!"

"Why, yes, yes it is. Do you think you might be able to scare up a few candles for it?"

"Yes!" She pounded down the back stairs.

I sighed. There would be no easy way of getting Samuel to leave now that Vinnie knew he was here. At least she would be happy.

The front door rang again. "There's our goose," I said.

I stepped around Samuel and his tree and opened the door. Mr.

Poe, hatless and wind-tossed, stood on the porch, holding a large fir. My soul leaped at the sight of him, so red-cheeked and handsome, happiness lighting his dark-lashed eyes. My joy quickly shrank into fear. Was it safe for him to be here? Where was his wife?

"There's our goose," Samuel said drily.

Edgar's smile turned into a scowl. "I didn't know he would be here."

By now, Eliza and her brood had come to the hall, the littlest holding hands with Ellen.

"Two trees," little Johnny said stoutly. "That's silly!"

"Maybe you ought to take yours to your wife," Samuel said. He met Mr. Poe's cold stare with a shrug, then kissed Ellen.

"How is she?" asked Eliza gently.

"Sleeping. Soundly. Her mother is with her."

Eliza glanced at me as if wondering whether to invite them in. It was Christmas Eve. A time of peace and good will, a time, as Samuel said, of amnesty. My children would be thrilled. And maybe the presence of my husband would placate Mrs. Poe should she hear that Edgar had come. I nodded in resignation.

"You may both stay for supper if you'd like," she told them.

"Thank you," said Samuel. "But it's up to the lady." He looked at me.

Vinnie ran upstairs, waving a fistful of little candles.

I blew out a sigh. "Stay."

"Hurray!" shouted Vinnie.

The awkwardness at the supper table was only mitigated by the children's excitement over the Christmas trees, which had been duly decorated and exclaimed over before we sat down to eat. Samuel talked too much; Mr. Poe too little. Mr. Bartlett and Eliza tried to pick up threads of conversation only to have Samuel run away with them or Mr. Poe to snip them short. It came as a relief when Mr. Poe put down his napkin and, gazing at the children at the table, said, "Do you know the tale 'The Fir Tree'?"

"Is it for children?" asked Vinnie.

"The man who wrote it, Mr. Andersen in Denmark, thought of it as such. It's about a Christmas tree."

The children leaned forward, Eliza's boys barely containing their wiggling.

"Are you ready?" Mr. Poe looked around with those dark-lashed eyes. The children shrank back into themselves.

"Good." He glanced at me, then began.

"Once there was a young fir tree growing in the forest. He was a handsome tree, proud of his green branches. All the birds and animals said how tall he stood and how very straight. No other tree was as green and straight.

"I have a tree!" exclaimed little Johnny. "In my garden."

Mr. Poe nodded at his outburst. "This little tree, I'm sorry to say, was not happy. He had noticed that every year come winter, men would march into the woods with their saws and take away one of his brethren, even though the other trees were not nearly as fine as he was."

"Why?" asked little Johnny.

"Shhh," said Eliza. "Listen."

Mr. Poe continued. "The little tree asked a sparrow where the other trees were going. The sparrow, who had been to the city, said, 'To people's homes, where their branches are stuck with candles and their tops are crowned with a golden star. Children dance around them and sing. A more wonderful sight I have never seen.'

"From that day on, the fir tree could not be content. Why was he not chosen to go to the city? If he were taken, he would shine brighter and dazzle the children more brilliantly than all the other trees combined."

"Like our tree!" crowed little Johnny.

"Hush," said Eliza.

Mr. Poe glanced at me before continuing. "Each year when the men came, he lifted his branches to the sunshine, showing off his beautiful green color and perfect form. Each year, the men passed him by, crushing him with their ignorance. He then tried all the harder to stand straighter, to hold out his boughs better, to display his extraordinary bright greenness. *Pick me!* He thought. *Pick me!* And still they did not notice him until one year, when he had almost given up, they *did*."

Vinnie clapped, setting off applause from Eliza's sons. Their sister, Anna, glared at them, intent on the story.

Mr. Poe thanked them, then went on. "Yes, he was happy, too. All the way into the city, he dreamed of how important he would look with the candles upon his boughs and a star upon his top. Children would come from miles around to admire him.

"He was taken into a house and nailed onto a stand. Ouch, yes, that hurt, but he didn't mind. It was a small price to pay for his upcoming glory. The candles came next—so tight around the tips of his boughs, and so very heavy, too, but he was strong, he could lift them up! Then he was crowned with a golden star: King of the Forest! He was beaming with pride when the candles were lit and then with a *swoosh* the parlor doors flew open and the children ran into the room.

"'Oh!' they cried. 'It's the most beautiful tree in the world!'

"His heart nearly burst with joy as the children danced and sang around him. He didn't care when drips of wax singed his handsome boughs. All he could think about was what came next, *for then he would truly be the happiest tree alive.*

"But then the candles burned down and the children stopped dancing. The people went away, closing the doors behind them, leaving him in the smoke-tinged darkness.

"The next day, he was dragged up to the attic, his star catching on the steps, where he was dropped down, *bang*, in the dust.

"He lay there many years, his branches turning brown, his needles crumbling, his torn star getting covered with dust, until one day, a rat gnawed at his trunk."

"'Stop that!' cried the little fir tree.

"The rat gave him a grumpy frown. 'Who are you?'"

Mr. Poe held up his chin. "'The most beautiful tree in the world.'

"The rat sat back on his haunches. 'You don't look so beautiful.'

"'I am beautiful,'" said Mr. Poe in his soft and frightening voice. "'I was told so on the happiest night of my life, but I did not know I was so happy at the time. I thought there'd be more.'

"Footsteps sounded on the attic stairs. A man came and chopped the tree to pieces, then took them downstairs and put them on the family room fire. The tree sighed as the flames went up, each sigh as sharp as a pistol shot. The children, playing nearby, stopped to listen. With each pop, the tree sighed with the memory of his days in the forest, of the days when he was growing big and green, of the Christmas Eve on which he'd shone so bright. One of the children found the torn paper star, lying on the floor, and pinned it on his breast. He ran off to play, wearing the star that had adorned the tree on what had been the happiest day of its life."

The gathering at the table had gone silent except for Vinnie's sniffing. There was fear in the eyes of the children who were not actually crying.

"Some tale, Poe," Samuel said.

"It's Mr. Andersen's, not mine."

Samuel gave him a disgusted look then turned to the children. "Who would like to hear 'A Visit from Saint Nicholas'?"

A tearful cheer went up.

Mr. Poe did not stay for the lighting of our tree. I walked him outside when the family was waiting for Mr. Bartlett to finish dessert so they could leave the table and let the festivities begin.

"Such a sad tale," I said.

"I did not mean to upset the children, but it's not a tale. It's me. If I had known that our night together would be our only one, I would have not have let you go that morning. I would have shanghaied you on Astor's boat to China, or whisked you off to a castle in Scotland—taken you to a place where you could be mine forever more." He settled my thick paisley shawl higher upon my shoulder, protecting me from the wind. "Now I must content myself with the memory of the only night I had truly lived."

"You are the toast of the town, Edgar. You are followed by admirers on the street. You have sole ownership of your literary journal. You have everything you ever wanted."

He narrowed his eyes in pain. "I have nothing without you and you know it. This night of joy is a torture to me."

I drew in a breath. "How is Virginia?" I asked.

"Must you destroy any shred of happiness that we might find tonight?" He sighed. "I'm sorry, Frances." I could feel him trying to lighten his voice. "It's Christmas."

In the glow of the streetlight, I could see the bleakness in his eyes. "I wish that it didn't have to be this way," I said softly.

"Virginia will not last long."

"Don't say that! Do you think I will wait like a ghoul for her to die? No, Edgar, it's wrong."

"But when she dies—"

"We cannot think like that. It poisons what is good about us."

I felt the pain in his silence. How I wished to bury myself against him, the wish made more intense by knowing I could not. Why are we doomed to crave most that which we cannot have?

A horse clopped by, its clouds of breath snatched away by the frigid night.

"I am not the heartless creature that you think I am," said Mr. Poe.

"I know you aren't."

The bells of the Dutch church in Washington Square tolled nine, their sonorous clanging infusing the night with melancholy. It was Christmas Eve. Good husbands and wives were chuckling at their exuberant children, dashing around the house until it came to tears. In the morning the loving couples would smile at each other as their wee ones raced to their stockings hung by the fire to find a doll or top or ball. They would eat their toast and marmalade, smiling at each other in sweet contentment, then afterward, upon bundling the children in boots and mittens and mufflers, would take a walk, during which they would nod to neighbors fond of both them and their family. Such a simple dream. And so impossibly beyond reach of Mr. Poe and me.

I was shivering from the cold. He drew in a deep breath, then tucked my shawl tighter. "We must be patient, my love."

I sighed. "Oh, Edgar."

"You must trust me. It will be right someday."

Vinnie appeared at the door. Mr. Poe's hand slid from my shoulders.

"Mamma! They're going to light the tree!"

"Yes, Vinnie."

"Now, Mamma!"

"Yes, Vinnie. I'm coming."

When I turned back around, Mr. Poe was striding down Amity, a single dark figure on a street bright from the festive lights burning from within every house. He looked as alone as an orphan on Christmas. That was exactly what he was.

Winter 1846

Thirty-three

A new year, a new start. I was at the desk in the Bartlett's front parlor, trying to resurrect my writing. I *had* been a writer, before becoming consumed by my love for Mr. Poe. If I were to become known again as a serious poet, and not just for the gossip spun around Mr. Poe and me, I must produce something of worth soon. Now, more than ever, it was important for me to make my bread at it.

I put down my pen, bracing myself as a wave of nausea broke over me. I had been feeling sick for the past ten days. I had thought at first it was indigestion from all the rich Christmas foods, but when it had not gone away after a week, and a general weariness began to overwhelm me, I began to worry about other possibilities. A consultation with the calendar solidified my fears.

Now a fresh onslaught of panic-tinged nausea induced me to snatch up my pen again. I glanced outside as if grasping for a lifeline. In the street, the children were throwing snowballs under the bored supervision of Catherine, who did not share in the maternal instinct that Mary once had. Eliza was, at this moment, at the domestic help bureau, to see about getting a replacement for Mary, who would not, she had written recently, be coming back. Mr. Bartlett was up in his study, working on his dictionary, I presumed. I had the morning to myself, something, I reminded myself, that I would not have once a baby came.

I shied from this sobering thought. I must create a shivery story that would help me be independent. As much as I did not relish the macabre, the public taste called out for such. I *would* impress Mr. Morris and his gelatinous curl. I could do anything that I set my cap to. I had to, now.

The image of Madame Restell swam into my mind. I saw her swathed from head to toe in furs, totting up her accounts upon an evening at her rosewood desk. She was stacking coins into even piles of gold, when she began to hear voices.

The practical side of my writer's brain intervened. Voices? Whose voices would this Madame Restell character hear? I thought of the women who must cross her door each day: Servants impregnated by their employers. Women with child by abusive husbands. Women in intolerable situations whose last desperate hope was to place their lives in Madame Restell's untrained hands. Women who died on her table.

I had written three much-crossed-over pages, when Mr. Bartlett said, "New poem?"

I jumped, tipping over my inkpot. It splashed onto a finished page before I could catch it.

"Sorry!" He whipped a handkerchief from inside his coat and began blotting. "I'm sorry, I think I've ruined it."

I caught my breath. The page I'd been working on was destroyed. Could I remember what I had written?

He peered at where he was dabbing. "Not a poem, I see. What's it about?"

A snowball hit the window, startling us both. "Hey, knock it off!" he shouted.

We could hear the children's laughter through the glass. Catherine moved to scold them, making them laugh harder still.

He turned back to me. "So what is it about?" he asked again.

I pursed my lips.

"A secret?" He grinned.

I shook my head. "Not really. But it has been tricky. It's about a character based on Madame Restell."

His face changed color with the alacrity of an alarmed squid. He turned as red as Vinnie's mittens.

I'd offended him. Why had I not believed that a piece based on Madame Restell would offend everyone? I could never sell it.

I moved to stuff the remaining page into my leather notebook. "It's a foolish project, really. Mr. Morris at the *Mirror* wanted me to write something ghoulish. I'm not very good at it."

"No." He stopped my hand.

I looked up.

He pulled away when he saw my discomfort. "You'll smear your pages."

"It doesn't matter. He won't buy it."

He stared out the window as I put away the manuscript and capped the inkpot.

"What do you know about Madame Restell?" he asked.

"I suppose what everyone else knows."

He swallowed, then turned a darker shade of red. "What does everyone know?" He stared back at me in defiance when I tried to read his face.

The corners of his mouth turned down severely. "I told her not to go there. They would have butchered her. Didn't she know that I would not have that on my head?" His shoulders drooped as if a weight had slid off them. "I love her. I love that child. How could she have given it away?"

Bang! A snowball hit again. He jerked as if shot. "Blast you kids!" He raged to the door, but not before I saw the tears glittering in his eyes.

The chatter of the children, cheerful from plastering each other with snow all morning, allowed me to steal surreptitious looks at Eliza as I ate my soup at the noontime meal. Mr. Bartlett had taken his lunch up in his study—he had taken pains to avoid me after his startling revelation. Surely Mr. Bartlett did not mean that Eliza had gone to Madame Restell. Even though she had gravely suffered with the loss of her children, Eliza wanted more, I knew she did. I feared that he wasn't talking about Eliza. But if it wasn't Eliza, who was it? They'd had a child together?

I spooned in my soup. It seemed impossible that Mr. Bartlett should have a lover. Yet who would ever dream that Frances Osgood, daughter of a well-to-do Bostonian and a fixture of New York's brightest literary circles, would have lain with a married man in a hotel? I was living proof that what we do in private is often unbeliev-able.

After lunch, I decided to walk over to Miss Lynch's house to see if she was having her customary Saturday night conversazione in spite of the snow, which was falling again. I felt the desperate need to do normal things, act in normal ways, as if clinging to normalcy would make my pregnancy go away.

Stinging crystals of snow were sprinkling down as I shuffled along the shoveled sidewalk, my skirts crushed within the narrow two-foot high tunnel made in the snow. Within moments my toes ached from the cold radiating up through the soles of my boots. The snow had a deadening effect on sound, muffling the scraping of my skirt against the ice tunnel, muting the steady huffing of my breath. The unplowed streets were still as death. Save for a single cardinal huddled atop an iron fencing paling, I was the only creature out laboring in the frozen landscape.

I neared Mr. Poe's home, one of a row of cheaper houses built flush with the sidewalk. Had he gone out today? I marveled like always at how brazen he had been to move his family so close to the Bartletts'. How it must have hurt Mrs. Poe to know that a mere stone's throw away, her husband had been wooing another woman. No wonder she rarely went out, even had she been well. In the face of such humiliation, I would have withdrawn, too.

Yet, as I minced down the frigid tunnel, hating myself for causing such misery to Mrs. Poe, so ill in body and mind, the imp in me could not help but think: Was Mr. Poe at home?

The instant I was beside his window, I turned to look in.

I met the dazed face of Eliza's girl, Mary.

I stared at her, shocked, for one long moment before she fell away from the window as if someone had drawn her back.

"Mary?"

The curtains swished closed.

Before I could think, I knocked on the window. "Mary? Mary?"

My call was swallowed by the silent snow.

My heart thumped in my ears. There was no mistaking—it was Eliza's Mary. Yet she looked so strange, her expression so vacant. Although she looked straight at me, I wasn't entirely sure that she had registered my presence. Something was terribly wrong.

"Frances?"

I nearly jumped from my skin.

Arm in arm to keep their balance, Mrs. Ellet and Reverend Griswold had turned the corner from MacDougal and were hobbling toward me at top speed. A more unwelcome pair I could not imagine.

I glanced over my shoulder.

"Frances!" Mrs. Ellet demanded. "Wait!"

The angry look on her face made me want to do anything but.

"I should have known you'd be sneaking out here to get your letters when you thought no one could see you. What did I tell you, Rufus?"

"Letters?" I asked. "What letters?"

Slowly Reverend Griswold smiled with half of his mouth. "I think you know, Mrs. Osgood."

The malice in his expression shriveled my insides. "I don't."

Mrs. Ellet leaped in. "Don't you play dumb with us, Frances. Mrs. Poe read me one this morning. You all but ravished Mr. Poe on the page. It was *disgusting*."

"But I have never written such a letter!" It was true. I had written love poems, dozens of them, all for "publication," and yes, I had ravished and been ravished by Mr. Poe, but not once had I written a lover's letter. Not even the notes that had accompanied my poems spoke of my love for him. My poems had done my talking.

"Poor deranged woman—she *laughed* when Mr. Poe came home and ripped it from her hands. When I told him what I thought of you and your indecent letter, he told me that I had better take care of my own letters."

I turned toward the window, ill. I saw movement behind the curtains.

"*My* letters were just sweet poems," she cried. "They weren't really to *Poe*. I simply wanted him to publish them in his journal. They were to any man"—she noticed Reverend Griswold's frown—"to my husband."

"What did Mr. Poe do?"

"I told you. He insulted me." She clamped her lips shut. Her mouth quivered until the words came boiling out. "He's a fraud. Worse than a fraud—a moral bankrupt! I can't believe that I ever admired the man. I am warning everyone I know about him. . . . And you! I am warning them about you, madam!"

Reverend Griswold smiled smoothly. "Surely this is all a misunderstanding."

So this was how our affair was to be discovered, by a letter I had never written. Mrs. Poe must have concocted it to damn me to a well-known tattler and her husband's enemy. A curious calm, cold and heavy as a blanket of snow, fell over me. There would be no more hiding now. There would be no more affair. Only a mournful and never-ending remembrance of a rare and precious love.

"Well!" cried Mrs. Ellet when I smiled. "I don't see anything that is the slightest bit humorous about all this. I don't know about you, but *I* want my letters back." She marched up the steps and rapped on the door.

I watched in numb fascination for it to open.

No one came.

She pounded on the door. "I saw the curtain move!" she called. When no one responded after another rapping, she shouted, "Mr. Poe! I know you're in there! Come out here this minute and give me my poems!"

The snow consumed her cries.

She turned sharply. "Are you just going to stand there, Rufus? Do something!"

He drew up his shoulders in a shrug. "If Mr. Poe is not home—"

"He's home," snapped Mrs. Ellet. She raised her voice to the door. "Coward, hiding behind your women! I'll be back!" She latched on to Reverend Griswold's arm. "Let's go."

I reeled away from them and strode, slipping, for home. The children spilled onto the street just as I reached the Bartletts'. I opened the gate, shaken now of its cap of snow, and started up the stone steps.

I felt a blow on my neck.

I turned and found Ellen, covering her mouth with her mittens. "Sorry, Mamma. It was an accident."

Pieces of ice slithered inside my collar and down my back. I hardly felt them.

The day turned colder around two o'clock, driving the children inside. A horse-drawn plow had come down Amity but there were still few travelers upon the street. I sat at the front parlor window, with a pen poised idly in my hand. I was too agitated to write a word but used it as an excuse not to sit downstairs in the family room with Eliza and the children until I could sort out what I'd seen.

What could Mary be doing in town? She had been seen off to Ireland months ago. But there was no mistaking her wide blue eyes and dimples, nor the mole so prettily punctuating her cheek. It was her and something was wrong with her. She'd been unwell for much of the time since Mr. Bartlett had brought her home, smudged and coughing, the day of the Great Fire, but she had never looked so strange. To think that she had been in charge of the children—had she been hiding a grave illness?

But why was she not in Ireland? Why was she at the Poes'? And yet, I was hesitant to tell Eliza that I'd seen her. For all of Eliza's claims that she would welcome Mary back, I had the uncomfortable sense that Eliza would not relish this news. A fresh wave of nausea swept over me.

Outside, squinting up at the house, was a small boy wrapped in layers and layers until he resembled a child's rag ball. He pushed open the squealing gate and began to trudge up the steps. I met him at the door, letting in a freezing blast.

From within the muffler swathed around his head, he piped, "A message for Mrs. Good-good, ma'am."

I smiled. "I think you mean me." I took the folded paper. On it was written "Mrs. Osgood" in Edgar's orderly hand. I opened it quickly.

I'm at Trinity Church. You must come now. Your life depends upon it. Hurry, my love.

Edgar

Alarm shot through my veins. Mr. Poe had never been so bold as to send a message before. What crisis had prompted this?

The boy peered up at me from a gap in his muffler.

"Come in." I shut the door. "Wait."

I ran upstairs to fetch my reticule, and while I was at it, my hat, muff, and coat.

Why Trinity Church? Trinity was a good mile to the south. But it was only a few blocks from Mr. Poe's office for the *Journal*, and a church was one of the few buildings open to the public at all hours, although would Trinity be today? The rebuilding had not yet been finished.

Muff under my arm, I rushed back downstairs, tying on my hat. I paused to give the boy a half dime. Catherine came up from the basement, then pulled back in surprise.

"Who's this?"

"He brought me a message from a friend. Let him warm himself before the fire. Do we have an extra bun for him?"

"I don't know—"

"Tell Mrs. Bartlett that a friend needs me," I said, going to the door. "I'll be right back."

Outside, the air had turned bitter. I hunched into myself, trembling more from anxiety than from the cold as I minced and slid toward Broadway. There, on the busiest street of town, few had braved the elements. A sleigh jingled by, then a beer wagon on runners, pulled by sturdy shaggy horses straining against their halters. I passed only a handful of citizens, so huddled into their clothes that their faces were hidden.

What mad scheme of Virginia's had Edgar uncovered? I could not live with myself if my children or the Bartletts were endangered.

I forced my way through the alien landscape. At Broadway and Prince, the doors of Mr. Astor's mansion flew open. Oblivious to my shock, four Chinese servants ran down the steps, carrying a burden between them. They spread out on the sidewalk, each taking a corner of what turned out to be a blanket, from the center of which scowled the ancient Mr. Astor, in a nightgown and fur cap. Using the blanket as a sort of trampoline, they proceeded to vigorously toss him in the air. The pompom on his cap flying, his fur-slippered feet kicking, and his ropey octogenarian jaw grimly clenching, the richest man in New York endured each hearty bounce. Then, as if given a signal, the Chinamen ran together and folded him in, then trotted back up the steps.

"Good for blood," said the Chinese doorman, seeing my astonishment. "Live long time." Then he banged the door closed, leaving me standing in the wintery wasteland.

Disconcerted, I journeyed on. I passed the Astor House, where a single doorman shivered into his blue livery at the top of the steps. I shuffled past Saint Paul's Chapel, past Mr. Brady's closed studio, past the City Hotel and some venerable mansions whose original inhabitants had long since departed. On frozen feet I came to the grounds of the Trinity Church graveyard. I tipped back my head. Severe, haughty, built in defiance of nature, the spire of the bell tower of Trinity, the tallest structure in the city, pierced the stark white sky.

Something felt horribly wrong.

I let myself in the churchyard gate, its hinges shrieking from the cold. The monuments, the names of those they commemorated obliterated by shrouds of snow, watched in mute disapproval as I crunched my way through the skeletal trees. With a jarring caw, a crow landed above me, sending down a dusting of snow.

I peered around anxiously for Edgar, my movements watched by the curious crow, who hopped heavily from branch to branch as if to get a better view. Compelled to be out of its sight, I ducked into the stone side porch of the church, then pushed open the heavy door and spilled into the sanctuary. I inhaled cold, stale air.

The hushed cavernous vault was empty of pews. Bloodred light oozed through an apostle's stained-glass cloak. Many of the other windows were still yawning holes in the wall, hastily nailed over with wood. In place of the altar, in what would be the holiest part of the church, stood workbenches and sawhorses. No one would be worshipping here today or any day soon.

I noticed a red ribbon upon a nearby sawhorse. Drawing closer, I saw that a paper had been tied to the sawhorse's spine.

Mrs. Osgood

Again it was in Edgar's handwriting. I plucked off the paper and opened it.

Please come upstairs. Quickly!

I looked around. There were no stairs. How did one go up? It was strange enough that Edgar had called me to an unfinished church on such a winter's day, stranger still that he should insist that we meet upstairs. I felt a rush of angry fear. Why could he not meet me right here?

I heard a muffled thud. I held my breath, listening.

The building moaned with the wind. I told myself that what I had heard overhead were green timbers, contracting in the blast, even as my throat constricted with foreboding.

Something scurried above.

"Edgar? Is that you?"

Outside, the wind keened. It forced its whistling way through the boarded-up windows. The building groaned as if in sympathy, then fell silent.

My breathing echoed in the vast chamber as I inched forward. I saw that the main door to the sanctuary had been propped open with a piece of lumber, and beyond that, in the vestibule, one of the carved wooden Gothic panels of the wall hung loose. A secret door?

The vestibule, as dark and close as a cave, was achingly cold. In a cloud of my own breath, I pulled open the heavy panel. A tightly spiraling stone staircase, like that in a medieval tower, wound up into darkness.

Drawing a jittery breath, I clung to the stone block walls and began to climb.

Up I spiraled, around and around, until at last, breathless, I came to a door. I pushed it open then stood upon the threshold of a space not yet visible for lack of light.

Thump!

The sound came from above.

"Edgar?"

Why wouldn't he answer?

I smelled sawdust and new-cut wood as my eyes struggled to adapt to the light seeping through rosette windows. There were three of them, as wide as a carriage, high up on three of the four sides of the walls. A long ladder had been propped up under one. In the dim, I could just make out what looked to be bales of cotton heaped in the center of the chamber. Otherwise, the frigid cavern was vacant.

I felt a gentle stirring in the air above me. I looked up. In the darkness I could feel more than see a massive log of a pendulum, as large as a stately tree, swinging sedately to and fro.

Where was he?

My gaze caught on a faint scrap of red across the way: a ribbon, binding a rolled-up piece of paper, affixed to the ladder under the window.

A rush of wings dashed at my head. I batted wildly, then shrank back.

"Edgar!"

A pigeon sailed past the gently swinging pendulum, then beat the walls with splayed feathers.

Holding my throat, I saw that one of the bushel-size petals of the rosette window had not been covered with glass as the others had been; the ladder was directly beneath it, perhaps put there for its repair. The poor creature must have flown through the opening but couldn't find its way back out.

The paper beckoned silently. I hesitated upon the rough plank floor, then went to it, grasped it, and plucked it free.

I opened it and held it to the light.

Wait for me.

I gazed up the ladder to the open window high above. I didn't like this game. I didn't like it at all. This was no way to treat a woman— one carrying his child, I thought with a pained gulp, although he didn't know that yet. If Mr. Poe cared for me, he wouldn't tease me like this.

Mrs. Ellet had said that if you really wanted to know what Mr. Poe was up to, read his work. He had not denied it. As an author, did I not know firsthand how very much of me was in each piece of my fiction, whether I meant for it to be there or not?

His gruesome stories in which innocent women were killed flashed through my mind: "The Murder of Marie Roget." "The Black Cat." "The Fall of the House of Usher." Even in "The Oval Portrait," the woman had to die when the artist reached his success.

Madness spreads like a drop of ink in water. Soon one does not know who is mad and who is not.

Mr. Bartlett had warned of Mr. Poe's capacity for violence under pressure, coupled with his moral confusion. Want and sorrow and Virginia's madness had pushed him to the brink, and then, when he reached out in desperation, when he needed me the most, I had kept him at arm's length. Had his mind crumbled under the strain? If he could not have me in life, did he mean to possess me by death?

From above came the soft thud of the pigeon beating itself against the wall. The massive pendulum stirred the air as delicately as breathing.

My gaze went to the cotton bales. Someone had positioned them below the pendulum as if it were in danger of falling. I was looking up, up, up into the blackness to where the pendulum was fastened to a rope as thick as a sailor's arm, when I heard shouting in the distance. It wafted into my tomblike room like a call from another realm.

"Frances! Wait!"

My heart smashed against my chest. It was Mr. Poe. He meant for me to stay so that the pendulum could crush me. Had he not written such a tale? It was me he wanted to kill. Me.

I scanned the room frantically. There was no way out but the stairs up which I'd climbed. He could be upon them before I could get out. My only hope was to reach the window and scream for help.

I began to scramble up the ladder.

I could hear Edgar's footsteps at the bottom of the staircase. "Frances! No! Stop!"

My foot slipped on a rung. I banged my chin and bit my tongue.

"Frances!"

Tasting blood, I righted myself and skittered upward. Just short of the window, the ladder stopped. I would have to jump for the ledge. Clinging to the wall, I pulled my shaking self onto the top rung.

"Frances, no! *Please!*"

My heart leaped from my chest as I lunged onto the circular sill. I wriggled out the opening, sweat pouring down my body in spite of the deep cold.

Icy granules pelted my face, my head, my neck. I saw Battery Park in the distance; the dome of Castle Garden; ships moored in the harbor, with sails furled tight against the snow.

Far below me, a lone sleigh inched its way down Broadway.

I opened my mouth. My scream would not come, though I strained until my head grew weightless. I could feel my soul split from my body. It looked down upon the pitiful figure on the ladder, so desperate and scared.

A bubble of speech burst from my lungs.

"Help!"

The sleigh driver looked around as if he heard, but not thinking to look up, drove on.

My soul slid into my body. I yelled with all my force. "Help! Help!"

Mr. Poe dashed to the top of the steps. Seeing me on the ladder, he launched himself toward me. "Frances! Look out!"

I gazed up just as the minute hand of the clock hit my neck.

I fell backward. All went black.

I opened my eyes. The log pendulum swung sedately in its appointed path. Mr. Poe's dark-rimmed eyes came into view. He smiled tenderly, smoothing my temple with leather-gloved fingers. My head was cradled in his lap.

I tried to roll free of him, setting off a pain in my shoulder.

He frowned as if worried. "My darling. You took a terrible fall."

Remembering the sight of the gigantic oncoming minute hand, I shrank away from him.

Mrs. Clemm bustled up behind him, her perpetual frantic look amplified with emotion. "Let her go!"

I shrugged free of Mr. Poe's arms and threw myself into the protection of Mrs. Clemm's embrace. "Don't come near me!"

He reached out to me. "Frances!"

I shrank into Mrs. Clemm. "Don't!

Slowly, the concern on his face melted into anguish. "Frances, no. Do you think that I meant to harm you? Oh, my darling. Oh, my darling." The light went out of his dark-lashed eyes. I could feel his soul receding into its shell. "Oh, my love, you thought it was me."

Mrs. Clemm stroked my arm. "Do you think you can walk, dear?"

"What are you going to do with her?" Mr. Poe demanded.

"Where is Mary?" I drew away from her. "What happened to Mary?"

"Oh," said Mrs. Clemm, "she's at the house."

Mr. Poe drew a sharp breath, then lunged at his aunt. He wrestled me from Mrs. Clemm's arms. I wriggled free and faced them both, not knowing who to trust.

"Frances," said Mr. Poe wearily, "whatever you think, it's wrong. Muddy has become very . . . ill."

I blinked. It could be a trick. "Ill?"

He sighed deeply. "When I went to the asylum this spring, I was there to place her in their care. I only got the idea for a story set there after one of my many trips. But Virginia flew into pieces when she heard that I was arranging to commit her mother, and she was so ill with her weakened lungs, I feared she could not bear the strain." He sighed again. "Virginia needed her mother and I could not deny her."

Inside her white widow's bonnet, Mrs. Clemm's face crumpled with fury. "Monster! How could you think of doing that to me? I took you in when you had nothing. I gave you the apple of my eye— Virginia is worth two of you! She could always lead you down the primrose path."

Mr. Poe spoke soothingly as if to a child. "Muddy, I know you're trying to do what's right for Virginia now. I don't blame you for trying to mesmerize her. Of course you would want to forestall her death. None of us want her to go."

"You do!"

"No. I don't. Although she tortures me to my core. She is the me I would be if I'd never grown up. But she remained as a child—easily wounded, spiteful, vindictive, crude."

"I knew you wouldn't help me to save her!"

He breathed in with a shudder. "Transferring her soul into Mary's body is not the way."

Mrs. Clemm gave him a guilty scowl. "It could work."

"Muddy," he said, nearly whispering, "it's madness. You are basing your attempts on fiction. 'The Facts in the Case of M. Valdemar' is just a story. You cannot catch Virginia's soul when she dies any more than you could transfer her soul into Mary."

"Why Mary?" I asked. "Why poor, innocent Mary?"

Mrs. Clemm looked down with a sheepish grin. "Because she was available. I couldn't believe my luck when I found her drifting along our street this morning, mooning around for Mr. Bartlett. Who would come to the aid of a servant girl whose master couldn't keep his hands off her? Poor thing, she couldn't think straight after giving up her baby. You've never seen such a desperate creature! All I had to offer her was a hot meal and she was mine." When she raised her face, her round blue eyes had gone black with hatred. "Don't worry, I was going to let her go once we got you. I just needed her for practice, or in case Virginia's health did not hold out until I could harvest you."

Harvest?

"So you thought you'd kill Frances in the manner I had dreamed up in 'The Predicament,' " he asked bitterly, "by the strike of a church clock's hand?"

Mrs. Clemm laughed. "I knew I could get you up that ladder, you stupid, gullible girl—your type has had the brains bred right out of you. I just didn't know that Eddie'd be the one to do it for me, shouting at you like that."

She turned to Mr. Poe. "I did not want to kill her, Eddie. Just wound. Just enough to nurse her back to health in time to transfer Virginia's soul into her when Virginia's body expired. Then, just for fun, I'd have sent her back to those snooty Bartletts." She chuckled. "So when you *thought* you were dallying with your whore, you would really be dallying with Virginia."

She ignored my look of horrified incredulousness. "That's all Virginia ever wanted, Eddie, just to be treated like a wife. Why couldn't you have taken her in your arms once in a while?"

Mr. Poe shook his head as if trying to release an imp from his brain. "Muddy, Muddy, you are more ill than I knew. Souls cannot be moved around from body to body like so many peas in a shell game."

"I talked to that nice Mr. Andrew Jackson Davis about it. He said that the principles are sound."

"He's a charlatan."

Her face contorted. "You think you're better than us because your mother was from Boston. She thought she was so important. Leaving you that picture of Boston, writing on it that all her friends were from there, that you should turn to Boston if you needed help. Lot of good they did you! My brother, David, was the better of the two of them but she never respected him. She's the one who drove him to drink. He'd still be alive if she hadn't have ruined him, just like she ruined you, putting such big important ideas in your head."

"You don't know what you're saying," he whispered icily.

"I don't have to listen to this anymore." Mrs. Clemm trundled toward the stairs.

Mr. Poe sprung forth and caught her arm. "You're not getting away with this!"

"Let go!" She fought against him, the lappets of her bonnet swaying. Her reticule fell to the floor, releasing a hammer that went sliding across the boards. A hammer meant for me. I sagged to my knees as if my bones had turned to jelly.

I looked up at Mr. Poe, the pain in my heart so sharp that I could hardly breathe. "But how did you know to come save me?"

The regret and wonder in his dark-lashed eyes cut through my heart. "Virginia told me."

Winter 1847

Thirty-four

We were on our way to Yorkville. The snow fell from the bright gray sky in soft pats, dampening the bearskin robe Samuel had tucked around me, moistening my frozen cheeks under my fur hat. It settled heavily upon the fields, upon the bare branches of the trees, upon the bony backs of the cows huddled at a fence. As our sleigh went jingling under the crooked spreading bough of an ancient oak, a sodden mound of it slid down onto our heads. Samuel laughed and shook the snow off his shoulders, reins still in hand.

"I'm sorry, darling. Did you get wet?"

"I'm fine." I brushed at my face with the beaver muff he'd given me at Christmas a few weeks earlier.

"Well, it's nothing that a sherry flip can't fix. Don't worry, we haven't far to go."

I smiled complacently. I could play the role of Samuel's well-bred wife to help him climb up into the rarified circles of New York society to which he aspired. I owed him that much. He had insisted that I live with him and to claim that the baby was his when he had found out that I was with child, a lie that I would have resisted had not Mrs. Ellet loudly and publicly announced that I had written scandalous letters to Mr. Poe. Once I had a child without a husband, who would have believed my claim of innocence? Even Miss Lynch and Miss Fuller, thinking they were acting as friends, had gone to Mr. Poe's house to demand them back. Not even they believed me when I protested that the letters didn't exist.

It touched me that my friends had tried to shield me. In truth, I would have welcomed my shame. I deserved it for doubting the only man who truly loved me. But for my girls, for the well-being of his child, I'd had to permanently sever all ties to Mr. Poe, and pretend that he meant nothing to me. I'd had to laugh it off as a joke when the poem he'd written to me in Boston, 'To Her Whose Name Is Written Within,' a poem I kept at the center of my heart, was read as a valentine at Miss Lynch's, sent by Edgar, evidently, the week before our falling out. I had come to realize that you must do what you must for your children, even if it called for the sacrifice of your very soul.

Now I listened emotionlessly to the runners slicing through the sodden snow. I thought of the girls back home with our serving girl, Lizzie, who I hoped would change the baby before she got too wet. I wondered which of Samuel's society ladies would come calling on me while we were gone, and dreaded having to go through the motions of returning the favor of visiting them. Out of old habit, I thought about writing, then winced at the numbness in my head. Odd how a brain cannot be goaded into creativity without a soul to give it a nudge.

"A good crowd," Samuel said.

Up the road, sleighs were jammed higgledy-piggledy before a white-painted frame building. It appeared that much of fashionable New York had escaped along with us to Wintergreen's, a roadhouse in the hamlet of Yorkville, several miles outside of town. A venture inside confirmed this. Crammed shoulder to shoulder in a room redolent with the smell of woodsmoke, perfume, and wet fur were Roosevelts, Fishes, and Rhinelanders, busily snubbing the New Money folk whose loud laughter rang from the rustic rafters. Among them, I saw Reverend Griswold enter with Miss Lynch. All sipped upon hot flips and toddies as a harried young man in an apron threaded through the crowd with a tray of steaming cups, while a violinist fiddled in a corner and a collie worked the patrons for pats.

The drink soon worked its magic. I found myself happily chatting with Mr. Phineas Barnum, the famed showman himself, who was enjoying new social cachet having had audiences with Queen Victoria while in England the previous year. I thought fleetingly how Mr. Poe would have been amused by my conversationalist. It occurred to me that I should suggest to Mr. Barnum that he add a bust of Mr. Poe to his pantheon of heroes. I chased away the thought with a gulp of warmed sherry.

"What was the queen like?" I asked. Out of the corner of my eye

I could see Samuel, beaming his relentless charm upon the young Schermerhorn girl. Although she kept haughtily turning away her head, her cheeks had gone rosy with pleasure. Would I ever become accustomed to this marriage of convenience? I breathed deeply and smiled at Mr. Barnum.

"The queen's much like any other mother," he was saying. "Mostly she just wanted her children to get a good look at the general." A grin lit up the bulbous features bunched in the front and center of Mr. Barnum's great shiny egg of a head. "Tom gave the performance of a lifetime. He played with the little ones and sang for the queen, then engaged her poodle in mock swordplay before backing out of the room at a run. Now that's an entertainer!"

"I must come see his show sometime."

"I admire him. He took being small and made a mint out of it— well, I helped him with that part—but he's the one who milked it. The hamming it up is all him. For anyone else, being little could have been a disaster, but not him. He glories in his size." His exuberance flashed into seriousness as he looked me in the eye. "It takes a lot of spunk to spin gold from heartache, Mrs. Osgood. A lot of drive. Most of us can't do it. It's a mean world, Mrs. Osgood, mean and spiteful."

I nodded, sipping.

Still, he did not release his piercing blue gaze. "Fortunate is the person who can succeed in extracting honey from such a flower as this life, whose root and every petal is bitterness. Are you that person, Mrs. Osgood?"

Had he read the sadness in my eyes? Yet I did not wish to flee from him. What *was* the secret of turning bitterness into honey?

I felt a tap on my shoulder. I turned around to find Reverend Griswold, holding out a glass to me in his fawn-gloved hand. "A toddy to warm you, Mrs. Osgood?"

I shivered at the sight of his handsome smug face. "I have a drink already, but thank you."

"My timing has always been off with you," he said. He took a sip of the drink that he offered. "A pity."

"Nice gloves," said Mr. Barnum. "Where'd you get them?"

"Brooks Brothers. On Catherine Street. I buy them by the box. I have rather a fondness for hand wear."

I was trying to remember where I'd seen a Brooks Brothers glove box when Miss Lynch came up behind him. "Hello, Frances," she said. "Hello, Mr. Barnum. I see you have found the most beautiful woman in the room."

Mr. Barnum laughed. "You caught me out, madam. I haven't yet ascertained as to whether she can sing or dance." He winked at me, but not before he shot me a private look of sincere encouragement.

"She's a poet," said Reverend Griswold, not catching Mr. Barnum's playfulness. "She would never besmirch herself on the stage. Have you not read her collection that came out last year? *Cries of New-York*—a rather interesting title."

The book had done well. The scandal Mrs. Ellet had stirred up had increased the public's appetite for the poems of Poe's lover. No one had taken it seriously. I smiled to myself. Now I knew how Edgar felt, finding his success from a poem that he felt trivial.

"I gave it my best reviews. Got it seen by all the right people." Reverend Griswold turned to me. "You can thank me now, dear." He smiled expectantly.

It came to me where I'd seen the glove box: Mrs. Poe had kept her poetry in it. Had Reverend Griswold been visiting her? Had he been fanning the flames of her jealousy in hope of getting at me and Edgar? I swallowed. He could have written the love letter that Virginia had read to Mrs. Ellet, the one that had served to sever us forever.

No, no. It couldn't possibly be. It was too thin of a connection. A coincidence.

"Look at her turn her face down in modesty!" exclaimed Reverend Griswold. "I've made her a star and still she's shy of her creator."

Miss Lynch crumpled her elfin face in a frown. "I wish this past year had worked out as well for Mr. Poe. It was as if he had hoped for his own ruin. He lost his magazine by antagonizing anyone who might have written for it. Could he have made any more bitter enemies than by writing a series of articles for *Godey's* about his friends, painting them only in the most critical light?"

"'The Literati of New York City,'" Reverend Griswold cried. "'The Little Lies of New York City' is more like it! Poor Willis! 'Neither his nose nor forehead can be defended: the latter would puzzle phrenology.' And what Poe said about Bryant was unconscionable. He wasn't kind about Miss Fuller, either. What he said about her long upper lip was inexcusable."

Miss Lynch unconsciously brushed at her own lip. "It was obvious that he wanted to provoke. He was like a wounded animal, lashing out. It was heartbreaking, really."

"You're too kind," said Reverend Griswold. "They were personal attacks, plain and simple. Why would he want to cut himself off from everyone like that?"

"Self-promotion?" suggested Mr. Barnum.

"Well, you can't blame *me* for ruining him," said Reverend Griswold. "He's done it all by himself. Soon he'll have no one in the world on his side." He slid me a sidelong look. "I've heard Mrs. Poe is close to death."

"They're in a very bad way," said Miss Lynch. "She's on her deathbed and he hasn't even the money to buy firewood to keep her warm. I understand that some admirers took up a collection to buy blankets."

Reverend Griswold sniffed. "It didn't have to be this way."

I tried to keep my voice from shaking. "How is Mr. Poe?"

"Poor Edgar?" Miss Lynch grimaced. "Not so well. He seems to be declining as quickly as his wife."

"Too bad," said Reverend Griswold.

"Don't gloat," snapped Miss Lynch. "When he goes, America will lose one of its most original minds. We will all be poorer without the likes of Edgar Poe." She looked at me. "I fear the both of them have but only a few days."

"Where is he?" I asked.

"You don't know?" She seemed surprised. "In the village of Fordham, north of here a few miles—in the middle of nowhere. I went to see him a few months ago." She sighed. "It's a terrible scene. At least it will be over for him soon."

I blindly thrust my glass into Reverend Griswold's hand. "Take me there, Anne. I must go to him. Now."

"Now?" bleated Reverend Griswold. "What good can come of it? For your own reputation, I beg you to reconsider."

"Tell Frances's husband that she's gone, will you, Rufus? As for

anyone else, they won't know unless you talk." Miss Lynch glanced at
Mr. Barnum. He shook his head as if to deny his involvement.

Miss Lynch handed Reverend Griswold her own teacup. "Surely,"
she said as he juggled the three vessels, "one of your many dear
friends will give you a ride home."

She bid Mr. Barnum good-bye, took my arm, and walked with me
toward the door. "Honestly, Frances," she said as we shrugged on our
coats. "I was wondering how long it would take you to ask."

At first appearance, the tiny cottage, perched upon the crest of a
steep hill and sheltering in a grove of bare trees, appeared to be
charming, with its wide porch and rough shingle roof capped with
snow. But then I saw that no smoke curled merrily from the chimney.
The steps were piled with snow, the windows glazed over with frost.
Was anyone living here?

Miss Lynch glanced at what must have been a look of dismay on
my face. She hopped out of her cutter to tie her horse to a tree. "I'm
sorry. I know this must not be easy."

We crunched through the snow and up the steps and across the
porch. Miss Lynch knocked on the door. We waited. Behind us, her
horse pawed the snow, snorting. A pair of crows cawed in the bare
trees.

"Maybe they've left," I said.

"Oh, they're here." Miss Lynch knocked again.

Someone tugged the door from the inside, sending a sheet of ice
from its surface. I glimpsed the starched white lappets of a widow's
bonnet through the sliver of opening.

"Go away!" bleated Mrs. Clemm.

"We're here to help," said Miss Lynch.

A round blue eye appeared in the opening. She saw me. "Help?
She's the one to blame!"

"Let us in," Miss Lynch demanded. "Now, if you please!"

Wrapped and pinned within a ragged plaid blanket, Mrs. Clemm
opened the door and stood aside, glowering at me.

We stepped directly into the kitchen, a low-ceilinged room domi-
nated by a cold iron stove. Miss Lynch went over to it, opened the

wood grate, and then stepped over to inspect the empty fireplace. "You've got no wood."

"He's freezing us!" cried Mrs. Clemm. "He is trying to kill us all by freezing us."

"Do you know where I can buy wood?" said Miss Lynch.

Miss Clemm nodded. "The Jesuits. In the village."

"Take me there."

So desperate was Mrs. Clemm's need that she left immediately with Miss Lynch, without a further thought of me.

I was alone in the frigid kitchen, my only companion the acrid smell of long-cold ashes. My feet burning from the cold, I crossed the wide plank floor to the adjoining room—a parlor, bare of a rug and bereft of furnishings save for a little shelf of books, a rocking chair, and Mr. Poe's small, fine desk. I heard a scratching.

I glanced around wildly. A branch was scraping against the window-pane. Why was I so nervous? It was just a little cottage in the woods. But where were Mr. Poe and his wife?

"Hello?" I called out.

I took one step forward and listened. From behind the door on the other side of the room, I heard a raspy choking sound. A person laboring to breathe? The strangulated inhalation rose with a wheeze, then after a perilously long pause, subsumed into a bubbling exhalation. Then the process began again, each respiration seemingly the person's last.

"Mr. Poe?"

I received no answer.

Shaking more from anxiety than from the brutal cold, I inched across the creaking floorboards. I stopped at the door, drew a breath, then put my hand upon the knob. The handle chilling me through my glove, I eased the door open.

Immediately to my right was a tiny closet of a room, just large enough to hold a bed barely larger than a child's cot and the narrow chair beside it. The bed was spread with a patchwork quilt and on top of that a butternut-colored cover—Mr. Poe's military greatcoat. On its skirt sat his tortoiseshell cat, serene as a sphinx, rising and falling with the terrible respirations of the person beneath it.

The upended collar of the coat obscured the person's face.

Swallowing, I leaned forward until I got a glimpse of black hair splayed upon the pillow, then, one more inch forward, I saw a visage more skull than face.

Virginia smiled.

I covered my mouth.

She did not move. Indeed, to speak seemed to take excruciating effort. "I knew . . . you'd come."

"Mrs. Poe! You need help!"

"No. Come . . . here."

Shivering so hard that every muscle ached, I drew nearer. The cat hissed.

I flinched back. Virginia latched on to my arm.

"I wanted," she gasped, "to be you."

Inwardly, I writhed from the pinch of her fingers. Or was it from guilt? "I can get a doctor. Please, let me get a doctor, before it's too late."

She dug her fingers tighter. "Help him. Help him. He doesn't know . . . how to be alone."

"Virginia, please, I must go get you help."

She stared fiercely, her lungs bubbling with fluid. "Help him. Then you have helped . . . me."

I heard the slow approach of footsteps. I turned to see Mr. Poe ducking down the low flight of stairs just behind me. He stopped when he saw me. He was so pale and thin that I gasped.

Virginia fell back on the bed. Her fingers slid from my arm. "Now . . . I am free."

I watched her drift into sleep, my heart aching. I followed Mr. Poe into the desolate little parlor.

He sank onto the rocker, his head upon his hands. "I cannot forgive myself."

Kept from him for twelve long months, I drank in the sight of him, although what I saw wounded me to my core. His illness had hollowed his cheeks and lined his noble forehead. His wild black curls were shot with gray. When he looked up at me, his eyes burned in his pallid face. Tears sprang to my throat.

I dropped to my knees before him. "Edgar." My voice broke. "What has happened to you?"

He hungrily searched my face. "Fate."

I took his hand. The sight of his beautiful fingers, so sensitive, so intelligent, made me want to weep. I had thought he was one of his murderers from his stories. I could never forgive myself.

He lifted his hand to my face. As if he had heard me, he said softly, "It's true what they say, you know. No matter how fictitious, writers' stories are always about themselves. Not that we know it when we're writing them. Far from it, usually. Do you think that I thought of myself as the murderers and madmen in my tales?"

"You are the kindest, gentlest man in the world. I was mad to think otherwise."

He brushed a wisp from my cheek then put down his hand. "Don't punish yourself. We had all gone mad."

We gazed quietly at each other.

"But I have learned something about myself," he said, more firmly now. "In story after story, my dark heroes must come undone, whether it be by the imp of the perverse, the wronged sister, a vengeful cat. But it's not the imp or sister or cat who destroys them. No. It's their guilt. My guilt. I was writing about me after all."

"We all make mistakes."

He laughed mirthlessly. "Do we all marry our little cousins because we're lonely? Do we all keep her at arm's length when we realize that she's weak and childish, scorning her every touch? Do we all throw in her face the woman she could never be, and upbraid her for her pitiful attempts to emulate her superior? She loved me, and I was cruel."

I bowed my head, absorbing my part in his shame. How many times over the past year had I punished myself by recounting the instances in which I had blamed Mrs. Poe for deeds she had not done? I saw now that her mother had been part of every scene in which I suspected Virginia. It was Mrs. Clemm who had pushed me into the water, Mrs. Clemm who had arranged for the ice to crush me. Surely it was she who had used Virginia's coughing as a means of distracting Catherine while lighting the gaslight. The acts that Virginia herself had committed—ruining my daguerreotype, hanging it on their wall—were the ploys of a desperate child and no more. I had been looking at Virginia through green-colored glasses and seen a monster because I needed to.

But there was one other thing—

"Edgar," I asked gently. "Who had started the fire at Madame Restell's?"

Mr. Poe frowned. "What fire?"

"Before you moved."

He shook his head. "I don't know. I was at my office when it happened. Why?"

I stared at him, trying to understand. Had Virginia burned her hand while lighting the fire? Or had she burned it while pulling her mother back from it?

He sat back, seeming to withdraw into himself. After a while, he said, "I hope that I go with Virginia."

Anger flared up from my gut. "Go? Edgar! No. You cannot cheat at life. You must deal with the cards you've been given. You have to go on, Edgar. The world needs you. The world needs your mind."

"What good is my mind if I haven't a soul? You took it, Frances. No—I gave it to you. I wanted you to have it."

"Then we must go on, as empty as we are."

His eyes were wells of pain. "Why?"

I drew a breath. "Because we have a child."

He stared as if he could not believe it. "I heard it was Samuel's."

"I had to say that," I said softly. "For her sake. But even Samuel knows the truth."

Tears filled his eyes. "I have a daughter? We have a child?"

"Yes, Edgar."

We clasped each other tight. I savored the beating of his heart, the dear musky smell of his skin, the feel of his arms around me.

After a moment, he loosened his hold to look at me. "What did you name her?"

"Fanny Fay."

He nodded slowly as if becoming used to its sound. Soft light flickered within the dark frame of his lashes, warming his broken face, until at last, a smile nudged at his mouth. "You sure you don't want to call her Ulalume?"

My laughter threatened to spill into tears. I hid my face against his shoulder. I loved this man.

Tenderly, he lifted my chin. "I've made a lot of mistakes in my life, Frances Sargent Locke, but loving you isn't one of them."

I kissed him softly. He tasted like the salt of tears.

When he pulled back, I could hardly breathe for the lump in my throat.

"Frances?"

I nodded, unable to speak.

"Do you think you could tell little Fanny about me?"

My soul cried out, desolate to leave its mate. "Yes, my dearest darling. Of course."

He gathered me to him. I listened to his heart, memorizing its sound, then let him go.

He was hers now.

The baby was crying when I arrived back home. Although immediately tensing from the internal alarm triggered by her cry, I rushed to the desk that I kept by the parlor window. I uncapped the inkwell, a crust of dried ink crumbling from the lid from disuse. I dipped in a pen then impatiently scribbled to get it to flow.

The maid, Lizzie, ran up from the basement, wiping her mouth on her apron. "She just woke up from her nap, ma'am."

"I'll get her."

"Are you sure, ma'am?"

I needed to write quickly, before I forgot, for into the drained silence that Miss Lynch had been wise enough to honor, an inspiration had come. As the runners of her cutter had sheared through the snow, drawing me homeward, a poem had formed itself in my mind. A voice whispered from that inner place that every writer knows and no writer understands, the voice for which all of us live.

Now I said absently, "What, Lizzie? Am I sure? Yes—just one moment."

I jotted down phrases, some images, key words, so I would not forget, then put down the pen. Thinking twice, I snatched it up and scratched out at the top of the page: Fanny's First Smile.

The baby's calls grew louder. I dropped the pen and, with my still-tender heart swelling with gratitude, flew upstairs.

I found her standing unsteadily in her crib, holding on to the rails. When she saw me, she rattled the bars and crowed with excitement.

I lifted her to my breast, inhaling deeply her dear infant's scent. There was the sweetness of a meadow in it, of unfurling flowers, of pure human joy. It is the smell, I realized, of hope.

"Hush now," I murmured into her rosebud ear, "hush now. Mamma's here. You're not alone. You'll never be alone. You're mine, forevermore."

And the child, gazing at me with dark-lashed eyes, laughed.

Author's Note

In his better moments he had in an eminent degree
that air of gentlemanliness which men of a lower order
seldom succeed in acquiring
—RUFUS W. GRISWOLD, *Memoir of the Author,* 1850

When I set out to write *Mrs. Poe*, my intention was not to write a "shivery" tale. I was interested to know how Frances Osgood might have come to be the lover of Edgar Poe—a notion some Poe scholars still deny. The plan was to let recorded events and letters, and Frances's and Edgar's own writings, show me the way. I was also ready to fall in love with the Edgar Poe, known to be sexual catnip to the ladies in his time. But I didn't know that I was writing a dark story.

Maybe I was naïve to think that a novel about Poe would not end up being heartbreaking. As every American high school student knows, E. A. Poe's work contains some pretty black material. But the more I researched, the more I found that Poe didn't just write frightening stories, he lived them. The horrific aspects of his childhood described in my book are all true. He endured deep personal loss and grinding poverty his whole life. In fact, I was careful to try to stick to the facts about the lives of Edgar Poe and Frances Osgood as closely as possible throughout the book. To my mind, the action that I made up could have actually happened. The vast array of materials at the New-York Historical Society, the jaw-droppingly detailed *Gotham* by Edwin G. Burrows and Mike Wallace, the meticulous documentation of Poe's daily life in *The Poe Log* by Dwight Thomas and David K. Jackson, and simply tramping up and down the streets of lower

Manhattan, chasing down historical leads, served as my guide into the world of Frances and Edgar. I came to be awed by how they both kept going in the face of constant adversity.

As tragically as I imagine Frances and Edgar's affair had ended, what happened in real life after they parted is even more relentlessly devastating. Life could be cruel and short in the mid-nineteenth century, and the people in our story serve as a sad illustration.

Virginia Poe died on January 30, 1847, of tuberculosis, or consumption, as it was known then. She was twenty-four years old. In the years after Virginia died, Edgar Poe wrote some of his greatest poems, including "Ulalume," one of my inspirations for this book. In that poem, the narrator and the woman who is my soul, Psyche, come upon a star of great beauty. They have been in despair—the narrator described his heart as being "volcanic"—so at first such a glorious sight brings them much needed relief and joy. Then they come to realize that the star is none other than their lost loved one, Ulalume. Once again they are plunged into grief when they realize that Ulalume is unreachable. It was, to me, Poe's most emotionally honest poem. I felt as if I could understand his relationship with Frances—and the utter anguish he felt at their parting—once I began to study the lines. Was Poe the narrator? Was Psyche actually Frances, and Ulalume their daughter, Fanny Fay? I like to think so.

Two years after Virginia died, on October 7, 1849, Edgar Poe followed her to the grave at the age of forty, his original mind quieted forever. Seven months after Poe's passing, Frances Osgood died, on May 12, 1850, of tuberculosis. She was thirty-eight years old. Upon her death, her husband, Samuel, ever the entrepreneur, collected her poems, including those to Edgar Poe, into a volume. It sold well. Samuel himself long outlived everyone in his family, finally joining them on the other side in 1885.

Frances's child Fanny Fay died at sixteen months of age on October 15, 1847, cause unknown. Tellingly, in "Ulalume," written in December 1847, the narrator and his soulmate mourn the death of their beloved Ulalume in the month of October, in his "most immemorial year." I theorize that Poe was referring to 1847, when he lost both Virginia and Fanny Fay, and had his final parting with Frances. He was to live for only two years after that and Frances just a little longer.

Could it be possible that their rift, and then the death of their child, had shattered their health?

Frances's other daughters, May Vincent and Ellen, died on June 26, 1851, and August 31, 1851, respectively, perhaps to tuberculosis, losses I found particularly hard to take. "Vinnie" was not yet twelve and Ellen had just turned fifteen.

Maria Clemm served as Edgar Poe's executor. Although Rufus Griswold's hatred toward Poe was widely known, she turned over all of her nephew's works to Griswold upon Poe's death. Questioning why Maria Clemm would leave Poe's legacy in the hands of someone who was determined to destroy him ultimately shaped my story. "Muddy" died, destitute and alone, in 1871, in the Church Home in Baltimore, Maryland. The Church Home was a charitable Episcopalian institution that had formerly been the Washington Medical College—the place where Poe had died under mysterious circumstances nearly twenty years earlier.

Griswold would go on to commit the most vicious character assassination in the history of American literature. It began two days after Poe's death. Griswold, under a pen name to which he soon confessed, wrote a eulogy in Horace Greeley's *New York Tribune* that began, "Edgar Allan Poe is dead. He died in Baltimore the day before yesterday. This announcement will startle many, but few will be grieved by it." Griswold continued to ruthlessly smear Poe until his own death, spreading countless fabrications about Poe's drug addiction and madness. Among other falsehoods, he recounted seeing Poe flailing his arms and shouting at the wind and rain, or throwing curses at imaginary foes as he walked down the street. He doctored Poe's letters to make them look more hostile. He claimed Poe had deserted the army. He even went so far as to insist that Poe seduced Muddy. One begins to wonder who was actually the unhinged character in this scenario.

Griswold's biased biography of Poe was the only one widely available until 1875, by which time Poe's reputation was stained irrevocably. Yet from these ruins arose the public's enduring fascination with the dark and dangerous Poe. Unwittingly, Griswold had created and then amplified the legend of the very man he wished to destroy.

In spite of his great efforts, Griswold never got the girl who provoked his campaign to crush his rival. He died in 1857 of tuberculosis, alone in a room he had decorated with pictures of himself, Frances Osgood, and Edgar Poe.

Now, of the three, only Poe has gone on to immortality, thanks in part to Griswold. But to rediscover Frances Sargent Osgood, one need only read her poetry. There, between the pages, her wit and passion gleams, as does her everlasting love for Edgar Allan Poe.

Fanny's First Smile
By Frances S. Osgood

It came to my heart—like the first gleam of morning,
To one who has watched through a long, dreary night
It flew to my heart—without prelude or warning,
And wakened at once there a wordless delight.

That sweet pleading mouth, and those eyes of deep azure,
That gazed into mine so imploringly sad,
How faint o'er them floated the light of that pleasure,
Like sunshine o'er flowers, that the night-mist has clad!

Until that golden moment, her soft, fairy features
Had seemed like a suffering seraph's to me
A stray child of Heaven's, amid earth's coarser creatures.
Looking back for her lost home, that still she could see!

But now, in that first smile, resigning the vision,
The soul of my loved one replies to mine own:
Thank God for that moment of sweet recognition,
That over my heart like the Morning light shone!

—*Graham's Magazine*, Thirtieth Volume, January 1847
to June 1847, page 262

Acknowledgments

While need might be the mother of creation, the mother of this book could be said to be my agent, Emma Sweeney. The moment I proposed the idea for it, she took me and Frances under her wing and helped us to grow, offering wise suggestions during the many drafts, cheering us on, and, most important, bringing the manuscript under Karen Kosztolnyik's exquisite editorial care at Gallery Books. Karen's steadfast (and to me, heartwarming!) belief in this novel and me from the start, and her patient, steady hand in helping me to develop the story to the fullest, are the stuff of a writer's dreams.

In addition, I owe a huge debt of gratitude to the entire Gallery Books/Simon & Schuster team for their generous support and hard work in the making of this book. I am touched and profoundly thankful for the vocal enthusiasm for this project so kindly given by Carolyn Reidy, Louise Burke, and Jennifer Bergstrom. Thank you to Stephanie DeLuca, Liz Psaltis, Natalie Ebel, and Ellen Chan for the many miracles they have wrought. And thank you, too, to Alexandra Lewis and Heather Hunt, for their tireless editorial assistance. I am so lucky to be a Gallery gal!

The research for *Mrs. Poe* has been particularly fascinating and fun, thanks to those who have taken the time to instruct me as I visited the places critical to the scenes in the book. Thank you most warmly to Tony Furnivall for taking me on a tour of the Trinity Church bell tower, and allowing me to poke my head out the rosette window. Besides giving me a bird's-eye view of lower Manhattan, it was a thrill of a lifetime. Thank you to Angel Hernandez at the Poe Cottage in the Bronx, New York, for allowing me to join in his school tour and giving me my first glimpse of Virginia Poe's deathbed, and to P. Neil Ralley, who supplied additional information there. A big thanks goes to Joseph Ditta at the New-York Historical Society for lugging out all sorts of old maps and books which proved to be invaluable in retracing the steps of Frances and Edgar. I am grateful, too, to Roberta Belulovich and Margaret Halsey Gardiner and the rest of the staff of The Merchant's House Museum in Greenwich Village, for helping me to re-create what life would have been like in 1845 at the Bartletts' home just a few blocks away.

I am fortunate to have great support on the homefront as well. Thank you to my local core team of friends/boosters, Ruth and Steve Berberich, Karen Torghele, Jan Johnstone, Sue Edmonds, and Thiery Goodman, as well as to my large and lusty neighborhood book club of twenty-plus years. Thank you to my dear neighbors, Diane Prucino and Tom Heyse, for the use of their mountain home for when I needed to hunker down and get things done. A hearty thank you to the friends from afar who have so kindly spurred me on: Stephanie Cowell, Rudi van Poele, and Marie-Paule Rombauts. Thank you, too, to Steve Levy and Marilyn Herleth and the editorial board of JAPA for their kind support, as well. Many thanks to my sisters and brothers, Margaret Edison, Jeanne Wensits, Carolyn Browning, Howard Doughty, Arlene Eifrid, and last but definitely not least, David Doughty, for standing behind me and occasionally feeding me. And thank you, most deeply, to my husband and daughters and their families, for their constant nurturing, care, and laughter.

All of you have made writing this book, in Poe's words, "a dream within a dream." Thank you.

Mrs. Poe

Lynn Cullen

Set in the fascinating world of New York's literati scene of the 1840s, *Mrs. Poe* tells the story of Frances Osgood, a poet desperately trying to make a living as a writer in New York, a difficult task for a woman—particularly one with two children and a philandering husband. When Frances meets Edgar Allan Poe at a literary salon, he seems dismissive of her work. However, a few days later, she learns that Poe has given a lecture praising her poems and then asks to speak with her about poetry, striking up an unlikely friendship. Although both Frances and Edgar try to deny their feelings, they become increasingly obsessed with each other, leading to a passionate affair and endangering Frances's reputation. During this time, Frances has also become the confidante of Virginia Poe, Edgar's much younger wife, who, despite her appearance of innocence, seems to be subtly threatening Frances. As the stakes escalate, Frances must decide whether she can walk away before it's too late. This captivating novel is based on the historical fact that Poe and Frances Sargent Osgood published a very public exchange of love poems in 1845, the year in which "The Raven" catapulted Poe into literary stardom.

Topics and Questions for Discussion

1. Cullen begins *Mrs. Poe* with two epigraphs. In the first, Osgood is recounting her first meeting with Poe to Reverend Griswold. In the second, Poe describes Frances Osgood. How do these two quotes set up the novel? Were Cullen's representations of Osgood and Poe as you expected after reading the epigraphs?

2. Although Frances narrates the story, it is named for Mrs. Poe. Why do you think that Cullen has chosen to call the novel *Mrs. Poe*? Did the title affect your reading of the story? How?

3. After Frances meets Virginia Poe for the first time, Eliza asks her, "What does she seem like? Sweet? Sharp?" and Frances replies "Both, oddly enough." (p. 55) What does she mean? Do you agree with Frances's assessment of Virginia? Why or why not?

4. Miss Fuller tells Frances, "Beneath that pretty society-girl surface, you strike me as the striving sort." (p. 163). Do you

agree? What reasons does Frances have to be "the striving sort"? What are your initial impressions of Frances? Did your feelings about Frances change throughout the novel? In what ways?

5. Of Poe, Reverend Griswold says, "I find that there is nothing about Edgar Poe that is remotely like the rest of us. He is a predator, plain and simply. A wolf in wolf's clothing." (p. 123) Why do you think that Griswold feels such animosity toward Poe? What do you think of Griswold? Discuss his interactions with Frances.

6. After Frances learns that Poe has praised her poetry in a lecture, the two meet to discuss writing. She tells him, "I find that the thoughts spoken between the lines are the most important part of a poem or story." To which he replies, "as in life." (p. 36) How does this apply to their relationship? Are there other instances in the novel where this is true? Discuss them.

7. The subject of marriage comes up frequently in *Mrs. Poe*. Eliza tells Frances "Wedded bliss is a tale made up to keep the species going" (p. 278), and Margaret Fuller says, "for every married person [at Anne Lynch's conversazione] there is a story of rejection and betrayal." (p. 77) Discuss

the marriages in *Mrs. Poe*. Why do you think Eliza feels that wedded bliss is simply a story? And why does Frances stay married to Samuel even though she knows he is a philanderer? Do you think that Frances is justified in making her decision?

8. At one of the conversaziones, Poe says, "Desire inspires us to be our very best." (p. 169) Do you agree? In what ways, if any, do Poe and Frances improve because of their relationship?

9. Margaret Fuller warns Frances to steer clear of the Poes, stating that Edgar is "not what he seems" but rather "a poor boy much damaged from the trauma of his childhood." (p. 193) Do you agree with her assessment of the Poes? What do you think caused her to drop the idea of running a profile of them? Do you think that Margaret is acting as Frances's friend, as she claims? What makes you think so?

10. Were you surprised by Samuel's return? Although he is "maddeningly agreeable" (p. 230) with regard to Frances's relationship with Poe, he is critical of her work. After reading one of her poems, he tells her, "There was a time when you would have made fun of a poem like this." (p. 240) Why does Samuel's statement bother Frances so much? What do you think of the poem that he critiques?

11. Frances thinks that Virginia Poe is out to do her harm. What evidence supports her suspicions? Were you surprised when you found out the truth?

12. The Poes invite Frances to attend a play called *Fashion* with them. How does the plot of the play mirror their outing? Why does Poe apologize for his wife?

13. In several of his conversations with Frances, Poe makes references to stories that he has written, including "William Wilson" and "The Oval Portrait." How does Poe use these stories to communicate with Frances?

14. Poe reads "Al Aaraaf," the poem he wrote when he was fourteen, at the Boston Lyceum, claiming that he wanted "to see if they could tell the difference between a child's verse and a masterpiece." (p. 260) What do you think the real motivation behind his decision is? Do you agree with Mrs. Ellet that he called "down the wrath of the Boston circle" because it terrified him to do so (p. 271)? Why?

Enhance Your Book Club

1. The New York Literati scene of the 1840s serves as a the backdrop for *Mrs. Poe* and many luminaries of the period appear as minor characters within the book, including Henry Wadsworth Longfellow, John James Audubon, Walt Whitman, and Margaret Fuller. Discuss their famous contributions with your reading group and share some of these writers' works, creating your own conversazione.

2. Read Griswold's eulogy of Poe from *The New York Tribune* here: http://www.poeforward.com/poe/texts/griswold-poe-obit.html Then discuss Cullen's representation of Griswold. Was his writing as you imagined after becoming familiar with Griswold in *Mrs. Poe*?

3. When Frances first reads "The Raven" she says, "What trickery. It's just a word game." (p. 17) Read it here: http://www.heise.de/ix/raven/Literature/Lore/TheRaven.html, then discuss it with your book club. Do you agree with Frances that it's trickery? Or, do you think, like much of the literati in *Mrs. Poe*, that the work is an enduring classic?

4. To learn more about Lynn Cullen, visit her blog, read more about her other books, and find out how to invite her to your book club, visit her official site at http://www.lynncullen.com

A Conversation with Lynn Cullen

You've written nearly twenty books throughout your career. How does the publication of *Mrs. Poe* compare?

Each book comes from where I am in my life when I'm writing them. When my daughters were young, I wrote children's novels and picture books. I penned my first young adult and adult novels when they were in high school—and planned our family vacations around the research. After they left home, I wrote *Reign of Madness*, which might look like an adult historical novel but was really my exploration of the relationships between grown daughters and their mothers.

Then, in September 2011, my husband became ill with a life-threatening case of encephalitis. Already he was a casualty of the Great Recession and not working, and now he had a long stint of recuperation ahead. I was on my own when it came to supporting our family and terrified. As any writer can tell you, income from writing is not exactly steady. So the day my husband came home from the hospital, I was pacing in my office, wondering how we were possibly going to survive, when suddenly, I thought "Poe." I have no idea why. A coincidence? (We know what my Poe would say about that.) I Googled Poe and stumbled upon the story of Francis Osgood, the abandoned young mother who exchanged love poetry with him. Many scholars suspected that she had a love affair with Poe, some going as far as to suggest that Poe was the father of her child, Fanny Fay. In Francis Osgood I had the perfect character into which I could pour my own fear and determination. Frances Osgood survived and so would I.

Frances Osgood is an intriguing figure, not least because, in her time, she was just as well known for her own writings as she was for her friendship with Edgar Allen Poe. What drew you to her?

Frances Osgood was the perfect person for me to write about. Not only did she allow me to work out my own fears of survival but she gave me a chance to talk about what it's really like to be a writer, since she was a poet. She let me pour into the pages the joys and terrors of writing life. I also thought it would be fun to fantasize, through her, about falling in love with the mysterious, wounded, sensuous Poe. (I had learned that he was sexual catnip back in the day.) I let my imagination go to work on Poe as a cross between Ralph Fiennes as Heathcliff in the BBC film version of *Wuthering Heights*, Colin Firth in the movie *Bridget Jones's Diary*, and Johnny Depp in *The Pirates of the Caribbean* (but sober) and voilà, I understood Frances's obsession.

After Frances finishes writing "So Let It Be," she says, "I sat back, wrung out, as I always am after I have brought forth a true and honest work, regardless of its subject or length. It is as if producing a creative work tears a piece from your soul." (p. 100) Is your writing process anything like hers? Can you tell us about it?

Frances's writing life is my writing life. I tried to describe the pain and the joy of having work ripped from the part of your mind that is a mystery even to you. I wanted to get across how when the writing flows, it's a high that makes an addict out of you. You can just feel the exhilaration whooshing through your veins when you have a breakthrough with a true and honest scene. A few happy tears are sometimes in order. When the writing doesn't come, you feel as bleakly desperate, hopeless, and unloved as if all your friends have left you for smarter, more desirable people. Your brain fills with mud. You can't enjoy sunshine. To take the ups and downs of writing, you have to be tough as rawhide; yet to create, you have remain as open and sensitive as an exposed nerve. As I tell my friends, writing is my therapy and it also causes me to need therapy.

How do you research your books?

Research is pure pleasure. First, I read everything I can get my hands on, not only about the main characters but about the setting, daily life, and other people from that time. I have bought at least seventy books for *Mrs. Poe* alone. In the case of this novel, I then spent time combing through the eye-popping collection of material from the 1840s in the library of the New York Historical Society. Next comes the best part. Before I set out to write the book and several times during the actual writing, I visit the settings. I go to the places where my characters were known to have lived, worked, and played in real life. I have made a point of visiting the site of each scene in my books, even though the place may have completely changed. It's a thrill when they have not. In the case of *Mrs. Poe*, I tramped the streets of lower Manhattan and Greenwich Village so thoroughly one week in late April that I tore the meniscus in my knee. Many other times, I trotted up the steps of Miss Lynch's home on Waverly Place. I stood over the bed where Virginia Poe died, in the Poe Cottage located in what is now the Bronx. I strolled through Washington Square at night, peeking through the trees and trying to imagine seeing the light shining from Samuel Morse's window while E. A. Poe put his arms around me. (This is where having a husband comes in handy.) I explored the parlors, kitchen, garden, and bedrooms of the Merchant House Museum in Greenwich Village, grateful that a house very much like the Bartlett's still exists. I even climbed up into the clock tower of Trinity Church and stuck out my head through the rosette window, as did Frances. What good luck it was to write a book set in 1845 New York!

Like Frances Osgood, you have written works for both children and adults. Does the process differ? If so, how?

When it comes to research and attention to detail, there is not much difference between writing children's and adult books. I take the same care choosing each word in all my books. However, there are so many less words in children's books that it takes far less time to write them. You have to commit several years of your life to writing an adult novel; researching for a historical novel only adds to the time commitment. Novel writers are the marathon runners of our field. No wonder so many need "hydration" during the long and arduous slog to the finish.

When Frances tells Reverend Griswold that she has not read Margaret Fuller's column about John Humphrey Noyes, he chastises her, saying that she must keep up with the news because "As an important woman poet, it is your duty to speak out against false prophets." (p. 205) As a writer yourself, do you think that it is the responsibility of the artist to speak out against "false prophets" as Griswold suggests?

I think all serious writers are articulating their personal philosophies in their stories, even if the book isn't overtly about a political agenda. I don't know if it's so much that artists feel a responsibility to speak out—it's more like we just can't help ourselves from sharing our views!

Poe tells Frances, "Our job [as poets] is to raise questions, not to answer them." (p. 53) As a writer, what questions were you hoping to raise with *Mrs. Poe*?

Thank you for asking—I have a ton of unanswered questions: What *is* that animating essence in each of us that is traditionally called a "soul"? How does this animating essence contribute to our individuality? Is it communicating with other souls on a level that we don't often pay attention to? Do animals, other creatures, even rocks, as the Swedenborgians believed, have souls? Is our soul the part of us that is responsible for always keeping us craving what we cannot have? Does the human's—and all creatures'—universal need to be loved spring from this part of us, and why? What *is* love? I think I better stop now.

Since its publication in 1845, "The Raven" has become a canonical text. It has inspired other writings ranging from Vladimir Nabokov to Ray Bradbury, and has even been parodied. Why do you think the poem has had such an enduring appeal?

"The Raven" is catchy and vivid. It's a movie in words. Also, Poe's legend as a frightening, half-mad genius (thank you, Rufus Griswold!) brings a darkness to the poem that has thrilled people for centuries. In addition, its immense popularity in Poe's day helped cement it into the American memory. We picture Poe's raven almost as automatically and as mindlessly of its origins as we say "okay." Personally, I don't think it's his most honest work. For authentically expressed anguish, see "Ulalume."

***Mrs. Poe* is based on historical facts. When recreating the relationship between Poe and Frances, what liberties did you take?**

As a historical novelist, the game I like to play with myself is to try to make sure that everything that happens in the story could have actually happened. I like to fill in the gaps of recorded history but try very hard not to bend the facts. But since I'm a novelist and not a Poe scholar with decades of Poe study under my belt, and since so much has been recorded about him, I might have inadvertently gotten some things wrong. (Poe scholars: forgive me!) It wasn't my intention, though, to write a biography about Poe or Frances Osgood, fictionalized or otherwise. My aim was to take these two personalities as I came to understand them, put them together, and see what sparks flew.

What would you like your readers who are interested in Edgar Allen Poe's writings to take away from *Mrs. Poe*?

Mainly, I hope readers will think about how his difficult life shaped his writing. He was a wounded beast and his own worst enemy, but he put everything he had into his work. What I think Poe strove for hardest was simply to be loved.

What are you working on next?

It's a secret just yet. But I promise to keep raising unanswerable questions. And there will always be people in my story craving something they shouldn't have.

About the Author

LYNN CULLEN is the author of *The Creation of Eve*, one of *The Atlanta Journal-Constitution*'s best fiction books of the year, and *Reign of Madness*, nominated for the Townsend Prize for fiction. She is also the author of award-winning children's books and the young adult novel, *I Am Rembrandt's Daughter*. She lives in Atlanta, Georgia. Follow Lynn Cullen on Facebook or visit www.lynncullen.com